Angelic Rage

Billy Scott

This book is a work of fiction. People, places, events, and situations are the product of the author's imagination. Any resemblance to actual persons, living or dead, or historical events, is purely coincidental.

© 2005 Billy Scott All Rights Reserved.

No part of this book may be reproduced, stored in a retrieval system, or transmitted by any means without the written permission of the author.

First published by AuthorHouse 03/11/05

ISBN: 1-4184-6876-2 (e)
ISBN: 1-4184-3117-6 (sc)

Library of Congress Control Number: 2004091002

Printed in the United States of America
Bloomington, Indiana

This book is printed on acid-free paper.

What Readers are saying about
"Angelic Rage"

"Angelic Rage" is fantastic! The captivating combination of real versus unseen good and evil will definitely KEEP you turning the pages. The spiritual realm is mind boggling and this will have you looking over your shoulders!

Miriam C Spiller,
Cardiovascular ultrasound

"The Angelic Rage" let me say it is truly extra ordinary, fast paced, completely engrossing. The story's characters come to life fully, catching you up in it's compelling good verses evil story and entangles you in it's world.

Sheila M Cutter
Deputy Sheriff

"What a great idea," the ultimate GOOD vs. EVIL horror story! It will leave you on the edge of your seat...ready to PRAY!

James C Appel
Deputy Sheriff

Dedication

This book is dedicated to;

Wayman L Rogers~ a great shepherd of the flock and a man who believed in acorns turning into Oak trees.

Acknowledgments

Miriam ~my best friend without your help it would not have been possible. Thank you for the help with the first seven edits, you are a raven in the wilderness, T.f.p.

Shontae'~ your laughter is a light to my heart.

Joshua~ who said, "Don't worry dad; Someday."

Jody- Thank you for the last edits.

A word from the Author,

I pray this story bless you greatly. And that you look at spiritual warfare in a new light.

ONE

From the dark corner of the alley a flash of light, orange, red, and amber glow burst in the night. The blue hues ignited, burned upward and then slowly down the matchstick as the gentleman in the long gray overcoat lit his cigarette. His face became visible only in time intervals, as the flashes of neon above the diner glowed. He paced back and forth, lurking in the shadows, moving quickly to keep his feet and body warm, but never taking his eyes off his prey. Across the city street, the last couple was exiting the diner. He refused to let his plundering eyes wander away, but did only for a brief instant to ensure that no one else was around. He seemed to become anxious when the couple exited. The air was cold and crisp as the steam and smoke were exhaled from his body. He made puff rings in the dark

Only one man remained inside. The view was clear from where the man in the gray coat stood. Tossing his half-smoked cigarette onto the gray, dismal snow, he stepped on it, extinguishing the flame. Whispering he said, "Now I got you." He stepped out of the shadows and into the dimmed lighted area of the sidewalk. He moved closer to the diner, walked between two parked cars, and placed his right hand into his coat to pull out a concealed item.

"Eeecck!" was the sound screeching over my shoulder. There it was, the reason I was here. I turned, looking backward into the alleyway. In the blackness of the pitch, my eyes, more keen than any human, watched the shadow of the night rent itself into a hole from hell. Out of that dark hole stepped Zolan. Zolan; the once great guardian of the Trees of Eden. He and I were the two angels assigned to make sure Adam never ate of the Tree of Life, although Adam had eaten of the Tree of Knowledge of Good and Evil. Like myself, I knew Zolan never relinquished his sword.

He retained not his once beautiful appearance, but now was disfigured. His mighty stature is all I could remember. He stood as tall as I, nine feet according to man's measurement, but the curse had definitely changed him. The once elegant wings that glistened like the purest snow were now hideous, dark and bent, outstretched like a bat. His face had become contorted and ugly. His legs were covered with wiry like goat hair. I guess because his garment of purity was taken from him. Yes, he was different in appearance, but he still had all his power and strength. I had seen him in battle in ancient times, and he is a formidable foe. Yet, here he was, coming toward me. Yes; even right at me! But wait . . . he just passed me by as if he . . . no, it cannot be.
He did not even see me.

Out of the shadows of the darkened alley, Zolan crossed the city street as if he had an appointment to meet with the man in the gray coat. He was staring through the Christmas decorated diner windows, especially at the young man who was sitting at the counter alone. His objective target was in view. The young man wore a black leather overcoat, and a red scarf hung around his neck. He was much younger than the man standing outside the diner.

Whoosh! Whoosh! Faster than thought, two imp-like creatures had burst through the dark hole in the alleyway behind me. Now standing beside Zolan, they had moved as if time had stood still, faster than the naked eye could conceive. They began screaming awful obscenities toward the man in the gray coat. Their shrieks reached the high heavens. The vulgar language was deafening and ear piercing. Even my ears were being bombarded by their profanity. The man became suddenly agitated but did not know why.

I saw the item which he had concealed inside his gray coat, for he had pulled it out into full view now; a black nine-millimeter, semi-automatic Beretta pistol. Slowly raising it, he took aim at the young man inside. Zolan was shouting the commands, and the man in the gray coat was acting like a puppet on a string.

"Take aim!" Zolan shouted.

Humans hear us only as a whisper, the voices of the unseen. It takes a lot of energy to break the barrier between the two worlds; the realm of the natural and the supernatural.

"Cock the hammer!" he commanded.

And so he did, but I was motionless, frozen, as if I were inside a box. A box that was invisible even to my eyes. Why? Why couldn't I move? What was holding me back? I wondered why no one had prayed.

Swinging doors opened from the kitchen doorway. A young waitress was entering into view. She brought out a plate and placed it on the counter in front of the young man. My senses were so attuned; I could smell the sizzling sausage and eggs even from where I stood in the alley across the street.

"Squeeze slowly! Do it now, do it now!" Zolan commanded.

"Judy? Is that your name?" asked the young man.

"It is unless someone changed my name tag, dearer," she replied.

"Dumb question . . . huh? My name is Paul, like the apostle." She raised an eyebrow.

"Judy, do you think I could sweet talk you out of a bottle of ketchup for my eggs?" She smiled hopefully thinking that her son would be as polite and handsome as the young man she was now encountering. She removed a small rag from her apron pocket, wiped her hands, reached under the counter, and placed a bottle of ketchup in front of him.

"Here you go, darling, goes good on the home fries, too."

Across the country, in the town of Boise, Idaho, Justin, a young teenager, lives with his mother. His father passed away several years earlier. Justin kneels down beside his bed to pray. Being involved in the youth group had made him into a prayer warrior. He always believed the battlefield of faith started by bowing your knees. While praying, he hears the still, small voice of whispers say, "pray for Paul." So the young teenager, feeling the Holy Spirit move on him, becomes ignited with zeal in his innermost being. He recants scriptures that alone his own mind would never retain, but by the help of the Holy Spirit, he is now able to recall. No longer asking for things in prayer, Justin begins to command them to come into existence using faith. As he speaks of Paul, he perceives a strange feeling of danger for his once, long ago teacher. So with tremendous determination he releases words of great faith, quoting God's Word . . . "Whatsoever thing you bind on earth, shall also be bound in the heavens," and "Whatsoever thing you loose on the earth, shall also be loose in the heavens."

Justin cries out, "I bind you, devils of darkness, and I loose the angels of the most high God in heaven, by the name of Jesus!" Finishing his prayer, he crawls up into his bed, and whispered, "I hope you're watching over me, dad. Someday, you and I will get to play that game of catch." Rolling over on his side, the boy looks at the nightstand table where a picture of himself, his mom and his dad sits. A tear rolls down the edge of the nose of the young prayer warrior and gently falls on his pillow. His eyes grow heavy as he falls asleep.

Freedom! I was set loose! I could move. Someone somewhere must have prayed. I was no longer confined to the invisible box. I reached down to my side and lay hold of my sheath, as I grabbed the handle of my flaming sword.

"Do it now, squeeze the trigger! Squeeze the trigger!" Zolan cried out in a terrible screech. A thundering voice of hoards . . . a voice that use to be the sweetest for the ears to hear, but now chilled . . . like fingernails on a chalkboard.

"In the name of Lord of the Host of heavens!" I swung my flaming sword. Swoosh, swoosh, was the sound of my blade.

"Awhhh!" one screamed, the other hissed, as my sword cut both of Zolan's imps in half. The tormented banshees were now banished to the place of wretchedness and despair, to the place known as Tartarus. All that was left of them is the dissipating gaseous form from whence they stood. I enjoyed taking them first because of their cursing of the Holy One. Zolan turned to face me. He was now aware of my presence, shrieking and retreating while covering his eyes. My raiment, or my clothes rather, which were normally golden bronze in color, had become gleaming, brilliant white. This happens when I am ordered to commence in spiritual warfare by the power of faith, usually by someone's prayer.

Zolan's eyes were not accustomed to seeing light, nor had they been for quite sometime. While Zolan was cowering on the ground, I laid my hand on top of the gun the man in the grey coat was holding. He lowered it slowly, dropping it there between the parked cars into the muddy slushy ice.

"What was I thinking?" he murmured. "They'll send someone after me, I'm sure. I must have been crazy to take this assignment." He placed his hands deep inside his long grey coat, took one final look at the young man sitting at the counter, and turned and left.

"You!" Zolan said. "I remember you! You're Septuagint!" To hear his voice made me squirm.

"Yes, Zolan, we once served on an assignment in ancient times in Eden, the Holy-Garden."

"Aaah, don't say those words! The Garden! The place where God fell in love with them, giving them everything they wanted. Ah yes, I do remember. I remember the test these humans failed also. But even after they failed, God still loved them. That's why we were on an assignment, not because He loved us more, but them. Why?" Zolan asked.

"Zolan, you know they are created in God's own image. And the spirit of life that is in them is His breath. They were created below us so as to learn how to attain perfection. We, unlike them, were perfect in the day he created us."

"Why, Septuagint? Why are you here at this very moment to torment me with your beauty? Make me remember my once self?"

"No, Zolan. The beauty you see is only the reflection of God's handiwork in me. I am but a messenger, as you once were."

"Once were? And am I not still a messenger? I am still a messenger! But now I give my own messages to these descendants of Adam!" Zolan replied sarcastically. The drool was dripping from his fangs. I was in utter disgust at the state in which he had become.

"Sure you do, Zolan. I saw you do it, but under whose orders Lucifer, the ancient dragon? We all know he is the ringleader for all the fallen ones."

"Enough, history! What is it that you want, Septuagint?"

"I am curious as to one thing. What was so important about that young man, who was not doing anything but eating his breakfast? Why did your boss want him terminated?"

"Septuagint, it was because he. . . " The floor of the spirit world began to quake. Behind Zolan's cloven hooves, an opening of flame and smoke filled the darkened night.

"Aaaaahhhhhhhhhhhh!" he screamed. The hand of the once powerful cherubim reached up and grabbed Zolan right before he could answer me. I had forgotten how big cherubim's were, the guardians to the steps of the throne, even fallen ones. Zolan's nine foot stature was but a matchstick size in the hand of his commander. His eerie screams were horrifying as he was being plucked from my view. I am sure the failure of the assignment was being discussed.

"More coffee, Paul?" asked the waitress.

"Why, yes, Judy, I think I will. Would you bring some more cream too, please?"

Paul smiled, but inside his spirit it felt like something had just happened. Judy was saying something, but his thoughts were diverting his attention elsewhere. He turned his head, looking to his right, but seeing nothing, just an empty diner, not a soul around. Looking left, to the glass window and into the dimly lit street, across the corner, he saw a shadowy figure. As a man in a grey coat was walking away from the diner, Paul thought to himself, *poor soul, the air is so cold outside I hope he isn't homeless.* Paul began to pray silently.

"Dear Lord, hear this prayer. Please assist that man walking in the cold night."

"Is something wrong? Did I lose your attention?" asked Judy.

"What? No, no, not at all. You were saying?" asked Paul with a grin.

"I asked you what brings you here to Washington, politics or people. You know, like family?"

Leaning over the counter with a damp rag in her hand, she reached toward Paul's coat. He reacted to her forwardness, a little surprised. He moved backward.

"Its ok sport, you just dripped a little egg on your jacket. You really should order your eggs hard boiled instead of sunny-side up."

"Oh, yeah clumsy me. I should be shot for something like that, huh?" Paul said.

I had to smile when I heard what the man in the diner had said, for surely he did not know how near his fate had come.

"Huh? Oh, business. I'm here on business. I'm conducting a revival meeting on Sunday at St. Thomas Church."

"Revival, you're a minister?"

"Yes, I'm afraid I am," Paul replied while removing his scarf and revealing his white collar of the cloth. Throwing the damp rag on the counter, Judy exclaimed,

"Well, just when you meet one that isn't stuck on himself or isn't fruity as a fly, is young and good looking, wouldn't you know it, he's married to the church. I can't win for losing!" Judy walked back into the kitchen. Paul just grinned, and took a bite of his eggs.

●─────────────●

(Ring . . . Ring . . . Ring.) A man's hand reached out from under the covers and picked up the telephone.

"Hello?" he spoke in a gravelly voice adding "this better be good."

"Tom, this is Steve. You better come down here to Forty-Fourth and Decker Street. We've got two more."

"How bad?" asked Tom.

"Real bad. Same as the others, but with a twist."

"Fine, I'll be there in a few. Give me forty-five minutes."

"Oh, and Tom, can you bring coffee? Looks like we're going to be here awhile."

"Yeah; yeah, bye." Tom hung up the phone and crawled out of bed. Slipping his feet into his favorite house slippers and shuffling slowly toward the bathroom, he said out loud to himself, "Time to make the doughnuts, time to make the doughnuts."

TWO

"What a lovely December morning we have here in Washington, D.C. If you're going out this morning, please dress warmly. Today's high will only be reaching the mid-to-upper thirties. Seems old man Mr. Frost is going to be sending us a cold breeze from the northern states. Although it will be cold, we will see no chance for showers or snow flurries until later in the . . ." (Click). Tom pushed the button on his car radio.

"The President will be announcing his details concerning the summit meetings with Syria and Israeli officials on Tues . . ." (Click)

"Politics, politics, politics. I have to get out of this city," Tom said to himself while reaching down and turning off the car radio. He was only a few blocks from Decker and Forty-Fourth when he whispered under his breath, "Dear Lord, I could use some help with this case. If you're not too busy up there, think you can lend a helping hand?"

Pulling his vehicle up to the police barricades, he proceeded slowly, as a small crowd was already gathering. Rubberneckers, they stretch their necks like chickens looking over a wire fence. The curious types never really see awful events, but only hear about them on television or read about them in newspapers, the kind of newspapers that make money by exploiting the truth and turning it into sensationalism for a buck.

"Hello, Sarge," said one uniform officer.

"I see Curious George is here. Make sure all the reporters, especially George, stay away from the crime scene. I don't want to see him or anyone else trampling in the red snow," Tom replied.

The uniform officer understood the tone of Tom's voice. He stood up straight and saluted, saying, "yes sir."

The red snow, I thought to myself. That was an unusual phrase to describe a tragic event. While thinking of the colors, I looked down at my clothes and noticed that the brilliance of white was fading back to golden bronze. I looked further down and saw the white snow was now mingled with a bright red color. I now understood the meaning of this one; they called sergeant.

What a pretender I saw before me. He acted so mean to those around him. Not hateful mean, but talked so sharp, quick and formal. He did not seem to act that way with the one called Detective Steve. I could perceive past their flesh. I saw their innermost being, the spirit part of them, in these creatures called humans. Some of the Pneuma humans are dark, but some of the Pneuma humans are like our Creator, praise be His name. I wondered who prayed for this one called Tom, Why did I feel so compelled to stay close to him? Turning the corner of the brick building, I sensed evil was near. The red snow was all around. Two bodies in long coats adorned the city's dirty alley. Their coats were laid open.

"They're both hookers, Sarge. I busted both of them about a month ago."

"Oh mercy, Where are their heads?" asked Tom.

"Look up, Sarge," Steve replied. All present looked up to see the horrifying site on the fire escape. The corpses laid in the red snow with a pentagram of the fallen one carved into the flesh of their bellies.

My clothes began to gleam. I turned and looked behind me. I let my eyes search the crowd around me until I targeted it with accuracy. Across the street, on top of a iron-rod fence, he sat there frozen still, not moving a muscle. But I was aware of him. He looked like a grotesque gargoyle of old, hoping I would not see him. His name was Grief. I knew why he was there. He was waiting to follow the electric pulse of negative energy in the telephone lines, sniffing out its signal to the home of the mother of one of the victims. The young girl had run away from home because she felt unpopular in school. The only way she felt loved was to become sexually active, not really knowing true love. And a not so understanding father had thought it best for her to find her own home, which she did, on the rough city streets.

Whoosh! Gone . . . too late for me to move. Grief disappeared and I did not want to leave Tom's side, not for a moment. Somehow, I was drawn to him.

"Ok, have a report on my desk by five o'clock. Send any samples over to the lab. I want photographs of all angles, and snap a few of the crowd. You know, sometimes the perpetrator likes to hang out and watch his work being admired. Someone have the coroner's report sent up to me as soon as possible," commanded Tom. "Hey Steve, you said on the phone there was a twist. What were you talking about?"

"Yeah, we found this in the fur coat pocket of the white woman. The Jamaican woman didn't have anything." Steve held up a clear, plastic baggy marked as evidence "A."

"A watch?" Tom raised an eyebrow with a unconcerned look. "Sooo, what's the twist?"

"Take a look at the inscription. It reads: To Maggie, all my love, Senator John L. Tinnimen."

"Oh, that's just great, Politics! This just keeps getting better and better. Now what's a twenty-something year old murdered hooker doing with a senator's watch?"

"Maybe ole John was a real John," Steve said. Tom smirked at his odd humor.

"Maybe we will go see this Senator."

"You mean Senator John-John?" Steve replied.

"Knock it off, wise guy." Steve nodded holding back his smile.

Crash! The sound of heavy cans hit the floor. The back door to the alley was ajar. Officers turned and placed their hands on the handles of their weapons drawing and pointing in the direction of the door, one of the patrolmen shouted, "Come out with your hands up!"

As he walked out of the back door of the pizza parlor, hands half-way raised, the man in the light brown long overcoat held a small notepad and pencil in his hand and said,

"Did I hear you say a senator's watch, as in Senator Tinnimen?" asked the reporter.

"George, are you stupid or what? You could have been shot. You're interfering with a police investigation," Steve said.

"I do apologize, Detective. The front door to the pizza parlor was opened and I was just looking for the restroom."

"I bet you were, George," Tom said.

"He didn't get the name Curious for nothing," Steve added.

Tom pointed down the alley toward the street and said, "Get this reporter back behind the crime-scene tape and have someone seal that door!"

As George was being escorted away by a uniformed officer, he said, "Hey, not so rough!"

"George, you better keep that info under raps until you get an official release or I'll come and find you."

"Come on Tom, you know me, I wouldn't do anything that wasn't law abiding."

"Mmm-hmm." I watched as the one called reporter was being led away. My eyesight is not limited. I see both the natural realm and spiritual world. He had an imp on his shoulder. They are the common kind, always around, half monkey and half bat. Its tail was hanging down the back of its carrier, the one called reporter. The creature had its spiritual claws imbedded deep into George's skull, constantly whispering lies into the ear of its host. The imp used his wings to cover the carrier's eyes just directly above the nose, veiling him or her from seeing truth.

It was aware of my presence. It only turned once and glanced in my direction. Growling evilly at me, it knew I was not in battle mode, for my robe was diminishing from white to bronze in color. But all the same, it was aware that I was a guardian angel. After his snarling hiss, a questionable look appeared on the imp's face. It was one of curiosity. Maybe he did find a suitable host to cling to. Maybe this George was taking on the characteristics of his invisible, uninvited guest.

T H R E E

Tap . . . tap . . . (pause) tap, was the sound knocking on the old, hand-carved wood door of the guest room. The corridor was empty, and only the color of the sun shining on each of the tiny pieces of the Picasso stained glass window illuminated the floor. The sun rays of the art work filled the long narrow hallway.

"Come in, good morning," Paul said.

The door opened slowly exposing a not so very large, simple room with a single bed, a crucifix attached to the wall above it, a lamp with a small table-stand beside it. Near the foot of the bed and under a window was a small roll top desk and wooden chair with coaster wheels.

In the corner was a standup dresser for those who had brought more than one change of clothing. The comfortable leather reclining chair, which was used for extensive reading, was clearly visible, and a floor lamp stood beside chair. On the table laid an open black Bible, King James Version, marked with a red ribbon. The closet door was no wider than three feet in diameter. This was a very simple guest room for devotional study.

"Good morning, Paul," said the kindly elderly gentlemen, adding, "My name is Bishop Davis. First of all, it's a real pleasure and a treat to have you here with us, praise God. Secondly, my wife has instructed me to invite you to join us at breakfast in the galley."

"Love too."

"I am really looking forward to hearing about all your endeavors in Israel."

Paul extended his arm to shake hands with the Bishop, and, upon contact, Paul felt the hair on his neck stand up. Paul knew in his spirit the man standing before him was a great spiritual warrior.

"I'm pleased to meet you Bishop; I am looking forward to meeting your family and having a great fellowship breakfast. Just give me a second or two and I'll be right down."

"Very well, see you in the galley. And God bless you this morning," replied the Bishop.

As the Bishop turned walked away, his footsteps growing fainter, Paul looked upward and said, "Dear Lord, thank you for one's such as these."

●——————————————————————●

"Nancy this is Tom. No, I am going to be here in my office for about an hour and a half. I need the files brought up here on the pentagram killer. Yes, I know. But it looks like the same M.O. It must be a copycat. That or we electrocuted the wrong one. No, it's just a hunch. Thank you." Tom hung up the phone, unaware of anyone else's presence.

I could see he was very intellectual, a man of taste. This space he called office was pleasant. A top floor view overlooked the metro area, even if it was only slushy streets. The park across from the building was covered in snow. Several children were building a snowman in the center of the park.

"Septuagint!" the voices said. Whoosh! I turned with lightning speed. How could I have let someone come on me like that? My face sparkled. It was my old friends. I had not seen them for what seem to be an eternity. It was Rejoice and Glee. These two, whom now stood before me, are the King's most beloved of messengers. To the left of Glee was the wall of Tom's office, which only seconds ago was but a empty wall with nice pictures. But now "The White Door" was there. It is the doorway of time. I now realized how Rejoice and Glee had come upon me so quickly. I had only used 'The White Door' a couple of times. I love that kind of travel. It is even quicker than my wings, which are as fast as thought.

I said, "My friends what brings you here?"

Rejoice and Glee both started to run around in a circle, laughing and giggling. Their speed generated a whirlwind in Tom's office, causing some papers to fall off the edge of Tom's desk. Because of Glee's presence in the room, Tom could do nothing but laugh, instead of using the curse word he wanted to use.

"What? What is it my friends?" I asked.

They both stopped; Looked at each other, and began to grin. Both of them paused, turned and looked at me and shouted as loud as they could.

"Revival . . . revival. . . revival!"

Oh yes! The sound of the battle cry was ringing in my ears.

"You have been ordered, by the archangel himself, Michael, to come with us and slay them all in the spirit," Rejoice said.

The White door opened. It folds space and time-dimensions. You can travel from this place across universes just by passing through it. The other side of the door was opened to a large room. It was apparent that the room in which we stepped into was a kitchen. Glee moved in first, then Rejoice and finally me. There was a place to eat and a long table with a bench on which to sit attached to both sides. I had seen that kind of table in the city parks, but this one was three times longer. A cloth of white and red checkered linen covered it. Six place setting were at one end. Four bowls of fruit were atop of the middle of the table, from one end to the other all adorned with four sets of salt and pepper shakers. The woman placing the food on the table was an elderly lady in terms of time for man. The curse of the fall of man (only able to live in the human shells called bodies for approximately seventy years) was visible in her. She had grayish hair and wore a yellow dress. A red apron was wrapped around her full figure. Her hands were the kind I had seen on those who are close to departing this world, wrinkled and tough like leather. As I looked pass the shell of flesh, I saw the light within her. It was a giant light! I became aware of the presence of the Sovereign Being, which resided in her. The Holy Spirit himself was evident, not only in her, but in all four of the ladies who were in this room. The footsteps grew stronger as a elderly man was coming down the wooden steps of this place. He too had the light shining in him.

"Is he coming down Bishop Davis?"

He patted his hand against the air saying, "Yes, yes, he said he would be here in a few minutes."

Rejoice stood behind one of the women and clapped the woman in front of him was so moved, she reacted the same. I laughed, unable to control myself, as Glee got in on the act. It was as if they were double teaming each one of the ladies.

Glee Stood behind the one called Ophelia, and started to say "Oh, goodie, goodie," Ophelia repeat the words aloud.

I could see that this was going to be, at the least, a very interesting morning.

"Senator Tinnimen, the press conference is ready, sir." The words were spoken by a young lady dressed in business attire. She looked very conservative in her petite wire framed glasses. Jenny started to close the door behind her, the door to a very nice office with a large oak desk. Behind it was two windows looking down on the city streets and the court house steps.

"Oh yes, thank you, Jenny," replied the senator. "I will be right there." The senator turned his head back towards the window, one arm folded across his chest. Tapping his lower lip with his index knuckle, he looked down at the steps, observing the bustling crowd. A hand reached up to the right shoulder of the senator, a hand with a golden ring and an emblem of a pentagram. He turned and looked at the man.

"Sir, I am sorry for your loss. But what are you going to tell the press?"

"It is only politics, I will tell them the truth." The man coughed a half persuasive laugh,

"I don't think so . . . The truth will only lead to an investigation. We have a pre-made press release available. It will cover up any ties to you, Senator."

"Damn it Kirk, she was my family! Don't you think it was bad enough, for her, to have to live the way she did. Now she's dead. And I am supposed to just pretend she was nothing to me?" The senator wiped his eyes as he shrugged Kirk's hand from his shoulder, turned and walked around his desk.

"If you read your own statement, Tinnimen, you will be committing political suicide. Not just for you, but for all who are in the party."

"I don't care anymore, do you hear me?" Kirk slammed his fist on the desk and exclaimed with rage in his eyes.

"YOU WILL READ THE APPROVED STATEMENT OR YOU WILL ANSWER TO THE SOCIETY!" A demon now appeared from below the floor, invisible to both men it stood behind Kirk towering over him like a big brother. Its name was Fear. The senator, unable to see him, felt the demon's presence. An eerie darkness had filled the room. The demon grabbed Tinnimen by both arms, holding him, overshadowing him.

The senator wanting to calm Kirk down, said,

"Yes, Kirk, I understand now. I will read what you want me to read. The society doesn't even have to know." The senator walked around the leather chair shrugged his shoulders, "What was I thinking?"

"Yes, what were you thinking?" An evil snarl appeared the face of the demon, Fear, and on the face of Kirk.

•―――――――――――――――――•

The footsteps on the hardwood floor grew louder as Paul Zoe came down the steps and entered the galley. "Good Morning, everyone," Paul announced as he entered the room.

Glee moved so fast, I almost didn't see him. Around and around Pastor Zoe he went. I looked inside this guest of honor, seeing the Pneuma inside him. It was surely bright; This guy was definitely exercising his spirit. When he turned, I saw his face.

"Hey, I have seen this one before. I was sent to stop a man from shooting him."

"Praise God, he is the reason the Lord sent us here," Rejoice replied.

"Good morning Pastor, I hope you're hungry for some breakfast," Ophelia said.

"Yes I am, but why don't we start off our day with prayer?"

"OH, I like this guy," I said to the two angels with me. "His thinking is surely in the right order."

"I knew you would, Septuagint," replied Rejoice.

"Septuagint, Get ready, your sword is flaming," Glee said. The way he giggled made me start laughing. I drew out my sword.

Pastor Paul, the bishop and the four ladies all gathered in a circle and held hands. Paul began leading the group in prayer and a sweet peaceful presence filled the room. I looked upward and was able to see between the two worlds the natural and the supernatural. I saw the ceiling open up like a big hole was there, moving outward, exposing the morning sky. Then the sky itself opened up to Heavens glory. I saw the oil being poured down from the King's throne, showering everyone who was present in the room. Then the order came to my mind like someone had spoken it gently in my ear. I swung my blade of fire, which is a representative of the Word of God.

Paul prayed for revival and laid his hands on the Bishop's head. The spirit of fire, and holiness of my sword, now cut the bishop in half. Not the flesh of the real man, but only the spirit-man or Pneuma-man, that lives inside him.

Imps, I abhor Imps, I thought to myself, as one jumped out of the bishop's flesh, not his spirit man, but his flesh. "Aaawwweee" it cried, and with a grunt it sneered at me. It was hiding in his elbow. Its name is Arthritis. The creature moved into the shadows of the floor and disappeared as the bishop fell to the ground. Never before had the anointing of the Holy Ghost been so strong on him.

Paul continued to pray, and then he ordered Heaven to send a legion of angels to come. At that command of prayer, the solid walls of the back room of the galley faded into nothingness. I then witnessed twelve thousand angels appearing in the distance walking toward the earthly building, to the place where the wall once stood only seconds before.

A small portion of the army of the Lord had just arrived. I could see this man of God was preparing to take a city in spiritual warfare. Somehow, I felt I would not be in the major battle, but only as a spy for the forces of good. I was here for a special assignment.

Again I had to laugh at Glee. He moved so fast, all I could see was a streak of bright, white light. Glee encircled the interior camp of Warrior Angels. All of them aware of Glee's workings began to laugh. Rejoice watched Glee's actions and he too was moved as light, and the whole encampment began to worship. The hunger for food on the table had vanquished, but now a uncontrollable frenzy for the food, known as the Word of God, had become the focus of the group's hunger. Jesus had said, "Man shall not live by bread alone, but by every word that proceeds from the mouth of God."

An atomic-like cloud, only brighter, moved outward in a perfect diameter of a circle, toward the outskirts of the city. The smoky veil of Glory was filling the entire city as it once did in the tabernacle of Moses' camp, when the Lord led Moses and the people from slavery from the hand of Egypt's bondage. What a glorious morning this was turning out to be. I wanted to see the effects on the city from a better point of view, so I flew upward and outward away from the church on the corner. I moved with great speed to a distance far away from the metro area. I could see the capital and the Washington monument in the background. It was a sight to behold . . . not the city made by human hands, but the Glory . . . Oh yes, the Glory! The Shakina Glory was falling from Heaven's throne on top of the church. I could see angels arising and descending through the smoke of the Glory. Many angels were involved. They encircled the bottom of the smoke ring, standing as guards of the Glory. No evil was going to penetrate this barrier that was apparent. Well, it was if you had my eyes.

F O U R

"Senator Tinnimen, so what you're saying is the victim was given a twenty-four karat gold watch by a burglar, who broke into your house and stole the watch, but didn't read the inscription? Don't you think that's kinda thin?"

"No, I don't."

"So you didn't even know the girl, is that right?"

"Come on, you expect us, the bearers of the world news to believe that?" asked George.

"Well, George, I can't tell you or any of these other reporters of the great American press, what to believe. I can, and I am, telling you the facts as I know it . . . That's all. No more questions," replied the senator. The senator turned to his assistant in conversation while walking down the steps to his limo.

"That must be how the press received its name. Because that is sure what they do, press you," Tinnimen said.

"That's what they get paid to do, John, and to be a senator, they want to know everything that a Presidential hopeful does and everything he is involved in. That's the price you pay, along with your soul to the devil, because the devil is in the details, my dear Senator," Kirk said, smiling with a malicious grin. As they entered the limo to drive away, a slight drizzle of snow and sleet started to fall from grayish clouds.

Next to the enormous column which supported the building's overhang stood George. His lying Imp was whispering in his ear. Its voice carried an overlapped sound of many voices speaking at the same time. "Your stories will make you famous," whispered the Imp. George just looked downward at the steps, pondering the voices he now heard in his head, noticing the wet steps and the dry foundation under the overhang, upon which he stood.

●────────────────●

"Knock . . . knock, you busy?" asked Detective Steve Brodie,

"No, not at all. Come in," replied Tom.

"Here's the coroner's report. The instrument that carved the pentagram was the same diameter as the type of dagger we found from the old case. Bad news is, the dagger that we had in evidence is missing."

"What! No way. That's just great! What's next,"

"Sorry to interrupt, Tom, But I am leaving early before the heavy snow hits. I have to make sure my kids are ok. Here are all the files you requested. Is there anything else?" asked Nancy.

"No, that's fine, thank you Nancy, We'll see you tomorrow, if you don't get snowed in. Be careful.

"Bye, Nancy, Steve interjected with a smile.

"Goodnight, Steve. Tell Lori I said Hi." As she walked away Steve gave an alluring gaze to her attractive legs.

"Hey, hey, let's keep our eyes focused on the matter at hand," Tom said.

"I thought that was a matter at hand," Steve replied.

"OK, funny guy, if you don't behave, I am telling Lori on you."

"Oooh, Papa bear Well, don't pull any punches on my account."

"I won't. Now go find out who had the last command for the property room, also when the last log file was dated. I want the names of anyone who entered that room. Narrow it down for every officer, look what they were checking in and out. I want to know who had access to that dagger. And I want to know pronto!"

"Yes sir."

Steve thought to himself, I know I am friends with him, but I know right now he is being the boss. I wonder why he always takes these cases so personally. These cult cases really get to him.

"Oh, and Sarge, call Lori for me. Tell her you're making me late. Don't mention anything about Nancy's legs not even jokingly. She is jealous enough as it is." Tom laughed as he threw a bean-bag frog toy that he uses as a paperweight at Steve. Steve shut the door before he was hit. He turned and laughed as he walked away knowing the face he made eased the serious attitude from Tom.

•———————————————•

Night was falling on the city's capital. In a dark, run down industrial area of the town, at a large warehouse, many cars were pulling into the parking lot. The neon sign on the front of the building was flashing green and purple colors. It read the "Melting Pot." The building was large like a football stadium. The crowd was filled with young adults. The chatter of many peoples voices and a thumping noise in a continuous rhythm, echoed throughout the district's area. Six very tall and muscular bouncers guarded the door's entrance, keeping all who waited to enter behind a red velvet rope. It aligned a red carpet as long as the building. Inside was a circle embedded in the floor sixty feet wide and six feet deep. The nickname for this circle dance floor was called the pit. A stage for a band to play on was occupied by a gothic group. Each member dressed in all black attire, with the number six hundred and sixty-six tattooed to their foreheads. The air was filled with a strange stench of burning herbs and chemicals. The young people were jumping up and down inside the pit, squeezed in like sardines in a tin can.

Some people were running up to the center of the stage, on a solid ramp that looked like it was made for the handicapped to roll a wheel chair up or down. Once atop of the pit area, they flung themselves into the air and onto the others, as a mockery of the casting of souls entering the premises of hell. Others were banging their heads into the skulls of anyone standing next to them. Some wore leather bands with spikes wrapped around their knuckles, punching anyone within arm's reach. Wounds invoked, and they laughed at their victims as blood gushed, truly symbolic of the demonic torture of souls in the abyss. Iron cages hung in different areas of the building. Inside were women, stripped of clothing, revealing their flesh for all to see. "Crack Slash," was the sound of a whip. A task master was administering torture, but the screams from the tortured were not to stop . . . or for mercy . . . but cries for more. "Give me more, master, give me more!" the voices of agony in this temple of evil worship. In one corner, open acts of sexual deviation were being conducted. Above them, in the invisible realm, their puppet masters were pulling the strings, laughing at them in a hideous thunder.

Mocking copulations these once illuminated beings now creatures of darkness were perverse in understanding. Fallen angels, now demons, were ridiculing these humans.

A homeless man in rags knelt down in front of a parked car. He picked up a half-smoked cigarette butt, it was a little soaked, but still long enough that he figured he could dry it out and smoke it later.

The imp, known as addiction, whispered in his ear, "Go ahead! No one is watching, pick it up. It will be just what you need. Smoke it you will get your buzz. Forget your pride."

So the homeless man acted on the voices he heard. As the man reached for the butt on the ground a black limo drove by, splashing muck, mud, and slushy ice, into the air, soaking him with the bitter dampness of the cold. He raised himself upright quickly. Shaking the water and ice from his coat and face, he clenched his fist at the black limo, now fading into the dark street, Cursing obscenities as it disappeared into the night. The imp mocked his weakness, sneered and shouted, "You fool!" He turned and walked into a forgotten alley of darkness, too cold to sleep. He wandered the frozen walkways, waiting day-break, hoping to find an opened fast food restaurant to thaw his limbs from the extreme cold.

Inside the limo, which was warmed to a perfect seventy degrees, was the Senator. He was looking out the left side of the window. Far off in thought, staring at the buildings passing by, the Senator demanded, "Where are we going, Kirk?"

"To a place called the 'Melting Pot.' There is someone who wants to meet you. Someone very important to the society."

"Who is this person, that he is so important that I have to meet him in the middle of the night? Why doesn't he come and meet me in my office?"

"Protocol, sir, protocol."

"Forget protocol Kirk, who is this guy?"

"Who?" Kirk said with a laugh. "The question, my dear Senator, is not who . . . but what is he? And you're going to find out very soon. So sit back and SHUT YOUR MOUTH!"

The senator sensed that Kirk was speaking with a power greater than himself. The demon, Fear, was still close to Kirk and enveloping his presence onto the senator. The senator turned his head, looking outward toward the city . . . looking at the lights twinkling in the black of night.

F I V E

Oh God! Please hear this, I will give myself the time to be a better husband, better father . . . just please, let it all be ok.

I stood at my high point above the clouds, now only silvery on the top edge, by the light of the full moon shining. I saw the city in broken segments, when the wind gave opening to the cold flurries falling on the white ground. I never knew what cold was like, not having a flesh and blood body. I have only known this spiritual body that was created for me to reside.

"Septuagint, assist!" I heard the command as clear as if someone was standing right beside me. My clothes began to shine a bright white. The command came straight from Heaven. I turned to look behind me at the vast, open space of white clouds. To the southwest, far off in the distance but higher than I was standing, I saw the assignment to which I was being beckoned.

"Roger that, tower. Negative, repeat no pressure to the right hydraulic wheel base. We are declaring an emergency."

"Copy that, flight four-one-two- seven, you are cleared for emergency landing on runway three-nine'r alpha. Vector on current pattern hold. Barring is zero-two-four. Runway crew has been notified. We are on code three standby alert, ready to assist. Good luck, Captain, and God be with you. Enter downwind."

"Ladies and gentlemen, this is your captain. I need everyone to return to their seats, and please fasten your safety belts. We are experiencing mechanical difficulties to the landing gear. It seems we are going to have to arrive on the belly of the plane. Again, please put your seats in the upright and locked positions, and be prepared to exit in an orderly fashion as soon as it is safe to do so. All stewardesses please return to your seats also."

"Oh God, please hear this. I will give myself the time to be a better husband, better father. Just please, let it all be ok. I will even go back to church and truly seek your presence."

Those were the words he uttered softly below a whisper. He was unaware I was sent by the Lord and standing right in front of him. Unaware I was here to assist. Unaware that the Lord is always attentive to the cries of the saints. I wondered if he would make good on his promise. I've never known what it is like to die. Neither did I understand fear, not like they do. But there is that one place . . . yes that one place. I shudder at the thought. That place angels do fear to tread. I never want to go there. The place of outer darkness, the place where there is no love of God. Maybe that's the emotion these human beings were experiencing.

I watched as he gripped the arms of the seat, slowing the flow of blood, his hands turning to a pale white, and his knees moving up and down in nervousness. It was clear to see the anxiety he was facing. In a few moments of their time it would all be over. The plane descended with the landing gear in the up position. All the crew was hard pressed to the back of their seats. The co-pilot was reading aloud the instrumentations descent. "Twelve hundred, eleven hundred, one thousand, nine hundred,"

"Brace yourselves, men," the captain interjected.

"Seven-fifty, six hundred, four hundred," a button on the control panel that had just been blinking red turned to green.

"Captain, we have pressure!" said the co-pilot.

"Landing gear down now!" the co-pilot pushed the green button as the captain pulled back on the steering column, lifting the nose of the plane slightly upward. The wheels began to unfold.

"Two hundred, one hundred." the wheels were still unfolding, but the timing was critical, the plane was descending rapidly toward the pavement. The long stream of neon blue runway lights was now buzzing pass and growing closer with each moment.

"Fifty, forty, thirty, twenty."

"Oh man! This is going to be close," said the navigational co-pilot. He squinted his eyes and flinched up his body muscles anticipating the impact.

A solid thud was heard as the wheels locked in solid position only milliseconds before the touchdown. The plane's wheels hit the ground, jolting the passengers in a harsh bounce. The front nose of the plane continued in a forward descent, striking the ground. The pilot pushed the levers forward causing the engines to roar spinning the turbines in reverse to slow the speed of the plane.

"Flight four-one-two-seven, to tower. We have made a safe landing and currently request permission to taxi."

"Roger that. After departure please see the commanding officer in tower."

"Copy that tower. Over and out," said the captain. He removed his headphones and let out a big sigh of relieve. "Now that was a little to close for comfort for me," he said, looking back at his co-pilot.

"Whew! You aren't the only one."

His pale hands rushed with blood after he released his grip on the arms of the plane's seat. The crew and the captain wanted to celebrate, but unknown to them the real hero was the man in seat twelve 'A' a Christian who had called out to God. "Thank you, Lord," he whispered just under his breath. I smiled as I removed my hand from his shoulder. Still he was unaware of my presence, I turned, looking up the aisle, only to see that I was needed elsewhere. There before me, invisible to all except me, was the White Door. One step, that's all it takes, is one step. Through the doorway I entered. I was now inside a fast food convenience store and gas station. Looking back into the White Door, I could still see the passengers exiting the plane. The man in the row twelve seat 'A' was still a little shaky, but he would be fine. Fading into nothing the door disappeared. So there I was, looking at HoHo's, Twinkies and potato chips. A man was working at the counter, making notes on a paper pad. Why was I here? No one was around . . . My clothes had turned back to bronze, so I decided to sit. I imagined myself on the ceiling's rafter beams, and so I was there, looking down at the store, empty of all but the man working at the counter. I must have arrived ahead of the event that was to take place.

•―――――――――――――――•

Two men entered the store wearing black hoods over their faces. I had seen that kind of mask before, but it was long ago in times past, called history. I remember the Englishman who had repented of his sins for what he was ordered to do. Yes, the place was in England. The young warrior had fought for her country, the girl known as Joan of arc. I remember that hooded man, how he cried behind the black mask, not really wanting the young saint to suffer death. Executioner; Yes that's the name given to those who wear the black hood. Why were two of the executioners here now in this place at the same time? I see a third person entering this space. He did not see the two with the black mask hiding in the back of the store. Wait! I knew why I was called here. It was Tom Allen, the police officer I had been drawn to. Tom was getting milk out of the cooler. One of the men in the mask moved into the room, from behind the swinging, smooth steel doors. The other one crouched down behind one of the aisles, so as not to be seen by Tom. Being in view by the man working at the counter, he put his finger to his lips, gesturing to the man not to say anything. I knew it was time to act.

I was standing beside Tom. I laid my hand on his shoulder and whispered, "Danger!" Tom remained calm, turned around, and walked right out the door. He spoke to the man at the counter saying, "I left my wallet in my car. Be right back."

Tom got into his vehicle, pulled the gearshift down to 'R' and drove it backward in the parking lot out of range of the front door. He picked up the radio that was sitting on the front seat and called for backup.

●────────────────●

"You can't do this! You can't! I have a family! I was just doing what I thought you wanted me to do." A nod from a man sitting in the executive chair was the go ahead. Whap! Whap! A heavy thud from the huge enforcer struck the blows to the face of the man sitting bound with handcuffs. The room was dark except for the glow of a small lamp on the table, and the glow of the large fish tank across the room of this office. The sound of the faint, thumping noise of the bands playing in the front half of the warehouse, known as the "Melting Pot," was muffled by the soundboard insulation.

The man in the executive chair raised his finger in an upward gesture. Without saying a word, the enforcer grabbed the shoulder and the chair to which the man was bound, and raised him upward from the floor. The shackled man was now bleeding profusely from the nose and mouth because of the lead in the black leather gloves the enforcer had struck him with. He repeated his pleas with dire desperation.

"You can't do this! I'm a cop!"

Once again the nod of judgment had proclaimed its sentence. The sound of cracking filled the empty room, as the teeth of the bound man snapped and broke into many pieces. His head turned quickly to the left, as the blow struck him on the upper right side of his face, causing deep lacerations to the mouth. His lips swelled like a over inflated rubber tire that was about to burst. Thick, red blood oozed down his chin and neck and onto his leather coat.

Haw, haw-haw, was the laughter of the once warrior angel, now demon. He was there whispering the commands to the man in the executive chair. He was no longer an angel but had changed in eons past, at the casting out of Lucifer. His name is Fury, the one who has an unquenchable thirst for blood. His ranking in the army of darkness is that of a ruler. The order ranking, starting from the lowest is Principality, then Powers, then Rulers, then Wicked Spirits in the heavenly realms. So Fury was third up the chain of command, and his spiritual troops of fallen angels were posted all around this place called the "Melting Pot," the den of sin.

•─────────────────────────•

Tom had exited his vehicle. He drew his weapon and squatted down behind the driver's door. Two police units had arrived. Officer Murphy was missing, and this was his zone, and Tom knew it. Considering why one of his own did not show to a call, Tom thought, He'd better have a good reason for not being here. The first unit took up a location at the back door. The other police officer parked in front, not far from Tom's unmarked police unit. The two cars made a barricade for both officers to hide behind. Tom looked over and the thought of seeing this young officer was consoling. But still, Tom recognized that the officer beside him was only a rookie, a rookie who had been on the streets for less than a year. He wondered if he would hold up under the pressure. Could he pull the trigger if he had to? Would he know when to fire or not? What if the suspect had seen the units pull up? What if they send out the store's worker? A million and one questions went through his head. When was the last time he had spoken to his kids? Did he do enough to help his ailing parents? Is the gunpowder still good in the bullets, what if I get a misfire? Are there any civilians behind me in the line of fire? Will I die? Do I have my bullet proof vest on today? Ok Tom! Get a grip on yourself! You're the leader here, so lead.

"O'Rork . . . Use the P.A. system after they exit the store, not before," Tom instructed.

"Ten-four, Sarge," replied the rookie.

Inside the store, I watched, as the two suspects rushed toward the man working at the counter. They pointed their guns at the man, demanding money from the cash register.

"Should I blow him away?" one asked.

"I don't know about that, we came for the money, man, not to kill anyone." He raised his gun to the man's head.

I waited because I knew they were going to show "the hidden ones" that were residing deep in the black spirits of the two executioners.

Whoom, Whoom, Ah ha! There they were, finally showing themselves. They always come at the last moments to watch. Looking down at my side, I saw my sword flaming.

Ice and sleet flung into the air, as the long black limo made a sharp left and accelerated through the curve. Inside, Kirk and the Senator swayed as the turn proceeded into the parking lot filled with many cars.

"Where are we?" asked the Senator.

"We're here," replied Kirk.

The Senator looked out the right side of the window, seeing the neon sign which was flashing the "Melting Pot"

"The 'Melting Pot' . . . sounds like a witches' brew," the Senator commented.

Kirk replied with a condescending look.

"More that you know." The limo proceeded to drive alongside the building. Arriving at the entrance at the rear of the building, two guards in long coats stood at a large, iron gate. Both were holding chain leashes and two beautiful, large purebred Doberman Pinchers, snarling at anyone who might approach the secured area. The gates swung inward as a gesture of welcome. The guard motioned his hand to say, come in. The limo continued into the management controlled area reserved for the V.I.P's. Kirk exited the vehicle, and then the Senator, as the driver held the door open. The Senator turned his coat collar upward to protect his neck from the cold breeze.

While pulling on half of the pentagram to open the door, Kirk turned, looking back toward the Senator and asked, "Are you ready for your first use of the Poniard?" Kirk knew he was being sarcastic, making a mockery of this political windbag's rhetoric. He Knew full well the high and mighty Senator had no idea what a Poniard was.

SIX

"Hello, Septuagint."

I had just started to pull my sword from its sheath. I turned and looked to the right. Beside me, he had appeared, Xenophon. His stature was huge, and beautifully splendid.

"Would you like some company, Septuagint?"

"Yes sir that would be nice."

"Well, I know if I didn't come, you would surely be here for awhile."

I smiled, comforted by his company. Xenophon was a Cherubim in the ranking order of the army of the Lord. The ranking order for the Host of heaven is as follows; Angels are the messengers, the guardian spirits or attendants for God's plans on Earth; Cherubim are second in the order of ranking, next to the seraphim, and most times confused with a cherub, Seraphim, who is an angel of the high order and an awesome creature to behold. He has six wings, and words cannot express his magnificent glory. He is the protector to the steps of the throne; Arch-Angel is the highest in the rank of Angels. I remember many archangels but only three are well known to man. Michael, the commander of the army of the lord; Gabriel, the messenger of God; Lucifer, the angel of music and praise. His name means light bearer, and light is the ancient word for praise. He had a job and that was to bring the praises to God. But he started stealing the praises for himself, he was the most beautiful of all the angels, but because of his sin and his desire to be worshiped, he fell from Heaven's glory. The event is now known as the fall. The number of all the angels in heaven cannot be counted, but of that vast amount, Lucifer fooled one third into following him. His appearance changed from beauty to repulsive ugliness. So did the appearance of the one third of the angels that followed him now called demons. Only three names were given to man, and then only for historical purposes, so as not to have them fall down and worship angels. They are but creations, like humans, who were made to worship the Creator, "Praise be his Name." I have free will and could have gone down in the fall, yet here is my stand, I choose good. I am but an angel still earning my rank.

Xenophon said I would be here awhile, what did he mean? His words alone had merit, he knew something I didn't. But I did know he wouldn't have shown up unless

. . . Whoosh, whoosh! Out of the bodies of the black hooded executioners appeared the two demons. Stepping away from the back-sides of the men standing at the counter, the tall one holding the gun to the man at the cash register repeated the words just before the demon exited his body.

"Yeah, I am going to blow your head off!"

One of them I recognized. His name was Deprive. The other one I did not know, but I did realize why Xenophon was there now. In my zeal to vanquish these evil beings, I may have been a little over zealous. The one demon that came out of the smaller man was in the rank of darkness, a 'Power Demon'. I had no idea he was inside the smaller man. I would have guessed a Principality, or an imp, but not a Power Demon.

"He's mine!" Xenophon shouted.

"Be my guest." I would definitely have been here awhile if I had tried to do battle with this one, just like Xenophon had said.

"Aweeeeee!" I heard the screaming, as Xenophon used only his raiment as a weapon. He allowed the full glory to shine through his clothes. By the time the power demon realized that the glory was shining in the room, it was too late. He was vaporized on the spot, sent back into the dungeons of darkness known as the abyss. Swoosh! Was the sound my blade made while cutting the upper half of the spiritual body of the demon known as Deprive. And in the nick of time too, for the man holding the gun had just cocked the trigger. Deprive was but a misty vapor forced back to the shadows of darkness.

"O'Rork, he's going to shoot him. Use the P.A. now!" commanded Tom.

"Stop! This is the police! Come out with your hands over your heads! Do it now!"

At the very first word "Stop" from the P.A. used by the rookie officer, a spine tingling chill sped through the bodies of both the men in the store. The tall man quickly turned, looked out the plate glass window, and saw the lights flashing an echo of red and blue streaks, across the blackness of the night.

●────────────────────●

The door to the back office of the "Melting pot" started to open. He raised his lip and growled, unseen by human eyes. Only half of his spiritual body fit inside the room. Fury's vast size of a power demon was immense. His waist and upper body protruded up from the floor, while the other half was still somewhere submerged in the earth. His arms were muscular, similar to a giant man on steroids. His hands were huge with bony fingers and fingernails like claws of an eagle. His head resembled a boar. Razor-sharp teeth pointed upward from his jutting jaw. He was always slightly bowed forward from the weight of the long bull horns atop his head. Behind his tremendous shoulders were the wings of an enormous bat folded inward.

Kirk and the Senator entered the room. Fury whispered in the ear of the man sitting in the executive chair. "They are here, take care of business."

"Senator, how nice to finally meet you," said the man in the executive chair. The Senator looked directly at him, turned seeing the bound man half-beaten and bleeding in the other chair.

"Nice to meet me who are you? What is this? What's going on here?"

Fear made himself into a long chain of grayish, dark smoke, and slithered on the ground wrapping around the feet of the Senator and sliding upward like a snake around his body.

Fear whispered in the senator's ear.

"Your life is done if you don't follow and obey."

Realizing the dreadful situation he was in the Senator's knees began to shake, as he stood there speechless in the presence of the man before him. The spirit, Fear, jeered at him with a haunting laugh. Fury then shouted at Fear.

"Yes, that's it! Make him tremble. I hate these human beings."

Fear unwound his Smokey form back into the grotesque figure he was. The two demons stood back with their arms folded, to watch life imitate the art they were painting.

"My dear Senator, this is the one who killed your step-sister, and now it is your turn to return the favor. Since I have him for you, you will slice his throat."

The senator shook inside upon hearing those words. So did the bound man. The man in the executive chair said to Kirk,

"Hand him the poniard." Kirk moved towards the senator and handed him the dagger.

•───────────────•

The glass door opened slowly. The tall man came out first and his partner followed. "Put your weapons on the ground," commanded the rookie officer, O'Rork.

The two would be robbers complied with the orders.

"Turn and face the store's window, and keep your hands on top of your heads, fingers interlocked." again commanded O'Rork.

And again the thieves did as they were told. Sgt. Tom Allen pointed his weapon towards the criminals. The other officers approached slowly and proceeded with the pat down. After searching the robbers for any other weapons, the officer handcuffed both of the men. He then removed the black face hoods that had concealed their identities. Both men were placed inside the patrol car and transported to the county jail for booking.

Xenophon smiled "Good work, Septuagint," and he instantly faded from view.

Tom was getting into his vehicle, and I wanted to go with him, to see where he was living. I was now a little more curious about him especially after seeing that this one human was so determined to do good deeds. There was something about the spiritual light that was in him. I noticed that it got a little brighter every time he seemed to come in contact with the presence of evil. I wondered if he could have been in the heavens at one time. Maybe he decided to come to earth to live as a human? Maybe he was on an assignment that I was not told about? Could it be he was here on a mission too? Only time will tell.

"Good Job, O'Rork. Have the paperwork on my desk in the morning. I will sign off it then. If you see officer Murphy, tell him I want to see him in my office in the morning." Tom said.

S E V E N

On the other side of town, the Senator held in his right hand the dagger known as a poniard an instrument used for ceremonial rituals. Now he stood behind the man who was limp from the beating that had been inflicted upon him by his captors.

"Don't worry Senator, he is a dirty cop. Isn't that right officer Murphy?" asked the man sitting in the executive chair.

The demon, Fury, was shouting curses at the Senator taunting him in the spiritual realm to make him agitated. The Senator did become angrier as each word spoken by Fury pierced his eardrums. The Senator grabbed Murphy by the hair pulling his head backward then raised the dagger upward to strike.

●─────────────────────●

Tom was driving and I was sitting right beside him. Sometimes I think he is aware of my presence but I am unsure. I would have liked to reveal myself to him, but I was restrained from doing so. He was pushing a button on the dashboard to warm himself from the chill in the air. I comprehend the idea, but was still unable to understand the concept of the loss or gain of body heat, being that I do not have one. So many things I wish I could understand, the small things they do . . . like chewing gum, or roller-coasters, or why they go 'Mmm' after drinking the liquid they call coffee. They are a curious race. I have watched all their generations from the start. I have seen many centuries come and go that are only moments to me, but years to them. There are things that are available to this new race that were unthinkable to their fathers, such as the ability to harness energy or release it. Tom reached down and turned a knob on the dashboard radio, but across the country, in a silo called Mx four deep in the earth, a hand reaches for a different kind of knob.

"Mock test one. On three, two, one. Simulation mock, turn key left. Mock simulation turn key right." the hand reaches over the counter with computerized equipment, and lifts a sealed red button encased in bulletproof glass.

"Simulate launch" The major said.

"Launch simulated, Sir, I got to say I hope we never have to release these birds. Every time we run though this drill, I get a chill to the bone.

"Sergeant, if you're having any kind of second thoughts of noncompliance with your functions in this unit, you need to seek a transfer to some other unit. Is that understood?"

"Yes sir, Major! No second thoughts here, sir!"

"Good. Carry on."

The observing general exited the silo launch room, stepping through the ten inch thick steel doorway into the corridor.

Approaching the general from the other end of the long corridor was an information office in a tan uniform. He was carrying a chrome briefcase. As he neared him, He addressed the general with snappy salute and said, "Sir, you have a phone call from Eagle one."

Raising the briefcase, he opened the latches, lifting the case top towards the general. Inside was a red phone and a computerized dial pad for accessing a secure code. The general dialed in his issued military code and then lifted the phone.

"Yes sir, the test was a success. The new codes for operation Angelic Rage will be implemented next week. Everything is on schedule as planned."

"There will be a mandatory meeting in my office on Friday, nine a.m."

"Yes sir," said the general as he up the phone, and the information office, which was still standing at attention, shut the case and secured the latches. The young officer was able to see that even this war monger of a general was disturbed by the proceedings of this new operation. He saluted the general as he preceded on his way though the corridor.

•———————————————————•

The red light had now turned to a glowing green, as snow gently fell. Tom reached over and turned the windshield wipers on, clearing off the soft snow. It was quickly melting into water as the car's heater warmed the inside of the glass. The night was cold and the streets were empty but ahead in the distance, the church parking lot was notably crowded . . . not unusual but different, more full. Tom removed his hands from the steering wheel and rubbed them briskly. Warming them, he then grabbed the steering wheel again. What's going on here? This is a Wednesday night, he thought to himself. That's quite a crowd of people. Tom parked his car in front of the building, and leaned forward towards the steering wheel. He tried to see the sign posted in front of the church between the up and down motion of his windshield wipers. The sign read, "St. Thomas Church. The new Azusa Revival with guest speaker Pastor Paul Zoe."

Tom opened his car door and looked back down the empty street. He saw nothing but the street lights, and just a handful of cars far off in the distance. Turning up the collar of his overcoat to offset the chill, he shut the door to his car and walked around the front to the sidewalk. He could hear the voice of the pastor emitting from the building. Opening the big wooden door, Tom walked in and could see the crowd was bigger than he ever had expected. It looked as if it were a rock concert more than a church service. The overflow was all the way back into the vestibule area. But, unlike a rock concert, he took note; no unruliness was going on in here. All were attentive to what the pastor was saying. This event was peculiar to Tom. He could see the man who was speaking was standing on the first or second step. A line was formed all around the inside walls. The people were young and old alike. Walking slowly, the ushers were assisting them to the front of the steps to where the pastor was standing. The sound of an organ was playing a sweet melody of the song called, "Just as I am."

I had followed Tom inside. I loved this place, the feeling of being at home with family and friends. The house of the Lord has always been to me like a cabin you go to on vacation. So this place was a home away from home to me. I could see things in the spirit that these humans could not. Such as all the angels who had gathered here at this one special moment in time. As I walked with Tom up the isle, I could see angels I had not seen in centuries.

Tom whispered, "Excuse me," as he bent over to step into the pew to sit down. He sat beside a man in a grey coat. I looked at the face of the man. I smiled as I recognized him. He was the man who I stopped in the street with the gun. But now he was here and tears of repentance were rolling down his cheeks. I looked upward toward the ceiling and there many angels were standing in the air. We are not bound by natural laws like gravity, although we do sometimes obey that natural law just to be next to humans.

As I was looking, the mist, pure white smoke of the Glory cloud was beginning to fill the church. It is the peace that surpasses all understanding. Anyone who was in the place where it fell did not want to leave. I was standing at the end pew, where

Tom was sitting. A child in front of him turned around and looked at me.

The small boy leaned over to his mother and said, "Look mommy, angel, like in the book."

I smiled at the boy. She turned and looked my direction, but her eyes revealed a life of sin, and were unable to see me. But the heart of the child was pure innocence. He rested his head on his arm just gazing and smiling, as his mother hushed him to be still.

I listened as Paul Zoe the guest speaker was preaching about Jesus, and what happened in his ministry two thousand years ago according to human time.

He said, "If Satan had known what Jesus was about to do in the spiritual realm after he was crucified, the devil would have never provoked the crowd in Jerusalem to have him killed."

Paul explained in a easy going manner of speech, that Jesus was the Messiah. He pointed out how he was the only one who met all the criteria of all the predicted prophesies. And that Jesus is the anointed messenger from the Father God. He talked about how the anointing was passed on to each of his disciples, and all who believed became Christians.

Like all the other angels, I was intent on hearing this message. For us angels do eagerly seek the message which was given to the human race.

Paul continued teaching, saying, "When Christ who is your life appears, so also, shall you appear with him in glory." He went on to say, "When Jesus walked the earth, there was but only one God like man. The devil's only goal was to destroy him, and unbeknownst to the Devil or Satan, God's greatest work was done in the infirmities of his only begotten son. That by his destruction, the devil would be helping the creation of a whole new race of God like individuals.

Paul continued on saying, "A single seed that is dead and buried is like a sunflower, only then does it germinate and bring forth a new creation much larger than the seed itself. Within that new creation is other seeds that will skater and further that creation, all individual yet all of the same first seed. Being planted and then reborn. So are you by being reborn in Christ Jesus. As it is written, 'Therefore if any man be in Christ Jesus, he is a new creature, old things are passed away, behold all things are made new.'"

Paul continued to minister to the people. He taught about the Holy Spirit, he preached on healing, how it was written that, 'By his stripes, you are healed,' That by simple faith and believing the Word of God, you can receive your healing. Paul explained that he was no miracle worker, just a messenger that believed the Bible was true. And if he preached about Jesus, that signs and miracles would follow. He began to place his hands upon people asking the Lord to act on what the Bible had said.

Tom was listening intently. I saw the spiritual light inside him begin to glow brighter as Paul was ministering. Tom's faith was increasing and he stood up. He wanted to get in the line. Tom had never before seen a true man of faith like this Pastor before and he wanted Zoe to pray for him.

●────────────────●

Oh God! Oh God! Please don't kill me! I'm sorry, I'm so sorry!" Officer Murphy begged as the Senator's hand hesitated to thrust the dagger downward.

The two demons, Fear and Fury, were lurking in the shadows, snarling and giggling with a abhorrent laughter.

"Do it Tinnimen. Prove your loyalty to the society!" Kirk said.

Tinnimen looked at the beaten man then glanced up at the one sitting in the executive chair. He had just hung up the phone. One of his associates had brought in a chrome briefcase. He gave the nod of approval again without saying a word. A memory flashed in the mind of the Senator, a memory of his sister helping him up to the sink to brush his teeth when he was five years old. Then another when he was sixteen, she came into his room to console him about the girl that broke his heart.

But like a flash of lightening, Fury whispered,

"Remember the photo." and a memory of the last image of his sister filled his mind. The black and white police evidence photo, lying on a cold wet alleyway with a carved circle of the pentagram star etched into her skin . . . a cadaver with no head.

Wham! Wham! Wham! The dagger made a slurping sound as it exited the wounds of Officer Murphy. The blood squirted as each thrust was projected with cataclysmic force. Kirk squinted and reared his head as he saw the forcefulness the Senator used, but still managed to form a grin as he watched him cross the line between good and evil.

"Surely, dear Senator, you now have the true satisfaction of now knowing this very bad man will not be living on death row for years telling every scumbag dirt-ball all the gory little details of how he axed up your sister," The man sitting in the executive chair said, as he stood up and pulled a handkerchief out of his breast pocket and wiped the droplets of Murphy's blood that had squirted on his left cheek.

He then turned toward Kirk and added, "Give him the ring."

Kirk walked over to the maple desk, opened the top drawer and reached inside, pulling out a wooden box made of pine.

"It was especially made to hold twelve rings, but as you can see only two are left. So you should consider yourself very fortunate to be receiving one of your own." Kirk said. He remove one and reached down lifting the Senators hand, and placed it on his left hand pinkie finger. The Senator stared at the floor in a confused daze, he was in shock. The reality was just sinking in that he had just killed a man. He looked at his new ring as blood dripped from the knife. He dropped the knife on the floor. He peered at his new crown of victory noticing the blood that dripped on the tip of his right shoe.

Swoosh!–The demon, Guilt had appeared behind the Senator. He immediately grabbed the Senator and wrapped his arms around his head while jumping on his back and placing a heavy weight of sin on him. Fear and Fury laughed when they saw the Senator slump unknowingly as Guilt grabbed him and climbed atop of his shoulders and took his seat.

Guilt, seeing the other demons in the room, said in his horrible voice, "Will you be visiting often?" Then Guilt hissed his laugh, for he knew he had a host to cling to for quite sometime.

The man who had been sitting in the executive chair reached up with his left hand to shake with the Senator, and, by doing so revealed his own ring. It was the same kind of pentagram ring as the Senator's.

"There's a meeting in my office on Friday, at nine a. m. See you there."

As he was leaving the room, he said, "Kirk take care of our new friend, and see that he gets home safe."

"Yes, Mr. President, I will."

The music sounded out its Thump- Thump- Thump from the Melting Pot as the door was unlatched and opened by the Presidents bodyguards.

The Senator began to shake, saying, "I would like to go home Kirk." Kirk held the Senator by the shoulders to hold him up.

"Of course Senator," Kirk turned to one of the men in the room. "Wrap that up," he said, looking at Murphy's corpse in the chair.

"Kirk, I want to go now!"

"Yes sir, I do believe it is time to go. Yep, now is the time." Kirk smiled smugly.

"Yes sir now is the time. Now is the time don't wait for tomorrow friends, tomorrow is not promised, Today is the day of salvation. That is why today is called a present." Pastor Paul Zoe quoted, "You never know at what moment your life will end. And there is no hope for anyone if you die without salvation. So please my friends, if you have not accepted Christ Jesus as your Lord and Savior, do so now. If you need to renew your relationship with the Lord, please say this prayer with us. You have nothing to lose and everything to gain."

Tom felt a chill run down his neck. Somehow he wondered if his coming into this church was purely accidental or divine intervention of some sort. He bowed his head and began to whisper quietly,

"Dear lord, I remember as a child I accepted you, but I know I have backslidden far from you. Please forgive me and help me to understand what it is you really want from my life." Tom felt a lump well up in his throat as tears began to stream down his cheek. He twitched a smile, knowing he had not cried since he was five. He thought that he had run out of tears and had none left in his body, but now here he stood proved wrong. The line had moved forward and he was now face to face with Pastor Paul Zoe.

"Hello Brother, What is your name dear sir?"

"Tom, Tom Allen."

Zoe held the microphone in one hand, and place the other on Tom's shoulder, leaning in closer and speaking so only he could hear him. "Tom, I am sincerely glad you came tonight."

I was standing next to Tom on his right side and just a little behind him. Paul had taken about three steps backwards away from Tom but was still facing him. Paul was un-aware as most of the congregation, except maybe that little boy, that two of the Lord's angels were standing on both sides of him. The one to his left was named Sword of the spirit. The one to his right was named Defender of the Faith. Both were there to act on behalf of the word of God.

"Look mommy! The angel is standing right beside E-acher."

She tried again to hush the young boy, as the people in the first few rows all smiled intently looking but not seeing.

"Sshhh." the boy's mother whispered, "Can you really see an angel?"

I looked at him, and smiled, placing my finger to my lips as to say "quiet please." The boy beamed back and stood up in the pew, trying to mimic my actions by tapping his finger to his own lips. He then pointed at me, and leaned into his mother ear,

"He . . . right, there . . . seee."

Pastor Zoe began speaking to Tom by faith, saying, "Tom, you didn't just come here by accident, and you were wondering if the Lord has brought you here by divine inspiration. Tom, I believe God has a specific plan for each of our lives, and he reveals himself in wonderful ways."

Zoe's act of faith to begin to speak in faith, had now increased, and was granted what the Bible calls in First Corinthians the gift of discerning of Spirits, the ability to see into the spiritual realm. Zoe began to smile as Tom grinned, hesitantly uncertain about how Zoe could know what he just prayed only moments ago.

Zoe was now aware of his two assistants standing next to him. "Tom, are you ready to surrender your will to God's will?" Tom looked up into the face of Zoe.

"Yes, I believe I a..." Pastor Zoe did not even get the chance to actually touch Tom as he was beginning to step toward him when the two angels beside Zoe heard Tom say, "yes, I believe," they moved swiftly as Zoe began to raise his hand. They drew their swords faster than the speed of light, and charged into Tom, one to each side of him, and cutting to pieces the spirit man that lived inside Tom. His spirit-man was slain, and so what happened in the spiritual realm is reality. It took place in the natural realm as well. Tom's body fell backward to the floor as though he were dead. Twice shot and seventeen years as a police officer, Tom thought nothing in his life had ever been as powerful or real to him as that moment. In the natural counting of time, Tom only lay on the floor for what was seconds but to him it was an eternity, and a review of his life.

Zoe's grin turned to tears of joy, as the gift of insight was lifted from him. The church choir began to sing, "Just as I am lord, just as I am."

The iron gates opened slowly as the parade of limos departed from the back of the parking lot. Seven cars total, and the middle one was carrying the leader of the United States.

"Sir, mind if I ask you a question?"

"No. What is it?"

"Well, it's about the case, sir."

"Case?"

"Yes, sir, the chrome case with the phone in it?"

"What about it?"

"If you're receiving calls from that line, can't they trace that to you, sir?"

"Jack, you been a good agent, and your instinct for details are assured but no need to worry. Only three people are aware of the relay code from this phone, and I trust the other two."

"I see, so it goes directly to Air Force One's communication telecom."

"That's right. So no one can actually tell the exact location where I am."

"Sorry sir had to ask." The President nodded as he smiled.

"I understand Jack. Sometimes it's just the little things that get to you, isn't it?"

Jack adjusted his tie, and sat back in the limo, and said, "Yes, sir."

The Senator and his personal assistant, Kirk, had just exited the Melting Pot, when the Senator looked to his left and saw the last three limos leaving the gated area parking lot.

"Burrrr, it sure is a chilly night," Kirk said as he puffed out "O" rings in the frosty air. He turned up the collar of his pinstriped suit coat and wrapped a blue scarf around his neck. Slapping the on the right shoulder, he added, "Let's get you home, Senator, What do you say?"

Tinnimen, was still in shock, looked up at the sky, not really looking at any one thing.

"I wonder if He's really up there, I wonder if he saw what I did. Am I doomed?"

Kirk laughed making light of him. "Doomed, no... no... Your not doomed, you're leading the poles by a two to one margin ratio. Don't you know this was your entire destiny? Fate, that's what I call it, fate."

"Yeah, fate, and I just sealed it in blood."

He looked down at the tip of his shoe, seeing Murphy's blood on it. The driver opened the passenger side rear door for him, and Tinnimen got in. Kirk walked around to the other side opened the driver's rear door for himself. He patted the limo's roof a couple of times with his left hand, the same hand that bore a ring with a pentagram on the pinkie finger.

Jesting, as if he were in a good mood, said, "Home James."

EIGHT

Fury hissed as he quickly whipped around, turning the huge bull-like horns atop of his head toward the direction of the thunderous screeching voice. The former angel, who now was his demonic partner for all eternity, had cried out his name.

"Fury Beelzebub demands an immediate report! You are ordered to report to him right now," Fear said.

Fury turned his back to his evil accomplice, gritting his razor sharp teeth.

"I know, I know."

"Then why do you hesitate? Go!"

"I hate going down to that part of the regions."

He made a fist and pounded it into an open paw of a hand, then pointing his finger claw at him, added "And you know why."

Enjoying the fact that he outranked Fury, and that by giving him this order was tormenting to him, Fear expanded his shadow of a being. He make himself appear larger, over casting himself above Fury.

"What reason would that be you miserable spirit of angriness?" Fear asked.

"I hate going there because . . . Because he might make me stay in netherworld of Hades."

"You have no choice. Now go!" again Fury gnashed his fang-like teeth, cursing vile obscenities as he descended blinking his reptilian-like skin over his yellow colored eyes.

He passed through the earth's surface beyond the dirt, sand and hard rock, sinking downward into the pits of nothingness. Opening his scaly eyes which were accustomed to seeing into the blackness of night, he entered into the spiritual abode. A realm where there is no time; a place where all of the past, present and future are bound as one, the place know as eternity. He entered the domain called 'Outer darkness.' This is the place angels fear to tread. This is the place where lost souls are harvested, those who have separated themselves from the love of God.

Fury looked out into the vastness of emptiness, and saw other demons working in pairs of two. Here the lower ranking demons, known as the Collectors of the damned were at work. They are the ones who believe their punishment will be less-severe by bringing other lost souls down to hell. They form no real object of shape, only the appearance of shadows.

Fury watched two of them with a recently lost soul, who was fighting without hope against their sticky grasp. They clung tightly one to each side of the tormented spirit. The collectors believed if they didn't succeed that the torment of the newly damned ones would be their own misery. Fury knew this was just a lie made up by his master.

As they passed by him, a once human, now lost soul was being crated off to be placed in a confinement torture area. Fury laughed as the soul of the man was screaming out in horrid cries of terror. He recognized the being. It was the man who was once known as officer Murphy, someone who had abused the weak on earth for monetary gains. Now all those relic's and all his desires of lustfulness seemed like a total waste of his life. He remembered everything he ever did, and every hateful word he ever uttered. Realizing he would never be able to leave, the horrors of being condemned for all eternity started to fill his mind. Murphy screamed as the demon collectors bit into his spiritual body and tore away pieces of his spiritual flesh. To the lost soul, it was like seeing his flesh body, not truly realizing he was departed from it. The sting of death is victorious over the damned. Murphy and his hideous escorts were descending quicker than Fury, for he was in no hurry to return. Murphy tried to see around him but was unable, the blackness smothered him. Somehow his eyes started to become accustomed to the darkness and a small speck of orange and red flickering in the far-off distance. He was aware of the fact that he was falling downward. Murphy's captors tormented his mind, telling him he was on his way to hell.

Fury looked around and listened to all the screams echoing in all the directions of the blackness. He thought about the thousands and thousands of lost soul's those who continuously entering the depths of darkness, and he was glad, knowing he was not going to be the only one to suffer. He watched as further and further down, Murphy's screams grew faint.

Murphy's agony was just about to begin, the orange and red glow became clearer. There it was Hell, in the shape of a giant harlot, lying on her back in the mist of nothingness; a whore waiting to receive her lovers of sin. Murphy shrieked at the sight of the gates opening up to greet him as he gazed at the indescribable being.

It was big as a building, a power demon named Rokron. He ordered the collectors to take Murphy to the valley of pain. Murphy continued to struggle to no avail.

"This can't be happening. I'm dreaming," he said.

They dragged him down the long wide path cavern. He saw what his fate was going to be. In the area off to the side of the path were pits of holes, with cages over the holes. Inside the pits was every dreadful slimy creepy thing one could imagine. Towering high above Murphy, Rokron grabbed him by the neck of his puny spiritual body, lifting him up like a rag doll. Murphy's spiritual body in the hands of Rokron was like the size of full grown man picking up a coffee cup. Rokron took a whiff of the scent of fear coming from Murphy. The terror and shock he was now experiencing was overwhelming, Rokron threw Murphy into one of the confinement cages and sealed the door for eternity. In Murphy's mind he was in the flesh. He watched Rokron as he walked away squinting what he though were his eyes in the glow of the dimness, Murphy heard others screaming out loud as he stood in the pit his head and shoulders barely at the level of the path walkway. He grabbed the bars of the cage, trying to see across the path from whence a scream came. He could see another cage.

"Hey, Hey you there." he shouted. He saw the shape of woman, "Hey lady!"

She did not answer. She was holding something in her hands. It was too dim to see what she held. Suddenly underneath his feet he felt a rumbling he thought, now what, an earthquake?

"Somebody help! Get me out of here!" the icky slimy things that were moving across his feet and ankles had quickly vacated into the pocket-holes of the pit. The rumbling had made them flee. Murphy squeezed the cage bars tighter and thought to himself, "Oh, this is not good!"

He screamed out louder, "Get me out of here!"

Suddenly, underneath his cage, bursting flame engorged his feet and swept upward, covering his entire spiritual body of which he still perceived as his flesh body. He watched as what he though was skin and muscles were completely consumed by the flames. His knees buckled in extreme agony as he hung by the bars of the cage. The flames were all consuming, leaving nothing but an imaginary hollowed skeleton. The pain was so severe he could no longer scream out only gnash his teeth in excruciating torment. The glow of the flame devoured him fully, his spirit imprisoned in a skeleton. He watched in amazement as his flesh regenerated itself and grew back again and again, only to be ravaged time after time. At the first burst of the ignited flames he recognized the woman to whom he called out. Her stomach etched with Murphy's own signature. It was the woman he had slain on earth. Again the slimy creatures the worm that never dies had hid itself. Murphy tried to rattle his way out of the cage but found no way to open it. As he felt the ground trembling once again under his feet, he thought, 'Oh no, not the rumbling,"

He screamed the same words he had heard the woman scream when he had killed her on earth.

"Mercy, mercy!" but there was none to be given, the flames had busted upward again. His screams had turned into whimpering moans and gnashing of teeth.

●────────────────────●

What a beautiful experience, I thought to myself to watch Tom Allen realize how much he needed to be in right standing with our Lord, to take the step of faith by receiving Jesus as his personal Savior. The Glory cloud, a wispy mist, was still surrounding him. I could tell he was hearing from Jesus as Pastor Zoe continued to minister to others. I wondered if the young boy who was able to see me had a call on his life to ministry. I know the Spirit administers the gift of sight into the spiritual realm for the good of all, maybe in future years he will be pastor of a church. I remember a young man from the east, which was forcefully ousted from the church for revealing the truth about the spiritual gifts recorded in the word of God. His hands clenched with fervency as he explained the letter of Corinthians written by the Apostle Paul, that the manifestation of the Spirit is given for the common good of the church body. But certain members guffawed and hooted, wrapped up in the quirks of modernism, saying that the gifts were only for the apostles of Jesus' day. Unaware that Jesus is the same, today, yesterday and forever. The eastern man had told them about the nine gifts with desperate humility, but to no avail. His voice was as an echoing concrete to deaf ears. He explained the Message of Wisdom. Not just human wisdom, but divine wisdom, and the Word of knowledge, as having the same knowing of God, coming from within the person; The Gift of Faith, as a strong acute sensitivity, to believe that the supernatural law of order will supersede natural laws of order; Endowment of divine healing, and the Working of miraculous powers; Prophecy, different from wisdom, or knowledge, it is the foretelling of events God knows to take place, sometimes not for years to come; Distinguishing of Spirits, the gift to see into the spiritual realm, like the young boy who is sitting in the pew; The ability to speak in different kinds of Tongues; and the interpretation of Tongues, the comprehending of what was said in a unknown tongue.

    I watched as Pastor Zoe was being used to minister in many areas in all kinds of the gifts. I beheld many of the angels gathered in this place listening intently as he spoke. I looked down and became aware my clothes were gleaming and becoming the purest of white. I was being called elsewhere, but I really did not want to leave Tom. Zoe had begun vigilant prayers as the choir sang from the loft. I heard the beckoning growing louder and more intense, until finally it was upon me.

    The light was now surrounding me, and then he said my name.

    "Septuagint," it was the voice of Xenophon. " I am sorry to interrupt you but this is a special assignment. It won't be but a moment of time. Orders have come."

"Orders?"

"Yes, they are personally for you."

"Blessed be, the name of the Lord. What am I to do?"

"I will explain to you in thought," Xenophon said.

And immediately my under standing was complete. I was transported across the country to California. High on a mountainside I stood, looking down a narrow road on steep curves banking sharply to the right. A car was hanging over the edge. The vehicle tittered as two wheels held onto the twisted metal of what was once a guardrail. The passenger's door was shut, but the driver side lay open. Desperate screams of help, rose intensely, filling the night air, reaching a crescendo.

"Help me, P-Please someone help me!" she cried. She was a young woman, no more than twenty years of age.

The car jostled, slipping closer to the edge. Her white blouse, spattered with speckles of red blood, was snagged from the back, on the frame of the side window. Dangling in a mid-air state over jagged rocks, Feet twitching, one shoe on, the other was missing. She hung helplessly suspended above a three hundred foot drop. Oozing, warm liquid ran down her thigh from the wound received to her lower back. She repeated her pleas in dire hopelessness. I began to move toward the mangled heap, when I heard Xenophon said, "Wait."

"But why Sir?"

"You shall see in a moment, and then understand. Enjoy the tour home." and as fast as he appeared he had faded from view.

I thought, My tour home?

"PJ, I love you," she whimpered, just as the wreck inched in a tightening jolt.

"Awe" her screams echoed from the cannon walls. The car slid over the cliff. Her blouse ripped from the snag, and she was flung awkwardly forward, spiraling downward toward the peaked rocks. Her final plea had exited her lips as she closed her eyes unable to watch her descent.

"Lord Jesus, Help. . ."

Whack! She had not be able to say the last word, 'me'. The snapping of her legs, then every major bone in her body followed. Her head struck the stony earth. The car preceded missing her by inches, and continued to roll the down the sloping hillside. A ka-boom explosion, followed by bursting flames, was heard and seen from across the valley. The fire lit up the night sky, like diamonds shining on black velvet.

I was now standing beside her limp body, when I saw it, that glaring stare. The stare these humans of earthen-clay have just as they are about to step out of these shells their spirits are encased in. Her chest wheezed, as the air was began to be expelled from her lungs. A gurgling, bubbling sound audible as the blood filled up her lungs. Both of her arms broken, she was unable to lift herself as she began to drown in her own blood. She was only able to slightly open her right eye. That's when she saw me standing near. That moment between life and death, right before she left her physical existence. A grin slightly spread across her swollen jowls covered in red stain. Then the long, exhaling sound of a dying breath, forcing itself from the contorted figure of what was once humanoid. Her spirit was then ejected from the mangled corpse.

She stood looking at her hands in disbelief, seeing the transparent ness to herself. Then glancing up, at the wreck and her own body, she covered her mouth taking a gasp.

Time froze for her, but not for me. My clothing was gleaming bright light. Something else was nearby. I drew my sword, wheeling it as I searched around. I looked up near the top of the bent twisted guardrail, and there I honed in on its presence I saw it, the membranous wings wafting. The jaundiced glow of his peering eyes, he was Chaos, and this was his work. Hissing, as he looked down from atop the ridge.

"She was not supposed to cry out to the Holy one! This is your doing, Angel. If you had not been near, she would not have called on his name." he said shaking his fist, as he stood humiliated.

Before he could blink, I appeared behind him with my sword drawn high to strike. He was turning swiftly around as my blade was moving downward. In reflex action he held up his left forearm, and tried to outstretch his wing, it was too late my blade had smote him, as I was giving him an answer to his sarcastic remarks.

"Yes, but she did, and Praise be the name of the host of heaven."

The sulfuric stench of gas was all that remained with the distant eerie cries of cursing rage.

I appeared again at the bottom of the ridge before the young woman had even known I had moved.

"Greetings, Child of the King."

She turned around, startled a bit by introduction.

"OH, Hello, I'm sorry, I don't know what happened, I. . . I . . . think, I was in an accident. But it seems like it was a dream, and you...,You were there. That's strange, I don't feel anymore pain. But

I remember, I felt it in my whole body. Hey, am I dead? Just a minute, who are you?"

Her spirit was beautiful to behold, a flower of magnificent color. I reached out and took her by the hand. She looked into my face, and became somewhat impressed with my glow.

"My name is Septuagint, and I am an angel of the Lord. I am here to escort you home."

She smiled somewhat dazed, unable to stop looking at my gleaming essence. The peace that surpasses all understanding had enveloped her. And her mind was now at rest. I knew now why I was going back. . ., back home to heaven. This was an escort mission, but most of all, I was going to get to see Jesus again. We turned and walked through the time-tunnel, a walkway of review. The end of the tunnel is long journey, but the concept of distance is short. Reaching the other side is like no time at all. The girl was asking all sorts of questions,

"Will I see all my family or my friends? Will I get to know some things or everything?" I just smiled at her enquiries. She was quickly becoming so excited with joy and a little overwhelmed. She was asking questions before I could convey the answers. I knew the closer we get to the light at the end of the tunnel, all things are made known. Soon, all she wanted to know was being revealed to her spirit. Figures of shadowy bright light were standing at the tunnel's edge. As we approached closer, they became clearer. A spirit of a woman who had left the earth many years prior, was standing with outstretched arms and came rushing toward the girl

"Tabatha," The woman said.

"Granny? Is that you . . . Granny!" She ran to embrace the woman.

I continued reaching the outskirts of Heaven's edge. I took a big sigh, and thought to myself, Home. . . I am home.

"Hello, Septuagint," the woman said to me, as Tabatha held her around the waist.

"Greetings, to you Mrs. Davenport."

"I just wanted to thank you, personally, for walking my precious granddaughter home."

"It was my pleasure, she is a brilliant spirit. I am sure she has much to share. Peace be with you."

The foundation layers of stone are multi-colored. The grass and all the colors here are brighter than anyone on earth can imagine. All is perfection, and all is complete. The flowers sing. The trees sing. The heavenly hosts sings.

I was truly home. I was filled with inexpressible love looking towards the center gates made of pearl. I walked the path toward the streets that are made with the purest gold. Entering in, I beheld the masses of souls saved by the blood of the lamb. They stood as far as the eyes can see to the left or right. They were all arraigned in robes of white linen, silent, all intently watching him who sat upon the throne, the creator of all things that were made. Ascending the steps, crystal clear as glass and sparkling like diamonds, I approached my high Commander.

"Hello, Septuagint," was the words spoken.

As I neared him, He smiled.

The love that is shone from His face is transcending. Like a sound wave, throughout all heaven and all the universes.

The crowds began praising and singing in one accord, "Worthy is the lamb, worthy is the lamb to be praised."

Michael the arch angel approached me and wrapped his mighty arm of strength around my shoulder.

"Welcome back, Septuagint. You are to be commended. We have many things to discuss, let us go to the Halls of Meeting."

I bowed toward my Lord Jesus, as I stepped backward from His presence, not wanting to take my eyes off him, as I said the words,

"You're Majesty!" Jesus smiled and again I was brimming with the warmth of his love.

Tabatha and her grandmother stepped forward as Jesus rose up and hugged Tabatha, Saying her name, and then, "I love you, and welcome to heaven."

Michael and I were walking toward the Halls of Meeting, as he said,

"It's still amazing, isn't it? It's still wonderful to behold his Majestic presence. And oh, how the masses gather and love to just gaze at him."

"Yes, it seems like an eon since I have seen him myself. But just one look and he fills you up with the love of God." Michael grinned.

"I know Septuagint, I know."

"Michael, I have to tell you, it is really an unbearable thing to be away from here." Michael's smile turned into a look of seriousness.

"Septuagint, I understand, none of us ever want to leave but . . ."

I could tell by his hesitation, what he was trying to say. I knew it would pain him to issue me a direct order, so I spoke first.

"I really do not want to go back to the testing ground, sir, but I am ready to serve any way I can." I raised my sword upward, and shouted, "To battle for the Lord, and the host of heaven!"

I looked down seeing a flower surrounded by the deepest jade colored grass. Somehow the life force within it acknowledges my presence and opens stretching out its petals, releasing the sweetest smelling scent of lilac. I smiled as a greeting gesture, to it.

Michael placed his hand on my shoulder and said,

"You are a good soldier, Septuagint."

"I knew this current mission was but a temporary one."

"How is your other assignment coming?"

"Tom Allen?"

"You know, he will need your assistance very shortly. He will play a vital role in times to come."

"How long, before I have to return?"

"I am sorry my friend, but it is imperative that you return immediately. But seeing our Lord will sustain you until your mission is completed."

I walked to the edge of heaven, leaving the gates behind me. Looking over the boarder into the vast emptiness of space. The porthole of time appeared. I departed back to the testing ground, Earth.

N I N E

Ring . . . ring. . . rin- Tom swiftly snatched up the phone.

"Hello?"

"Sarge; sorry to bother you. We've got another one. It's one of ours." Steve blurted out quickly.

"Who is it?" Tom asked, holding the phone between his shoulder and ear.

"Tom, its Murphy. We found his body by the smoke stacks of the ole' factory, the one on Market Street. Homicide crew is already there."

"I meet you there in a few . . . anyone notify the family?"

"Not yet, we wanted to let you know first."

"Fine, contact the Chaplin and have him meet us there."

"I tried that, Sarge. I thought you'd want him there. But Tony, he made the contact call, told me the Chaplin was out on vacation. Is there anyone else you want me to contact?"

"No, wait a minute yes, send a patrol car over to St. Thomas Church and ask if Pastor Zoe is available."

"You got it."

Tom hung up the phone as he pushed the button on the toaster. He reached for the coffee pot and poured a hot cup.

Meanwhile Steve pushed the end button on his cell phone as the cold wind wisped over his face. The smoke stacks located at Market Street were emitting gray puffs rising up to meet the rolling clouds in the sky. The crime scene located in the dismal industrial area, was being chalked by one of the detectives.

"Hey Steve! We found this in his upper left pocket," Dougin said, as he held up a plastic baggy containing a business card.

His other hand, wearing a latex plastic glove, gripped a mutilated, half-chewed cigar. "Sorry 'bout the blood, it was running down his neck and soaked through the clothing."

Steve took a good look at the object, his face registering displeasure, as he began reading the words written on one side, as he held it up to eye level. The Melting P... The rest of the words were covered in dark, coagulated black blood and illegible.

"Thanks, Dougin. I'll pass it along to Sarge when he gets here." He said with a scowling look, as he sipped coffee from a star-foam cup.

The coroner was zipping up the body bag that contained the corpse of Officer Murphy. Nothing remained on the ground except the chalked outline. Steve looked at his watch, noticing when a car pulled up to the scene. He marveled, thinking to himself, how does he do that? He always makes it in forty-five minutes. A couple of detectives were still taking dirt and tire tracks samples to build a case.

One glanced up and said to Dougin, "Aw oh, here comes ole' grumpy butt." Dougin looked back over his shoulder, taking notice of Tom's car pulling up to Steve.

"Just do your job fellow's and stay out of his way this morning." Dougin said.

The snow was melting in little gathered pockets, the sky casting dreary shadows with short breaks in the clouds. The air temperature was an all time high of only forty-two degrees. Tom was exited his vehicle and adjusted his collar upward to keep the brisk wind off his neck.

He asked Steve, "Where is he?"

"Morning Sarge. He's over here. I've got a patrol car on the way to St. Thomas. They should be getting back to us any time now. Also, there's a slight break in the case. See the old guy over there,"

Steve pointed to a homeless man wearing a toboggan cap, long overcoat and gloves with the finger tips missing. The man was pacing back and forth hugging himself trying to keep warm. "He lives under the overpass of the highway, up under the rafter beams, in a cardboard box. Low rent housing." Steve shrugged his shoulders.

"Yeah," Tom expressed a questionable look, like what else?"

"Well, he was here last night when he saw two guys pull the body out of the back of a limo, they dumped the body over there."

"A limo . . . Huh? Was he the one who called it in?"

"Not really, he didn't have any change for a phone call, he told the clerk at the liquor store. He was the one who made the call. Patrol came by, they met with the old guy, and he pointed out the drop."

"I see, bring him down to the station, and follow up there. Get him some coffee and breakfast, whatever you have to do to get him to cooperate." Tom said, as he turned around and quickly walked right through me, not realizing that I was there.

I looked back as I saw him get a pad out of his car. He pulled a silver pen from his lapel coat pocket. He wrote a note to himself of the events that had taken place. Walking over to the white chalk line he viewed the scene, picturing an image of the Officer Murphy laying on the ground, and trying to think of what he was going to say to Murphy's family. He shook his head with a grievous look as one of the detectives was kneeled near the scene and took hair sample with a pair of tweezers.

Tom strolled over to the concrete embankment, and stood looking out over the moving muddy river. Thoughts of the prior night's arrest filled his mind. The question he was asking himself was where was Murphy when he was not in his assigned area. Tom drew a visual image of Murphy being stabbed. The thought sickened Tom. He spat on the ground, as if he was vomiting the sickness out.

"Hey Sarge, I'll meet you back at the office." Steve yelled, as he departed in an unmarked patrol car.

Tom just waved his hand in reply, not even looking back, his mind cluttered with the events that bogged his every thought. He was unaware of the amount of time that had simply passed by, then he heard a voice come from behind him.

"Hello Tom."

The words just hung in the air, as Tom glanced down at his watch and turned to see who it was that had spoken to him, a little surprised at the time he let slip away. He thought the voice was a detective, but instead he saw Pastor Paul Zoe standing a few feet behind him.

"Pastor Zoe thanks for coming."

"I'm sorry to hear about your officer, Tom. Was he a close friend of yours?"

"Not really, I barely knew him personally. But whenever we lose one in the field, I always feel a deep remorse for the family and loss they will suffer. Hope you don't mind me sending for you. I think I could use some of your spiritual guidance talking to his family. But if you don't think you're up to it, I can have a patrol car drive you back."

"Nonsense, I like to help in anyway I can. We're brothers in Christ now. And family needs to rely on each other whenever possible."

Tom smiled at Paul's willingness to help. As they began to walk back to the car past the chalked outline, Tom's slight smile faded back into a stern look.

Meeting Kirk in the hallway of the oval office, Senator Tinnimen walked towards the secretary sitting at the desk.

"Good morning, Senator," Kirk said.

The senator turned to see him rising up from a chair. The senator drew a deep breath and scowled a bit and said,

"Morning Kirk. So what is this last minute emergency meeting about? I am sure you know. You seem to know just about everything."

"Well sir, I wouldn't be a good information aide if I wasn't properly informed, now would I? First thing, to bring you up to speed is we have a slight problem."

The senator despondently shook his head. "Problem, what problem is that Kirk?"

Kirk took the senator by the arm and led him away from the office door.

"The locals have a witness. He saw your limo leaving the scene where Murphy's body was dumped."

"What!"

"Shsss, remain calm sir."

The Senator was losing all color in his face, turning pale white. He reached down for the arm of the chair that was placed against the wall, and just flopped down into it. With his other hand, he reached inside his suit coat pocket to pull out a Rolaid antacid tablet.

"Get me some water, Kirk"

"But of course, sir."

Kirk walked about five paces to the water cooler removed a paper cup and filled it. The Senator placed the tablet in his mouth and chewed it. Kirk handed him the water. He quickly drank it and crumpled the cup in his hand.

"So now what?" The Senator asked.

"Don't panic. We have someone on it now." Kirk grinned a smug smile.

"Listen, my friend, my tail end is on the line here You'd better be right, cause if I go down, so do you," the senator said, as he quickly rose up and poked Kirk in the shoulder.

Kirk moved a step back and brushed his shoulder as if rubbing of the threat.

"Senator, there is so much more on the line than just you going down. And, if you did, you should be asking just how far down would you be sinking." Kirk laughed as if he knew some childish secret. "Just remember, that dirty flatfoot died because he didn't follow orders, not because of some long lost sister of yours. Loyalty, Senator, Loyalty, that's all we respect."

Tom reached in his pocket to retrieve his keys. Feeling a plastic baggy he pulled it out and looked at the business card inside that read the Melting Pot. He knew the location and thought to himself that he wanted to check it out first.

"Paul, there is something I have to do first. Would you mind if I let one of my associates go with you to Murphy's house?"

"What ever you want, Tom; If that's the way you want to handle it; Fine by me."

"Thanks, I will meet up with you as soon as I'm able."

Tom turned to one of the uniforms and asked him to drive Pastor Paul Zoe to Murphy's house.

"Just wait outside until Brock gets there."

"Sure thing, Sarge; Come on Pastor, this way." He opened the car door for Paul; Paul clasped his hands and blew into the thumbs and then rubbed them together keeping warm. Zoe whispered a prayer for Tom as he got into the car.

"Dear Lord, send your angels to watch over him."

Tom opened the door to his car and picked up a microphone to the police radio. He hung his elbow on the edge of the car's window fame, and the other elbow on the roof of the car.

"One Yankee seven to dispatch."

"One Yankee seven, go ahead." Tom watched the other patrol car pull away.

I watched as my clothes of bronze begin to gleam as an answer to prayer. I looked out above the water and three figures from the invisible realm were materializing into view, walking towards me. Their arraignment was of fine linen and each had a golden sash wrapped around its waist. The one in the middle was a step in front of the others, and he spoke first.

"Greetings in the name of the Lord, Septuagint."

I was now able to recognize them. It was three of the elders from the twenty-four Holy Counsel members. I folded my hands in the center of my chest, and bowed my head in acknowledgment.

"Brothers of light, what brings you here?"

"We are here for the greater good. We must inform you not to change future history."

I again bowed my head in understanding of their request, but when I looked up they had faded from quickly from my view. I pondered the thought, that future history is already recorded and that it could be changed. I understood that I was not to impose on man's freewill.

"Senator Tinnimen! How good of you to join us this morning. Care for some coffee?"

"Thank you, but no." The man at the window made a gesture at his cup in hand,

"How about you Kirk?"

Kirk shook his head rejecting the coffee, and shifted his eyes toward the Senator standing off to the side of him. The man seemed to understand the message from Kirk.

"Wonderful commodity . . . The Colombians produce . . . Coffee that is. You know Senator some things just can't be duplicated in this country. Oh, we try, but it never is exactly the same. The Columbians with their Juan Valdez, the Arabs with their oil. In turn they just want a little help with their revolts. You know, few guns here and there. Well, this time we have a special request from one of our Arabian allies."

"Since when did the Arabs become our allies? Was I asleep when this was on CNN?"

The President was now facing the Senator, and pointed over toward the corner, just over the left shoulder of Tinnimen.

The Senator looked back seeing a man wearing a blue turban and a white suit made from the finest Italian tailoring. His skin was olive bronze and a lustrous gold watch adored his left wrist. A gold bracelet, huge as a jail-keepers handcuff, hung on the other. He sported two golden rings on his right hand, and his other displayed a diamond as big a cherry. But what caught the Senator's attention was the pentagram ring on his pinkie finger. The Senator expressed a slight smile and nodded his head in greeting.

"Senator Tinnimen, if I may introduce you, please say hello to King Oculus."

Kirk just stood back watching.

"Kirk you've already met the King."

Kirk stepped forward and extended his hand.

"Yes, sir, we met prior, back in '95, Istanbul."

"Ah, Kirk, how good to see you again."

"Senator now this news is not released yet, but King Oculus has presented a plan for reunited the split countries of Iraq and Iran. The two are meeting at the negotiating table as we speak. The ancient world of the great country known as Persia is soon to be rebuilt. Now what do think of that?"

The Senator shook his head, in disbelief, "Well, that I guess takes some real kind of politicking. I never had the honor of meeting a King before," Tinnimen extended his hand to shake.

"Pleasure to meet you sir."

Oculus pressed both his hands toward the other as if he was going to pray, and bowed his head ever so slightly in greeting, then shook hands with him.

"The Honor is mine."

Tinnimen looked into his eyes and a chill rushed down his spine. His eyes flashed black as coal. Pitch as the blackest night. It was weird . . . strange, that olive skin and jet black mustache and bearded goatee. He had the look of a holy man but his presence was numbing. Tinnimen thought even that thousand dollar white suit could not cover up the evil that was emitting from him.

"Gentlemen, if you will please excuse us, the King and I have some things that we need to discuss. You will be informed shortly of a meeting that will be forth coming." the President opened the door, ushering the Senator and Kirk out.

"Thank you again," The President shut the door as soon as they had walked out.

The senator stood in the secretary's office and placed his hand near his mouth, holding his chin with his thumb and middle finger. He paused and turned to his assistant, Kirk.

"Who is that guy, and what were you doing in Istanbul?" Kirk grinned and replied.

"He kinda makes your skin crawl doesn't he? It's like knowing you're meeting the next world leader. He'll make Hitler look like a Cub-scout."

"What did you say?"

"Nothing; just mouthing off."

The senator felt a jolt of fear rush up his backside. He knew the words Kirk spoke were possible. As the senator turned to walk out into the hallway, he displayed a puzzled look on his face. He turned his head back to look at the white door, and allowed himself to realize that the few moments of that man's presence was real.

But while he was staring at the door, a Power demon of darkness had poked its head out through it. A high ranking unholy membranous bat winged monster from the place in the neither world region, known as Shoal Hades. It was glaring right at the Senator, irritatingly tapping his talons to a unheard beat unheard by anyone in the flesh. His name was Gopher. He growled and hissed as the Senator stood there.

Then he shouted at him. "LEAVE OR YOU WILL DIE!"

Tinnimen suddenly felt an insidious terror within that if he didn't walk away his life was in serious jeopardy.

Shaking his head as he walked away, Gopher snarled, as he thought to himself, "Meddling fool, I will have your soul put in the hottest pit."

●———————————————●

"Why do they do that?" Tom asked aloud.

I was taken by surprise by his sudden outburst, as I was unseen to his eyes.

"Why do they rig a perfectly good car to do something so stupid?" He asked again aloud.

I looked around to see if someone else was in the car. I almost answered him, thinking he was actually talking to me. For a second, I forgot he does not see me. But I, too, was at a loss of understanding of that human action of which he spoke. We both watched as a bouncing car continued down the street, a hydraulic low rider. Tom turned the steering wheel of his car pulling into an empty parking lot.

TEN

A huge neon sign hung over the building called the "Melting Pot." Tom drove to the rear of the majestic parking lot. He neared the rear of the building and pulled up to two huge iron gates. Water splashed as his front tire struck a small sink hole in the faulty asphalt. The splashing sound had startled some feeding pigeons feasting on stale popcorn, the remains of a snack tossed aside by someone who had attended the frivolity and chaos of last nights festivity. Tom observed as the birds took flight and came to rest on an adjacent buildings tin roof.

Seeing the parking lot barren and the huge gates were locked with a padlock and large chain, he slapped the steering wheel and said,

"Dag gone it!"

Holding the top of the steering wheel he laid his head atop of his hands, and drew a deep breath, exhaling slowly. Frustrated he leaned back on the headrest and for a brief moment closed his eyes.

Crash! Tom's eyes suddenly popped opened wide alert, and aware of his surroundings. His training and quick thinking had kicked into high gear from the loud noise. Letting out a sigh of relief, he was looked back over the seat, toward the street where the sound originated from.

A car had driven by and thrown a bottle on the side walk causing it to break. He turned back again, seeing the pigeons had flown to the roof. Below the gentle popcorn pickers, a tilted window opened outward from the top. Tom carefully scanned the corner edge of the adjacent building. On the corner edge he saw something; Some thing that peaked his interest. He thought "Bingo!" as his eyes, gaining a fixation on a camera that was attached to the building next door, he saw it pointing toward the melting pot parking lot.

I watched as Tom swiftly circled around and pulled into the parking lot on the other side of the gate. A man was walking into a door of the warehouse. The front had a large garage door on it. The sign read, "JOE'S AUTO SALVAGE & PARTS."

Tom exited his car and asked, "Are you the owner of this place?"

"Yep, I am, I'm Joe. Something, I can help you with Mr.?"

Tom smile and nodded yes.

"Does that thing work?" Tom pointed up at the camera on the edge of the building.

Joe looked up as he was wiping his hands.

"Yeah, it works. But I sell auto parts, Mr., Not cameras."

"Was it on last night?"

"Yep, I keep it on to make sure none of them young dopers and drunks come over here and jump the fence. You know, try to break into the biz and rob my place. Why you so interested in the cam. You a cop?"

"Yes, I'm Detective Tom Allen, Metro, I am investigating a case. Would you mind if I take a look at the film in your camera from last night?"

"Sure; No problem. Come on in." Joe finished cleaning his hands with the red colored oil rag, and stuffed it in his back pocket.

"I appreciate your cooperation."

Joe and Tom walked up to the building's door. But I stayed outside. Something was amiss. My attire changed from bronze to blazing white.

"Eeeecck," it screeched. The air whisked with motion from his wafting wings, the membranous contortion flapping against the space of time. It was an imp, ancient according to man's time but a youngster in the time of creation. He must have just come from the depths of Hades he had the stench of death, and was still blinking his jaundice bulging eyes. Stretching outward his wings, he cried out with a hideous voice,

"Warning Septuagint, you should come, follow the way of freewill, and leave that human to us. His demise has already been plotted, by ones stronger than you."

The foul spirit began to laugh, as my sword began to quiver and flame. I knew it was time to strike. I drew my sword as he drew backwards, his dark wings bracing his forward perpetual motion, skidding to a midair stop.

I shouted, "in the name of the Lord!"

Whhhooossh! He fled in a subsonic speed, but I was hot on his trail. Upward and eastward, the chase was ensued toward the dark and grayish colored clouds. He was trying to lose me in the water vapors. Swissh! I wielded my swift blade. My sword nipped his wing tip, as he screamed curses. I struck a second time, downward through his blackened hide of an evil entity. A viperous gas of sulfur exploded, as echoing screams bellowed out vile obscenities.

I realized the chase had carried me thousands of feet up in the air. Looking downward, toward the earth, I decided to walk back. Like walking on stairs, I descended one step at a time.

I pondered the word of the wicked imp. What did he mean by his demise was already plotted? Could this be tied in with the three from the counsel who gave me the order not to change history? Was Tom in danger?

I saw the building 'JOE'S SALVAGE'. I walked right through the building, still descending. Tom was standing behind Joe, Joe was sitting in front of a T.V. monitor looking at the video tape. It was displaying Senator Tinnimen getting into a limo, and two men placing a large cylindrical object in the trunk. It then pulled out of the gated area of the parking lot.

"Thank you Joe, I am going to have to take this, for evidence."

"No problem, just don't mention my name."

"Don't worry we won't call you, unless it's absolutely necessary No one knows about your cam' except me and some pigeons."

"Pigeons; what?"

"Never mind inside joke; Thanks again." Tom walked out and Joe escorted him to the car. Joe turned to walk back in as Tom's car pulled out of sight. He looked up at the camera on the side of his building.

"Coo, coo."

Hearing the sound, Joe looked up and saw a pigeon sitting of the edge of a tilted, open window on the second floor above the camera.

"Ah, pigeons!" Joe smiled.

●───────────────────────────────●

"Why do they run like roaches, as if a light was turned on?" asked a voice that sounded like a freight train.

"It's called a mock test. They must report to the place where they are assigned by the one called 'General'. In this underground cavern they call a bunker, when they hear the sound of the siren, that thing that is making the loud noise from the wall, that is when they go to work, I have been watching them now for what they call the space of time, for a year. Is everything ready?" Fury asked.

"Yes, the new leader of annihilation is ready. I watched as he was berthed, we destroyed his innocence in his childhood as instructed. His only parents are hate and envy. He was trained in all the ways of eastern religions. He was given power by the riches of a Kings concubine. He has taken a seat on a throne that was over thrown by force." Deceit answered, and bowed before him.

"Who is he?" Fury asked.

"His name is Oculus, a new ruler of ancient Babylon."

The over head intercom blurted out an announcement.

"Attention all personnel. This is a mock test. This is a mock test. All personnel report to post. No unauthorized personnel will be allowed on blue level six. Commencing count down at 'T-minus thirty seconds' on mark, Five . . . Four . . . three . . . two . . . one . . . Launch.

"I want to see this new leader. Where is he?" Fury asked."

"He is above us on the earth's surface, in the place called the white house, with the one called President. Oh, but begging your pardon, my lord, you can not get near him."

Fury turn enraged and backhanded the demon, throwing him into the cavern wall.

"What do you mean I can not get near him?" Fury grabbed him, and lifted the smaller demon up to his eye level, and gnarled at him. Deceit, gulped a swallow as Fury's giant hand enveloped his throat.

"Please, my most unholy lord, if tho will loose your servant I will try to explain more plainly."

Fury released his grip.

"Lucifer has assigned him guarded by Gopher, fear of a revolt, I suspect from his own followers."

Fury guffawed, and shouted,

"Gopher, I don't care, take me to him. Gopher, mmm, he is my next challenge."

"But . . ."

"Just lead me to him. Now!"

Deceit bowed down, not wanting to be struck by fury again.

"As you say, oh prince. What of this place shall I come back here and do your bidding?"

"We shall see, first I will speak with this Gopher, this power ruler."

●────────────────────────●

"Septuagint."

I looked behind me in the back seat of Tom's police cruiser.

"Hope!"

"Greetings, Septuagint. It is so well to see you again."

"Why are you here?"

"New orders; You have to come with me and document a permanently recorded event. It will take place any moment now. We must go by order of the Highest; Praise his name."

The car was sill moving, but it seemed to stand still as if all mankind's time had stopped for us to travel elsewhere. Hope and I used thought travel. It is fast, but I would have liked to have used the white door.

●────────────────────────●

We were now standing in a building, somewhere in Jerusalem. There were several men in the room gathering for an important meeting at the home of a Jewish rabbi. It was evening time. The lights that were on from the corner lamp were glowing with a golden soft illuminating essence. The rabbi was sitting in a large brown leather chair. It was next to a large bookcase with ancient looking texts locked behind a glass door. The conversation was loud, and the rabbi was motioning with his hands, patting the open air, as to hush the discussions of several men present. Each was talking over the other's voices.

"I know, I know, now tell me, what is it you have found out?"

"He is here! I tell you. I have seen him!"

"Mark, please! Let me hear this from Joel,"

"What? My eyes have seen him! Is that not witness enough for you, am I a blind man? If not for me, no one would be here! Ok, ok, I'll sit here in the corner and be a good little boy."

Joel stood up, as he began to address the others in the room.

"The premise of this meeting can only be based on the Code, which has only been discovered in our life time of history. As we all know, Mark was in Egypt, covering the photography for his newspaper journal, when he had the opportunity to take this photo of the man we all know as King Oculus. After the war with America, Iraq has joined with Iran to return the ruler ship of one govern leader. Oculus is the man. Our sources in intelligence decided to run his name in the Code. This is what we found in running his name in the Code."

Joel pointed his finger to the ancient document that laid on the table. The men leaned forward in a semicircle to view the words that crossed the path of the man's name Oculus.

"Alas!" One cried out as he read it.

"It has come. We are at the pinnacle." said another man.

"Petra. We must prepare. It will be the only safe place," someone else added.

The rabbi sat very still, tapping the finger tips of his right hand to the tips of his left hand, as if he was going to pray. Gathering his long white beard in his right hand, he gently pulled repeatedly downward, stroking from his chin to the end of his beard. He pondered the magnitude of the events which had fallen upon him and his people.

"What do you think they will do, Septuagint?"

"I am not sure, Hope."

"You are aware these men are the leaders in the matters and affairs of Jerusalem, even though they are not of a politic persuasion?"

"What is it you have called me here to record?"

"Listen carefully."

The rabbi stood up and spoke. "If it is him, and we do not attempt anything, we fail. Then Israel will be on our hands. And if we do, and what is written happens, then we are the ones predestined to fulfill the written will of God."

"So what is the vote?" Mark asked.

One by one the seven men voted by ballot. When they had finished, the rabbi looked painfully at Joel and said, "Call him, we are either making history or fulfilling it."

"We will commence the details later. But we know now that we will never let another Hitler come into power, as before."

"Septuagint, you look puzzled."

"Never in all my existence, has my raiment not turn white when something was going to happen that might be evil."

"Maybe that's why you were here, To record this event as a second witness. Maybe it is not an evil event, but a divine judgment."

"That is possible, but only the Creator is able to determine divine righteousness."

"I am being called elsewhere. Goodbye Septuagint, it was good seeing you again."

I watched as Hope spread his feathery white ivory wings in a full stretched out formation, leaving nothing but a blinding long streak into infinity. The colors of a rainbow prism dispersed a spectrum of light following the trail, catching up to the immeasurable speed of which Hope departed with.

I too turned around toward the northwest and traveled back to America to complete my assignment with Tom. In the moment of an eye's twinkle I was back in Washington, D.C.

E L E V E N

Tom had just arrived at the police department's headquarters. As he walked in and sat down in his chair behind his desk, unseen and unnoticed to his eyes, I appeared.

"Nancy, has Steve come back yet?"

"Haven't seen him; Do you want me to tell dispatch to call him in?"

"No, I still have some paperwork to catch up on. When he get here, have him come see me. Oh, and contact the district attorney's office and let me know when you have them on the line. We're going fishing, fishing for a Senator."

Tom grinned; a sly smirk as he tossed a video tape up in the air and caught it again. He leaned back in the chair and put his feet on the edge of the desk. But, in only moments, he adjusted himself up to the desk.

I watched Tom fill out some papers. Nancy shouted from just outside the door.

"Tom, Ira, is on line two."

Tom snatched up the phone quickly.

"Got it, Hello, Ira."

"Well, well, how are you, Tom?"

"Doing fine, Ira, how are Jody and the kids?"

"Great. Sammy got a winning goal in the home hockey game last week. But let's cut to the chase Tom. You don't call me at work unless it has to do with some kind of legal issue. So what is it?"

"Ira, I need a search warrant for a limo and the home of Senator Tinnimen's house."

"What? Are you nuts! Tom, you better be sure of what you're implying here."

Tom tossed the video up in the air.

"Oh, I know exactly what I am implying."

"That's some pretty powerful feet to be stepping on. So you better be sure you have Probable Cause established."

"I do."

"Bring over what ever you have, let me review it. If it is, then I issue the warrant."

"Thanks, Ira. I'll be over as soon as I can. I'm waiting on Steve to get here."

"Hope you know what your doing pal."

"I do. Oh, and Ira, don't mention anything to anyone yet. I mean no-one."

"Got cha."

Tom hung up the phone and leaned back and placed his hands behind his head again.

●────────────────●

Placed in specific locations the room was dim, but warmly lit, with glowing chandeliers. The bartender had adjusted his red snap vest while viewing himself in the huge mirror behind the bar. He turned and picked up a damp rag and began to dust the maple wooded bar counter top. A barrage of brass and expensive decor adorned the hotel bar's establishment. A man wearing a green flight jacket and white tee shirt entered from the hotel lobby. Dark sunglasses seem out of place in a room with no need of such vice. His blue jeans were ironed and matched his dark leather boots. Boots that heavily clunked on the hard wood floor with each step taken. The barkeep took notice of the shine of the bass reflected from the chrome colored case he carried. The barkeeper nodded an ignored greeting as the man walked by. The man in the green flight jacket make contact with another gentleman in a black suit sitting at the bar, and motioned with his head to go sit in the back area of the bar. The man in the suit swallowed his last gulp, setting the glass on the bar. The message was understood.

"Get you another sir?"

"Bring two of these to the back table."

"Yes sir."

The man in the suit followed the man in the boots to the rear of the bar to the table.

As he pulled out a chair to sit he asked the man in the green jacket,

"It looks like it might be warm today?"

"Yes, blood temperature."

"Good. Now that we have that out of the way and know who we are, let's get down to it. So you're Scorpion?"

"Do you have it?"

"Yes, it must be done right away. The orders are from the top."

He reached into his coat and pulled out a tan envelope and laid it on the table. He slid it across toward him. As Scorpion reached out to receive the package, he looked down to see the man wearing a pentagram ring.

"I didn't know the organization reached into the CIA."

"It reaches everywhere, my friend. Your overseas account will be credited by half by noon tomorrow, the other half to follow when the job is done."

"Just like last time."

"Sorry we didn't get to meet then."

Scorpion unzipped his green jacket to reveal his tee-shirt, which had only showed the white part of it until then, but now enabling the whole logo to be seen. The man in the suit grinned, seeing the yellow smiley face and the words underneath which read 'Have a nice day'."

"Cute, real cute." he said, smiling himself.

Scorpion re-zipped the jacket picked up his case. "If the other half of the money is not there when the job is done pray you never see this smiley face again. Because I assure you, it won't be a nice day at all. Ask those who knew your predecessor." The smile quickly ran away from the face of the man in the suit.

Tom placed his key in the door to his house. His day was coming to an end. The quite little suburb of the metro area was his refuge. He was dragging and it was apparent. He felt as if all his energy was zapped. All he could think about was getting into that unmade bed. No matter how unkempt it was, he knew it was going to feel so good. Opening the door and tossing his keys on the living room table, he picked up the remote control to catch the evening news. The announcer was speaking as they were cutting to the live camera action.

"As you can see behind me, the streets are littered with stones, one on top another. These stones, here in this pile are a monument to the ones who died fighting . . . fighting for the same cause as all their forefathers had. The city, of that dome of the rock Jerusalem as always laid the foundation as a backdrop for wars. The people who live here have vowed to defend it even if their defense is only a stone."

The newscaster turned to the camera man and said, "*Go ahead pan, around,*" then went back to talking to the viewers.

"Now, the city streets are empty. No one is out throwing any stones. The people of this land have come to terms of peace. And a new leader has arisen among the people, a man of dual heritages. His father was of Arab decent and mother of Jewish decent, he was adopted into royalty by chance. He has now shown great leadership in the Arab world by bringing together the ancient land of Persia. He is today's man of peace. History tells us that Abraham had two sons. One was Ishmael and the other was Isaac. Now Ishmael became the Arab nation, and Isaac became the Jewish race. The two have been fighting for rights to the land since the dawn of time. Now a leader of both great nations is born. So today, by the words of this new leader, no one is casting stones. Reporting from the streets of the holy city of Jerusalem, I'm Mark Bogman, C.N.N. World News."

Tom turned off the T.V. his head was cluttered with so many details. All he wanted to do was sleep.

Tom woke to the sound of banging on the door. He wanted to curse the unannounced guest. The night had come and gone in a blink. Opening his eyes, but not moving, he stared at the ceiling, hoping that the intruder at his door would leave. He looked over at the alarm clock sitting on the edge of the table.

Knock...knock...knock.

Tom opened and closed his mouth a couple of times, noisily smacking his tongue against the roof of his mouth. He cupped his hand and sniffed as he huffed out a harsh breath. It took every thing in his power to drag himself out of his comfort zone.

Knock...knock...knock!

"Yeah! Yeah! Yeah! I coming.

Tom sat up on the edge of the bed and slipped on his over sized house shoes shaped to look like bear claws. He grabbed his robe from the back of the green wooden chair with tan woven straw-like material. Covering up his flannel pajamas, and rushing to the door, He tried to reach it before whoever it was knocked again.

KNOCK...KNOCK..KNOCK!

Tom yanked it open swiftly. He was in no mood, and very sleepy. The sun was coming up and peeking over the edge of the roof tops from across the street, shining an eye piercing beam right into Tom's eye, agitating him all the more. He raised a hand palm outward, as if giving an English sloppy salute, to cover his eyes.

"WHAT! What do you want?"

His one eye was still half opened, the other half shut, before he perceived who it was standing before him. His vision was only of a dark shadow, then his vision suddenly came into focus.

"Good morning to you, too." came the sarcastic reply. Steve looked down at Tom's slippers finishing his greeting, "Papa bear. Don't you ever answer your beeper?"

Tom stood back, opening the door for Steve to enter.

"I must have turned it off last night before I lay down."

"Nice shoes."

"Don't start."

"What, I just said nice shoes."

"Everyone wants to be a comedian."

"Here, cream and two sugars. I have something else for you too."

"What?"

Steve reached into his jacket to remove apiece of paper folded long ways. He tossed it onto the coffee table. He sat down in the big recliner chair across from Tom. Tom propped up his feet on the coffee table to drink his coffee.

"What's that?"

"The search warrants for the limo of one U.S. prime suspect in a murder investigation; otherwise know as one Mr. John L. Tinnimen."

Crash!

The window shattered behind Steve as the echoing sound of breaking glass filled the room. Steve slumped over in the chair, not moving. Tom spilled coffee on himself, dropped the cup and reached over to the end table for his gun.

Instantly, I was standing on the billboard sign. It was located across the highway, but high enough that it was over the rooftops of Tom's neighborhood. I looked and I could see Tom's house three quarters of a mile away. I could see the front window that was shattered. I watched as the man standing on the platform next to me dismantled the high powered rifle scope. Then he dismantled the rifle itself with precision timing and placed it back into a silver suitcase containing a heavy, molded padding to hold each piece. My clothes turned from bronze to brilliant white. My sword trembled and burn. I knew a demonic spirit was near.

I turned and behind me there he was, Murder himself.

"Septuagint, you're a long way from home, aren't you?"

I held my sword above my head, over my left shoulder, gripping both my hands in the manner of a Samurai Warrior.

"You still have to come and join the rebellion. Why care you about these inferior creatures?" he added.

I stood in the ready position to strike. I watched as he drifted off the edge of the billboard sign. He moved slowly, like a cloud, over the busy highway of cars. He then evaporated into a misty dark cloud.

I saw what he did as he was returning back to hell. He compelled a driver to sway, and drift into another car's lane of travel, side-swiping the vehicle. He had caused the driver to crash into another, forcing that driver to slam into a brick wall barricade. It killed two humans, both who were unsaved by the Blood of the Lamb.

I heard their screams as the collectors of the damned appeared. They emerged at the edge of the earth's surface and dragged those human souls kicking and screaming downward into the abyss.

Climbing down the ladder with his silver suitcase, I watched the assassin depart, making his getaway on a racing motorcycle.

I returned to Tom's home. An ambulance was pulling up to the front walkway.

Tom was shouting from the doorway.

"GET YOUR TAIL ENDS IN HERE NOW!"

Police vehicles were arriving from every direction, but the big puzzle was unraveling now. I knew why Murder had cause a wreck on the highway. The fastest route to the hospital for the driver would have been that way. Just when I was about to whisper in the ambulance driver's ear not to go the freeway but to take the side streets, I remembered the voices of the elders,

"Don't change history."

TWELVE

The butler adjusted the edges of his coat sleeves and straightened his bowtie, as he opened the huge wooden door to the foyer area entrance.

"Good morning sir, may I help you?"

"Hello, Peter. Is the Senator in?" asked Kirk.

"Is he expecting you, sir?"

"No, he isn't, Peter, but its a matter of importance."

"One moment, sir; If you will wait here in the study, I will let the Senator know of your arrival."

Kirk was escorted into a large room with oak bookshelves which covered a long wall. In the center of the room was a cherry covered desk at which the Senator wrote most of his letters. Across the desk were two chairs facing large twelve foot windows, which overlooked the lawn with a marbled fountain spewing water up into the air and back into the bird bath.

Footsteps growing louder sounded out on the empty marble tiled floor.

As the Senator entered the study he said, "Good morning, Kirk. What brings you here at this time of the morning?"

"Senator, bad news travels quickly, I'm afraid. Our inside man, Scorpion made his move earlier this morning, but the target was missed."

"What? What target? Scorpion who?"

"I had told you earlier, sir. We had someone taking care of that problem of yours."

"Oh really."

The Senator walked around Kirk and took a seat in the chair behind the huge desk.

"And, to top it off, information has come in from one of our inside men, that he . . . Scorpion, made his hit on another police officer."

"What! Are you out of your ever-loving mind! Oh, for the love of Pete!"

"Of course this will put the whole D.C. area on high priority. We won't be able to make another attempt for awhile."

"Attempt, another, who is it you're after? No, No... I don't want to know."

"He is a cop."

"I TOLD YOU, I DON'T WANT TO KNOW!"

"Fine, but we also have it from one of the women; she belongs to us and works in the D.A. office, that he has already been issued a warrant to search your limo."

"My limo? What? Do you know what kind of scandal that will bring?"

"He has been delayed. Maybe. That man's tenacity is like a flint."

Tinnimen was shocked. The words Kirk had just flung out went into empty space of air, and just hung there.

"He is on his way here, now? What in the world am I suppose to say? You idiot! You're responsible for this. You're supposed to have everything under control. You and all your powerful friends. What the hill of beans were you thinking of giving a go ahead to hit another cop right after the one was . . . I can hardly say it, murdered."

"Remember who held the poniard sir."

"I know! So, Mr. I'm on top of everything, tell me, what am I suppose to do? Offer him tea and crumpets? This man is on his way to look me in the face, and oh, he will see, I promise you this Kirk, I will not be anyone's patsy. If I go down so do you."

●─────────────────────────────●

"Hey! Hey! Watch it up there!" the paramedic shouted to the ambulance driver.

"Steve, hang on partner! Don't give up on me," Tom said.

The driver shouted back to the paramedic, "Sorry, I have to go in the median. There is an accident up ahead, all traffic is backed up."

"South Central, we are en-route with a gunshot wound. Victim is white male age thirty-four, blood pressure is sixty over forty. Wound entry is from the back, right shoulder exiting the front left pectoral, Administering I.V. fluids one milligram of epinephrine and oxygen. Have trauma unit on stand by, for code blue. Victim is also police office."

Using his thumb, the paramedic raised Steve's left eyelid and looked down into his pupil with a small pen light, then checked the other.

"Good, we still have some response. Steve! I want you to squeeze my finger, do it now partner."

Steve squeezed the paramedic's finger.

"Great, he's a fighter. Means he won't give up easily."

"Where are we?" Tom asked.

"E.T.A. is about five minutes," the driver replied.

"He is slipping away. Steve, Steve, can you hear me partner? Steve stay with me man. I'm losing the pulse!"

"Don't lose him!" Tom said.

"Starting C.P.R."

The paramedic began using a defibrillator to jump start a rhythm of his heart again.

●────────────────────────●

"Who are you?"

"Greetings in the name of the Lord."

I smiled at him. He was now very pleased to be in my presence. All that was around us in the natural world had faded away. We were now in an open field as far as the eyes could see. The yellow flowers were waving into the wind and the temperature was as perfect as a spring morning.

"Would you like to talk and walk a bit?"

"Me? You talking to me?" he was curiously looking around.

"Yes Steve you; My name is unimportant now, but I have been informed it is not your time."

"I was just talking to my friend, Tom . . . that is his name. But it seems as if I must have blacked out. I heard a crash. It came from behind me . . . and, hey I was shot. Am I..."

"No. You are not dead. You must go back now," I said as I interrupted his question.

"But I like it here. I don't want to go back."

"You are needed more there than you are here."

"Did you hear that? I don't see anything, anywhere for miles, nothing but these flowers, how could I hear that?"

I watched as he looked around for the voice.

"You won't find it Steve. What exactly did you hear?" I asked.

"Listen, there it goes again. You know I don't have any kids, but it seems as if I knew it was meant to be speaking to me,"

"What did you hear, Steve?"

"A voice, it was the voice of a little girl, maybe five or six. All she said was the word 'Daddy'. But I know I am not a father. How come I feel she is calling me daddy? Wait . . . there it is again."

I watched as he quickly looked around again. He turned and chuckled a little.

"You don't hear it."

"What did she say this time?"

"She said, 'Daddy, I love you'." he turned and looked at me clearly now. "Hey, just a minute, you're a . . . you're a... Wow! Look at those wings!

Those are huge. How could I've missed that? I'm trained to notice details, you know.

I smiled and took a quick glance back at both my wings, just for effect. "Really?" I said.

The voice cried out again.

"Daddy . . . I love you."

"Hold on, I changed my mind. I do want to go back, that is the voice of my unborn child, isn't it? I do want to see my child, please sir, is it too late?" I was beginning to tell Steve just as his spirit moved back into his bodily shell.

"No, it's not too late Steve"

"Steve . . . Steve . . . can you hear me? Come on buddy, stay with me now. You're in the O.R. You're going to make it. Hey I think he is coming around." said one of the trauma workers.

The peaceful place was gone. The commotion around the operating room was filled with the sounds of beeps from the heart monitors. Metal tools were hitting the metal plates. Several voices were talking at the same time. But the thing Steve felt the most was the pain in his upper chest from the surgery. Steve was mumbling something as he was becoming conscious. The Doctor leaned down and placed his ear near Steve's mouth.

"Angel . . . Angel." he repeated.

"Maybe it's his girlfriend's name." said one of the nurses.

Tom was pacing back and forth in the corridor just outside the operating room.

"Tom?" said the voice of the elderly lady. He turned to see who it was.

"Hello Tom, I am sister Ophelia, from the church." she paused. "We met at the revival meeting."

"Oh, yes, How are you?"

"Are you ok? You look upset."

"Fine just fine. A close friend of mine was hurt. He's in O.R., Gunshot."

Ophelia turned to one of the staff nurses and whispered something to her. The nurse went into the O.R. room.

"Tom, I'm having one of the staff go and see how your friend is doing. She'll be right back."

"What do you do here, Ophelia?"

"I'm in charge of nursing management. Staff supervisor. Your friend is the police officer, right?"

"Yes, he is."

"I heard the call come in on the radio. Are you a cop also."

"Yes, I'm his sergeant."

The staff nurse was returning from the O.R. Tom turned and was attentive to what she had say.

"He's in stable condition. He woke for a moment, but the medication has put him back to sleep, he needs the rest. It looks very good, sir. You can come back and see him in about six to eight hours. He's going to be fine."

"Well, Praise the Lord." Ophelia said.

"I agree to that," Tom replied.

"South Central has some of the best doctors here, Tom. Your friend will get the best of care. If you like, I can even contact Pastor Zoe to come over and" Ophelia was Interrupted by Tom.

"Pastor Zoe! Oh, I have to get back in touch with him."

I was standing next to Tom when I saw the White Door open in front of me. It had appeared from no where. One of the staff nurses had walked toward me, passing right through it, not knowing it was there. An angel I had not met before came into the corridor by walking through the wall to my right. A human spirit was next to him.

"Greetings in the name of the Lord." he said.

"Greetings," I replied.

"My name is New Found."

"I am Septuagint. It brings me great joy to meet you."

He was awesome creature to behold. A rainbow of color surrounded his presence and the love of God was emanating from his very essence. The human spirit that accompanied him was very excited, jumping up and down, praising the Lord.

"I wish we had time to talk, but I am on an escort mission, and I can not be delayed. You see, this is one happy soul. In life, was a person known to the others of humanity as a paraplegic. His earthly time ended moments ago."

"What were the events?"

"His parents were involved in an auto accident on the tracks of a train. They were unable to get to the back seat in time and so it was recorded. As you can see he is very happy to be out of the shell which held him confined, a prisoner of soft clay."

"Praise to the highest. I will not hold up this happy reunion waiting." I turned to the boy spirit and said, "Welcome home, my friend."

"Thank you sir, will you be joining us on the journey to heaven?"

"No my young friend, my work here is not yet complete. But I am sure we will meet again."

I watched as they departed. I observed the angel New Found and the boy walk though the White Door and into the Tunnel of Review. As they walked a slight distance, I had wished that I could be returning myself to the Father's house. I gazed as the White door faded from sight.

THIRTEEN

The unusual tone of a melody chirped out the quaint song of 'Take Me out to the Ballpark.' Kirk reached under his coat to his waist, un-clipping the pre-star-trek tri-corder and swiftly answered his melodic cell phone.

"Hello? Yes sir, I am here now. Yes sir, It's for you, Senator. This is a secure number."

The Senator displayed a puzzled look as Kirk handed him the phone.

"This is Senator Tinnimen."

"Tinnimen, I need you to relax. Everything is being taking care of." Tinnimen's puzzled look turn to pale grey as he recognized the voice. The voice added, "We have been made aware of everything, and we will take care of every little detail." The Senator was quite dizzy from the rush of adrenaline. All this news was coming at him all at once. In the foyer area was the sound of sharp staccato footsteps of a woman's high heel shoes quickly approaching.

Kirk turned toward the senator and asked,

"Are you expecting anyone sir?"

Before he could answer back, busting into the room like a hurricane raging with a gale, a woman stormed in shouting.

"John! Is it true? Is it True?

All this news I have been receiving?"

She was mad as hornet that had just been swatted. And she was ready to sting anything or anyone that moved. Carrying a newspaper in her hand she slapped Kirk out of her way, plowing a path straight toward Tinnimen.

"What news, Dear?"

"Don't!, Don't you do that!, Don't you dare play coy with me John. I know you better than your mother."

She slammed the paper down on the desk and opened it up. A whole article was circled in red pen. The header read, 'GOLD WATCH FOUND ON DECEASED PROSTITUTE."

"Maggie, there's a perfectly good explanation to all this."

"I bet there is!" defensively, she crossed her arms, pausing to hear his next reply.

"Maggie, there's something I need to tell you."

"Well, I am all ears, this had better be good. I have already spoken to my attorney this morning."

"Nick! You spoke to Nick? Listen, Maggie, this isn't what you think."

"Excuse me, Maggie, one moment please,"

Tinnimen raised the cell phone to his ear. "Sir, I will have to get back to you, regarding this matter."

"Tinnimen, make it quick, we need to finish this."

"I will." Tinnimen pitched the cell phone to Kirk. "Kirk, please wait outside. I will be there in a moment."

"Of course," Kirk walked out to the garden.

The Senator lifted a cork from the square crystal etched bottle. The brown liquid flowed over the ice he had just taken from a bucket with tongs, and clanked as it melted.

"Drinking this early John? Really!"

"I have a feeling I am going to need it this morning. Maggie, the woman was . . . well, she..."

"Yes, go on."

"Maggie, she was my step sister. I never spoke of her to you. But I guess now is a good time to do so."

The hissing noise surrounded him, as oxygen was force flowed through the tube into the plastic mask held by an elastic band that was strapped over his head.

"Hey, look who's waking up! Hey buddy, how you feeling?" Tom asked.

"Feel like a freight train ran me over. What happened? One minute we were talking in your house. Next minute, the lights were out."

"You were shot, Steve. I believe it was intended for m'waa,"

"I took a hit for you? Oh, that's it! You're buying donuts till I retire."

Tom laughed, "You got it buddy, Krispy creams right? I might even throw in a cup of coffee."

Steve pulled the oxygen mask off his face he displayed a serious look, and asked,

"Just whose buttons were we pushing, that they would take a chance of making a hit on a cop?"

"I don't know pal, but I'm sure gonna find out."

"Does Lori know what happened?"

"Yeah, she's right outside the door. I'll send her in. I'll catch up with ya, little later." Tom pointed his finger at Steve and asked, "Oh, and by the way, who is this angel chick you keep calling out for? I wouldn't let Lori know about that if I were you. Might not want to fall asleep with her in the room." Tom laughed again as he exited the room. A puzzled look came over Steve's face, and he thought to himself,

"Huh?"

•─────────────────────────•

The shadowy hideous beast turned and growled when it heard his name spoken. Scowling unspoken displeasure, his large talons scraped the air behind him as a warning to all whom might try to approach him uninvited.

"Gopher!"

"Who dares call my name?"

Fury was large in size himself, but in comparison to Gopher, his stature was puny. The Great winged creature reached out and snatched Fury, and handling him like a toy.

"You dare say my name!"

Fury understood this was not his time to challenge this stenching force of evil, and in pretend humility, humbled himself before Gopher.

"I have heard said, you were in charge of the unholy one. I come my prince from seeing the Dark One. He has commanded that you allow me to see the new leader, that I might influence my presence on him. For I am know in the realms as FURY! SEEKER OF BLOOD."

Gopher released his grip and turned his back to him, showing his repute to Fury. He stood up unhunched, folded his powerful arms, and deviously asked him, "If you have seen the Dark One, surely he has given you the code word to say to be allowed an audience to the new leader."

"Oh, yes my Prince, I know the code word, it is Fallen Angel."

Gopher turned swiftly and backhanded a closed fist, smashing Fury in the grossly contorted face with such enormous energy it caused him to fall with pain.

"You lie! Wicked one! There is no code word. I was testing you!"

Fury gathered him self up. He was as tall as a mountain, being a power spirit, Muscular in his own right and not one to be intimidated. But when Gopher who was a Principality for the air, stood upright, his presence covered an entire city.

"Go from here, Fury; before I command you into the nether regions. Nothing is here for you to see. If you are needed, you will be summoned."

Fury was hotter than a poker that was purged in the coals of fire and his temper began to rage. But seeing Gopher's over-whelming presence and feeling the power of his blow, Fury decided to leave. He thought to himself, 'I will entice his anger just once to show my own power to this prince.'

"Yes My prince, I will leave. Forgive my intrusion," Gopher snarled. "It must pain you to no-end knowing you followed the Dark One Lucifer, and lost that entire splendor you once had."

Gopher raised his lip even more, revealing a bloody fang. Fury knew he was getting to him, for his tongue was a sharper sword. He had brought back the memories of ancient times, only making Gopher angrier. "I had forgotten how big and powerful your hands were. I had heard stories of your works in times past." Gopher was now clinching his fists. "Yes, Go-pher this, or Go-pher that, I remember now. Your hands helping with the creations, given by the orders of Jesus, before the fall, you use to be ALMOST as big as Michael, who still has those pure stretched out wings of ivory snow feathers, Oh, I'm sorry, you don't carry those wings anymore, do you? You only have those contorted membranous branches of sin sticking off your backside to fly with now."

The underworld rumbled as Gopher slammed his clawed fist downward, pounding his fist into his other hand. Gopher threw his head backward looking up and screamed, "F...U...R...Y! Curse you, curse your hide. You have antagonized me with memories long enough! Leave me now!"

Fury left Gopher's presence laughing hideously knowing he had done the damage he intended.

•─────────────────────────•

"Step sister, you expect me to believe that?" Then, remembering that John's father had been married more than once, Maggie began to lower her tone, wanting to believe what he said.

"Yes, it's true. She was my older sister. The stuff in the paper about a burglary is a cover up. The part about the watch is true. She was holding a Christmas gift I bought for you."

The chimes of a grandfather clock had sounded out filling the large room with elaborate bonging. The deep sound of the clock had momentary caused Senator Tinnimen to pause his conversation.

But before he could continue a different kind of ring sounded out, It was the front door. The butler again viewed himself in the foyer mirror, as was habit, making adjustment before presenting himself to any guest of the Tinnimens'.

"Good Morning sir, may I help you?" he said as he opened the door.

The man at the door held up a badge, and Identification. He was not alone.

"Washington Police Department! We have a search warrant for John L. Tinnimen and all the premises."

"Sir; are you aware of whose house this is?"

Tom pushed the butler aside and was escorted by seven uniformed officers and a mobile crime scene lab crew as he step inside.

Maggie heard all the commotion in the hall and now was more interested in what was going on at the entrance of her house than the conversation Tinnimen may have had to offer.

"What is going out there?" Maggie asked, as she started walking from the library into the huge foyer area.

Tinnimen looked out the French glass doors at Kirk. He motioned for him to come in.

"The Police are here!" Tinnimen said through gritted teeth.

Kirk gingerly walked toward the mansion house. In the hallway, Maggie was introduced to Detective Tom Allen.

"Mrs. Tinnimen?" Tom held up his I.D. again.

"Yes; What is this all about? And why have you found it necessary to invade my home unannounced?"

"Is your husba...Ah; Senator, Detective Allen, Washington Metro. I need to ask you a few questions sir."

Maggie became indignant and said, "You can't just barge into house like this."

"Yes, I can Mrs. Tinnimen. I have a signed warrant from the D. A. and Judge residing. And enough Probable Cause to do so or I would not be here. And I WILL search this place until I am blue in the face." Pointing to two of his officers Tom instructed them to start up stairs. "You guys from crime lab unit, get to that limo's trunk first, Rest of you men, take the downstairs.

"Sir, do you know who I am? I have a lot of polic...." he was cut off in mid sentence.

"I know exactly what I am doing and I sure do know WHO you are." Tom turned to face Tinnimen. He didn't like him and it showed. He poked Tinnimen in the shoulder blade while saying, "You Sir, are the prime suspect in a murder case."

Kirk had just walked in. "Ah, and what do we have here? One-snot nosed press secretary?"

Tom turned to one of the uniformed officers and said, "Take all these people into the library. Have them all sit down. Don't let anyone leave."

"What is going on here officer?" Kirk asked.

Remembering his face on a video tape, Tom answered him. "Shut up; dirt bag. I'll ask the questions around her. Now get in there and sit down."

"I'll have your badge for that remark!"

The demon, FEAR rose up from the floor. Now standing behind Kirk, it was moving toward Tom to over cast his shadow on him. But FEAR look up and stopped in his tracks. The wicked spirit saw me standing behind Tom. My clothes began to gleam solid white. I shook my finger in a tick tock motion as if to say,

"Uh ah!"

"Septuagint," Oh, how I cringe when they speak.

"Why are you here?"

I took one step toward him now. Crossed my hand over my waist and laid hold of my sword. Fear backed away, knowing I was about to smote him into the abyss. Unaware to Tom, I placed my other hand upon his shoulder. Tom began to laugh and said.

"You, have my badge? You pond scum, I am about to make sure, the only thing you're ever going to have is a four by four cell, with a room mate named Big Bubba for the next sixty or so years. Now get your keyster in there shut that pie hole you call a mouth, before I shut it for you!"

Fear had backed away from Kirk as I took another step forward.

"Septuagint, you have no right to do this." Fear professed.

"You're a liar! I have all the right in heaven's glory. Leave my presence now!"

Fear sank into the shadows of the corner knowing I was more than able to take him. And he was alone.

Kirk somehow felt the power of evil was no longer around him. In fact a presence was felt that was strange and intimidating to him. He looked at Tom, there was something . . . yes something . . . he couldn't put his finger on it. Kirk knew whatever it was, it was stronger than his will of evil. Kirk decided that this might be a good time for him to remain quite.

"John, I want to know what's going on and I want to know right now!"

Kirk interrupted and jumped into the conversation.

"Maggie I don't think this is the time to deliberate anything. Wait until you've had the opportunity to speak to a lawyer."

"Just what do you know about this Kirk? Are you involved in all this?"

Tom mockingly interjected,

"Oh yeah, do tell, Kirk; Do tell."

"I don't know what you're implying, Detective."

I looked inside Kirk's spirit, it was black and empty, cruel and evil. If I were unrestrained, I would have dashed him to pieces with my sword.

"Hey; Sarge, jackpot!"

"Officer Mince, escort these three people to the police limo. You know what to do first, don't you?"

"Yes Sarge." Mince reached into his upper left shirt pocket and removed a card and began reading from it.

"You are under arrest. You have the right to remain silent. Anything you do or say"...

His voice grew fainter as I followed Tom up the steps to where one of the crime scene officers was.

"General, Air Force One just landed," said the secretary.

"Thank you. I'll be right there. Shut the door behind you. That will be all," the general replied.

The young man saluted and left.

The room; A room of four wood paneled walls. A metal desk and file cabinets, two metal chairs with green padding on the arm rest that faced the desk. A double window side by side with pull-up blinds. The General stood up and turned to the man who was standing at the window, staring out at the vast runway. He was watching a plane that was taxied to a moving plat form with steps.

The General asked, "Are you sure you can make this happen?"

"Most assuredly, we already have our people in place."

The General put on his military hat and yanked on the edge of his uniform coat to straighten it out. He didn't look back at the man at the window and said,

"I don't need any mistakes; it would be the end of your life and mine. I hope that is understood."

He reached for the door and departed quickly. The man at the window replied an answer to himself,

"Yes, but there is always risk, my friend." he pick up his brown attaché' case and exited the room.

While exiting the building he heard the intercom announce an alarm drill.

'Attention all personnel this is a mock test, this is a mock test.'

He looked back at the speakers on the building, then outward toward the large presidential jet on the runway. On the runway he could see several men at the foot of the plane. The General was greeting the President and other dignitaries. He watched while getting into his car. His cell phone rang.

"Hello. Yes, he is willing to help. They are arriving now. Oculus is here. Have the money transferred. Fine;" He pushed the end button on the phone.

Tom wiped the banister railing of the stairs with his index finger while walking up the steps.

"I wonder if I can hire their maid?" he said aloud.

Making a right at the top of the stairs, A voice called out . . .

"Hey; Sarge, in here,"

One of the detectives was inside the master bedroom, kneeling down on the floor near the closet, wearing a surgical rubber glove. He was holding a shoe. His other hand held a cylinder object, flat on one side with a neon tube on the other.

"Check it out, Sarge." He waved the tube along the side of the shoe, the black light revealed traces of blood stains that were smudged. "Looks like he tried to wipe it off,"

"Bag it and tag it," Tom said.

I felt my clothes change, as the anointing welded up within me. They were already white, but now began to glow. I sensed the presence of an evil spirit in the room. One of the detectives standing near the dresser drawers had moved it, pulling each drawer and dumping the contents out on the bed. He used the black light over each item, looking for more traces of blood.

The presence of evil was coming from behind the dresser, but the detective was standing in front of it. A wooden pine box lay atop of the dresser and several different types of jewelry were displayed on a blue velvet pad.

The Detective lifted up one of the rings, "Sarge, got one that has a pentagram on it."

Hissing sounds were exhuming from behind the dresser. Not physical sound, but sound that can only be heard by the spiritual. As the detective handed the ring to Tom; it popped its ugly little head from around the side of the dresser.

"Seppppp'tuui' aaa' gent!" it hissed out my name. It was the imp called GUILT. It trembled asking "What are you doing here?" I drew my sword immediately. "Sssuuurrely, you would not waste your strength on me, would you?" seething through his fangs. He had a long tail and sharp, nasty talons.

"What are your orders! I adjure you in the name of the Lord, answer now."

"Awwh! Unfair messenger! To use that charge, I will tell, I will tell," His tongue was forced to speak. "I am ordered to follow the ring and it's wearer," Guilt replied.

"That is all I needed to know; In the name of the host of heaven!" I shouted, as I swung a fierce blow of my flaming sword. slicing the horde of hell back into the abyss. A dissipating puff of stench and sulfur filled the air. He screamed as he departed, "you have not stopped me, only delayed me!"

"Perfect. This is just what we needed to tie the Senator into the other killing. I think we may have the pentagram killer, boys. I am going to head back, but I first want to go check on Steve. You guys finish up here and get as much as you can."

"Hey, how's Steve doing?"

"To tell the truth, Jeff, I am amazed. I thought he was a goner there for awhile. But he pulled through with flying colors. He was actually awake when I left."

"Tell him we're all pulling for him."

"I will."

Tom exited the room; I was following him down the steps when I heard someone say my name.

"Septuagint!"

I turned and looked back at the top of the stairs.

"Come with me."

It was Oracle, an angel of unquestionable wisdom. I didn't ask why, I knew if he was here, he was sent by the highest.

"Greetings in the name of the Lord, it is nice to see a friendly face."

"I have been instructed that your are on a two fold mission."

"Yes sir, I am. that one is my current assignment. His name is Tom Allen, but I am also here as a recorder."

"The latter is why I need you. Come with me and record this event."

When I turned back and walked up to the top of the stairs, the entire top floor had faded to nothingness. I followed Oracle as he led the way. We had only to take one step from where we were and arrived. We were now in a huge open field, an outdoor event.

"Why is this mass of people here?"

"To be deceived,"

"By whom?"

"The one sitting on the right of that man is known as the President, the other is King Oculus. He is chosen by Lucifer to rule a short period."

"What is the event, I am to record?"

"His event,"

As Oracle pointed to the back of the crowd, we were immediately moved from where we stood to a new location at the back of the large crowd. A small hole camouflaged by a brush of trees near a tunnel completely horizontal from one side of the hill to the other. There was only a one foot by two foot opening on the side that faced the crowd. It was also covered by brush.

As I looked at a man lying in the tunnel, I watched him adjust a long scope on a rifle. His face was painted same as the grass.

"Why? Who is he?"

"His name is David. He is an Israeli soldier, but today he is a mercenary and will not live after this event."

As the one called Oculus stood to address the crowd, I saw David take aim and fire. Oculus fell to the ground. He laid dead on center stage.

One of the secret service agents had just exited a port-o-pot, and saw the flash from the hill's edge under the brush. Seeing the commotion going on near the stage, he ran to where the shot and flash had come. When he reached the top of the hill, David had just exited the tunnel from the other side. He was running out to the parking lot full of cars.

"Stop; You're under arrest!" The agent shouted.

David ignored the warning, but it was too late. The booming sound of a forty five auto rang out and filled the air. David slumped over the hood of a car and fell dying. The agent's bullet penetrated David's heart. As he neared his death, I saw that look, the same one I had seen countless times.

Oracle moved nearer to him as David stood up, looking down at his own corpse on the ground.

"I am Oracle; I am here to take you before the counsel. You have to come with me."

Oracle grabbed David by the hand before he could say anything, and immediately picked David up, several feet above the earth's surface. David was speechless at the astounding beauty of Oracle's presence. Oracle turned towards me.

"Septuagint, have you recorded all?"

"Yes," I replied.

I was about to ask him why he lifted David so quickly, then I saw for myself. Two demons from hell, the collectors, had just arrived, and were going to snatch David's soul down to Hades. He had just committed an act of murder. But I thought about it.

The act itself must have been predestined or Oracle would not have been here to intercede. The collectors were outraged for not retrieving David's spirit. Now they would have to answer for their blunder. I watched Oracle smile at me with such love that it emitted the pure joy of the Lord. I thought about Tom, and knew I had to get back to where ever he was.

    I turned to my right and the White Door appeared. I stepped through, and I was inside the hospital where I had seen the angel New Found.

FOURTEEN

The cry of a baby screeched out from the cubic room as a young mother held the child, trying to smoothes her young during an injection to do good and fight fever but the pierce of a needle was never the joy of any toddler. The smell of sterilized fumigant filled the hallway, the same hallway bustling with nurses and people walking this way and that way. Tom turned to the side as a couple of nurses passed by, and placed his hand on the wall asking Lori,

"How's he doing?"

"He's resting now."

"Lori, I never had the chance to tell you, I am truly sorry. I never wanted any of my guys to get hurt. I wish it were me instead of Steve. I hope you know that."

She patted Tom on the chest.

"I know that Tom. I need some coffee. Would you like me to get you something from the cafeteria?"

"No thanks, I think I'll just go in and sit with him for awhile. Maybe I can catch the news."

Lori grinned and wiped a tear from her eye.

"Ok, I'll be back in a bit."

I watched Tom as he looked up and down the hallway. He lowered his head and whispered a silent prayer. But his prayer was a spiritual prayer so it sounded out in the spiritual realm as a thundering voice reaching all of heaven's end.

"Dear Lord Jesus, help me in what ever it is I am involved in here. Lead my footsteps. Please help Steve recover quickly. Amen."

Tom cracked the door open slowly to the room. Peeking in, he saw Steve was awake and turning on the T. V. The News was just coming on. A young reporter was holding a microphone. He was standing in front of the platform. It was surrounded by police moving the crowd back.

The announcer said, "the man of peace, is dead. Assassinated like so many other great leaders of the past. Once again, King Oculus was shot while making a public address to the masses of people here..."

Steve lowered the volume.

"Hey buddy, how you feeling?" Tom asked but was interrupted by Steve.

"Get over here. Take a look at that."

"Yeah, I heard. Someone shot Oculus."

"No, not that Tom, Look!"

Tom turned to look at the T.V. and camera was zooming in a view of the corpse of the king being covered up. "What Steve? I have seen dead bodies before."

"Some detective you are big dummy. Look at the close up of the hand, Tell me, what you see?"

The camera panned back outward before Tom could turn around again.

"What? What did I miss?"

"The ring, it was a pentagram ring. You know the one with the star in it. He had on the same dang on ring! This case goes all the way up to the top brass."

"Now just calm down here buddy, lets not start any conspiracy stories just yet. Are you sure you saw a pentagram ring?"

"I was shot in the back, not in the head. Tom, I know what I saw. It was the very same as the one in the case we are working on. I bet you anything that our Senator Tinnimen can lead you to that guy right there. I wonder if Tinnimen has one of those little rings."

"Nope, I got his. We found it today during the search of his house. He's now preaching politics to inmates at our county jail."

"Be careful, I have a feeling this isn't over yet."

"Know what you mean, check back with you later."

Lori was walking in just as Tom was starting to leave.

"Hello, some boss, you are Tom, not letting your number one guy get any rest."

She took a sip of her cup.

"Naw, he was awake when I came in. But I have to run anyway. Take care of him. I think I'll give him a week off work."

I watched from the corner of the room as Tom exited the room. Lori turned to Steve and said,

"Honey I have something to tell you now that, well now I know you're ok. I was going to tell you later, but I want you to know it now."

"What is it hun?"

"I'm pregnant, Steve you're going to be a father."

"What, Really?"

I started to walk out the door, but I wanted to remind Steve of the conversation he had with me when his spirit was with me in limbo. So I flashed my wings, only a millisecond, for him to see. The memories flooded his mind.

•————————————————————•

The brisk wind chill had dropped the temperature several degrees. The air was crisp to his lungs. Tom knew the case was not over, although the suspect a Senator was now behind bars. He realized Steve was as smart as they come. And if he said he saw the same ring, then there was another ring. Wanting to clear his head, Tom dug his hands deep into his pockets and decided to take a walk. He walked across the street from the hospital, and into a park. He knew that the sandwich shop was only a few blocks west of the park. Pounding the pavement, the loose change in his pocket made a jingling sound with every down step of his left foot.

Keeping a cadence as he walked, his thoughts carried him back in time when the heat was incredibly exhausting. Yeah, he thought Yates. That was the name, how could I forget, Yates, Drill Sergeant Yates. With each marching step and jangle of the change in his pocket, the more vivid the memory became. Drill Sergeant Yates, walking beside him as he had done so many times during basic training.

"You eyeballin' me boy?" Yates would shout.

"No Drill Sergeant!"

"You better be looking straight ahead Private Allen, because if I even think that you had the gaw to look at me, Private you and all your platoon will be marching up that hill until the crack of dawn! Is that un . . . der stood pri...vate?" Yates barked out each word.

"Yes Drill Sergeant!"

Tom thought about how hot it was that day. He remembered the sweat rolling down his face, keeping in step with his fellow army recruits of his platoon, carrying that heavy army issued backpack that weighed a ton. But that backpack was no where near as heavy on him as Yates was.

"I can't hear you private! Did you just address this United States Army Drill Sergeant with the vocal command of a squeaky mouse?

Where you from boy? Florida? You been hanging out down in Disneyland with that big mouse? Is that why you're so squeaky?"

Tom raised his voice. He wanted to turn to look at the face of the man who was keeping in step with him and yelling questions at him. He slightly turned, but the rim of the Drill Sergeant's military hat was only millimeters away from his face.

"Don't you dare look at me, boy!"

"No Drill Sergeant! I am not from Florida! I have never been to Disneyland! I don't even like that mouse, Drill Sergeant!"

"Platoon Halt!" the Sergeant shouted. And all stopped.

"What did you say Private Allen! Yooou don't like the mouse!" Some of Tom's fellow cadets wanted to laugh but knew better. "Everybody likes the mouse! The mouse is an American icon! Are you an American or some kind of Russkie in the mist? Don't you eyeball me Allen!"

"Drill Sergeant, maybe I can learn to like the mouse, Drill Sergeant! I don't know..."

"You don't know? Are you unsure of yourself private? We won't put up with double mindedness in this army! You make a decision boy and by the Will of the Almighty, Bless His sweet name, you stick to that decision soldier. Is that clear? Did I say something funny? Are you trying to provoke me private? Wipe that smirk off your face right now private, or you will march the whole day under our hot Georgia heat! Would you like that, private? Would you like to march this whole base till sun up?"

Tom was tired, but somehow he found the energy to shout at the top of his lungs, like a soldier who was going into battle screaming a war cry.

"NO DRILL SERGEANT, I would not like to march the whole day!"

"Now that's funny, Allen, You sound like a real soldier. Are you sure you don't want to change your mind?"

"NO DRILL SERGEANT!"

Tom had almost forgotten where he was going. The thoughts had seemed so real to him. He even forgot about how cold it was until his hand touched the metal door handle of the sandwich shop.. As he shook the sleet off his shoes, he looked behind him at the hospital top floors which towered above some of the smaller buildings. He realized that he had marched the way through the park, not recalling seeing any of it. As he was looking back, he figured the trajectory of the bullet that had struck Steve must have come from a high angle. He made a mental note to himself to check it out when he got back home.

"Don't just stand there with the door propped open. Come in, come in."

Tom saw she was talking to him. He walked in and let the door shut behind him. The place was small warm and cozy. The hard wood floors had added a down home motif to the atmosphere. The neon sign was blinking in the window the words "OPEN CAFÉ", little tables for two were covered with red and white checkerboard clothes. The chairs were wooden with some kind of weaved straw like material to sit on. Tom shook the sleet from his overcoat off at the entrance of the door. At the same time he looked down at the floor mat that read, "Some of the nicest people cross this threshold."

The counter was a soda pop type, and round chairs adorned the place. All were empty. Tom had let the chilly air rush in like a home invader and the young girl working the counter was rubbing her bare arms.

"Burr, that is cold. Can I get you a cup of coffee?"

"Yes please, black."

"Are you hungry? We have some of the best philly cheese steak around."

"That sounds pretty good. I'll have that. Thank you."

Tom surveyed the decor behind the bar and on the walls. He noticed a group of caricature pictures that were all done in charcoal pen. Laurel and Hardy, Abbott and Costello, Charlie Chaplin, Buster Keaton, C.W. Fields. The photo memorabilia lined the whole wall. Tom was quick to note that all the pictures were of comedians of yesteryear.

"That's really cool. I love all those guys."

"Really? So do I, My father's favorites. I remember watching all the old reruns at the movie house my dad use to own. But he retired and sold it."

"Well, who ever the artist 'M' is, sure did a good job of recreating the like likeness of those old comedians."

"Thank you, I appreciate the compliment, not too many people nowadays even know who those guys were. Younger generation. The laughter they gave to the world was just wonderful."

"You're 'M'? Awesome work!"

"Yes I'm 'M', but you can call me Marcy. So what is your name?"

She reached out over the counter extending her hand. Tom shook hands and admired the softness of her skin.

"Tom, Tom Allen. Nice to meet you Marcy,"

He said as he smiled. He lost thinking that someone so pretty and lively was here in this cold capital, working at a small café "So why you working here? I mean, you're a great artist. You're pretty enough to be in the picture biz yourself. They must pay you good."

"No, they don't pay me at all. I own the place."

"Really?" Tom thought 'oh yeah, a young waitress owns this place.'

"You only happened to catch me working here tonight, because I gave Jodie, the girl that works for me, the night off to go home and get some Christmas shopping done."

His eyes zoomed in on the business owner's license which he knew would be posted behind the bar, since they sold beer and wine. It read, "Owner; Marcy Stewart." He raised an eyebrow.

"So what kinda work, you in Mr. Tom Allen?"

Tom thought for a second before answering and smiled. Knowing that most people's first impression of the title Police leaves a bad taste in some civilian minds, and not wanting to scare this lovely lady away, He played on her sense of humor.

"I'm an art critic"

Marcy leaned over the counter top, lifting her leg up flirtatiously, and with the index finger of her right hand tapped Tom on the tip of his nose.

"I don't think so...Mr. Policeman."

"How did you know that?"

"I saw a flash of your badge on your belt when you were taking off your overcoat."

"Observant. Why did you ask?"

"I wanted to see if you were one of those guys who has a big head and spurts it right out, you know the arrogant types 'I'm a cop' you know the one's who think they are so cool, because they carry a badge."

Tom grinned.

"I also wanted to see if you would tell me little white lies."

Tom's grin now turned into a big smile. Not only was she beautiful, but she was cunning and witty. He knew right then he liked her attitude.

"So Marcy, what time do you got to be home and take care of the man of the house?" Tom was trying to determine the answer of his latter question in a roundabout way.

"Oh, he expects me around eleven."

Tom made a disapproving grunting noise as took a sip of coffee she had sat before him.

"Hmmm."...

"But to answer the real unasked question, Tom, he has four legs and goes arf, arf,"

She smiled as Tom raised his eyebrow again, purposely holding the cup up to his lip to hide his grin. But it did no good. His smile extended outward, pass the brim of the his cup. A drop dribbled down his chin. She taunted him as she smiled, and walked back into the kitchen through the wooden swinging doors.

"Missed some."

Tom watched her walk away, while quickly grabbing a napkin from the bar counters to wipe the coffee running down his chin. As she entered the kitchen area, a man in white slacks and apron was cleaning up the grill. He was putting the spatula and utensils away in a large pan.

"Joey, I need one Philly please. I know you were done. But do it for me, please. Oh, and make it a good one. Thanks"

The old cook looked up at her and smiled. He had heard some of the conversation between his boss and the man sitting at the bar.

"This is where it always starts. Love over a good sandwich, kids always falling for a smile and a Philly." Joey thought and chuckled at himself, he had made a pun. 'A smile and a Philly.' Yeah Marcy was a Philly alright, pure thoroughbred.

FIFTEEN

In Israel, on the other side of the world, the rapid knock on a door was heard. An elderly gentleman answered. His steel, long grey beard was trimmed, yet touching his chest. He wore a white shirt with a black jacket and matching slacks. Adjusting his glasses he asked, "Yes, May I help you?"

"Mr. Shearson?" the delivery man asked.

"That's right, I'm Mr. Shearson."

"Please sign here, sir."

The man pointed to the "X" next to the long blank space. Shearson signed the paper and the man handed him the brown envelope.

"Thank you sir, Have a good day."

"Mmm hum." Shearson replied and shut the door.

He walked back into the study, and sat down at the desk. The room motif was adorned with ancient books locked behind glass door book shelves. He picked up a letter opener with a lion's head carved on the end of the handle. Carefully pressing the tip under the corner edge, he curiously opened the large envelope. The front of the envelope had only his name and address on it. The Demon Guilt had followed the package from America. He was lurking in the corner of the room, waiting for Shearson to read the news. The opportunity to invoke his presence again on a human had excited the leering cretin. The letter was written in an ancient text and the language had been long forgotten. Besides Shearson there were probably only a handful of people who could decipher the words. Tears welded up in Shearson eyes and streamed down his face as he scanned the letter.

Assignment completed. Target destroyed. But it is with deep regret, I must inform you, that your son David is dead. He was and shall be remembered as a true soldier. My deepest condolences to your and family.

Sincerely,
General T.

The loss of his child overwhelmed him. He crumpled the paper, and rent his shirt in two. He laid his head down weeping into his arms. "Oh... my God! Have Mercy!"

Guilt stood back away from the bearded man. The old man's cry for the Lord had spooked him. Guilt decided he had better not stay in this place and departed swiftly, looking over his shoulders for any warring angels who might have heard the old man's cry.

•———————————————————•

The alarm had sounded and the morning was passing. I watched Tom sleeping, but I knew there were many things to be done. I leaned over and shouted his name.

"Tom!"

"Huh?"

He jumped and turned, rolling the covers back quickly. The startled awakening had jarred him. He wondered what time it was. Placing his feet on the floor, he slipped on his house shoes with a bear's head. He recalled how Steve had laughed at them.

He scuffed his head as he rose up, "Time to make the donuts, Time to make the stupid donuts. Why do I always have to make the donuts?"

He walked out of the bedroom passing the living room to the kitchen. Tom saw the bullet hole in the window that shattered, and remembered that he was going to check the angle from the shot. He grabbed a long string from the closet and some masking tape. Securing one end of the string to the glass, and holding the other, he walked over to the place where Steve had been sitting. He sat down and held the string to almost the exact place Steve had been hit, and secured it to the chair. Tom reached to the upper shelf of his closet and pulled down a pair of binoculars. He looked through them to the place where the shot may have come from. He could see the angle only left one spot open, the high billboard sign across the interstate.

"Yeah, I will go and check that out right after breakfast," he said out loud.

I wondered how that happened, as I watched Tom move about his home. I did not understand it. But being an angel, there are many things these humans do that I don't understand.

Tom walked back into the kitchen and drank a cup of coffee. I moved nearer to Tom to try to figure out how it happened. He then walked into the bathroom and picked up his toothpaste. He applied a little to his tooth brush and raised it up to his mouth. I knew right then, that what I trying to understand, he was too.

"What the . . . ?" Tom shouted, as he leaned closer to the mirror. I was still at a loss for words not knowing what the two black circles around his eyes were. "Ah man, Steve! I am going to get you for this buddy!"

Tom rushed back into the other room and picked up the binoculars and looked at the eye pieces. "Shoe polish . . . Nice one." Tom started to laugh at the joke Steve had pulled on him.

•―――――――――――――――•

The door opened, and one of the secretaries peeked in, but didn't step in.

"Linda, he's here, and staff is following him."

She shut the door as quickly as she had opened it. Linda moved from behind the desk stood up and adjusted her skirt. Smoothing out the wrinkles and walking over to the door, she opened it and stood at the doorway's entrance.

"Good morning, Mr. President," she said as he and staff entered the office.

"Good morning, Linda." He turned back to the man who was walking with him, completing a sentence of the conversation that was taking place as he had entered. "I want to know how he got past all the security. I want to know how he got into the States, who he was linked to. I need the Ambassador of Persia here, now. I want to know who fronted the money. I want the answers and I want them now!"

Linda closed the door behind him as he and staff entered the Oval office. Shortly, the General entered the secretaries' office where Linda was sitting.

"Good morning, sir."

"Morning, Linda. Is he in?"

"He's in an important meeting, sir. I will announce you." Linda pushed the intercom button. "Mr. President, General cooper is here to see you."

"Tell him I will be with him momentarily, Thank you, Linda."

"Sir, if you would just have a seat, the President will be with you shortly."

"I think I'll just step out side and get a sip of water from the fountain."

The general walked out of the office into the hallway, removed his hat and placed it under his arm as he leaned down to sip a drink.

"General Cooper how nice to see you in this neck of the woods, So, how's the affairs of the world going?"

He looked up to see who was addressing him. It was Brice Noland, Head of the Central Intelligence Agency.

"You tell me, Brice. Seems you know where the next battle field is going to be played before I do. I guess you should, you end up starting most of them, don't you?"

"Now, Now, General, such a sharp tongue, not a very pleasant thing to say. Maybe you're getting a little rusty in the noodle in your senior years. Maybe need to slow down a bit, huh?" Brice leaned down to sip from the fountain himself.

"Just what are you really saying, Brice?"

"Nothing, General. Just be careful who you're seen with nowadays. I guess you heard about Tinnimen being arrested on murder charge of one of metro's finest."

"Yeah, I heard, and I'm not buying it. Why are you telling me this, Brice? What's the connection? You of all people never gave out info, unless it is to bait someone into biting the hook. Is that it, Brice? You trying to get me to bite?"

"Paranoid, are we?"

"Listen to me, Mr. C.I.A. I was working the world of spies and politics before you were a gleam in your sweet daddy's eye. So don't even try to play your mind games with me."

Brice sarcastically raised his hand in a sloppy salute and chuckled.

"Yes sir!"

The door to the office opened and Linda stepped out of the doorway as the General raised a graying eyebrow at Brice.

"General, the President will see you now, sir."

"Thank you, be right there. Excuse me, Mr. Noland," He looked Brice in the eyes with a piercing stare. Brice adjusted his red tie and pulled down on the coat end of his black suit.

"Have a great day, General."

Brice stepped back and stretched his arm toward the oval office like he was the one man welcoming committee as the General walked in. Brice stepped up to the fountain again and, taking a drink, said to himself. "Old war goat."

●─────────────────────────────●

"Septuagint," I could hear but not see. It was the voice of Xenophon.

"Greetings, in the Name of the Lord."

"Septuagint, come up here now. You are needed to record this."

I was immediately taken by thought travel to the highest pinnacle of where Xenophon was. We were somewhere in outer sphere of space, next to an unmanned ballistic weapons station. I saw the cargo bay doors swing opened. We were only a few yards from it.

"What's happening, Xenophon? Why was I called to record this event?"

"It is critical to the plan of history."

The tips of the rounded objects were about the same length as Xenophon's wing span. The writing on the object was of the Islamic language. I could see the whole Earth, both the dark side and the sun shining on the bright side. A beeping sound was heard from the metal that was floating flawlessly in space. Suddenly, there was an explosion, and red flames erupted from the back end of the long tube. It was now launching toward the Earth.

"What was that, and where is it going, Xenophon?"

"It is a nuclear weapon. And it is heading for Israel."

On the Earth the air base was in a full scramble. Reserves were running everywhere. The alarm was sounding.

A voice announced over the intercom, "This is not a drill, Repeat this is not a drill!"

"Why are we still here?"

But before I could finish my question to Xenophon, two more of the nuclear weapons were deployed from the bay.

"Are they going to the same place?"

"No, that one is heading for another city."

I watched as the tube of destruction barreled its way through space, splitting the air in front of its nose-cone.

"Where is that one heading to? It does not seem to be going the same direction as the others."

"It is heading for America."

"America, where?"

"Washington, D. C."

"But Tom is there. Have I completed my mission?"

Xenophon looked at me.

"Behold," he pointed upward toward the true North where Heaven is. I looked up and there were thousands upon thousands of angels descending toward America and Israel. "There are still chosen ones the land that the Lord provided for the saints. Many still pray for peace. The Lord is not slack in his ways, Septuagint, and He has provided a way for them."

I watched as the first missile disintegrated. It illuminated a large section of the dark side of the Earth. Israel was now under attack. I saw the huge white cloud as it moved upward and outward. A reverberating sound echoed, chasing the expanding white cloud. Moments later, another burst of white consumed the dark side for only seconds of time, then repeated the same movements as the first.

The air base was sealed tighter than a drum of chemical toxic waste.

"Launch! Launch is a go!" a voice sounded out on the intercom. A huge steel plated door that laid flat on the ground suddenly moved back. Smoke was bellowing upward and rolling outward from the deep silo and within seconds the long range missile was heading toward its target. Its destiny was to obliterate the Islamic nuclear missile launched from space. The missile was nicknamed the Angelic Rage. Someone had written on the side of it the ninety first Psalm, verses nine to eleven.

"If you make the Most High your dwelling, even the Lord, who is my refuge, then no harm will befall you. No disaster will come near your tent. For he will command his angel concerning you to guard you in all your ways."

I watched as the missile Angelic Rage raced to intercept the other that was heading toward the earth. But I also wanted to get back to Tom.

Then it happened, a huge bang. The two had collided. The missile Angelic Rage had crashed into the target. It had exploded in the outer regions of space. When seen from space, it was on the edge of the dawn's morning.

Tom was driving to work, when off to his left toward the sunrise he saw the bright light flash in the sky just over the edge of the darkness. "What th . . . what in the world was that?" Tom thought. He spilled part of his coffee onto the floor mat as he had hit the brakes. He pulled over into the emergency lane, as had many other spectators. The highway was now jammed with those who had exited their cars to see the huge ring of light and it's dazzling colors.

Tom's radio station sounded a warning tone.

"We interrupt this program to bring you a special news bulletin from the national emergency broadcast channel. Today, at approximately nine thirty two eastern standard time, two ballistic missiles where launched from the space station Andromedia, striking two regions above the Israeli government territories in space. All three launches were intercepted above the earth's atmosphere and destroyed. It is unknown if the United States was targeted at this time. The blast of the intercepted missile was visible to the human eye as far as mid western states eastern standard time this morning. This just in..."

Tom adjusted his volume on his radio, peering into the rear view mirror, seeing that traffic was starting to back up as far as the exit ramp, which led him to the highway.

"It seems, Israel was the prime target of this morning's attack, but both missiles were aborted or either self destructed before entering the Earth's atmosphere. The White House and all staff are on high alert. We have now been told that America, was a secondary target in today' attack. Military forces will be making further announcements momentarily." Tom reached down pulled a blue light from the floor board and placed the large magnet on top of the roof above the driver's door. He turned on a switch under the dash board of his unmarked unit, which let out a loud whooping siren squeal. The traffic was now starting to pile up heavily so he maneuvered to the emergency lane trying to get off at the next exit. He braked then quickly yanked the steering wheel to the left, then counter steered back to the right, while at the same time removing his foot and stomping the gas pedal. Tom wondered about many things. The people he cared about . . . Steve and his wife, Lori. Pastor Paul Zoe, his new found spiritual leader, and his parents who lived in

Kentucky on the old horse farm. But his mind also pondered about Marcy.

Tom thought, "I wonder if she is even awake? She is so beautiful." Tom picked up the cell phone while continuing down the emergency lane. He saw an exit ramp and it was all clear. The cars were piled up like a long daisy chain for miles, bumper to bumper, and made a swishing sound as he passed each one. Leaving the blue emergency light on, Tom reached down and turned the siren off. He punched in a number and heard it ring on the small speaker box that was mounted in the center of the floorboard. A tender female voice answered and said.

"Hello?"

"Hello, Marcy?"

"Yes, who's calling?"

"Marcy; this is Tom, from the café', last night."

"Oh yes. Well, when I gave you my number, I sure didn't expect a call this soon, but it is nice to hear from you."

Tom was almost at the clearing for the ramp, when he cut sharply to the right, quickly stomping the brake and skidding toward the guardrail. A motorcycle and rider had cut in between two of the cars on Tom's left side, and directly in front of his path. He came to a complete stop but almost crashed into the guard rail.

"You big dummy!" Tom blurted out.

"Excuse me?" Marcy asked.

"I'm sorry Marcy, Not you. It was a crazy driver, but I guess I can't really blame him. The whole city is in a uproar."

"Uproar? Why, what's going on?"

Marcy picked up her coffee cup and took a sip as she adjusted the towel on her head. She spoke a little louder into the speaker phone, and sat her cup down to tighten the terrycloth belt that was wrapped around her waist.

"You haven't heard what's been going on this morning?"

"No, I just got out of the shower. I was getting ready to go do some Christmas shopping this morning."

"You might want to turn on the news this morning. That is why I was calling you. I also wanted to know if you would like to see me sometime today."

"Ok."

"Great, what time is good for you?"

"What?"

"What time is good for you to see me?"

"No, Tom. I was saying 'Ok, I will turn the news on.' But to tell you the truth, I wasn't expecting to hear from you until later in the week."

"Little too soon, huh? Well, I as a little worried about you, from what was going on. There may not be a little later on this week.

"Have you been drinking this morning, Officer Allen?"

"No."

"Ok, just checking, hope I didn't offend you."

"Not at all, but I still would like to see you."

"How about you meet me at the coffee shop on Lexington Heights, near the mall at eleven this morning? We can shoot the breeze over a cup and a croissant."

"Great. See you then. Bye Marcy."

Tom was still trying to maneuver his car around the bend of the curve on the exit ramp. He turned the volume back up on the radio to hear the latest update. Just as he hung up the phone with Marcy, the phone rang. He pushed the control button to talk on the speaker as he continued his exit. The morning traffic was still moving exceedingly slow. He weaved, in and out of traffic as others slowed to let him pass, the flashing blue police light visible atop his vehicle.

"Metro; Detective Allen here."

"Hey Sarge, this is Paul from the release desk. Listen one of your guys said to make sure I give you a ring if I heard any news on that political wind piper, Tinnimen."

"Yeah; what about him?"

"I just got a call from the top chief and frankly, sir, I don't like it. But who am I to not follow orders from the higher ups."

"Paul, what are you saying?"

"I just got a call from the White House, saying to release Tinnimen. He was granted a full pardon from the President himself. Full diplomatic immunity. Sorry Sarge, he walked out ten minutes ago with an entourage of attorneys and secret service escorts."

"What!" Tom was livid. He felt his blood pressure soar through the ceiling.

"Sarge, I don't know who it is exactly he knows up on the hill, but those guys came busting in. I mean the attorneys with a brass parade following. Oh, and Sarge, the brass was from our department."

"Did you get a copy of the release order?"

"Sure, signed by the President himself." Paul ruffled through some papers and pulled the file to the top of the pile. Opening it, saw the paper with the orders stating, 'To all officers of the land of the United States, the person known as Senator J. L. Tinnimen is hereby granted a full pardon by the Chief Executive in Office. The President of the United States of America; Yelpers; Sarge. I have it right here in front of me signed by the big Cheese himself."

I saw Tom slam his fist down on the dash of his car. I knew he was unaware of my presence. I also knew something was wrong right away, because my clothes began to gleam. I looked backward out the rear passenger door behind Tom. Off in the distance, I saw it, not as humans eyes see, but with spiritual eyes. It was Rage. And he was invoking his entity over the whole metro area. Tom was just one of many who was being suppressed by the power of rage.

"Lord, give me strength," Tom said.

I smiled, thinking to myself, good boy Tom, good boy. For by his prayer, I was able to over shadow him with my protection. Suddenly, he became calm in his spirit. While he glanced out the side window and seen other drivers yelling and cursing at one another, Tom began to wonder why the other people he was observing became so violent.

"Hum, road rage." Tom said.

I smiled at him, thinking well at least you recognized half of the name of evil.

"Give you what, Sarge? I didn't hear what you said."

"Nothing Paul, I'll be there shortly." Tom clicked off the speaker phone, and rolled down the window as he drove. My clothes were still shining and illustrious white. I looked passed Tom's flesh to see his spirit man. I saw it was glowing and growing inside him.

"Lord," Tom said, "I never was a big praying sort of guy. But if things start to get worse, I know it might be a little late, but I always intended on getting married someday. And Marcy sure seems to be a pretty lady. What do you think? If it's your will, Lord that love grows between us, I'll give it all I got. Ok?"

SIXTEEN

The office door closed swiftly. The sound of the latch metal made a clicking noise, causing the young woman who was running her finger tips over the top edge of the files to turn to see who had entered.

"May I help you, sir?"

"I would like to see Mr. Noland, please."

"Mr. Noland is in a meeting, sir, would you like to leave your name and number or make an appointment?"

"No, that won't be necessary. Just give him this."

The man reached inside his leather coat, and pulled out a small business card with nothing on the back. The secretary took the card and looked at it. There was no number, no name, no address; Just a yellow circle on it with a smiley face. She gave a ridiculing look. She thought 'this is a governmental institution, and this guy is acting like a well wisher, passing out happy face cards.'

The man could see her sarcastic impression. He quickly commented with a tone of authority. "Don't worry he will know who it's from. Just make sure he gets it."

"Yes sir, I will." she was a little intimidated by his tone.

●━━━━━━━━━━━━━━━━━━━━━━●

The Washington Metro police booking desk was unusually crowded for a mid morning. There was chaos from all the traffic accidents. The holding cells were becoming crowded from the drivers who were arrested for taking the matter of the law in their own hands. Sergeant Allen went almost unnoticed as he entered the building. Although the noise was loud, most of the officers were trying to listen to the news being broadcast, about the explosion that took place in space over the Atlantic. Tom noticed the group of blue uniforms huddled around the portable T.V. that was located behind the booking desk. Each person was worried if there was going to be another attack or retaliation strike from the United States. The look on the faces of experienced officers, who were trained to handle all kinds of crisis, expressed fear for something for which that none of them were really prepared. These people were fathers, mothers primarily family orientated type people, who were now aware they had to be in charge of their personal emotions and above all else to maintain order. Tom realized the terror of the people with whom he worked, knowing the truth was evident.

"Allen! Get in here now!"

Tom rolled his eyes upward thinking, 'Oh, man' He had forgotten about the "Head hunter." The voice, that voice. Tom knew it well, it was the same voice saying you're in big trouble Mr. When Tom glanced up, he noticed the group in blue, looking up at him.

"Get back to work . . . now!" Tom said.

"Sure Sarge."

Some of them just looked at Tom strangely as he started walking down the hall to the captain's office. The walk reminded Tom of a walk he took long ago back in high school. He had put crazy glue on the edge of the drawer of the 'not so liked' science teacher. Tom smirked at the thought of it, not the joke but how he got caught. He remembered one of his buddies telling him the teacher was coming and he quickly got to his seat, maybe a little too quickly. He didn't have the time to replace the cap on the glue. And when the bell rang for the next class, Mr. Stanton felt it strange that Tom was still sitting in his chair especially when he was only supposed to be in class for one session. At first, Mr. Stanton thought Tom was trying to earn some extra credits. When he asked him to leave the class room and Tom attempted to stand, Stanton was all the wiser. Trying to carry that desk to the principal's office was one heck of a chore, it being glued to his rear end. Tom walked into the captain's office with that same boyish smirking grin on his face.

"Do you find something funny, Detective?" the captain asked.

"No sir." Tom replied and quickly held a straight face.

"I know you were right with the Tinnimen case. But I want to know how you ended up getting the department a legal issue with the Senator's press secretary, Kirk whatever."

"I was not aware of a lawsuit Captain, or that he filed one."

"Look Tom, I like you and I am not going to rattle your cage over this. There were a lot of strings pulled here. And you better know who you're messing with. Now, off the record, I can't stand to see someone get off Scott free, especially in a murder case. I don't care who he knows in the Oval office. Murphy was a veteran officer. I went to the academy with his dad. God rest both of their souls. Stay the case. Find out why all the strings were pulled. I want to know who the puppeteer is. Is that understood?"

Tom looked the captain in the eyes. The grin was gone.

"Yes captain, I'll do just that."

"Dismissed." Tom turned slightly to the left to get up out of the wooden chair, His gun, which was in a hip holster attached to his waist belt, had wedged ever so slightly under the chair's arm, lifting the chair as he began to stand. For a quick instant, the thought flooded his mind; Crazy glue.

Time is not measured in the spiritual realm as it is in the natural realm. I was gone from Tom's side only according to man's time, a fraction of a second. But within that fraction, I was gone long enough to meet with Xenophon. I gave my report of Tom's prayer. The word angel means messenger. Xenophon was pleased to pass the report on. He also had another task for me.

Lori had covered her mouth, as her other hand crossed her chest. She was listening to the latest news update from inside the hospital room. Steve was recovering from the sniper's bullet wound. A bullet had passed completely through his flash. Steve had lost so much blood on the way the hospital that he flat lined and his spirit had left its shell of a body lifeless for several moments on an E.M.T. gurney.

During his brief brush with death, he became aware of a new way of thinking. For the brief moments of his pulse less state, he perceived that death is not the end, but just a passageway, a door. The real man the spirit of man continues to live. Not only does he live but is more alive when dead, than when he is in a bodily shell. Near death experience is unexplainable to those who never experienced it. Steve's memories were coming back.

The news reporter was wearing a blue coat and red tie. But the little lapel ornament is what caught his eye. A golden angel and he thought. 'No they are not gold they're as white as pure snow.'

White as cloud, Tom snapped back to reality, looked at his watch, ten-forty. Ten minutes to get there, five minutes to park, and five minutes to act like I am not some actor in commercial running late for a plane. He was contemplating and re-evaluating the chewing out he had received from his captain. The beeping of an annoying driver behind him had made him stop day dreaming about the great job the dry cleaners did on his white shirt. The mall café at Lexington Heights was surely going to be packed on a mid December afternoon. 'I'll never find a parking space,' he thought. "Great," as he saw a car exiting a space near the door of the mall. The outside tables were empty and the chairs were bent inward resting on the tables. Tom quickly glanced up into the rear view mirror after parking the car. He ran his fingers though his hair and smiled widely checking his teeth.

    He locked up the car and started walking toward the café, popping a stick of gum in his mouth as he adjusted his tie. Tom looked up and into the window of the café. He could see Marcy had already acquired a table. Her arms were bare skinned and lily white. She rested her chin on the top of the back of her hands, which were joined as if she were praying. She smiled when she recognized Tom, and started to wave her hand as a jester to him to hurry up and come on in. Tom's face suddenly burst into a smile like a Hoover vacuum salesman who just arrived at a house made with dirt floors. As he was waiting for the mini bus to go by so he could cross the parking lot to he sidewalk, the smile that came so quickly left just as fast. Tom's mind flashed back to the words his academy instructors had told him.

    "In times of a crisis, you will always revert back to the basic training you received."

    Although Tom was still standing out in the open and many people were passing this way and that, Tom's instincts had kicked in. While he was looking at Marcy through the glass, he saw someone else he recognized. But the glimpse was too quick. The bus had moved into view. He scratched his forehead. "What, did I see?"

The bus started to roll away from the stop sign. Tom had slowed down his pace toward the café'. As the window came into full view from the bus rolling away, everything slowed down as the anxiety surmounted in Tom. There she was again. Now in perfect view, the few moments the bus took to stop had given Marcy just enough time to start to rise out of the booth chair she was sitting in. As she began to stand, Tom looked directly into the café'. Squinting; his eyes to see something or someone else besides Marcy, she was now standing and started to pick up her purse and held up a finger as if to say to Tom, "ladies' room." She moved a little to her left looking out the window at him, but the smile was no longer on his face. That's it, that is what caught his eye, Metal, the metal not found on a car, but the metal of a gun barrel pointed right at you. And it was in the hands of a trained assassin behind Marcy. A few tables behind her a man in a leather jacket stood pointing a gun outward through the window at his intended target. Tom.

"Boom, Boom, Boom! The sound of a forty-five caliber echoed though out the café and the halls of the Mall. The window shattered in front of Marcy as a pickup truck passed directly in front of Tom. He ducked down low and moved with the direction of the truck to the right, getting closer to the doorway entrance of the Mall. Another shot rang out and struck the metal of the truck's cabin door frame. Marcy jumped with each loud burst of firing. She reached up to hold her ears, and thought someone had thrown water on her neck. She began to kneel down to the floor. The sounds from the shots were deafening. Her fingers were moist, as she looked at her hand and saw blood, and believed that a piece of shattered glass must have struck her.

A man, who was in the restaurant eating bowed his head and prayed when the shots rang out, "Lord protect us in our time of need."

Standing directly behind the shooter, unseen to the natural eyes, was PRIDE; he had surfaced to wreak havoc on the descendants of Adam.

This was war. Not natural war, but spiritual warfare. Because the man had prayed, I was now enabled to work on the behalf of prayer. My bronze colored clothes had burst into a gleaming light. Pride was one of the fallen ones. I had known him before the fall. All the glory that was given him now lay to waste. His appearance was ghastly, dark and disfigured wings.

I cried out, "Touch not the chosen of the Highest."

The gunman had moved to the edge of the bar, looking for his exit from the café. The demon, Pride, had turned to look at who had spoken. He saw me standing in the mist of glory. He knew that all things were governed and had an appointed time. He cowered at the light of glory that was surrounding me. His allied in darkness soon appeared, dominating his presence on the crowd in the café and Mall.

People were scattering and running for cover from the shooter. Tom had taken up a position just outside the door of the café, He quickly peeked in moved back to analyze the situation. His thoughts were on Marcy.

Spreading his membranous dark wings and raising up his hideous dragon talons, Pride wrapped his left arm around the shooter's neck and with his right, gripped the gunman's right wrist and twisted him back toward the crowd making him take aim in Tom's direction.

"Touch not the chosen of the Highest!" I shouted. But pride hissed into the ear of the shooter.

"Kill, kill 'em all now!"

I drew my sword. Swoosh, swoosh! I had struck pride twice before he even knew I had moved. He jolted forward as he turned into a vaporous stench of dissolving gas, causing the gunman to bend forward as if he had stomach cramps.

The gunman flinched forward and pointed his weapon downward.

I instantly was next to Tom and cried out into his ear. "Go now!"

Tom reacted on his instinct and circled the corner seeing the shooter with no aim. Tom shouted,

"Drop the Gu..."

Boom, boom, Tom fired twice as the gunman began to raise his weapon toward him. The shooter fell backward about a foot from where he stood landing flat on his back, arms over his head with the gun only inches from his fingers. Blood began to seep out from under the dead body.

Tom approached cautiously, not lowering his weapon, searching around for any accomplices. He looked over the banister railing to see the would-be killer. The corpse silently still on the flood wearing dark slacks, black shoes, a black leather jacket and wore a yellow smiley face tee-shirt cover in blood.

I was still standing in the mist of the café when Pride's allied, Fear, noticed me.

"Septuagint; I heard you were here now, I had spoken to someone you vanquished to the abyss."

"Fear; Leave on your own your own accord or I will strike you also!"

"There is no need for me to stay here but one. He belongs to us." Fear pointed his crooked claw like finger at the corpse. "I am only here to overshadow him."

"Do what you must. Then go."

"Septuagint; why do you fight for these mortals? Come join us."

The spirit of the shooter stood up and looked at me, holding his wounds but not the wounds of the flesh. His body still remained on the floor, an empty shell. He said with a hatred voice,

"Who are you?" He didn't have time to ask the next question. "What the world..."

I pointed toward Fear, standing behind him. He shuddered at the sight of the beast. Up, from the floor which he perceived as something he was standing upon, came the Collectors. His screams echoed as he was dragged downward. I though to myself, surely, Pride goes before a fall.

Tom finished surveying the surroundings of the café. When he had determined there was only one shooter, he put his gun in the concealed holster under his jacket. He scanned the premises looking for Marcy. His eyes locked onto a woman in a white cashmere sweater that was splattered in red. She was squatting under the table, her face buried in her hands, sobbing loudly. Tom realized it was Marcy. He bent down in position right behind her. Marcy was in a state of shock and Tom needed to bring her back to reality.

"Hey think the owner of this joint will let me have a cup of coffee?"

"What?" she turned, looking back, and saw Tom kneeling behind her.

"Why don't you let me help you crawl out of his hole, unless you dropped something here and can't find it?"

Tom smiled and winked at her. And for a second of the distraction, Marcy forgot where she was. Tom's quick thinking had proven useful. "Next time, how about letting me pick the restaurant?" Tom asked.

Marcy smiled, putting her hand into his, as he helped raise her up into a standing position. Her eyes were teary. Time had whizzed by. When Tom turned to assist Marcy to the exit door of the Mall, police officers from all districts were arriving to the scene.

The black Ford Explorer made a left at the light, and was being followed by dark van five vehicles lengths back. Lori adjusted the mirror after checking her lipstick. She saw the van, but was not really aware of it. Steve was looking out the passenger side window, admiring the Christmas decor up and down the street.

"Well, it sure feels good to get out of that hospital bed."

"I am so glad you were not killed."

"So am I."

"I'd hate to think of raising a child on my own."

"What?"

The memories came back to Steve; Lori grinned and looked at him.

"Its going to be a girl, you know." Steve said.

Lori turned and looked stunned she had not told him about the ultrasound results.

"Brice Noland?"

"What does he have to do with this?"

"We're not sure yet. We have some of our key people working on it now."

"I want to know all who are involved, and where all the strings tie into. Is that understood?"

"Yes sir, Mr. President."

"Some of my staff has informed me that Shearson is inbound to D.C. Any idea who is fronting him?"

"We were under the impression, sir that Scorpion was going to take care of that problem."

"Find someone we can trust. Get in contact with that Kirk character, the one who was working for Tinnimen. He might be useful. Tinnimen is marked. He was careless. I need that taken care of also, understood?"

"Yes sir, Mr. President."

The agent adjusted his tie, revealing the ring with the pentagram, as he extended his hand to shake with the President.

"Let me know as soon as it is done."

His FBI badge on his belt flashed a shine when he reached into his pocket for his keys. As he walked out of the office the secretary said,

"Good day Mr. Ashton."

He didn't reply.

S E V E N T E E N

She answered the ringing phone, "Good morning, Metro Detective Bureau, may I help you?"

"Huh . . . Yes, who am I speaking with?"

"This is Nancy, Metro Homicide, What can I help you with, sir?"

"Yes Nancy, this Pastor Paul Zoe. I was trying to get in touch with Detective Tom Allen. Is he in?"

"I remember you, you are Tom's friend. No, I'm sorry he's not in Pastor. Tom's going to be busy for most of the morning."

"Oh, so, he won't be in anytime soon?"

"I spoke to him a while ago. He called and requested the homicide crew to the mall, that means a case is under investigation, So I don't think, he'll be in."

"Ok, can you have him contact me on my beeper? The number is 231-4229."

"Sure no problem,"

"Oh Nancy . . ."

"Yes?"

"Smile, God loves you and so do I."

Nancy did smile as she hung up the Phone.

●────────────────●

The mall café was roped off with evidence tape. The crowd was lingering around to see what all the commotion was. Police cars were blocking all the traffic in the parking lot. The ambulances were just outside the mall entrance doors. Police were moving the crowd back and setting up barricades around the area. Tom told one of the officers to escort Marcy and the paramedic to the ambulance. Tom noticed that the news media trucks had parked outside the barricade and a news crew was setting up for live broadcasting. He recognized the lead reporter.

"Not curious George." Tom said aloud.

The young officer was standing next to the gurney that was about to be taken out to the ambulance turned toward Tom.

"Did you say something, Sarge?"

"Huh? No." The sound of a whimpering sniffle caught Tom's attention.

It was Marcy. She was still crying and in shock.

"I'll come see you at the hospital as soon as I'm finished here. You're going to be fine."

Tom smiled to reassure her. She tried her best to show a grin as she was being taken away.

"Don't worry Sarge, I'll look after her," the officer said.

Tom turned to look behind him as the body of the gunman was being covered up. Another young man in his late twenties was standing there watching as the body of the deceased was being removed. Tom watched the young man as he reached into his coat pocket and pulled out a stick of chewing gum. Tom noticed a badge on the waist of the young man, but it was a badge from the Federal Bureau. And he wondered, Feds, why would they be here on scene?

"Excuse me!" Tom shouted across the room.

The clean cut hair, nice suit, shiny shoes. Yeah, he's federal alright. The young man looked up at Tom. He kinda crunched a smirk on his face and rolled his eyes up then gave a nod of greeting and forced a fake smile at Tom.

"Yes, can I help you," he said with an air of arrogance in his voice.

"No, the question is . . . can I help you?" who are you and what are you doing on my crime scene?"

"Agent Jamenson, Federal Bureau."

"Ok, that answers who you are, but what are you doing here?"

"Just who are you sir?"

"Sergeant Tom Allen, Metro Police Homicide. Now answer my question. What are you doing here?" Beep, Beep, Beep, Beep. The sound interrupted the air of silence between the two men. One younger, twentish, sharper dressed, the other, older with the age of experience showing on his face. Both looked down at their waist and saw that the sound of an incoming call to their voice pagers had both sounded at the same time in unison. Tom and the young agent, Jamison, had reached down to remove their beepers at the same time. Both parleyed for the gambit, and looking at each other, said at the same time,

"Excuse me."

Tom walked toward the host table near the door's entrance reaching for the phone on the wall. He looked back to see that the young agent was already on his cell phone and walking towards him. Tom covered the end of the receiver with one hand looked at the young fed.

"I need to speak to you. Don't leave."

"Sorry Detective. I'm being called away by Presidential order. Here is my number. You can reach me anytime. We have cell phones as you can see." The agent handed Tom the business card, as he excused himself and exited the café.

"Hello," Tom looked at the card as voice answered on the phone.

"Detective Allen here,"

"Tom, you had a call from Pastor Zoe. He needs to reach you. He left a number for you to call."

Tom placed one finger in his ear as he held the phone with the other. He reached inside his jacket coat pocket, and pulled out a pen to write the number. He patted his coat pockets realizing he had no paper to write. He took the business card of the Federal agent and wrote the last name of the pastor and the number. (Zoe) 231-4229.

"Did he say what it was about?"

"No, but he sounded like it was urgent."

"Anything else?"

"Yes, Steve called, said to tell you, that you're going to be a God father, and to practice up on your Brando imitation."

Tom smiled.

"Really, At least that is some good news. Nancy, send them a bouquet of flowers and a bottle of champagne."

"Done; you can thank me later, with a day off."

Tom's smile grew wider.

"Thanks Nancy." Tom hung up the phone as he walked outside and around the corner of the Mall's entrance. He listened as the sound of glass crunched under his feet.

"Hello Detective Allen,"

Tom turned and looked up to see who was addressing him. He thought about the fake smile the federal agent gave him, as he duplicated the same gift for the reporter.

"Hello, George."

The camera crew guy reached out and took the microphone George was handing him. George proceeded to walk a bit faster to catch up with Tom as he headed out to the open parking lot.

"Detective, can I ask you a couple of questions?"

Tom thought to himself, 'I wish you wouldn't'.

"What is it, George?"

Tom looked back and saw that the camera crew was not following, only George. Still Tom did not break his stride.

"What is this off the record?" George was trotting to catch up with him.

"Detective, can you slow down?"

"I'm kinda in a hurry, George."

"Tom, yes it is off the record. It's a little personal." Tom stopped and turned, allowing George to draw near.

"You know, in all the years I've known you George, that is the first time you have ever addressed me common. What is it?"

George had a disturbed look on his face. The issue he wanted to discuss was hard for him to say, and even a hard nosed cop like Tom saw the difficulty he was having putting it into words.

"George, what's the matter?"

"Tom, I've known you a lot of years. I know how to get a story. I know how to tell a story. But I have been tailing you ever since the pentagram murders in back of that alley. I was there.

Tom looked at him with a hard stare.

"In the alley, I know that, I had you removed."

"No, no. I was there following you after that. You know, in the Church...." George's eyes were beginning to tear up, "At the revival, with Pastor Zoe. I saw what happened to you. Tom, I thought you were just trying to make some kind of atonement or something. But now I ..." he wiped a tear from his eye and pinched his nose near the tear ducts "I just wanted to say, I'm sorry for invading your privacy and I think, No, I know, that I have seen something happen that, well,... I can't explain it.

I stood high in the air looking down over Tom, and the one called reporter. My clothes began to gleam bright. My sheath commenced to glow bronze and the sword itself became afire. I could see movement all around the parking lot as cars came and went. The other men in uniforms were still at the building. My attention was now drawn to the one called reporter. He was standing below me next to Tom. But now I felt the power well up within me as I saw from the west, an Imp his name was Liar. He was flying toward the one called George approaching from his backside. The imp was below me several feet, but still above the heads of Tom and George. His flight was swift as he drew nearer and nearer to them.

"Tom, I would really like to hear what happened that night, was it real? There was a young boy and his mother in the pew, just in front of me. The boy was but a child, and he said he saw an angel standing next to you."

"Yeah, what's your point George?"

"Did you see an angel Tom?"

Tom looked at him inquisitively, wondering had the Lord given him the opportunity to witness?

I drew my sword of flame. I was ready to strike. I watched as the detestable beast of hell was approaching. His shrieks of cursing filled the air. But he was still afar off and had some distance to travel.

"Yes, George. It is real. I believe Jesus is alive and well. My life somehow was changed that night, I accepted Jesus as my lord and Savior."

George felt the conviction of the Holy Spirit as Tom spoke. George became choked up with emotion and tried to speak, pass the lump in his throat.

"Tom, you sound like a pastor."

"George, have you ever" Tom saw this was the time to act, and now was the time to say it.

"George, will you give you life to Jesus, by saying the sinner's prayer? I'll say it with you.

He looked up at Tom.

"Yes, I will."

The demon imp cried out "Nooooooo!" it was now in my striking distance. I diverted it to the north and the chase was on. I moved with the motion of thought as his bat wings flogged the air and long serpentine tail swished back and forth from left to right.

Gaining ground he glanced back and shouted, "You have no right, warrior angel."

He quickly turned his gargoyle face over his right shoulder peering with his jaundice eyes, desperately trying to out maneuver me in the air, cutting this way and that, To the left and to the right. The horrors of the abyss made him flap faster and faster. I raised my sword as the swishing sound of wind swirled by. We were darting left and right, in and out, of buildings, moving cars, up and down above and below the clouds at subsonic speeds.

"Septuagint, he is ours, why are you pursuing me? It hissed.

I was gaining, he was mine to banish. He cried out to his Master as a swift blow of my sword sliced him asunder, causing each half to fall to my left and right, a smolder trail of ash to each side of me.

"What do I do?" George asked.

"Hey man, it's so easy, just repeat after me, and you'll know it's real."

Tom smiled as he reached out to shake hands with George. He laid his left hand upon his shoulder, and led George in a sinners prayer.

"Dear heavenly father, I am a sinner, I realize that. Lord I confess your son Jesus as my savior. I believe you raised him from the dead for my sins. Please come into my heart right now and wash away my sins."

George repeated the prayer with Tom and peace of God filled his soul as never before. He now knew what Tom was talking about. George looked up at Tom through tear blotched eyes.

"Thanks, Tom. Thank you very much."

"George you need some spiritual guidance. I suggest you go back to see Zoe at the Church."

The cameraman, a long lanky fellow with wild bushy blond hair, ran up to Tom and George. "Hey what's going on here? George, this cop hit you or something?"

Still red eyed, George looked up at Tom and smiled.

"No everything's fine, kid. I'll be right there."

"Ok, George, but the station manager is on the horn and wants to speak to you A.S.A.P."

"Tell him I'll be right there." George turned back to Tom with a smile of gratitude on his face.

Tom understood.

"I have to go. Hope we get a chance to talk later."

"I'd like that, George." Tom pulled out his key to unlock his car door.

George started to jog toward the news truck and yelled back.

"Maybe after Church on Sunday."

Tom grinned as he got in turned the ignition and said,

"Thanks, Lord. I'm sorry for being so harsh on him all those times before."

●─────────────────────────●

Lori made a right turn on Galveston drive, Steve was still looking out the right rear view mirror as they were going around the bend of the curve. He noticed the black mini van swinging wide as it made the turn several cars back, and turning on the same street.

"Now, I wonder who that could be?"

"What Hon?" Lori asked.

"Nothing babe, nothing."

Steve reached down to his right ankle and unsnapped the holster to his 38 revolver. He looked at the chamber to make sure it was loaded, while making sure Lori was unaware of what he was doing. He asked how she had been doing while he was in the hospital. He did this ever-so-convincingly, so as not to frighten her. His tactic worked as she rambled on about new items to buy for the baby, preparing a room, and notifying all her family. Steve just gave a few 'uh huh's' as he kept checking the rear view mirror.

Ding . . . ding . . . The young gentleman looked up as the light came on. A woman's hand reached across him to touch the shoulder of the elderly man next to him.

The younger man quickly blocked her touch, saying,

"Excuse please, he is Rabbi. Must not be touched by woman."

"Sorry sir," the stewardess said, "we are about to land. Would you please wake the rabbi? The captain has turned on the seat belt sign and he needs to buckle his seat belt."

"I'll tell him, Thank you."

She smiled and proceeded down the isle.

"Rabbi."

"Yes?" He woke blinking his aging eyes behind wire framed oval glasses.

"Rabbi, we are arriving in America. Seat belt . . . for safety." The young man spoke in his heavy Israeli accent.

"Yes, yes, F. A. A. Regulations, like a seat belt will save you from a thirty thousand foot drop in . . . a tin can."

A man sitting across the isle over heard the conversation of the Rabbi and the young man next to him. He laughed, adding to his statement,

"First class tin can."

The rabbi leaned forward and looked at the man, stroking his gray beard. He watched the man pecking on a laptop.

"I make a funny?" Like comedian?" the rabbi asked. The man stopped pecking and looked over at the elderly man.

"Yes, it was funny."

"You can use; No charge, I give free."

The young man smiled.

"Thank you."

"You welcome!"

"Is this your first time to America?"

"No. I was here in nineteen forty-eight."

"That was a long time ago."

"Yes, long time."

"My apologies, sir, I didn't introduce myself. My name is David."

The young Israeli man sitting near the isle, looked at him, then at the Rabbi. The look of sorrow filled the rabbi's eyes as he heard the man's name.

"David? I have a son..." the Rabbi quickly corrected himself, "had a son named David. I am Rabbi Shearson. It is nice to meet you, young David. So, you are from America?"

"Yes sir, born in Missouri, Southern by the grace of God, but I moved a bit further South, to Florida. I live in Fort Lauderdale now. Well actually, a little North of that. A city called Margate, Florida."

"You're going home. Were you in Israel for business or pleasure?"

"Both, I had never seen Israel and always wanted to visit. But I was also there to study some of the ancient language. That's my major, foreign languages, and Israel has some of the best books on the ancient text."

"We have a lot in common David. I am a scholar of languages. I know seven of the ancient languages, I have written a couple of books on the subject."

David's eyes grew wide.

"Really, are you going to be in America long?"

"I am only staying a short while, my young friend. But you may contact me in Jerusalem at this address." The Rabbi handed him a business card as an announcement broke over the intercom.

"Ladies and gentlemen, this is your captain speaking. We are now arriving in sunny Ft. Lauderdale, Florida. The temperature is a breezy seventy-eight degree's. It is partly cloudy. We hope your flight was an enjoyable one on El-Al International. Please remain seated until we come to a complete stop at the terminal gate. And once again, thank you for flying El-Al."

As David received the card from the Rabbi, another man two rows back dialed his cell phone and gave the description of the young man named David to whom ever he was talking with.

"Yes sir, he handed him a card. No, I lost audio as the captain made an announcement of the landing. I suggest he be followed immediately after de-boarding. Yes sir, I will stay with the Rabbi. Do you have transport? Who? Desmont no I don't know him, sir. Small red rose on left lapel. Got it."

"I'm sorry sir no cell phone can be activated while we are landing. You'll have to turn it off, please."

He smiled at the stewardess with a smile of aggravation.

"No problem, forgot." The man shut the cell phone and placed it back into his pocket.

●────────────────●

Tom glanced at the window as he climbed the steps of his porch. He looked at the bullet hole and all the tape that now crossed in all directions holding the window in place.

'Wonder, how much that is going to cost me?' he thought.

Then speaking aloud, "Bet that isn't covered under homeowner's." He shook his head as he thought about the bullet that invaded his false sense of security. His fortress of seclusion had now been raped and violated. Someone, somewhere, knew who he was, where he lived, And was not afraid to come after him. Tom heard the dog growl as he entered the door. Chancy wasn't a big dog, a Maltese who had a few years behind her.

"Hey girl, how are you? How's my baby?" Ring . . . ring . . . ri.

"Hello?"

"Tom,"

"Hey Steve, so what's this about me being a God father..."

Steve interrupted his questioning.

"Tom, turn off the lights to your house!" Tom heard the urgency in Steve's voice.

"OK, they're off!"

"Yeah, I can see that."

"You can? What's up?"

"Don't go near the window."

"Ok."

"Quarterback in the pocket. Flank left, Ref on the sidelines."

"Got it," Tom hung up the phone and reached into his coat pocket pulled his weapon out. He got low to the floor and moved for the back door. He exited the back porch, went left on the side of the house, then ran into the neighbor's back yard and crossed two fences. He came out into the street, four houses down. He saw a red car with black tinted windows. He stayed low and circled the car, coming up around to the passenger's side door. He yanked it open.

"Hey Bud, what's with all the cloak and dagger?"

"Nice to see you again, too, Lori and I were followed on the way home from the hospital, Black mini van."

Tom looked at Steve and both said at the same time...

"Feds!"

"Why were they following you?"

"Not just me . . . Look." Steve pointed at a black van in front of Tom's house.

•———————————•

Standing next to the exit door of the plane as the passengers were disembarking, the stewardess was handing out the same repetitive fair well, "Thank you, Come fly again."

"Rabbi, I'll carry your luggage."

"Thank you, Joel. The limo should be here. You go ahead and see if it is out front. I will be there in a moment."

"Yes sir," Joel stood patiently, as he thought to himself. 'The un-herding of the people through the cat walk is like cattle slowly moving into grazing pens.'

"Papa!" She smiled, a petite woman in her early thirties with Light brown hair, wearing a pale green blouse, black slacks and black high heels. Her lipstick was a faint pink. Her eyes were puffy from crying. Shearson walked over toward her with outstretched arms. Embracing her and holding her waist with one arm, he cradled the back of her head with the other. He kissed her just atop of the right ear.

"My Sandra,"

"Papa, this is America. All my friends know me by Sandy, please."

"Ah, Sandy it is, to all the friends. But to me; still my Sandra. How are you, my dear?" She patted her father on the chest.

"I'm ok, but I," She started to cry.

"I know."

"... I never got to say goodbye."

"My heart aches for him as well. Did you see Joel? He came ahead of me."

"No."

"Let's go see if we can find him."

"Oh, wait Papa. Mrs. Cooper is here to greet you."

"Your Mother-in-law, here? Where?" The rabbi turned and behind him stood a attractive lady in her late fifties.

"Hello, Rabbi Shearson. It is a pleasure to welcome you to the United States."

He tilted his head in greeting.

"It is a pleasure to finally meet the in-laws of my daughter. Let us go. We can talk more in the limo." They stepped outside into the breezy warm sun-shine; Joel was standing next to the door of the long black limo.

"Joel, you remember Sandra, my dau... Ah, Sandy, my daughter?" The rabbi turned and smiled and winked at Sandy.

"Yes, Sandy, how have you been? You were a little bit littler last time I saw you."

"Joel, it's nice to see you again. And this is Mrs. Cooper; she is my husband's mother."

Joel smiled with a greeting as he opened the door for them to enter.

Tom was concerned. The black van was parked across from his home near the corner intersection. From atop of the hill, sitting in Steve's car, the view was clear.

"You know for a surveillance team they're pretty lousy."

"Yep, I would have guessed they'd have at least removed themselves' from underneath that street lamp's overcast."

Just as Steve finished his sentence another black van pulled up behind the first one. "Oops, got milk?"

"What?" Tom asked.

"What makes your bones breakable?"

"What are you talking about?"

"Two van loads of bad guys."

Tom looked up and saw the other van pull up, realizing the innuendo Steve had implied.

"Ok, it's time to play the game."

"You're not thinking what I think you're thinking, are you?"

"Oh, yes I am!"

Steve raised his hand and let it flop on the steering wheel.

"Back it up, lights off."

Steve followed the order and backed up in the darkened street and over the crest of the hill. Unseen by the black government surveillance van, he put the car in forward gear, turned right off Tom's street, and onto the next block.

"Pull over there." Tom pointed to the all night Quick Mart.

About three minutes went by and Tom gingerly came walking out with a small brown bag and a smirk on his face.

"Let's roll." But go around to the back street and stay about a block and a half away. When I give the signal, I want you to go by the van, roll down the window, and ask for the time. Then honk your horn loud and lay on it hard to wake up the neighbors. Take 'em for a goose chase."

Steve waited. As he watched Tom turn into the invisible prankster of their childhood days, Tom gave the signal, And Steve let the car roll past the parked cars. He made a left, heading up the hill on Tom's street. Steve pulled up next to the van with the dark tinted windows and followed Tom's instructions.

One of the men in the van said, "Hey, that's the guy we were following earlier."

The agent near the passenger window said, "Think we have been made, fellas."

"Ok, see what that clown wants," the driver replied.

The agent next to him rolled down the passenger window and said, "Yeah, what do you want?"

"What time is it? You yahoos..." Steve laid on his horn and turned on his siren.

The Federal agent driver said, "Oh man, do you believe this crap?"

"Stop him. Stop him now! Get out there and turn that siren off!" commanded the senior agent.

"I can't. He's too close to the van. I can't open the door."

"Oh, dang gone it, radio crew two, have one of them come up here."

"They're on their way now." The agent looked in the huge rear view mirror.

"Hey officer!" one agent barked aloud as he was walking from the second van toward Steve's car. But the cry went unheard as Steve held the brake and punched the gas, releasing the brake at the same time, causing smoking rubber and the squealing of tires.

"Get that arrogant son of a . . . (Bang!) The rear end of Steve's car had slid sideways, smashing into the first van's side door. He then pulled off as he released the brake fully.

"Oops, sorry 'bout that gents." Steve laughed a sarcastic ha, ha, as he pulled away.

The first van started to follow in pursuit, but the engine chugged and sputtered and came to an abrupt halt. The three agents got out of the van just as the second one pulled up next to it.

"Get in we'll come back for it later."

Steve was airborne as he hit the crest of the hill. Tom smiled as he watched the feds chase after Steve. He admired the work he did. A spud was spewing out the tail pipe of one U.S. officially disabled government van, now abandoned. Tom opened the sliding side door, in which his buddy Steve had just recently placed a good size dent. Seeing all the high tech equipment, Tom felt like a kid in a candy store. A brief case lay open and had three tapes with labels. One with Tom and Steve's name on it, one with the name of Shearson, one with the name of Zoe. Tom stuffed the three tapes inside his shirt pocket, opened his cell phone, and pushed the quick send button. Hearing the whining of the engines in the background and Steve laughing, Tom asked, "Are you having fun yet?"

"Yeah . . . they are going by me now. I did one big circle in the back streets. I'm coming around where I dropped you off. Man, those guys are going to be ticked off when they see we stung them."

"See you in a few. Hurry up, Speed Racer." Tom snapped his cell phone shut as he walked back down the hill and around the corner.

Tossing his keys on the counter and loosening his tie, he removed his coat jacket. He casually sorted the letters, hardly glancing at the stack of bills. As the hand with the pentagram ring touched the refrigerator door handle, the phone rang. Kirk reached inside, removed a bottle of wine, and poured a glass into the crystal made of rose color.

"Hello?"

"Is this Kirk Dagon?"

"Yes, it is. Who's calling?"

"Mr. Dagon, this call is being made for someone else. Someone who is of the same fraternity as you, do you understand?"

"I think so. What can I do for you?"

"Meet the man on the park bench at the address of sixteen hundred tomorrow at nine. Is it clear to you where the address is?"

"You're referring to the big house with the oval room?"

"Yes." Click . . . the phone went dead.

Kirk looked at his watch, then hung up the receiver.

●————————————————————●

"So, where we headed for, Chief?" Steve asked.

"St. Joseph's Hospital," Tom answered.

"The one on the East side?"

"That's the one, have to see someone."

"Well, anyone I know of?"

"Not likely. I just met her myself."

"Oh, I see, Nurse, huh?"

"Nope; nosey, a patient."

"Sorry, wasn't meaning to pry, just making conversation."

"Her name is Marcy. Someone I was meeting when the shooting broke out at the mall."

"Must be real nice for you to drive all the way to the East side."

"Hey," Tom pointed his finger at Steve who just turned his head and looked out the window. "She's a looker." Tom looked down at the radio and tape player in Steve's car dash. "Does that work?"

"Sure, what do you want to hear?"

"Nothing you got," Tom reached into his pocket pulling the three cassette tapes out, and sorted through the labels.

"I take it that's from the spud mobile."

Tom chuckled at Steve's comment. Tom chose the tape with Steve's and his name written on the label. Tom then turned the knob on the radio, raising the volume. Steve had a stern look as he heard the report from the tape. He wasn't surprised by the date they started the surveillance, but by the comments.

"Sanction both parties. Stop that investigation; Top priority."

"Hey, that sounded a little serious, Tom, and just who is that giving that order?"

"I don't know." Tom looked out the window. His voice pager sounded. He looked down at the number. "Now why do I know that number?"

He reached inside his coat pocket and removed a company card. It was the card the Federal agent, Jamison, had given him. Tom read the back of the card. It was the same number on his beeper: 231- 4229.

"Zoe."

"What Sarge?"

"Nothing, the number is a Pastor Zoe's. He's been trying to get a hold of me all day." Tom pulled the gray tape out of his shirt pocket and took a look at the name written in red on the label. It was the same name on the label as the name on the back of the F.B.I. business card.

"Now, I wonder why they are looking into a Pastor?"

"Maybe he's not a real pastor," Steve said.

"I think he's for real."

"Think he's a spy?"

"Didn't talk like one when I saw him."

"I didn't know you went to church, Boss."

"Yeah, and I don't tell you when I'm wearing my boxers with fire engines on them either, but that don't mean I don't wear them."

"The voice mail box you are calling is busy at this time. If you would like to leave a message please do so at the sound of th . . ."

"Hello?"

"Is this Pastor Zoe?"

"Yes, Tom?"

"Yes. Sorry I couldn't get back to you earlier, but I've had a very unusual day."

"Tell 'em to say a prayer for us." Steve adjusted the temperature setting on the dashboard.

Tom held up a finger as to say wait a minute to him, so he could hear all the Pastor was saying.

"When is your flight? Ok, we will be there in 'bout thirty or so." Snapping the cell phone shut and looking at the street signs going by, Tom looked at Steve saying,

"Go to the airport, Delta terminal."

"What about the hospital?"

"Zoe's leaving for Florida, needs to see me."

"Ok, airport next stop. Whaddya say we hear what the goons from the spud mobile have to say about Zoe." Tom glanced at him, and inserted the tape in the dashboard player.

●━━━━━━━━━━━━━━━━━━━━●

"I don't want to talk about it! Now please don't ask me again Maggie!"

"It's a disgrace, John. You're a United States Senator, and you're mixed up in something of this magnitude. I'm not going to have our name, our children's name, associated with murder. Driver, take us home."

"Yes, Miss."

"Maggie, just drop it, I don't want to discuss it. I was given a full Presidential pardon, and that's the end of it." The Senator reached into his pocket and pulled out a cigar, patted his pockets, looking for a light.

"Do you really have to do that? You know I can't stand the smell of those things." Maggie reached into her purse and pulled out a small pill placing in her mouth. Then she flipped open the limo's little bar and opened a small bottle of water.

The Senator tapped on the darkened half opened window divider and said, "Light."

"Yes sir." the driver said. He laid the limo's keys down, turned around with his gold lighter and ignited the cigar as the Senator puffed, and said,

"Go ahead and take us home."

"Right away, Sir." The driver put the lighter back into his pocket. Turning to face forward, he picked the keys up off the front seat, looking at the fuzzy little rabbit foot attached to the key ring. Then adjusting his hat, he reached with his left hand to hit the button, and watched as the privacy divider raise shut. He placed the key in the ignition, looked out the rear view mirror, then across the street to the bar where Mr. And Mrs. Tinnimen had just come from having dinner.

Only one man was on the corner, resting one foot on the wall and leaning with his arms folded. The driver squinted sternly as he was a trained bodyguard, and found it odd that the man was staring at him. He gave a little wave. The driver nodded like he was saying 'hey', and turned the key in the ignition.

The man across the street jerked his head rapidly to the left as the limo exploded with shrapnel fanning out in all directions. Flames of fire burst forth and metal pieces were thrown skyward and fell earthbound after the limo exploded with a violent force. The man across the street reached up, pulling the first left and then the right earplugs out of his ears, then walked around the building's corner out of sight.

The laughter was boisterous and hideous, as three persons stood up from the ground, shaking their heads and blinking their eyes. The Senator looked over to his left and saw Maggie his wife, who held her hand to forehead.

"John? John? Where are you?"

Tinnimen's eyes grew wide with fear, never taking his eyes off her as she faded into a transparent figure of light. John heard her speaking as if she as talking to someone else.

"Who are you?"

But he could not see as she evaporated into thin air into a glow. He still heard her speaking, but it grew fainter. The light that was near became dimmer, but the hideous laughter was grew more audible, stronger, more clearer as were the shadows of darkness. The Senator turned to the right and saw the limo driver standing, moving and swatting at something that was not there only the deep blackness behind him. The screams of terror echoed from him as Tinnimen watched him float backwards into the nothingness. Something had hold of his arms and legs, contorting his body like a rubber band.

The words his wife had spoken only moments before were now being repeated. Only this time it was not the voice of his wife, but the voice a demon mocking him.

"It's a disgrace, John, you're a United States Senator, and you're mixed up in something. I'm not going to have our name, our children's name, associated with murder," Then the horrible laughter sounding out into the dimness.

The senator looked down at his feet. He was standing on emptiness. Blackness was all around him. Still looking down at the absence of space under him, his eyes focused on the tips of his clean shoes. But now he saw something. A blotch of red appeared. First he thought someone was dripping red paint on the tips of his shoes. No, he thought, it's not paint. Blood, blood, blood . . . and it was moving and the blood began to cry out. He realized the blood was Murphy's blood, the police officer he had stabbed and murdered. The demon again repeated the words of Tinnimen's wife, in tormenting mockery.

"It's a disgrace, John, You're a United States Senator, and you're mixed up in something. I'm not going to have our name, our children's names, associated with murder."

Murphy's blood cried out, like Able's blood had when his brother Cain slew him.

"Why John, why did you murder me?" Tinnimen's mind snapped, and he imagined himself kneeling down, burying his face in his hands, screaming and weeping. Then all was still as silence, deafening solitude. The Senator lifted up his eyes, looking around and outward toward the darkness, squinting into whatever minute light his spirit projected. He realized he was not alone. Faces became more and more clearer as they neared. Not really the faces of humans, but the contorted faces of hideous creatures, the Collectors. The were huge in stature compared to Tinnimen. As he looked up, his anguish of terror overwhelmed him. He had looked behind the Collectors, past them upward. Even more colossal in stature was one demon that made the other seem, like a child compared to a full grown man. It was Murder. He stood leering down at Tinnimen. His mischievous glare froze Tinnimen as he stood leering down at him. Tinnimen saw the face of Murder as it morphed and molded into something new. He could not take his eyes off it for the terror in him. Tinnimen realized what the mold had become...a mirror image of himself on the body of this cretin creature. The senator screamed as the Collectors grabbed him and swiftly sucked him down into the abyss. Murder laughed at his screams reverberating into oblivion. Then, one last time, the demon repeated the words as Tinnimen was being dragged from view.

"It's a disgrace, John, you're a United States Senator, and you're mixed up in something. I'm not going to have our name, our children's name, associated with murder, murder, M...U...R...D...E...R,

The demon laughter of sin filled the darkness of the caverns of Hell.

•―――――――――――――――――――――•

"Maggie Tinnimen?" She turned toward the sound of the voice that had called her name.

The brilliance of the light had now faded into various colors of the brightest green, and her eyes had become adjusted. She realized that she was still in a sitting position but she was now on green grass.

"Please allow me." the voice said as her eyes focused on a hand that had reached down to assist her up.

"Oh, yes, thank you." She took the hand. She had not looked at the person who had assisted her. She was still enraptured by the beauty, gazing over the horizon's end of the mighty field and the majestic mountains in the background with the most beautiful sky.

"I'm sorry. I seem to be a little lost. I must have fallen asleep because I thought it was night time." Still in the motion of rising to her feet, she added, "Oh, you must have hurt your hand in the explosion."

She now came face to face with her assistant. He laid his other hand now atop of hers, revealing the other wound.

"Welcome home, my child."

"Je...you're Je-..Jesus!" She cried.

The Lord smiled at her and the overwhelming, immeasurable love of God filled her being.

•─────────────────────•

The traffic was moving slowly as Steve and Tom pulled into the airport terminal. Steve stopped in front of the Delta terminal. Both men were exited their vehicle, adjusting their coats against the coolness of the Washington wind chill factor.

"Tom, is that Zoe?" Steve pointed inside the huge glass terminal.

"Yeah, that's him."

"You going to tell him what we heard?"

"Not yet."

They both walk briskly toward the terminal doors, footsteps echoing on the solid concrete. Tom had just placed his hands in his pockets when someone behind them shouted,

"Hey; you two, Stop right there!" Both men looked at each other, then back over their shoulders.

"Sorry Pal, You can't park there."

Tom looked at Steve.

"Take care of this. I have to meet Zoe."

He continued to walk inside the terminal sliding doors. Steve turned toward the officer pulling out his badge and identified himself.

"Homicide."

"Sorry, Detective. Something go down here I don't know anything about yet? Anybody hurt?"

The uniform officer stretched his neck, peeking over Steve's shoulder. Tom was shaking hands with Pastor Zoe inside the glass window.

"No..no murders,"

Steve glanced back over his shoulder to see what the officer was looking at.

"Just getting some info."

Inside Pastor Zoe was extending his hand to shake with Tom.

"Tom, God bless you, Brother, I'm so glad I get to see you before I go."

"It's good to see you too, Pastor."

"There is so much. I don't know where to start. Here, let's sit here. I'm afraid it's going to be short. My flight is leaving in a moment."

"Paul you said there was something you needed to tell me."

"Yes, do you remember the man at the church the night we met; he was sitting next to you in a gray coat?"

"Yes, I do. Something odd about his left eye."

"Yes, yes, that's him." The overhead speaker broke in an announcement,

"Delta flight 2406 now boarding seat rows twelve through twenty."

"What about him Pastor?"

"That's my call to board, I can't miss this flight. Tom, here is a letter I wrote for you. It will explain all. The address is written in the letter. Go see this man. It is very important. I must go now."

"Ok. Thanks, Pastor. I'll check it out."

"Goodbye, my friend. May the Lord bless you."

Tom smiled as the Pastor waved a blessing toward him and shuffled off, with his coat and cases of luggage in tow, toward the gated terminal.

EIGHTEEN

Tom looked out at the tarmac and watched as his friend boarded the plane. Pastor Zoe was now headed Southbound to Florida. Tom slapped the paper against his palm and glanced down to look at the envelope the Pastor had given him. He read the words written on the outside of it.

"Confessions of hired hit man."

A shivering chill ran down Tom's spine as he stepped out of the warm terminal into the cool night air. He placed the letter inside his left breast pocket and plunged his hands deep into his coat pockets. Tom puffed out a long breath as he watched the smoke make a swirl like wind. His ears were turning beet red from the nippy air.

"Steve, let's go," he commanded.

"Yeah, ok, Sarge." Steve turned back to the officer who was working the detail and began to head back toward the car. "Listen, it was nice meeting you. If you ever get down to Metro, come look me up."

"Will do, Be careful out there." the officer waved Steve off as Tom shouted from the car.

"Steve, come on!"

"I'm coming. I'm coming. What's the rush?"

"Things to do, people to see, and my ears are freezing."

"Come on Boss. It isn't that cold out here."

"Yeah, it is, if you just walked out of a warm building."

●───────────────────────────●

"Is she the one?"

"I don't think so, but somehow she has a connection."

"Do you know how?"

"Dr. Kennedy, please report to emergency," sounded the overhead intercom. Nursing personnel were in the hallway taking vital signs from newly admitted arrivals. An orderly in green surgical scrubs was pushing a gurney out of the big swinging doors.

"No, not yet, but the Lord's plan will unfold."

"Septuagint, I have heard about the many battles you have fought and also that you are near to receiving a great commission for your faithfulness."

"A new assignment?"

"I was called back for an escort mission before I heard all the details it was being discussed in the halls of the Great Library."

"Did you hear when?"

"No, like I said, I was called back. Why do you think she has a connection?"

"I don't think it was her, but someone close to her must have prayed or interceded for her."

"It was predestined for her to meet Tom, your current assignment."

"Yes, but I'm looking forward to meeting the prayer warrior."

"It is an exciting job we do, is it not?"

"Yes, I will agree, it surely is."

"Mrs. Marcy Stewart?"

"Yes."

The nurse walked up to the emergency room gurney and pulled the hanging curtain closed to separate her from the other patients.

"Hello, sorry you had to wait so long. As you can see we're swamped, tonight."

"That's ok; The injection the doctor gave me let me nap a little."

"I have some good news. You're going to live, but you will have a little scar on your left ear which can easily be fixed with a little plastic surgery. So, as soon as we get finished with the paper work, you will be discharged. Ok, any questions about the medication that you need me to answer for you?"

"No, not really," Marcy said, as she shook her head and looked down at the medication.

"I was told the doctor explained about the stitches. He would like to see you in a week to look at them."

"I'll make an appointment for that."

The nurse patted Marcy on the shoulder as she began to open the screen curtain.

"Good. You take care of yourself now." The nurse walked up to the reception desk. Standing next to the bed, Marcy was putting her shoes back on. Unseen and unheard, were the two angels in the background.

"Can I ask you a question? Why do you hang out here so much?"

"You see, Septuagint, it is because these descendants of Adam come close to leaving the earth and stepping into eternity. Many times they become aware at the last minute of their life and pray. So where else should an angel with a name like mine hang out?"

We both smiled,

"I guess you're right. Hospitals are a great place for you."

"I have to go, Septuagint, someone is about to call upon the Lord."

"Goodbye, my friend."

I watched as the White door appeared and the angel named 'Hope' walked through it.

●────────────────────────●

Steve got into the car and turned on the ignition. Tom immediately turned the heater up to the highest setting.

"Everything cool?" Steve asked.

"What's that, a pun on tonight's events?" Tom asked. Steve laughed not realizing what he really said.

"We still going to the hospital, or do you want to just head back to the house? I can call Lori and tell her to throw some extra blankets in the spare room."

"Hospital, I need to see that Marcy is doing alright."

"Hospital it is . . . Chief."

"Stop calling me Chief."

"Ok . . . Pale face."

"How would you like to be writing parking tickets on Christmas?"

"Alright, alright, touchy-touchy."

Tom smiled as he turned on the overhead spot light that provided just enough light to read by. He pulled out the envelope Zoe had given him and Reached for an ink pen. He used the point of it to catch just under the edge of the flap, breaking the seal. He slid it across the top, leaving a jagged edge. He pulled out the letter and began to read.

Dear Pastor Zoe;

I am someone who came to hear about Jesus in one of your meetings. I'm writing this letter for two reasons, First, to say thank you for obeying the call of God, for if you didn't I would never have heard of the love of God.

Secondly, to warn you that there are some who desire you dead. I know this for a fact. I was sent as the assassin to take your life. You were a target in my sites the night you sat inside a café. Please take this warning seriously. I am a trained agent. You were not my first target. But I'm happy to say you were my last. I need to speak with the man who was sitting next to me that night of the service. I know he is a police officer. I heard the child in front of me say something about an angel. I,

too, believe I saw the same thing. I need to speak to him. If you can assist, please do.
>Signed,
>A new believer,
>And ex-C.I.A.

Tom turned the page and finished reading, realizing that the man he sat next to in church had been a mercenary, soldier of fortune. The eerie thought made him shiver.

Tom;

This is the letter I received from a Deacon at the church last night, who said a man asked him to give it to me. The new believer called me this morning and gave me the directions to a meeting place where he wishes to meet with you. Take I-95 North to Maryland, then to Elkton State Park. I'm not sure if that is near Chesapeake Bay or Baltimore. I hope you know the area. He said there are some camping sites just before you enter the state park. He said to meet him at lodge #23, tomorrow night at 7:30 pm, That it was a matter of national security and life and death.
>God bless.
>P. Zoe

Tom folded the letter and put it back in the tattered envelope. "National Security?"

"What is?" Steve asked

"Keep your eyes on the road there, Bub!"

Tom shouted as the front tire went off the curb and back on the road.

"Oops, sorry," Steve adjusted the car back onto damp road.

"This letter is from Zoe. He received it from a nutcase, or else it's a real letter from an ex C.I.A. agent, who wants to meet me. He says it's a matter of national security."

"Really," Steve rubbed his bullet scar.

The iron gates swung wide as the man in the black Corvette pulled up to the fence. His V.I.P. card allowed him access to the reserved parking area in the back of the Melting Pot night club.

The doorman opened the door for him as he walked in. The band was playing loudly and the club was packed. He wore black jeans and boots with a black tee-shirt. A long leather jacket that was reminiscent of the days of the Third Reich was draped on his shoulder. In his left hand was a black leather bag, and on his finger a pentagram ring. As he walked into the men's washroom, a woman was on the counter sink, embraced in a kiss with one man while her legs were wrapped around another. The other man was more interested in the white powder he was trying to sniff up his nose than the woman.

The man in the black shouted,

"Get out!"

The man who was kissing the woman, quickly turned and asked, "Who are you?"

He said nothing reaching into his leather coat. He pulled out a chrome plated forty five automatic and snapped the chamber back, causing instant fear in the three young people who left the room quickly. He laid the bag on the counter and opened it. Inside, was a shiny metal box and a clock in red zeros. He pushed the small button on the side. The digital numbers clicked to five minutes and started to count backwards. The man in black looked into the mirror, licked his finger, and brushed his blond crew cut up with two strokes. He placed the leather bag in the last stall behind a toilet. He walked out into the hallway, bumping his shoulder into a young man who was entering the bathroom.

"Watch it, Jerk!"

"What's your problem, Dude?" the young man asked.

"Out of my way!" he said, as he shoved the young man hard toward the wall. As he entered the hallway a young woman wasted no time in grand introductions, she approached him and placed her arm on the wall, cornering him, and then she kneeled down and up again, keeping her haughty eyes on his face.

"Hey Mister, you're very cute, want to go find a corner, snort a line, and do a grind?"

"Sure Baby, you go get us a drink. I'll be right back. I have to go get my cell phone from my car." he handed her a twenty dollar bill.

"Hurry back, woo-who! A real man!" She smiled and turned toward the crowded bar. He exited the building, got into his car, and began to drive away. He adjusted the rear view mirror, looked at himself, licked his finger, and brushed it upward at his blond crew cut. The Corvette fish tailed a little as he spun out of the parking lot. He was down the block at the next street when the explosion in the warehouse district erupted into a giant fireball. The C- four type explosives were more than enough to take down the whole building and all who were inside. He re-adjusted the mirror to see the ball of flame that looked like a small nuke explosion.

●━━━━━━━━━━━━━━━━━━●

Unplugging the stethoscope from his ears and tossing it on his shoulders the man in the white jacket said, "Ok, Mrs. Stewart, you're free to leave. You're doing just fine now."

"You didn't by chance get a call from a police offic . . .

A nurse inquired, "Excuse me, doctor, did you say Mrs. Stewart?" .

"I'm Mrs. Stewart."

"Hi; Mrs. Stewart, You do have a call. A Metro detective would like to speak with you."

"Speak of the de." Marcy held up a finger to say stop, and completed the nurses' sentence for her,

"An angel." The nurse took on a wide eyed smile and grin, turned and pointed to the phone on the corner of the nurses desk.

"You can speak to your angel right here."

"Federal Bureau of Investigation, please hold...Yes, how may I direct your call?"

"Code four, one, two, alpha."

"Yes, Sir!" She redirected the call.

"Jamison?"

"Yes sir. Is the line clear?"

"Affirmative, what's the status?"

"I arrived at zero eight hundred. Southern branch has joined me. We're outside of targeted zone."

"Is target there?"

"Affirmative."

"Hold your position. Start file. M&N Affair."

"Do your parties want a checkmate with the cleaner?"

"Negative, repeat negative."

"Understood, Sir." Ashton hung up his cell phone and looked out toward the white house. He pushed the button forward, raising the car's dark tinted window.

"Marcy?"

"Hello, Tom."

"How did it go?"

"I'm ok; I'm being discharged as we speak. But I forgot I don't have a ride home."

"Hold on one second, Marcy."

She overheard Tom speaking on a police radio. But somehow his voice echoed from behind her. She turned to see a uniform patrolman walking toward her and answering Tom on his radio.

"Marcy, look behind you," Tom said on the phone.

"Yes, I see him. Is this my ride home?"

"Yep."

"Thank you Tom," she whispered into the phone cupping her hand like a child telling a wonderful secret. She hung up the receiver and turned to face the officer.

"Mrs. Stewart, I've come to give you lift back to your place. Were you all done here?"

"Yes, I am, and thank you for coming."

"You don't have to thank me, homicide called and asked us to do 'em a favor, I think we owed them anyway."

" Well, I still appreciate it."

"Just don't ask me to turn the lights and sirens on."

Marcy grinned.

●────────────────●

The next morning Tom woke at Steve's house. His back was aching from the metal bar that was under the thin mattress of the hideaway sleeper sofa. Sitting up on the edge of the bed and stretching, Tom looked down at the borrowed pajamas he was wearing.

"Golf pajamas," he thought, Tom put on the housecoat that was a half size larger than him and made his way to the kitchen.

"Morning, Tom."

"Hey, Lori; thanks for putting me up for the night."

"Coffee?"

"Yes, please, black."

"You know, you're always welcome here Tom."
"Where's Hotdog?"

Lori laughed at his question. "He's in the bathroom shaving."

"I'm going to keep him out all night tonight."

"Tom, but why?" she whined out.

"Sorry, Lori; we got some traveling to do for work."

She stood up and carried her bowl to the sink, pointed a stern finger and shook it at him. "Tom, you better not let him get hurt, or you're going to be dealing with me."

Tom made a crucifix with his fingers to hold back her warning.

•―――――――――――――――――•

The large home in Margate, Florida was located on the corner adjacent to the carwash parking lot. A black van with tinted windows was parked next to the building. A white vehicle pulled up next to it, and the driver of the car got out of it and knocked twice on the van's back window. He was carrying two large cups of coffee as he entered the van.

"Here you go, fellows; Thought you could use some of this."

"Hey, thanks, I need some of this for sure."

"Yeah, I could have used some about three a.m. this morning."

"Anything new?"

"Nothing, nobody's come or gone."

"How's the sound?"

"The amplitude modulation peeked but became pretty stable after that."

"Did you recheck for anti buggers?"

"Yes, clear as a whistle."

"We got company," the driver of the van said, as a late model car pulled into the drive.

"Get the close ups first and run them by headquarters."

"Won't need to do that, I know who he is, that's General Cooper."

"No bluffing', the five star honcho himself."

"Jamison, you better let Ashton know about this."

"Just get the photos. Make sure the sound and tape is rolling as well."

"Oh, speaking of tape. Let me ask you something. Is it true one of the D. C. Teams lost three tapes to the locals?" The driver started to laugh, but then regained a serious composure as he looked at Jamison. He started to add to the conversation but burst out in a boisterous laugh.

"Yeah, I heard they got it up the tailpipe with a potato. Call it a spud-mobile," the agent was stooped over in the van and Laughed so hard he bumped his head on the roof of the ceiling. Jamison tried not to smile. He composed himself quickly.

"Just don't let it happen to you."

"Looky here," the driver said, peering in the binoculars."

"What is it?"

"Shearson coming out to meet the General."

Click, click, the agent snapped the photos as fast as he could.

•————————————————————•

The skylight window was brightened by the sun shining down, filling the hotel's grand foyer. A continental breakfast table was set for the guests. The desk clerk was going over the checkouts for the morning, and unseen to the human eyes were angels ascending and descending the eighteen stories of the open decor of the grand hotel. Some angels hovered atop of the one called Pastor Zoe. Paul Zoe, a humble man of prayer, who only hours ago was in

Washington D. C. had now come to Broward County, Florida, and was enjoying a wonderful breakfast as he silently prayed for the souls to be won to the kingdom of heaven.

"I hope your stay with us was an enjoyable one, Sir," the waiter said as he lifted the sterling steel top of the serving tray to reveal the warm biscuits and gravy.

"Oh, yes. Praise God, I had a great sleep, now this great food."

The waiter lifted his eyebrow, echoing the words 'Praise God' the man had just said.

"Are you from this area, Sir?"

"No my friend, I am from a small town called Salina, it's in Kansas. But I have traveled most of the states."

"That's interesting, what kind of work do you do?"

"Maryland? Why do we have to go to Marylan..."

Tom held up a finger to tell Steve to wait a minute as he answered the phone.

"Nancy, I want you to book me a flight to Ft. Lauderdale around ten p.m. tonight; Yes leaving from Baltimore."

"Lauderdale?" Steve interjected with quirky look on his face.

"Oh, and book Steve a seat also; Yes he, will be going with me."

"What?"

Tom waved at Steve to be quiet.

"Yes, Lauderdale; and assign someone in our unit to pick up Steve's car at the Baltimore airport. Instruct them to bring it back to D.C. and leave it at the department."

"No, I didn't. The whole building? How many died? Really. Yes, I know him. Joe's Garage too? Only part of it? What hospital is he in? Thanks, Nancy." Tom hung up the receiver.

"Let's go Hotdog. Grab your coat, long day ahead of us."

Steve shook his head and scrambled out the door, and said despondently,

"So I heard."

"Short pit stop first; hospital; Got to see a man about some pigeons."

"What?"

"I'll explain on the way."

Steve began to walk out to the car, but Tom turned to go back inside the house.

"I forgot my wallet on the dresser. Be right out. Go ahead and warm up the car."

As Tom entered the house and shut the door, Lori turned the corner from the kitchen.

"I thought you guys were leaving."

Tom glanced back at her then looked back out the drapes at Steve as he got into the car.

"We are; but first a little payback for raccoon eyes." Tom had a sneaky grin on his face.

Steve sat down behind the driver's wheel, his hands cupped in between his legs. He was shivering in the cold air, Steve saw the heater was on high setting, so he put the key in the ignition and turned it. Tom laughed. And Lori gasped as she put her hand over her mouth.

"Oh!" Lori peeked over Tom's shoulder out the window and said, "You're in trouble."

The baby powder Tom had poured into the vents of Steve's dashboard had just exploded into one big puff of baby powder smoke bomb. All the vents were pointed at Steve who now sat behind the wheel of the car with a dumbfounded clown

powdered face. Tom walked out and jumped into the car's passenger seat.
"Ok, road trip. Let's go."
Steve turned and looked at him trying to see thru the powdery eyelashes.

•─────────────────•

"I am an evangelistic Pastor. I speak at churches around the country."
The waiter shook his head in agreement.
"Must keep you pretty busy, on the road all the time."
"It's exciting; the best part is seeing someone making a choice for Jesus. Are you saved?"
"What do you mean by 'saved'? I think I am a good person, don't steal, I pay my taxes. You know, just play the good guy routine."
"Well, my friend, the Bible says, "for all have sinned and fallen short of the glory of God. And all our righteous deeds are as filthy rags before the Lord."
"Didn't know that, so just how do I get to Heaven?"
"The Bible also says, "God so loved the world that he gave his only begotten son, whosoever, would believe on him would not perish, but have everlasting life. Now the Greek word for life here means Zoe, the God kinda of life. By the way, that also happens to be my name. Zoe, Pastor Paul Zoe." He extended his hand to shake with the young waiter. "It's a great pleasure to meet you, young man."
"Thank you, nice to meet you too, Sir, name's Todd."
"Pastor Zoe."
The voice was coming from behind him. Paul turned to see a man walking towards him. He was

wearing tan pants and a blue embroidered shirt with a logo of the fish sign overlapping a cross.

"Good morning, Pastor, good morning."

"You must be Pastor Greg."

"That a' be me." Greg turned and addressed the waiter.

"Good morning."

"Good morning sir, would care for some breakfast?" Todd the waiter lifted the lid again.

"Oh, that looks great. I do believe I will. Thank you." Todd handed a plate to Greg.

"Well done, thy good and faithful servant."

Todd smiled at Greg's ability to make his voice so deep. He picked up one of the sausages and waved it like a magic wand then shaking it like a rubber pencil before chomping down on it.

Zoe looked at Todd and asked, "Would you like to come as my guest at Pastor Greg's church this Sunday? We would love to have you there."

"Me?"

"Yes; you. Considering you're my first new friend I have met in Florida, I insist."

"Sure, why not, I think I would like that."

"Then it's a deal."

Todd like the idea and the way Zoe spoke.

"We would be honored to have you visit, Todd," Greg interjected. "And you're welcome to come by the fair tonight. We sponsor one every year."

"Yeah, I've seen that, it's on Lyons road, isn't it?"

"Yes, just north of McNab road."

As Greg was speaking to Todd, Zoe watched another man approached them.

"Ah, David," Greg said as he stood up.

"Paul, Todd, this is David Sneed. He is our school's administrative officer and language professor."

David shook hands with the men at the table, but Todd picked up the platter and offered him some morsels.

"Would you care for some breakfast, Sir?"

"No, thanks, I ate on the plane this morning."

Todd closed the platter lid, and began to carry it back to the kitchen.

"I look forward to seeing you Sunday," Paul said.

Todd looked back and nodded. "Wouldn't miss it for the world; Sir."

Greg preformed his magic sausage wand trick, saying, "I'm holding you to that." then he over exaggerated the chopping bite into the sausage.

Todd smiled thinking, "Even geeks can sometimes be cool."

•—————————————————•

"Oh, stop pouting," Tom said.

"I'm not pouting." Steve wiped his face and scowled at Tom.

"What do you call it then?"

"Heavy meditation," Steve replied.

Tom laughed, "Ok, Mr. heavy meditation. Are you planning on meditating all the way to the hospital?"

"Nope."

"If you don't think the baby powder was funny, you should have seen me when I looked up brushing my teeth and saw the black rings around my eyes. Mr. Shoe polish."

Steve's stern face turned to a smirk.

"Ok, ok, truce. At least until we get back from Florida. Deal?"

"Deal."

"Now, do you want to tell me why we are going to the hospital?"

"Someone blew up the Melting Pot Night club."

"No way?"

"Not an amateur either. Nancy said, the bomb and arson guys told her it was C-four."

"Really? Big toes."

"Yep, not only that, our big fish got fried. Tinnimen, his wife, and his driver, were killed in explosion downtown in their limo."

"So, if they're dead, who's at the hospital?"

"Remember the tape I got from Joe, the mechanic next door?"

"Yeah."

"His place took some of the heat, but he's got another tape."

"So, Joe's in the hospital?"

"Yeah, Nancy said he's called four times this morning."

The dark van sat motionless next to the car wash building, but inside commotion was astir.

"We're getting a fax sir."

Jamison turned. He looked towards the back of the van at the agent sitting at the control panel of the latest computer technology and surveillance equipment.

"It's addressed to you, sir."

The printer faxed out two sheets which the agent handed to Jamison. One agent was using binoculars, watching the house.

"Subject two . . . white male, is moving the General's car. The garage door is opening, it looks like . . . hum . . . two female subjects, Sir."

"Hold your position. Stay on Shearson. He's the key." Jamison looked down at the faxed sheet and began to read.

"M & M Affair."

"Jamison, here is the information you requested concerning the connections of parties, Shearson has daughter named Sandra, married to Mark Cooper, son of General Cooper, Julie Cooper, spouse to General, maiden name Stineberg. Shearson is father to deceased assassin Israeli commando Unit. Shearson's wife, deceased. Possible leak is from General Cooper to Shearson. Runner is Joel, Top level Israeli Commando, Use EXTREME CAUTION.

"Hey, where did that guy go who was moving the car?" Jamison asked.

"Back into the house; Why?"

Just as the agent who observing the house had completed his sentence, a man gingerly walked around the corner of the building and stood directly in front of the van with his hands behind him, looking into the van.

"Who's that?" the agent in the back of the van asked.

Jamison looked up from the papers he was reading and looked directly at him. The driver let down the binoculars, turning to glance at him.

"Hey, that's him!"

"Him who?"

"Joel, that's Joel!"

"Ok, now I know why we're going to the hospital. But why are we going to Maryland?"

"Zoe's letter; We're going to meet up with the ex-C.I.A. mercenary."

"Oh, that's just wonderful, Mind if I start praying?"

"For you, that would be a great idea."

"Tom, you know when I was shot and I ah, you know, almost . . . well when I flat-lined."

"You mean died; Yeah."
"I think I saw something."
"What?"
"I think it was an angel."
"You pulling my leg, man?"
"No, really, no lie, all joking aside."
"Did he say anything to you."
"I don't remember, I was so transfixed on his appearance that I really don't remember much of what he said. I do recall something about the child crying out my name, well, Daddy."
"You know the night I went to see Zoe at the church, I thought I saw one, too."
"Well, if we ever get to see Zoe again, I want him to pray for me."
"Really, for what?"
"To keep me from all the trouble you lead me into."
Tom laughed.

Joel pulled his arms from behind his back and pointed the nine millimeter gun with a silencer on the end at Jamison. He fired twice, shattering the glass with an instant hole, striking Jamison between the eyes. The second shot completely broke the front windshield, but only the sound of glass breaking was heard. He then edged the gun's front site just slightly to the left side of Jamison. He pointed it passed him, and targeted the agent who was in the back trying to remove the headphones from his ears, and drawing his own weapon. But the angle was too tight for the agent to move. Joel squeezed the trigger, striking him just below the right armpit. The bullet penetrated, ripping his flesh, piercing his heart. The second shot struck him under his chin as he was falling towards the back of the van. The bullet traveled upward into his brain, assuring a clean kill. The driver fumbled only seconds, trying to get the seatbelt undone. Reaching behind him to his waist holster, he actually had his hand on his weapon and had just unsnapped it, when Joel turned smoothly with accuracy and fired. He struck the driver in the right eye, then again in the middle of the forehead. Joel lowered his arms ever so calmly in a straightway motion. Clasping his hands behind him, he walked over to the house where Shearson and the General were having coffee. Jamison's head tilted forward and blood trickled down off the edge of his nose, dripping onto the fax paper that now lay in his loose grasp in his lap, blotting out the line . . . "Joel, top level Israeli commando, Use caution."

A light breeze from the van's running air conditioner caused the paper to flap up and down slightly. It made a ruffling sound in the stillness of an early morning sunrise.

NINETEEN

The next morning Steve woke himself with the sound of a grunt from his own snoring. He realized the car was parked just off the highway as he watched Tom exiting the store, double fisted with two cups of coffee.

"Roll the window down."

Still waking from his neck wrenching slumber, Steve began to yawn as he rolled down the window. Tom passed a cup to Steve and leaned against the front of the car. Steve opened the door and decided to stretch his legs.

"How far are we?" Steve asked.

" 'bout an hour away."

"Think he'll still be there?"

"I sure hope so."

Tom opened a small bag and pulled out an egg and cheese bagel, rolled the waxed paper back, and took a bite.

"Hey! Where is mine?"

Tom mumbled and pointed at the same time towards the store.

"Inside, mmm...smack, smack. I didn't...mmm...know what you wanted," Tom uttered between bites.

A little annoyed, Steve frowned at Tom and walked inside.

Tom sipped his coffee as he watched the sunrise. The bursting colors of the horizon's haze made him think of the intercepted missile attack over the Atlantic. He thought of Marcy. He missed her and he wished he could be near her. The sound of the small cow bell above the store's front door distracted him from his thoughts. Tom turned and looked back at Steve as he exited the store munching on his own bagel.

"Alright Chief, ready whenever you are."

"I really wish you would stop calling me that."

"I thought you liked being acknowledged as the boss."

"Tom or Sarge will do just fine. Got it?"

"Ok, Chief...Uh, Sarge."

"Mercenaries, why did he have to be a murk?" Tom asked.

"What?"

"Nothing; just thinking out loud."

"Ouch." Steve rubbed his left pectoral.

"You ok?"

"Yeah just a little sore from the stitches, I may need to get my meds refilled before the end of the day."

"Just remember, don't take the sleepy meds until after we see the bad guy."

Steve grinned as he gobbled down the last bite of his bagel. He took a little jump off the edge of the sidewalk and turning towards the corner of the building, he threw his wrapper at a trash barrel like he was a N.B.A. basketball player. The wrapper struck the wall first and fell into the trash can.

"Two points! And the crowd goes wild!" Steve raised his arms and shuffled his feet in a pretended mocked victory dance.

"Nice shot, Kareem. Can we go now." Tom commented while getting into the car. "I think you can keep your day job cause real basketball goals are ten to twelve feet high, not four foot something, and, as you know, white men can't jump."

"I can jump."

"Yeah, right."

"I can."

"Ok."

"No, really I can."

"Sure, let me guess. You jump into and out of bed. No even better yet, you jump into the mix of a conversation." Tom started to laugh at his own mockery as he started the car and began to pull away from the store. Steve folded his arms defensively.

"I can, I can jump."

He straightened his tie as he walked down the narrow corridor of his apartment. His white shirt was clean, crisp, and starched. The red power tie was a sure winner. The pentagram ring on his left hand sparkled rays of light as the sun reflected off of it between the spaces of the closed blinds. Pouring a cup of coffee and walking towards the balcony, he opened the blinds, letting the gushing rays of the morning sun fill his residence. He opened his front door and picked up the paper which lay atop a welcome mat. Glancing over the headlines, he shut the door almost as quickly as he opened it. Performing his daily ritual, he walked out to the balcony terrace overlooking the metro city and sat down at the patio table to read. The front page headlines of the paper showed a picture of a blackened building covered in soot, the apparent rubble of a fire. Kirk adjusted the fold of the paper to read the headlines better.

"FIRE DESTROYS 'MELTING POT NIGHT CLUB' FOLLOWING EXPLOSION. DEATH TOLL UNKNOWN."

Kirk looked at his watch, noticing that it was eight-thirty. He had a meeting with someone at nine. Someone important, someone close to the top, at the address sixteen hundred. The White House, The slight breeze atop the terrace caused the newspaper to flutter. Kirk quickly snapped his wrist like he was casting a fishing rod, fly fishing. The open newspaper snapped back into place.

The Florida newspaper only carried a small article of the fire in Washington, but as the paper was snapped in the hands of General Cooper, it, too, folded into place. The General was already sitting at the table reading when Rabbi Shearson walked into the kitchen. The Rabbi opened the refrigerator and pulled out the bottled water.

"Good morning."

"Morning, Rabbi. There is never anything worth reading in these, even when it's news from another state."

"I know. It is just been two days since Oculus's death, but I fear tomorrow's news more than I feared the passing of my dear son, David."

"I hope you're wrong."

"He's not wrong. The Rabbi is a messenger for us. I too have seen his name in the Code."

"Joel, it's good to see you again. I didn't hear you come in."

Adjusting his shirt over the weapon he had just holstered in the small of his back, Joel quickly brought his right hand forward to shake hands with the general.

"Sir, it is good to see you again.," Joel said, "it is always nice to see a fellow soldier. Sorry, I didn't mean to sneak up on you, but I am afraid the battlefield is nearby."

"Really? Something you are certain about?"

Joel now stood at the kitchen's doorway with his hand behind him at military parade rest position.

"Yes; Sir. I am certain. Three targets were acquired."

"Military?"

"No governmental."

"Joel, you are my friend and bodyguard. I do not wish to hear or be apart of any of these sad affairs. So, if you and the General will excuse me, I will go say good morning to my daughter."

"But, of course." Joel moved from the doorway as the rabbi exited the room, then he turned back and walked towards the kitchen counter.

"Sorry," the Rabbi said as he picked up the bottled water and left again.

"Rabbi, will you tell my son to hurry down when you talk to Sandy?"

"One O'two...One O'three..."

"What are you mumbling?"

"Oh sorry...am I bothering you? Was just counting the fence posts."

"Fence posts?"

"Yeah, I mean, look how far these fence lines stretch. Didn't you ever wonder how long it took to dig all the holes in the ground to erect that entire fence?"

"No, Steve, as a matter of fact that has got to be the furthest thing from my mind."

"Sometimes, I think of the little things like that, Tom. I mean, it must have taken years to put up all those posts."

"Here is the exit and the cabin lodge is just passed it. So, now get your mind in gear about meeting up with a killer and watching my back."

"Ok, Chief."

Tom looked over and frowned at Steve for calling him 'Chief'. Steve pulled his automatic pistol out, checked the magazine, and snapped it back in place. He looked over at Tom and grinned at his frown.

"Wise guy, huh?" Tom asked.

"Love me, don't ya?" Steve replied.

The parking garage was empty, and the sound of a man's dress shoe walking across the smooth concrete pavement echoed throughout the area. Kirk rattled his pocket and removed the key to his car a new Mercedes Benz with a deep green shine. Exiting the parking garage, he turned on the radio and adjusted through several radio stations until he came to the middle of the news' broadcast.

"...is unknown, but believed to have reached a total of twenty-five hundred to three thousand who were in the warehouse night club, known as the Melting Pot. Police are looking for a white male for questioning, last seen exiting the club in a hurry by a young woman, who said, 'the would be suspect gave her a twenty dollar bill'. The young woman, who received burns on her back and legs, was reaching in her car when the explosion took place. The woman said she exited the building to get some cosmetics out of her car. When she looked up, the man who gave her the money was exiting the parking lot quickly, and then the bomb went off..."

{Click} Kirk changed the channel to listen to classical music. The snow had melted on the streets, and as he pulled out of the garage onto the city streets, he passed under an overhead bridge. Moments later, as he neared the park, Kirk turned off the radio. He could see that there was only one car in the area besides his. As he pulled up closer to the other car, two men got out and strolled up to the passenger side of his car. Kirk cracked the window. The two men were wearing ties and long coats. They didn't look like muggers to Kirk, so he opened the window. The elder of the two men spoke first.

"Mr. Dagon? Mr. Kirk Dagon?"

Upon hearing his name, he knew they were his contacts and unlocked the back and side doors, inviting the guests into his car.

"Kirk, we want to thank you for showing up this morning. My name is Noland, Brice Noland. We represent some very powerful friends who would like to meet with some of your friends." The guy in the back seat licked his two fingers and then brushed the short crew cut upward while at the same time saying.

"You seem a little jittery. You alright?" The blond guy asked.

"Just fine Excuse me if I am leery. I just lost my former employer, and I am hoping not to meet the same fate."

"Not at all; Mr. Dagon, Your name was recommended by some very influential people."

•———————————————•

"Septuagint,"

The voice of Heaven had spoken my name ever so sweetly, like honey on the lips of a lover. The sound alone filled my being with an eternal presence of bliss.

"Septuagint, go and record all. Then obey."

"Thine will be done, my King."

I moved on the wings of thought, to a building. Where I sat and observed. I was sitting on the edge of the balcony railing on the eighteenth floor of a huge hotel. I looked upward to the sun shining down into this open atrium. Below were many dining tables covered with clean crisp linen, each and every table was set with beautifully decorated dishes and mauve colored napkins.

Below, I saw three men who had just finished eating and are about to pray. I am given knowledge of all present; Pastor Zoe, Pastor Greg and David. But I have only previously seen one, Pastor Zoe. The three men sitting at the table each bow their heads and fold their hands in worship. I am very interested in what is about to be spoken, for I was told to record and obey. I believe one of the three is about to command me in spiritual warfare by praying with true faith.

"Dear Lord in Heaven, we thank you that you always hear the voice of your sheep. Father God, I ask that you give Pastor Zoe the guidance and a double portion of your anointing oil from Heaven. And Lord, forget not your servant, me, Pastor Greg. Thank you for blessing my church and all who worship your name. Amen."

"Yes, amen Lord. Thank you for Pastor Greg. Now I ask in the name of Jesus, to send your angel to watch over Tom. Lord, I know he is your servant, too. Lord, he is a babe in Christ. Keep him, Lord, and give him direction." I watched as all three men, now humbled themselves and prayed before the Lord for Tom. The stronger they prayed the more my sword began to blaze in it's sheave. Then Pastor Zoe said it.

"I COMMAND IT IN THE NAME OF JESUS, THINE ANGEL BE SENT TO WHEREVER HE IS, TO PROTECT HIM, LORD, A SHIELD FOR THY SERVANT."

At that command, I was immediately transported to be in the presence of Tom. I am now in the back seat of a car directly behind Tom. His friend, the one known as Steve, is present in the front seat with him.

"Awe, come on, Chief, You telling me you never once ever thought about who dug all those holes for the fences?"

"No! Steve, I never did, not once till now."

"Look, there are the cabins up ahead."

●━━━━━━━━━━━━━━━━━━━━●

"Let me ask you a question. How could you tell I was jittery?" Kirk asked.

"Easy Mate; You gotta death grip on that Corinthian leather steering wheel; Matter of fact, I think it died of asphyxiation ten minutes ago. Ha, ha, ha."

"Funny guy, huh?"

He adjusted his long jet black overcoat, licked his two fingers and brushing the short blond crew cut in an upward motion.

"Yeah Mate, I am a real riot. T.N.T., that's me.

A phone rang and the blond guy in the back seat reached into his coat and pulled out the cell phone. He pointed his fingers like a hand puppet he was going to make talk and opened his fingers mocking an explosion at the same time he lifting the phone to his ear.

"Hello..."

"Yes. One moment."

"Mr. Noland, it's for you."

"Hello. Brice Noland here."

"Yes sir." Brice shut the phone, turned around in the seat, and handed the phone back to the blond gentleman.

"We have to go now, immediately."

"Just a minute, who recommended me to you?" Kirk asked.

Brice extended his left hand to shake with Kirk with his palm upward. When Kirk put his hand in Brice's, Brice turned his wrist, holding Kirk's in a firm shake. Now Brice's hand was on top, revealing the pentagram ring. Brice Noland made sure Kirk saw the ring.

"Some of the same friends of yours are friends of mine."

Whoosh, whoosh, whoosh, whoosh...Kirk jerked his head in direction of the sound behind him. The sudden loud noise of the rotary blades of a helicopter had descended swiftly on the open area of the park's grass near Kirk's car.

"It's alright, Kirk. I am sure you will enjoy the new position you're going to be offered. Remember Kirk, you will be reporting directly to me. Your salary will be tripled. My associate, Miss Kelly, will answer any questions you may have. I will be seeing you soon. Have a pleasant day."

"Miss who?"

"Nice to meet ya, mate," said the man in the back seat.

"Yeah right," Kirk watched Brice and the crew cut guy leave the car then walked around to the black chopper, pausing a few feet away as a young lady exited the chopper. Brice handed her the keys to his car. Brice turned and pointed at Kirk. The woman, dressed in black high heels, long gray pinstriped pants and a long overcoat, smiled. She held one hand on a furry Russian style hat as the wind rustled the blades of grass on the ground. Some light patches of snow flung misty—water vapors in the air. The brief meeting was completed. Brice Noland and his associate got into the black chopper while the attractive lady began approaching Kirk's car. She walked around to the passenger side and opened the door.

"Hello, Mr. Dagon. My name is."

"Let me guess. Miss Kelly."

"Yes, that's right." She smiled at Kirk.

"Nice boss you have there."

"The job does have its perks."

"So how do I fit in to all this?"

"Can we go somewhere a little more comfortable, Mr. Dagon? How about I buy you a cup of coffee and I'll explain everything."

"Well I've never been able to resist a cup of java, especially when treated by an attractive lady."

"Great. There is a café near the hospital. Do you know it?

"Sure do." Kirk looked back over his shoulder as the black chopper pitched forward. Its long rotary blades hovered in place only a few feet above the ground, as the tail end spun around to the way point the pilot predetermined, then lifted higher and higher, rising as quickly as it had descended.

"If you will follow me, Mr. Dagon, I need to take the company car back to the office. So it's best if we take both cars."

"Hey, just out of curiosity, just where are they headed to in such a rush?"

"I am not sure, but I saw the pilot's manifest and I believe he was charted for Maryland. Why, you like flying?"

"Yeah, it's ok. But if I can avoid it, I will."

●─────────────●

Tap...tap...tap. Someone was rapping on the bedroom door.

"Come in, it's open," Sandy Shearson said.

"Good morning my lovely daughter," the rabbi said, "Where is Mark?"

"Hello, Papa. Mark had to leave early to meat with some people about one of the construction sites he is working on."

"Ah, that is too bad. Mark's father is here and wanted to see him. He will have to wait, all for enterprise."

●─────────────●

Both men looked out the windows of the opposite sides of the chopper as it lifted off the ground. Brice Noland was handed a sealed envelope from the pilot. It had red printing on it:

"TOP-SECRET-CONFIDENTIAL-
FOR BRICE NOLAND ONLY"

Brice opened the envelope and pulled the case file, turning to the photographs inside. The photo was a black and white eight-by ten. The picture was of a man entering a room with a number on the door Twenty seven. Attached to the photo was held a small square piece of paper with writing on it by a large paper clip.

"Brice, this is the agent you requested to be found. He is now under the assumed name, Camden Pelt. Last location was at seven-fifteen this morning, checking into Peaks Lodge, a motel outside of Chesapeake Bay near Maryland. His room number is twenty-seven. 'Agent has turned.' Use caution. Security level status is A-two.

"So, what's so important about this Kirk guy?" asked the gentleman with the crew cut.

"He is needed or he wouldn't have been spared from the little explosion you demonstrated on the senator's limo. Oh, and by the way, you goofed on the Melting Pot Job."

"How's that, the whole building was taken care of?"

"Not the building itself. A woman escaped and saw you leave the scene. When we get done with all this business, you will find her and tie up any loose strings."

"Yes sir." He looked down as Kirk's car and Miss Kelly's bent position looking into the car, faded and grew smaller as the chopper pulled away from the area.

●───────────────●

"Are you going to drive past it first, Chief?"
"Yep."
"Peaks Lodge, not peak season that's for sure, only one vehicle in the parking lot."
"Think it's his?"
"I didn't see any other way in or out. Did you?"

"Nope Ok Sarge, how do you want to do this?"

"I am going to drop you off out here by the road. I go up to the front desk, find out which cabin. You use the binoculars to read my hand signal of which cabin, and then circle around to the back till I can figure out if this is safe. Keep a close watch. If I pinch my nose; come running. I need back up, understand?"

"Got it; Tom, Be careful. I gotcha back."

"Let's do it."

Tom stopped short of the gravel driveway surrounded by pine trees and the snowy hills in the background. Steve got out of the car and buttoned his coat. He watched Tom proceed into the driveway and up to the main cabin. Steve watched Tom go in. Tom held up two fingers to his chest, and then with both hands he showed seven fingers. Steve got the message: room twenty seven. Tom backed up drove down the hill, and pulled in front of cabin number twenty-seven. He exited his car, walked up the wooden steps and knocked on the door. There was no answer. Tom gripped the door handle and tried to turn it. It was locked. He stepped to the left of the door on the porch to see inside the window. No one was present inside the one room cabin. As he started to walk down the steps to get back into his car, Tom looked around at all the empty cabins. He turned, looking to the back of the cabin for Steve, when he heard a strange sound.

"Psst, psst."

Tom turned again looking directly behind him at the cabin across the gravel road. In the doorway was Steve, with silver duct tape on his mouth. It was apparent he was handcuffed behind his back. Tom drew his weapon, but Steve was quickly yanked from Tom's view into the cabin.

"Walk forward, Detective. Take the clip out of your weapon and place it in your pocket. Remove the bullet in the chamber also. Do it now."

Tom complied. The thought of having to face Lori, if anything happened to Steve disturbed him more than anything else in this world.

Tom had nothing to fear. I looked into the cabin and into the flesh of the man who was holding Steve hostage. He had a born again spirit. He was a Pneuma-man, a child of God. Tom was unaware that I was here as his protector. Unaware of the men in Florida who had prayed for him; Unaware that the King Himself had ordered me to obey the commandments of prayer.

"Walk forward Detective."

"You going to shoot me?—Uh, I don't even know your name. What do I call you?"

"Just keep walking. You can call me Camden."

Tom walked up the steps and into the cabin. When he entered the cabin he saw Steve sitting, still handcuffed, on the edge of the bed, with a wide stripe of sliver duct tape on his mouth. "Nice backup, Ace."

"...ooorry," Steve mumbled, trying to speak through the silver mouth muffler.

"Here you go." The man in the tan leather coat and tan pants tossed a handcuff key to Tom.

"I had to make sure he was with you. Sorry Pal," he said to Steve.

"The registry said you were in cabin twenty-seven."

"Just a little change up to keep the hounds off the fox's trail."

"I see. So what did you want to see me for?"

"I have some information for you."

"You know I can't offer you immunity, only a state attorney can do that."

Camden started to laugh out loud. "Is that what you think I want? immunity? Sit down, Detective; I have a lot to tell you."

"Alright. I'm game."

"Mmm...mmm...mmm."

"You can remove that if you want."

"I don't know. On him it might be an improvement.

"MMM...MMM." Tom yanked the tape off quickly.

●────────────────●

"Pastor Greg, is everything set for the fair tonight?" David asked.

"Yes, praise God. Are you coming tonight, David?"

"You know me, Pastor. I've have to have one of Mrs. Cooper's pies."

"Oh, yes, Mrs. Cooper. I almost forgot. She told me her in-laws were arriving and her husband was coming down from Washington."

"Washington? That's where I just got finished ministering." Pastor Zoe said.

"How was the weather up there?" asked David.

"Must say, it is more pleasant here than it was there."

"Did you get to see the White House, Pastor?"

"No, David, I didn't get to see much of the city. I was really kind of busy with the meeting. The church there has a wonderful leader. His name is Bishop Davis."

"Well, if I ever get there I want to see it all." Pastor Greg laughed, "That's what I'll say when I get to Heaven. I want to see it all."

"I just want to see Jesus," Pastor Zoe said with a smile.

●────────────────●

"Joel, do you think you and the Rabbi would like to join us at the fair tonight? My wife Julie cooks pies for the event each year."

"General, it is up to the Rabbi, whatever he wishes to do. I remember your wife's cooking and, speaking for myself, I would love to go. I could use a night off anyway." The Rabbi and Sandra were coming down the steps when the Rabbi heard Joel say he would love to go.

"Go where, Joel?"

"I was just asking if you and Joel would like to go the fair. Julie cooks pies for this event each year. You know something for the kids."

"Children, I would love to attend," said Shearson.

"That's great, papa."

"This won't interrupt our schedule, will it?"

"No. Not at all, Rabbi," Joel said.

"Oh papa, you're always working. It is nice to know you're taking some time off."

"Yes, I think I need the time to forget about certain events."

The black chopper was moved in a direct line, heading north by northeast, when the cell phone rang. The man in the black leather coat answered.

"Hello? Yes he is. Who's calling? One moment, Sir, it's for you. It's the bureau, Ashton." The man in the black coat handed the phone to Brice Noland.

"Ashton, my dear friend, what can I do for you?"

"Shut up, Brice, and listen, Jamison and the team were hit just a few hours ago."

"Has that been verified?"

"No. They were on a three-zero check-in schedule and they all are two hours overdue."

"So what's that have to do with me, Ashton?"

"Brice, I need to know what you know, and I need to know it now! What is that thunderous sound?"

"I am in a chopper, Ashton. I can only tell you that one of the targets made it into the states last night. His bodyguard is a commando. If your team was on a three-zero check-in, and haven't reported in for two hours, then you know as well as me they're eliminated."

"Brice, I can hardly hear you. If that's so, who let him in?" Brice put a finger in his ear to hear.

"We don't know."

●────────────────────────────●

"Ooouch!"

"What a baby."

"That hurt, Chief!" The man in the tan leather jacket walked into the kitchen and poured himself a cup of coffee.

"Either of you guys, want coffee?"

"Right here," said Tom.

"No, thanks. I don't think I can *USE MY LIPS*, thank you!" Steve rubbed his mouth and glared at Tom walking into the kitchen area. Tom glanced at Steve puckered his lips and blew him a kiss.

"Love me back, don't ya?" Tom asked in a sarcastic tone.

"So you think I want immunity? Sorry to disappoint you there, Detective," Camden answered.

"What do you want?" Tom asked.

"I want to give someone I can trust the information that might save a life."

"And what information would that be?"

"Pastor Zoe, and anyone like him, is in great danger."

"What do you mean, anyone like him?" Steve asked.

"And what makes you think you can trust me?" Tom asked.

"I was there," Camden replied.

"There?"

"The night you confessed Jesus as your Lord and Savior, that makes you a Christian, Tom, and that's what I mean by anyone like him. Christians."

"The set up of the chess board is almost in place."

"Am I supposed to understand that?"

"Look, Detective, when you play chess you set all the pieces into place, and you move for position before you ever even think of taking the opponent's pieces. For the place of position on the battlefield determines the victory with the right moves."

"Ok, so now what?"

"I know Zoe gave you the letter or you wouldn't be here. I know you know I am an agent for the C.I.A. and that I am a trained assassin. Yes, it is true, I have done many awful assignments. A few nights before you saw me in the church service, I was sent on a mission. It became my last mission."

"Really? Your target wasn't the two girls I found in an alley by chance was it?"

"No. Your own man did that one, and he paid for it with his life. I believe his name was Murphy. I was sent to take out someone who was a known in the political arena as an E.S. an Earth Shaker. Someone, who moves people to pray to become Christians. A real evangelist, not the types who do it for money. As a matter of fact some of those kind are planted in positions by the company to destroy people's faith. What I am talking about is the real men who are truly called of God. You know; the ones who can demonstrate the truth."

"You mean like Zoe."

"Yes, he was my target."

"Why?"

"The easiest way to explain it, Tom is this. Power corrupts and total power corrupts totally."

"I don't understand."

"There are some wicked people who have climbed to high places in government. There is even a inner circles of the most wicked that call and pray to Satan. They have plans in the works even as we speak."

"That's the big toes, Chief," Steve interjected.

"Time is short. You must go to Zoe. I would have given it to him myself, but I needed to get the proof, and this is it."

TWENTY

Kirk followed the black Lincoln into the parking lot across from the cafe diner. He watched the very attractive lady get out of her boss's car as he was locking it with the remote control. A short burst alarm sounded echoing off the buildings across the street.

"How quaint," Kirk said as he offered his elbow outward, in a gentlemanly gesture. Miss Kelly just smiled and grasped hold of his arm with her elegant, black velvet gloves.

"Oh, it does look charming, doesn't it?" she said.

As they walked in, Kirk removed his coat and gloves and reached for Miss Kelly's.

"May I?"

"Oh yes, please."

Kirk had on his best manners, pulling out a chair for her to sit. He looked at the decor on the walls.

"I used to see those people on T.V., comedians of the early era of television. My, my, the whole place is decorated with them." The waitress came over, pulling a pen from atop of her ear.

"Hello. My name is Marcy. May I get you something to drink?"

"Two coffees, please."

•————————————————————•

"Wait a minute. You expect me to believe that a cop murdered those two girls?"

"It's true."

"How do you know it's true? Tell me something that will make me a believer.

"Ok, I will." Camden turned and opened a black duffel bag that was sitting near the bed on the floor. He pulled out a file folder with a rubber band around it, and tossed it on the bed.

"Here's your proof." Tom removed the rubber band and opened the file to reveal photo after photo of Murphy in the alley committing the horrible crimes. The photos were taken from above the alleyway.

"If you were there taking these photos, why didn't you stop this madman?"

"The deed was done. I got up to the rooftop after he had already killed them. I had to report what happened. Later, I heard about Murphy getting stabbed. Put two and two together."

"Why do you have the photos?"

"Copies to show to guys like you who think all cops are saints. It also helps to have a little insurance, at least for immunity sake."

———•———

"Goodbye, Ashton. I have to make an important call," Brice said.

Each push of the cell phone sounded out a certain tone. Brice held the phone to his ear, waiting for someone to answer. The other man sat patiently, looking out the side door of the chopper, watching the streets, fields, and trees all go by at an incredible speed.

"Funny, isn't it mate?"

"What's that?"

"Life, It goes by just as quickly."

"Yes, it does. Sometimes you just can't even afford to blink."

Brice held up a finger towards the blond crew cut guy as to say one moment. "Hello? This is Brice Noland. Secure this line, sector "G". I need two blackbirds inbound to target alpha. Extractions team of eight each bird. Yes! That's what I said. Eight each bird! What is the E.T.A.? Their estimated time of arrival! What is it? You can't hear me clearly because I am already inbound in a bird. Now get those choppers up and going. A.S.A.P."

"Ya think with all this technology they'd get a cell phone to work better, hey?" asked the man with the blond crew cut.

●————————————————————●

The coffee shop was a great place to get warm and look out the window at the park. The streets were wet but the snow was still covering the ground in patches where children had made snowmen, built snow forts, or attempted to make igloos. She wore a white silky blouse accented by big hoop jewelry on her wrist. She had gold rings on every finger. She was a captivating woman with a very pretty face.

Kirk watched her shake her hair from side to side after letting it fall free from being shoved up under the black furry Russian hat. She then leaned forward, placing her elbows on the table, with her chin resting on the back of her fingers. She looked out the window, then at Kirk and smiled.

"I love Christmas time, don't you?"

"Yes. I guess it's as good as any other holiday."

"I could spend all day looking at all the decorations." She moved her arms and sat back momentarily as the waitress placed the coffees in front of them.

"Can I get you anything else?"

"No, not at the moment, thank you," Kirk replied then turning to Miss Kelly. "So, what is this new position in politics I am suppose to fill?"

"Mmmm," she sipped her coffee. "You're going to love it. I read your file, so I know the work you did for the late Senator Tinnimen. Mr. Dagon, I can assure you, your new position is not so much mainstreamed out in the public. But your seat of authority is a lot higher than you were."

"Please, call me Kirk. So, I won't be out in the public face anymore. Miss Kelly, what if I don't want this job?"

"Mr. Dagon, I mean Kirk," she reached across the table and touched the back of his hand.

"Humans are creatures of habit, and from your past psychological profile, we know you would want, or best fit, this job. Besides, you never know when your car could go boom."

Kirk was listening but looking out the window when she mentioned that. He turned and looked her in the face. She batted her eyelids, smiled and picked up her coffee cup. Her hoop jewelry clanged on her wrist as she took a sip.

"I see what you mean."

The spiritual demon, Fear, rose up from hell, unseen to the human eyes. He now stood directly behind Kirk. Fear outstretched his wings of darkness, reached out his arms and wrapped them around Kirk's as if he were hugging him. Kirk had known the feeling of fear before, but now it was being impressed on him by this beautiful wolf in sheep's clothing.

●────────────────●

I stood on the porch with my arms folded across my chest, and watched Tom through the window, as he looked at the photos of officer Murphy decapitating the two women he had killed. It was then that I heard something coming towards me from the woods between the cabins behind me. I turned to look. I saw nothing. I watched the leaves move then some snow squashed and compacted like someone was there, but no form at all. Then as he neared, he allowed himself to be seen. It was... Xenophon.

"Greetings, Septuagint."

"Xenophon! Greetings to you, Sir; Are you here to give me new orders, sir?"

"No, I was sent by 'Defender of the Faith'."

"For what reason, Sir?"

"To assist you, Septuagint; These men are in danger of losing their lives. You must get them to leave now."

"I will whisper in the mind of the one known as Steve. He has heard my voice before."

I walked into the cabin room right through the wall and glass window. Steve was standing, leaning with his right shoulder on the wall, his arms folded and crossed.

"DANGER! GET OUT!"

•―――――――――――――――――――――――――•

"This is such a nice place to relax, and I am amazed at how you can go from one state to another and don't have to worry about bombings or shootings or even rock throwers," Shearson said.

"I thought you might like to go to see the ocean view. It is peaceful and very beautiful," said the General.

"I am looking forward to seeing my Sandra. When I lost David, I realized that the cost of the war is something unbearable."

"I am glad that Mark and Sandy are very happy. I am truly sorry for the loss of David."

"David would have liked a big car like this, I am sure. He was a comfort type of man instead of being a sporty type of guy."

"To lose one's family is the ultimate price to pay, Rabbi. You don't have to hide your emotions from me."

The Rabbi pinched his nose, lifting his glasses to stop the tears from rolling down his face. He patted at the air like he was patting the head of a child.

"I know, I know. Who is able to even think of this type of tragedy? What would you do if it were Mark?"

"I don't know, Sir. I don't think I could bear it."

The house in Margate, Florida was now empty. General Cooper and Rabbi Shearson were out of the house. Sandra Cooper, the Rabbi's daughter, now married to the General's son Mark, was out shopping with her mother in-law Julie. Joel, the Israeli commando and long time friend of Shearson, was the only one home. The screen door creaked when it shut as he exited the house. Joel looked to his left, and then to the right, as he began walking across the lawn, approaching the street. It was still early in the morning and not much traffic was going by.

Joel put on a pair of latex surgical gloves and smoothed each finger down to make the glove fit tight. Crossing the city street into the big parking lot, he hurried his steps as he came closer to the white van. The driver's door was unlocked as Joel opened it. He climbed in and shoved the body of the dead agent into the open center of the van between the seats. The engine was still running. The faxed paper the deceased agent Jamison held was still fluttering to the breeze of the van's air conditioner.
Joel reached over and pushed the corpse forward so no one would see the body. He drove the van, following the alleyway, stopping behind a dry cleaner's building. Backing the van up to the bushes, it blended very well with the other delivery trucks.

"Federal Bureau of Investigation, southeast branch. This is agent Terry Reos. How may I help you?"

"Agent Reos? This is District Commander Robert Ashton, Washington. I need to speak to your C.O. Calvin Rust. It's very important. So get him on the line now, please."

"Yes Sir, one moment, Sir." She pushed the button, placing the call from Washington on hold. As she stood up from behind her desk, her badge from the Federal Bureau of Investigation draped over the waistband of her knee-length, royal blue skirt. She was very shapely, fit and trim. She walked over to the office where a gentleman was shaking a pencil in between his fingers, and talking on the phone to someone. She adjusted her white silk blouse before stepping into the office doorway, and gently rapped on the frame of the door. He uncrossed his leg and turned in the leather chair towards the door to see who it was.

"Hold one second, please," he said speaking to the party on the phone. Setting the pencil down while covering the receiver with one hand, he looked at Terry Reos.

"Yes, agent Reos?"

"Important call; Washington, Line one."

"Thank you." He pushed the button for the incoming call.

"This is Calvin Rust. May I help you?"

"Rust, this is Robert Ashton, District Commander, Washington; I need a recovery team and I need it yesterday. I want you on it personally. Get to the car wash on State Road Seven, north of Atlantic Boulevard, in the city of Margate. Look for a white van and find agent Jamison. They were on a three zero check in and we haven't received anything in over two hours."

"Yes Sir, Commander. I will get on it right now."

"Report to me as A.S.A.P. This case is top priority."

"I understand, Sir. Goodbye."

He hung up the phone, stood up and adjusted his tie. He picked up his dress coat from the corner coat rack in his office. He put on his jacket, turned off the light, and pulled his door shut as he walked out. He was heading for the elevator when he yelled out.

"Agent Terry Reos! Grab your coat. Come with me. We have work to do."

"Yes, Sir." She picked her coat up from off the back of her chair and put it on. The blue blazer matched her royal blue skirt. She then picked up her overcoat and scurried to catch up with her boss.

The giant pine trees towering towards the blue sky began to sway. Snow drifts accumulating on the branches began to dump large mounds of snow as the black helicopters started their descent. The solitude of the parking lot of the Chesapeake Lodge was totally disturbed by the sudden invasion. Steve looked out the window to see what the turmoil was, "Camden, were you expecting any other visitors?"

"No, and I don't think they're here to socialize. That, my friend, is a professional cleaning crew."

"I never knew of any cleaning crews arriving in whirlybirds," Steve interjected.

"They're here for me. I know too much."

"That's great! They have the place surrounded, but they are heading to the cabin across the way, like I did. Got any suggestions on how we are going to get out of this?"

"Quick, get up."

"What?"

"Get up off the bed and help me if you want to live."

Tom put the photos down and stood up as Steve watched the group of men begin to surround the cabin across the way.

"What are you doing?" Camden moved the corner of the bedspread, lifting the rug.

"What is that?" Tom asked.

After Camden pulled the rug back, he pushed a button that was near the bed's leg on the floor. It released a latch that opened a trap door in the floor. Tom leaned over and looked down the long drop at the ladder attached to the cylindrical wall.

"Hey Chief, we might be in for some trouble here. They're getting ready to go in," Steve said, spying out the window at the men surrounding the other cabin.

"That my friend is an old K.G.B. escape route," Camden said.

"No kidding!" Tom exclaimed.

"We have to hurry. There isn't much time."

"Hey, once you're gone, we'll just walk out there and meet 'em," Tom said.

Steve watched as a man touched the microphone near his mouth and received orders on a headset.

"How many are there?" Tom asked.

"They will leave no survivors. You can't stay here," Camden said.

"I can't tell, but they are all military dressed. Pros Chief, Whoaahhh."

The sound of machine gun fire echoed and reverberated throughout the wooded cove. In moments, the cabin would collapse. Steve watched as the agents moved in, closing in the semicircle and firing nonstop. The wooden cabin was quickly becoming a pile of splinters and toothpicks. Camden grabbed his backpack and was swiftly moving down the long ladder, leading to the underground tunnel.

"Ok, I think you're right. I do believe you," Tom said.

"Hey Chief, let's go if we're going. They are starting to look around at the other cabins."

"Last man down pulls the little string to cover up the trap door with the rug," Camden yelled upward towards the light.

"Got it," Steve said.

Tom looked down the deep hole as he tried to hurry. He reached the bottom with standing room only, about two inches above his head. A long tunnel ran in both directions to the right and left. He heard footstep to his left growing fainter. Camden was hauling tail. Waiting for Steve, Tom tried to whisper loudly.

"Psst! Let's go. Get down here now!"
"Ok, ok. Let me pull the string for the rug." Steve pulled the string from inside the dim tunnel and the rug slid back into place covering the trap door. At the same moment, the front door was kicked inward by three military agents carrying machine guns. I watched as they entered the room. My clothes turned to bright white as the three men stormed into the small cabin. My sword began to flame as I beheld one of the soldiers with an imp on his back. It turned its head to the right and looked at me, then hissed.

"Angel of the Lord, what business have you here?"

Its squealing high-pitched voice sounded with the gurgling of shredded vocal chords.

"Thy name; imp? I command thee in the name of the Lord. Say it and whom you follow!"

"Aaaaahhhhhh, I will. My name is Chaos. I am under the command of Murder."

I drew my flaming sword and held it high, ready to strike.

"Angel, beware!" Chaos said, as I watched him dig his claws deeper into the skull of the agent host in the black S.W.A.T. uniform.

"If you banish me now, seven of us shall return, for he has killed. I lie not, I saw it. He shall be worse off than now. Besides, we shall leave this place."

The imp moved unnoticed on the man's back and whispered into the ear of the agent.

"Ok, nothing here. Let's go," the agent said, adding "I feel a terrible migraine coming on."
One of the agents picked up a coffee cup from the counter. He was about to look down into the cup when the lead agent commanded again, "Let's go."

The one with the imp stumbled to one knee from the pain that shot through his skull. His sudden action caused the other agents to walk over and assist him up.

"You ok?"

"Yeah, I'll be fine. Let's get out of here." The other agent, who was by the bed, stepped out of the cabin first, then the leader with the imp followed. The third agent took a last look around and unknowingly stepped on the corner of a photo's edge, sticking out from under the bed. The photo was of a Washington Metro police officer named Murphy committing a terrible crime. The imp looked back into the cabin. I still stood in the same spot unmoved. My garment blazed as white as the sun and my sword was held high. I was a protector, but the imp knew not what I was protecting. A simple rug, a hidden door, a hole in the ground, a tunnel, a man in the tunnel, a man called to serve God.

Revealing his fangs, the yellow-eyed horde of hell hissed at me. His host, the human agent, held his hands over the invisible claws that were deeply embedded into his spirit by the imp demon.

●────────────────●

Inserting the key into the car door, General Cooper locked the vehicle and set the alarm.

"This is where your wife will be later?" Shearson asked.

"Yes. She told me the booth was second to the last at the end of the row," Cooper said.

"I am so amazed at the difference in temperature in this region of the country."

"Well, Jerusalem is not a very big country, land size I mean." As the two men walked, Shearson shook his finger.

"That is very true, General, very true."

"I've read that it was predicted to snow up north around your other home."

"You mean Washington?"

"Yes, Washington."

"I believe I read that myself."

"My, my, what is all that screaming?"

The General looked back over his shoulder, and pointed upward at the teenagers spinning upside down in circles on the Ferris wheel ride.

"Thrill seekers, my friend, just thrill seekers."

"Ah, kids. This is the American way?" Shearson rubbed his beard as he looked upward towards the spinning ride.

"Rabbi Shearson?" The Rabbi turned to see who it was that had said his name. The voice was not familiar to him.

"I thought that was you," the young man said. The brief look of bewilderment quickly passed as the Rabbi recognized the young man's face.

"David."

"Yes, you remembered."

"David from the plane, The young linguistics major."

"That's right. How are you?"

"Great. I am having a wonderful visit."

"Of all the sites to see in south Florida, how did you end up here?"

"Oh, please excuse me. Where are my manners? This is General Cooper. My daughter is married to his son. I am staying with him and his family."

"General? The honor is all mine, Pleased to meet you, Sir."

"Nice to meet you; Do you help out with the church? I noticed all the stuff you're carrying out," said the General.

"Yes, I do what I can for Pastor Greg."

"Do you know him?"

"I had attended one of his services a few years back. But no, not really."

"Well then, this must be your lucky day, cause that is him coming now with the guest speaker for the next week."

"Guest speaker? Your temple allows other speakers to come in and teach?"

"Yes, Rabbi. Church services are a little different than temple."

"That is Pastor Greg on the left, and the man standing next to him is Pastor Paul Zoe."

"Did you say Zoe? His last name is derived from the meaning, 'the God kind of Life.'"

"Yes, that's right."

"I would very much like to meet this young man."

"So, while you are getting to meet everyone, I think I will go make sure my wife's booth is set up for her. I'll be right back."

"Sure, sure, go ahead. I will be fine."

"Ok. Remember if you want to find me, it's the second from the end. Nice meeting you, David."

"Nice meeting you, Sir." Pastor Greg and Zoe walked up to David while he was talking to the Rabbi. They both were watching the direction that the General was heading.

"Interesting man; I bet he had hundreds of war stories to tell," David said.

"Yes, I'm sure he does."

"Who does?" Pastor Greg asked.

"Oh good, we didn't have to wait to catch up with you."

"Now David, I'm not that busy. You can catch me anytime you want."

"How are you, Sir?" Greg stuck out his hand to shake and greet the Rabbi.

"I am...pleased...pleased to be here."

"Pastor, this is Rabbi Shearson. We met the other day on the plane. He is staying here in America with family. I believe he is related to the Coopers.

"Ah yes, Mrs. Julie Cooper, The pie queen."

"The pie queen?"

"Yes, wonderful cook. She wins almost every year. Oh, let me introduce a friend of mine. This is Pastor Paul Zoe."

The rabbi looked at Paul's face. And saw it was angelic.

●────────────────────────●

The flickering light faded as the breeze brushed across his hand.

"Hey, Chief. Get that zippo working. I can't see squat in this dark hole."

"Alright, give me a second."

"Man, we must have walked at least two miles in this sewer."

"Be glad we're walking, period. Think what would have happened if we didn't make it into this tunnel."

"Well, tonight I am having a drink in the memory of some Russian engineer."

"Yeah, well I think he deserves a double toast."

The lighter's flame that Tom held up blew out once again.

"What's wrong?" Steve asked.

"Sssssh!"

"I hear something...like water, lots of water." Tom lit the lighter again, only getting a glimmer of the edge of the door's frame. They had reached the end of the tunnel.

"This must be the place where Camden got out, because there isn't no more runway."

"Great, let's get out of here."

"Yeah, this is the spot. A breeze is blowing in, that's why my lighter keeps going out."

"Whooooaaaaa!" Steve moved quickly to grab Tom to keep him from falling. Tom was hanging onto the knob of the door that had just swung open, with a three hundred foot drop of nothing below him. A shear wall face was covered by a huge waterfall drop. The door of the tunnel was high above the ground, with a ladder beside the door that led in only one direction...up. Steve yanked Tom by the back of the belt and pulled him back into the tunnel. Both men stood inside the tunnel and looked down at the drop, then at the ladder that was attached to the rock face beside the door. It led to a port hole type exit. It was too dark from where they stood behind the waterfall to see how or where it would come out.

"You have two choices. Go back and hope the choppers are gone, or go up," Tom said.

"Can't go back; They might even be in the tunnel now," Steve replied.

"Ok. Up it is."

"After you; Chief. This thing looks fifty years old. You think it will hold the both of us?"

"Don't know. Guess we'll find out."

"Must have held Camden, unless he knew some other way out," The thought of what Steve said affected Tom in a peculiar manner. He looked down and to his left. He was about five rungs up. Steve still stood in the doorway high above the ground.

"Hey! What are you waiting on?" Tom asked.

"Just wanted to see if that's really going to hold you."

"Thanks for letting me get out here on the line before you made a decision."

"Chief, somebody had to be the leader. You get paid more than I do. I know how much I weigh, and I can guess what you weigh. I saw how thin that Camden fellow was. I'm just a little leery about the two of us on there at the same time."

"Alright, smart guy. See ya at the top." Tom climbed and followed the bend of the ladder as it curved backward and outward, away from the shear wall, then upward again under the overhang of the cliff. Reaching the top, he saw light coming in through a small circle area. It wasn't until he moved the brush out of the way, and ascended out of the hole, that he realized the hole was in the side of a tree; A tree that had been hollowed out and used for espionage.

"Glad you made it out." Tom turned to see Camden sitting under a tree.

"This is for you," Camden said tossing the package.

TWENTY-ONE

The black truck with dark tinted windows slid to a quick halt in the open parking lot of the car wash in Margate, Florida. The sound of two car doors being shut echoed off the brick wall. Agents Calvin Rust and Terry Reos looked around at the open area where three federal agents were supposed to have been on a high profile stake-out. The off street was quiet, but the main road had cars going by every few seconds. The sound of Terry's high heel shoes made a crunching sound as she neared the building's corner. She looked down to see a particle of broken glass with red liquid on it. "look at this," she said.

"What is it?"
"Looks like a broken windshield."
"What make you think it's theirs?"
"Fresh blood. Call in a homey unit."
"Homey? Agent Reos, you mean homicide?"
"Yes sir. What, you have no sense of humor?"

Rust smiled as he picked up the phone and rested his elbows on the car's door frame and roof, calling dispatch.

"Homey," he said out loud to himself, shaking his head. Agent Rust completed his call and was leaning on the passenger's front quarter panel of the vehicle. His arms were crossed, as were Terry Reos, who was standing next to him. The two agents were passing the time, waiting for the homicide crew to arrive, when a stocky man dressed in black pants and a gray shirt rounded the corner across the street. He looked up and noticed the man and woman just standing in the open parking lot.

It was Joel. He had just returned from dumping the van. He kept on walking down the sidewalk instead of turning into the yard of the Coopers residence. He knew he needed a better advantage point for viewing than being trapped inside a house.

"Sir, don't you need to contact Director Ashton?"

"Yes, I do. See if you can raise him on the cell."

Terry walked over to the truck and opened the passenger door. As she reached inside to pick up the cell phone, she looked up and saw the same man walking around the block. Instinctively, her eyes were drawn by that one split second look. As Joel glanced back at the truck, Terry noticed it wasn't just a look, but a field study, a way to absorb information in a glance. She knew. She was trained the same way at Langley, West Virginia.

•———————————————————•

"More bad news?" Tom asked.

"What makes you think its bad news?" replied Camden.

"Cause good new never comes in a package this size." Camden laughed at Tom's comment. He stood up, walked over to the cliff's edge, and looked down at the waterfall that made churning white foam at the end of the drop.

"How did you know about this tunnel? And by the way, thanks. I believe you saved our lives."

Camden turned and smiled at Tom.

"I actually had followed a spy all the way out of the tunnel and up that scary ladder to this very spot. He walked over to the edge and tried to shoot me as I came out of the hollowed tree. I guess he wanted me to fall behind the waterfall curtain. But I was quicker on the draw than he was. He now lies at the bottom of that river's bed."

"All these atrocities and you answer to no one."

"Oh, I answered to someone. Someone who knew everything. That man was the same one you answered to also, that night in the church back in Washington. That man was a Jewish carpenter."

"Why me, why this package?"

"I wanted to save a life instead of taking one." Tom looked over at the hollow tree towards the sound of rustling bushes. Steve was crawling out of the hole.

"Now that's what I call a secret passage," Steve said.

"No one followed, right?" Camden asked.

"Hey you! You could have warned us about the prize behind door number one. That first step would have been a dosey."

"I had confidence in you. Now look, the two of you are here and I was right. Now we must go."

"Go? Go where? Our car and your car are still parked back at the Swiss cheese motel."

"Not both of my cars; Only one, Now would you like a ride, or are you going to wait the standard twenty-four hour surveillance time for the last agent to leave before going back and getting your vehicle?"

"We're going with you."

"Sure we can trust him, Chief?"

"You want to wait out here in the cold?"

"Not really."

"Then let's go. My truck is just over the hill."

"Steve, I believe this belongs to you," Camden said, as he handed him a chrome plated automatic forty-five caliber pistol.

Turning back towards the hill, he started to walk up the incline. Tom and Steve both followed, reaching the top of the ridge. The three men paused and gazed down at the small bait and tackle shop. The black truck was parked at the rear of the store.

"There she is," Camden said.

"Well, let's hurry. My toes are going numb," Steve said.

Camden looked down at his hiking boots, then at Tom and Steve's attire. The shoes they wore were shiny, military, low-cut oxfords, not conducive to the climate or the territory.

"What? We didn't have time to go shopping before we left Washington." Tom looked at Camden.

"Whose?"

"Whose what?"

"Whose life is it going to save?" Tom held up the envelope package. All three men trudged through the snow drifts, slipping and sliding awkwardly down the hill.

"Zoe," Camden replied.

"Who did you say?"

"Paul Zoe!"

"The preacher?" Steve interjected.

"A Preacher not a Rabbi? I must get used to the difference," Rabbi Shearson said.

"Yes, it is funny all the names that we have in religions, isn't it? Rabbi, Priest, Pastor, Evangelist, Apostle, Prophet. Yet in truth, I mean the real truth, we all are just servants of God."

Rabbi Shearson looked over at Pastor Zoe. He stroked his beard and raised an eyebrow. Shearson like the way this young man spoke harmoniously, not lofty like his ideas were better but as if all who truly loved the Lord were as one.

"Are you in town for long, Rabbi?" Pastor Greg asked.

"I will be here till next Friday, my friend."

"Rabbi, have you ever been to a service on Sunday?" David asked.

"No, my young friend, I haven't. We have service on Saturday, the real Sabbath."

"Why not come to hear Pastor Zoe speak? He is going to be teaching on the end time prophecies."

"Now David that is something I am very interested in. I believe I would like to attend that meeting."

"We would be blessed to have you, Rabbi. See you Sunday."

•⎯⎯⎯⎯⎯⎯⎯⎯⎯⎯⎯⎯⎯⎯⎯⎯⎯⎯⎯•

The police band radio was scanning and monitoring all stations in the South Broward area. Special Agent Terry Reos handed the cell phone to Calvin Rust, but didn't take her eyes off the man in the black pants and gray shirt as he continued his walk. In her mind, she had built a composite sketch of the person who was now out of her view; His height, approximate weight, hair color, clothing, build. But what caught her eye was something else she had seen before. Special Agent Terry Reos was married for a short time prior to joining the Bureau. Her husband was of a Jewish descent. Terry had seen that jewelry before the Star of David. Joel wore the same star around his neck. It was easy to see on his sweatshirt. The radio silence was interrupted. The county unit was calling for backup and a homicide unit to report to the area behind the cleaners in the parking lot. A white van with governmental tags and a broken windshield was just reported.

"Calvin, we have something," Reos said.

"Hold on, Ashton. What is it?"

"County unit just found a white van with governmental tags about six blocks from here."

•⎯⎯⎯⎯⎯⎯⎯⎯⎯⎯⎯⎯⎯⎯⎯⎯⎯⎯⎯•

"Hello Jay," Camden said, as the three men entered the bait and tackle store.

"Howdy, Mr. Pelt. It's good to see you. Do you want the usual today?"

"No, Jay. Just need the keys. I will bring the other one later."

"Ok, Mr. Pelt. She's out back. I did like you asked and started her up on every Tuesday, Thursday and Saturday. I let her run for a good half hour earlier today."

"That's great, Jay. Don't worry. There will still be envelopes for you every tenth of the month."

"The Mrs. wanted me to tell you thanks for all you have done for us. The things we were able to do for our grandchildren sure wouldn't have happened iff'n it weren't for you."

Tom looked at Steve, then both men looked at Camden.

"What?"

The elderly gentleman behind the counter opened the cash register and pulled the drawer out, lifting the keys from underneath the tray.

"Here you go," he said.

"Thank you, Jay."

"What, you thought I had no heart?" Camden asked.

Steve and Tom looked at each other, shrugging their shoulders.

"I didn't say anything," Steve said.

"Yeah, ok let's go," Camden muttered, as he walked out the front door of the bait shop. Steve turned to Tom and made a funny face.

"Ok, a mercenary who is merciful." Tom smirked at the silliness of Steve's jest. He then shoved Steve on the back of the shoulder towards the door.

"Hey, let's not miss the ride, alright?"

"Sorry, Chief. My toes are cold. Mr. Piggy isn't going to no market and the second guy, he sure isn't getting any roast beef."

"You can warm up in the car."

"Alright, I'm coming." Tom walked out the door as Steve hesitated and looked at the old man behind the counter.

"I'm sorry. I just have to ask. How much does he pay you to start the car?"

"It's a secret young feller, but since you're with Mr. Pelt, I guess it's alright to tell. Ten thousand dollars a month."

"Wow! That's pretty good for turning a key."

The old man just smiled and adjusted his fishing hat. Tom got into the front passenger seat and began to open the envelope that Camden gave him. Inside were two envelopes. One said:

"Top-Secret-Presidential-Eyes-Only."
The other read:

"Brice Noland, Central Intelligence Agency."

Tom opened the letter addressed to Brice Noland.

<u>Brice</u>: The subject known to the agency as "Zoe", is now out of the D.C. area. New location; Margate Florida. Telecom requests further instructions.

<u>Reply</u>: The Cleaner is in route. Hold surveillance. Await orders. Christian converts to new order immense. Target to be eliminated. <Zoe>.

Tom felt queasy as he read the note. The only person Tom considered close to a friend besides Steve was now targeted by his own governmental agency, of which his own department was involved.

"Where we headed?" Tom asked.

Camden reached into his pocket and pulled out a pair of first class tickets to Florida.

"Here; Last little gift from a brother in Christ. Zoe is in Margate, speaking tomorrow at a church on Lyons Road, Find him."

I do not sense time as humans do. It is more like a videotape that can only be seen up to the part of the present or rewound to the past. I can move backward to past events that are important, or to the events of the present. But the future is only in glimpses and visions of hope. Freewill has much to do with the many paths that the future will lead to. I was still standing on the cabin porch of the Chesapeake Lodge, as I watched all the agents in black uniforms leave in their flying machines.

It was then that Xenophon called out my name.

"Septuagint, record this event. It is needed."

"Yes, my High Commander, appointed by the Lord of Hosts." I looked to my left and there, where the guardrail of the cabin once was, now faded to nothing as the White Door appeared. I stepped through, to a point in time in the past, where the event began. I saw a young man who was becoming a known drug-dealer in his neighborhood, and a local friend of his who had given himself to the Lord. The young man had told the dealer about the love of God, but all to no avail. I recorded the event of the young man being told of the love of God. I stood still in the same spot as time is advanced quickly for me. I am moved forward in years into the future of the young dealer now a teenager of seventeen.

The city streets were becoming dim as the sunset faded. I've watched it so many times, as I stood here on this corner. It spun around the Earth in what appeared to me as only flashes of time. I saw the drug dealer walking to the same spot, to this corner in front of me as he had on so many other occasions. Time slowed to the point of importance for me to record. I see the friend of the dealer. He was coming back home to the only one he had ever known, in the city where crime is always found. He was returning from a Sunday night church service that he had to take two different bus rides to get to and home from. I was able to see the natural realm of which he lives and the shadows of the invisible realm where demons tread. I am unable to fight anything I saw in the spiritual realm for these events are of the past.

"Hey Gary, how you doing, Bro?" Toby, the young drug dealer asked.

"Too blessed to be stressed," Gary answered.

"Ah man, not that same ole song again, Gary."

"Come on Toby, you know I love you like my family."

"Yeah, yeah, I know and Jesus loves me too, right?"

"Whatcha doing out here, man? You know the wealth you get out here selling that junk is never going to prosper."

"Gary, how did you get home?"

"I took the bus, you know that."

"Why haven't you got a car? Do you know what I drive? a B.M.W. Take a look at this. See this wad of cash? It's tax-free, Bro, tax-free. Now you've been telling me about this Jesus stuff ever since we were nine, but it looks to me like I am the one prospering, not you. All I have to do is stand out here and pass a few rocks, so some dumb schmuck can burn up his or her brain cells."

"Toby, you're just hurting people."

"Man, I don't make people come to me. They come on their own and they get what they deserve."
"You don't fool me, Toby. I know you. I know who you really are inside. You're a good man. You just need some direction, Jesus is the way, the truth and the life, bro."

"Oh no, here we go!"

Toby waved Gary off, stepping toward the street curb under the dim light. Wheels of a car squealed and white smoke rolled out from under the backend of a low rider car. Toby had his back to the street corner as the charging car came towards him. Gary grabbed him by the right arm and pulled him face down to the ground. The passenger in the low rider leaned out the window and pointed a gun, firing in the direction of the dimly street corner. The vehicle was turning the curve as Gary was struck by one of the bullets in the center of his chest. The young Christian was slammed backwards. His feet flew upward and his head struck the ground.

Toby turned to Gary saying,

"Get the heck off me man," before he realized that Gary had been shot and had given his life to save his. Toby raised up and pulled a gun as he looked down the darken street at a car speeding off in the distance.

"Gary, why did you do that, man?" Toby asked as his eyes started to tear. Gary lay on his back, his blue denim shirt soaked in a pool of blood that was spreading outward in a circle. He tried to speak as he fought for every breath.

"Toby, God loves you. I love you, and Jesus said 'no greater love is this, than a man lay down his life for friends."

"Gary...Gary! Ah, man!...no, not like this! No, Lord. Not like this, Bro!"

I saw the demons, Lust and Greed, as they laughed at the young martyr take his last breath. Then I saw the spirit of the boy stand up from the shell. I watched as he was carried up to glory by an awesome winged angel of the Lord. I still stood on the corner watching and recording Toby.

"I'm sorry, man...I'm sorry...God forgive me. He wasn't suppose to take any lead for me." Toby wept and repented to the Lord, holding the dead body of the only friend he knew in life as Gary.

I saw the Holy Spirit move into his being as he became a Christian, right there on the cold bloody street corner of an inner city.

Lust looked at Greed and said,

"I didn't know he was going to accept God."

"We had better get two more to take his place or Lucifer will hold us in contempt," Greed replied.

I watched as they disappeared from my view. I recorded all. Now the natural realm has faded from my eyes. It is only spirituality I see. Xenophon is appearing before me now.

"Greetings my friend."

"Greetings, Xenophon. Sir, may I ask what happened to Toby?"

Xenophon did not answer me. He only smiled.

●────────────────────────────●

"What's wrong?" Calvin Rust asked.

"Why? What makes you think something is wrong?" Terry Reos replied.

"Because you always start doing that when something is agitating you."

"Doing what?"

"That, you know chewing on the edge of your lip."

"Oh, I see. Studying my body expressions and associations, are we?"

"Well, it's a little hard not to notice."

"Mmmm, I bet."

"Get in the car. Did you get the address for the van's location?"

"Yes sir. Turn right and go up to the Chinese cleaners on the corner. Then just swing around to the rear of the building."

"It's just a habit of yours I noticed, that's all."

"Mmmm, ah I see."

"Not that I am looking at you all the time."

"Ok, Calvin you can stop there. Let it go."

"That's Mr. Rust to you, Agent Reos."
"Yes, Sir." Terry looked out the window and smiled.

●―――――――――――――――――――――●

The three black chopper birds headed to Langley, West Virginia. While on the approach to land, a cell phone rang. The man with the blond crew cut reached into his jacket and pulled out the phone.
"Hello."
"Brice Noland, please."
"It's for you," he said as he handed the phone to Brice.
"Hello. Brice Noland here,"
A few moments had passed with a lot of uh-huhs and not much really being said by Brice. Brice shut the cell phone and handed it back to the blond hair guy.
"Anything wrong?"
"I am to report to Washington immediately. Pilot, don't land. Fly directly to White House, east lawn."
"Yes, Sir, Mr. Noland."
The black chopper dipped forward as the pilot maneuvered the stick, swinging the back end of the chopper around heading west, towards Washington. Turning the other stick control, the speed was increased and the chopper quickly raised its ceiling height.
"Camden can play his little cat and mouse game, but we have plans for that preacher, and the time is now."

●―――――――――――――――――――――●

"Who's this Noland fellow?" Tom asked as he glanced over at Camden driving.

"Brice Noland is the engine in the C.I.A. He is also one of twelve."

"Twelve what?"

"One of the twelve, in the inner circle."

"What circle?" Steve asked.

"Let me start from the beginning to bring you guys up to par."

"Please do...I'd like to hear the whole story."

"Ok, here goes...Some certain leaders of this nation could care less about the country, per-say. They have a hidden agenda. The only reason they took office is because of this one belief they have. They were told to take the high positions for the clout it would have to advance the hidden agenda.

Two thousand years ago, Jesus had twelve disciples. The one who betrayed him, his name was Judas. But Judas had some secret friends on the side, the Pharisees. That hidden society has continued down throughout all history. Hidden members are everywhere in Harvard, Yale, from lay persons to the President, all part of the same cult, all with one goal."

The story Camden was telling was so intense and with such intricate detail, that Steve sat straight up and rested his elbows on the back of both front seats to hear better. This story had all the ingredients to catch Tom's attention also.

"This story seems a little far fetched, Camden," Tom said.

Camden reached into his pocket.

"Yeah, well I was part of that 'Society.' Not only part of it, I was in the inner circle. Recognize this?"

Camden pulled out a ring with a pentagram star on it. The star was in a circle.

"Yes I do, as a matter of fact," Tom answered.

"There are only twelve of them in the world."

"I have one," Tom said.

Camden looked at Tom and his jaw almost hit the floorboard.

"How did you get one of these?" Camden asked.

"I got it when Tinnimen was alive, the night I searched his house."

"Oh, so you're the same guy that got the Senator. I thought they shot you."

"No, that was me they hit," Steve said.

"I see now. You took his bullet," Camden said as he pointed his finger at Steve then at Tom.

"Yes, I did. What info do you know about that shooter?" Steve asked.

"I was told he was terminated in a café shoot out with a cop at the mall. That guy was psycho, always wore a smiley face tee-shirt when he was going to conduct a hit."

Tom turned and looked at Steve then at Camden.

"That was you?" Camden asked.

"Finish the story," Steve interjected.

"That was you, wasn't it?" Camden repeated.

"Yeah, Yeah...was I there?...So all these people are in key positions to do what they need to do when the 'event' takes place.

"Hold it, you're losing me. What event?" Steve asked.

"Listen guys, I'm just as new to being a Christian as you both are."

"I'm not a Christian yet. I've only seen an angel," Steve said.

"Anyway, even I know about the event called 'Rapture'." Camden said.

"What is that? Oh, ok, I see some sort of mass alien type exodus, right?" Steve said.

"That's it, in a nutshell."

"So, like everybody will be down here sinning, drinking and having parties?"

Tom looked behind him at Steve. Steve made a face and shrugged his shoulders.

"No pal, it won't be anything like that."

"Awe, bummer. I could have used a party", Steve said playfully.

"The 'Society' knows the man that's going to take possession of the world affairs is here on earth. The flip side of the coin is the extreme protectors will stop at nothing to halt the rise of this new world maniac.

"Why Zoe?" Tom asked.

"He is winning a multitude of souls for Christ," Camden said. "The more he wins, the less souls Satan has. Remember, Tom, these people speak and hear the voices of demons. I, too, was one of them. I was sent to take Zoe out of the equation. Now, I thank the Lord in Heaven for His mercy that saved Zoe and stopped me."

"That's an incredible story."

"Yes, but it is true. So it is also dangerous."

"Dangerous for whom?" Steve asked.

"Anyone not in the inner circle of the twelve."

•———————————————————————•

He stood on the balcony overlooking the city. The waiting was killing him. He stepped back into the living room as he listened to the silence. Then he heard it. The distant footsteps got closer, growing louder and louder. Kirk watched his door as an envelope was slid under the door's frame. He listened intently as the footsteps faded away. Still not moving, just watching, he could hear the sound of his heart beating. He picked up the envelope with the orders. He knew it was coming. Miss Kelly made sure of that. His belief of infallibility had come to a short stop when he realized the top brass would do away with anyone. Even him if that was needed. He thought about how Murphy, who worked for them, was killed, then Tinnimen.

Now included was the fear factor of the threat from Miss Kelly. Kirk Dagon was smart and he understood that his rise in the political arena came fast. But just as fast was his rise, he knew it could crumble, more than ever now. He wondered what was so important, what did he know or who, that the "Society" wanted to keep him around, a lackey for a now dead Senator.

●━━━━━━━━━━━━━━━━━━━━●

"Septuagint, do not worry. The journey will unfold for all your unanswered questions very soon," Xenophon said.

"Is Toby still amongst the living?" I asked.

Again, Xenophon just smiled as he faded from my sight. The "White Door" appeared here on this inner city street corner. I watched the newly born Christian teenager as he wept over the body of his young friend. But it was all events of the past.

I was now being called to the present via the doorway of time. I stepped in and I was no longer in the past, on some forgotten street corner. I was inside a building, a tabernacle built and sanctified as a Holy Sanctuary for worship. It was a very nice place, a welcome to my being as I saw a man standing up to give heed to another speaker. I recognized him. He was the one I had seen in the diner in Washington. The young evangelistic minister, named Zoe, which Rejoice and Glee took me to see. The same man Zolan tried to eliminate by influencing the natural realm via the use of an assassin. I watched as Zoe began to speak about the point of time known to them as the tribulation period. Pastor Zoe began to preach his sermon from the Gospel of St. Matthew, chapter 24 and verse 13.

"But he who stands firm to the end will be saved, and this gospel of the kingdom will be preached in the whole world as a testimony to all nations, and then the end will come." He then paused and stopped at the verse, 'Let those who are in Judea flee to the mountains.' Now, the only place I know of as a safe haven when these horrible events begin is Sela, which means rock. But the place is now called Petra, just south and somewhat east of the Dead Sea, in one of the most inaccessible places on Earth. Conformed in a deep basin high in the mountains, it is surrounded on every side by granite. The only way to reach this ancient city is via the 'Sik'. It is a narrow mile long gorge between towering red granite cliffs. No wider in spots than twelve feet, it opens into a wider valley, called the 'Wadi Musa,' and then that goes down to the Red Rose City. The first structure to be seen is the 'El Khazneh,' a royal temple tomb carved out of the rock face about one hundred and fifty feet high. I know a lot of you folks have seen Petra but didn't even realize it. Now how many here have seen 'Indiana Jones and the Last Crusade?' I see all those hands. Now do you remember the scene where Indiana had to go into the palace carved into the rock, and then had to get to the place where the royal knight was? That was Petra."

    I watched as the people shook their heads in agreement to what the pastor was saying. It was apparent most of the people here knew who this Indiana fellow was. Pastor Zoe continued.

    "My friends, you can hide in a rock or you can be with the true rock, Christ Jesus. You don't have to be left behind. You can make a choice to be with the chief corner stone, the real rock. The rock of your salvation."

    I was unseen but I was listening intently to what Zoe was saying concerning salvation. The scripture says in First Peter verse twelve, that even angels longed to look into these things. But I was interrupted by a summoning prayer. I traveled on the wings of thought. Instantly, I was taken to where the prayer came from.

"Dear sweet Jesus, please Lord, watch over my husband. Show him the way to you, Lord. Please keep him safe from harm...Amen." I could see inside her that she was a very strong believer. Her spirit was lovingly bright, kind and gentle.

•————————————————————•

The sign read "International Airport, next exit" He made a quick turn onto the ramp from the main highway and followed it around the bend to the terminal gate.

"Alright then; I guess this is where we part ways," Camden said. The three men exited the truck. The air was cooler and the frost from their breathing was seen with each puff. Camden reached out his hand to shake with Tom. "Find Zoe; Good luck and God speed." Steve was cold and had his hands shoved deep into his pants pockets.

"Cam, thank you for the inside track, stay alive. Oh, and thanks for making the tickets first class, not coach," Steve said.

Tom and Steve started to walk away when Camden called out to Steve. As he turned to look at Camden, Camden handed him his coat.

"It should fit. Besides, I have another in the truck."

"I can't take your coat, man." Camden started to walk around to the door of the truck as Steve held out the coat.

"You sure about this, Camden?" Steve put the coat on, as Camden smiled and waved,
pulling the truck away from the terminal gate.

•————————————————————•

Cutting the wheels to the left, he made a tight turn around the shopping center building. Two to three police units were already on the scene. The truck came to a stop, and Calvin and Terry exited the black vehicle with dark tinted windows.

"You know them?" The uniformed officer asked the other officer.

"Nope, sure don't." Calvin and Terry started to walk towards the van when the deputy held up his hand in the stop motion.

"Sorry folks, this is a crime scene. You're have to get back in your vehicle and vacate the premises." Calvin and his partner both pulled out their badges and showed it to the deputy.

"Sorry officer, this is a federal case. You and your partner have done a fine job, but now we are going to have to ask you to step back momentarily."

"Ah, ah, don't touch that please," Terry said to the uniformed officer as he was about to open the door of the van.

"F.B.I. Officer, we would appreciate your assistance by securing the scene via evidence tape till prints arrive."

Terry walked over to the van reached into her purse and pulled a little box which contained one pair of latex gloves. She put on the right glove and reached into the van through the broken window. The paper was covered with a few drops of blood but the message was very readable. Terry scanned the first part of the note:

"M.& M. Affair Jamison: here is the information you requested. But then her eye and attention was focused on the next part. Joel...Top level Israeli Commando. Use caution.

"That was him!" she exclaimed.

"Him who?" Terry started to run to the truck.

"Get in the truck! Get in, get in, get in, let's go, let's go! She turned to the uniformed officer in the patrol car and yelled out the window.

"Follow us now!' He felt the urgency in her voice and shook his head yes, as he squealed the tires, backing out of the way of the black truck.

"Don't let anyone in her but forensics," she shouted to the second unit as the truck backed out of the alley.

"Where to?"

"Back to the car wash."

"What are you onto, Reos?"

"The shooter. It was him."

"Why do you think so?"

"The Star of David, the muscular build, the look he gave, the field study look. All of it."

"Star of David? Muscular build? What does all what mean?"

"The shooter is an Israeli Commando. Jamison just got the fax about a guy named Joel. I bet you ten to one odds that the guy in the gray shirt is Joel, the man who walked around the block when you were calling Ashton.

"You're sure, aren't you?"

"I am so sure I can taste it. I'll go so far as to say after seeing the driver in the van, shoved on the floorboard, that Joel did that and was just getting back from stashing the van."

"This guy may be armed to the teeth. If you're right, we are going to need more backup. If he's a commando, I don't want to go in blazing blind-sided."

"I understand Calvin, but this guy killed three agents already. Are we going to let him get away?"

"No, but we are not going to get killed, either."

●─────────────────────────●

I am called by the power of prayer, and so I am here. I am standing on the grass next to a sidewalk that leads around the bend. There are many homes here. I do not have substance as humans do. But I have the free will of imagination. I picture myself leaning next to this shady tree, and so I am. A man is hiding within this tree. He is wearing dark pants and a gray shirt. He is one of the chosen ones from the tribe of David. The sirens are growing louder as they get closer. A black truck is being pursued by a police car. Both are driving at a high speed, as they shoot out of the alleyway from behind a car wash. I look up at the man who is high in the tree. I imagine myself beside him, and I am. Someone dear to the Lord has prayed for this man. A hedge of protection was requested. The two vehicles went in different directions around the small block of houses. The police car even came to rest right under the tree of where the man was sitting. Then the black van approached from an opposite position.

"Must have got away," the uniformed officer said to Calvin Rust.

"Let's go back and recheck that van."

TWENTY-TWO

"Can I get you anything sir? Juice or soda?" the stewardess asked.

"I'll take a pillow, if you have one," Steve said.

"Ok, let me check. I'll be right back."

"Man, I hate these things."

"You scared of flying?" Tom asked.

"I'm not too keen to the idea."

"We will be in Florida in four hours."

"I miss Lori," Steve said.

Tom was looking out the window but his mind was back in Washington, at a little café. He was thinking of Marcy and a Philly sandwich.

"I'm kinda hungry," Tom said.

"Hey Chief, this is first class. You can order something to eat. I think they shut that blue curtain and feed us. You know why they shut the curtain?"

"Mmmm?"

"Because they only give stale pretzels to the others. If they knew you were eating steak, there would be a riot."

"Can't really say too much about airline food."

"Here you go, Sir," the stewardess said, while giving Steve a pillow.

•―――――――――――――――――――•

I watched as the man in the black pants and gray shirt climbed out of the tree. He cut in and out of back yards, crouching behind trash cans, and, dog houses. He hopped a few fences also, till he arrived at the back door of a certain house. Then he went inside. He was safe from harm. The 'Veil of Protection' had seen to that. I completed my task.

I was curious about Tom. I wanted to see him. And so I traveled on the wings of thought. I was appearing at a terminal airport when I saw Tom and his friend, Detective Steve, exiting from the gate. Immediately, my clothes became astounding white.

I saw it. It is the imp, Addiction. He and three other demons, Paranoia, Fibber, and Confusion, were all swarming a young teenager. Their hideous chatter and laughter ceased when Paranoia saw me walking with Tom and Steve. I drew my sword, and all four raised their arms, cowering in the corner over the teenager. I wanted to strike but I was not able to move from the invisible box. I had wondered why no living human loved the teenager. Why did no one pray? I would have gladly moved on the behalf of prayer and removed those imps. I wished someone had prayed.

"Hey, Chief; what's the agenda?"

"First, we rent a car. Second, we rent a room. Third, we get some suitable clothes for the climate and something for Sunday night church service. Then, we go get some food. How's that sound?"

"I say we get the food first and get everything else next."

"That works for me, too."

"I am glad Camden let me use his coat. Hey, he left something in the pocket."

"What?"

"I think...yeah, it's that ring."

"Let me hold on to that."

"Here you go," Steve said as he passed the ring to Tom.

Ring..., ring,.

"Hello," Tom said as answered the cell phone.

"Tom, this is Nancy. A lady named Marcy has been trying to reach you since yesterday. She says she needs to talk to you, and that it was urgent."

"Did she leave a number where I can contact her?"

"She said you can call her at her café."

"Ok, Nancy. Oh, about picking up the vehicle at Chesapeake Lodge. Better wait a good forty-eight hours, ok?"

"Tell her I said hi," Steve said.

"I heard him. Say hello for me too. Bye Tom."

"She heard you. And she said the word is gargle."

"Gargle?" Steve looked puzzled as Tom turned away and smiled.

●────────────────────────●

"May I help you, Sir?" The ticket agent asked.

"I have first class reservations for Florida."

"Your name, please."

"Ashton, Robert Ashton."

"Yes, Sir. There you are. Your plane is departing in about twenty minutes, Sir. Gate G-four."

"Thank you." Ashton picked up the small black attaché case and began walking down the terminal to the gate. As his hand slipped into the handle, the ring of the pentagram was clearly visible on his left ring finger. He wore a black pinstripe suit with a matching vest. He had a shoulder holster which was concealed from view. He had jet black hair with a touch of grey in the temples. Ashton was the perfect poster child for the F.B.I. His eyes held a sternness that was eerie to look at. The kind of eyes that looked right into the depths of your soul, revealing all your past. Arriving at the terminal gate, Ashton reported at the desk and informed them that he needed to sign the log for firearm transport. The steward understood that he was a law enforcement officer.

"Ok, sir. I just need to see your identification and then have you sign right here." Ashton opened his wallet containing his badge and credentials of Director of Federal Bureau of Investigations.

"Thank you, sir. You can just hand this slip to the stewardess on the plane and she will inform the captain of your presence."

"Thank you," Ashton replied, with his eyebrows lowered in a scowl.

The overhead announcement was made. "Flight 427, departing gate G-four, is now boarding rows one through seventeen." Ashton walked over to the small podium and handed the tickets to the airline worker.

"Welcome aboard. Your seat is number two next to the window. Have a nice flight." She handed the ticket back to him. Ashton just smiled as he walked down the ramp, thinking to himself that he wished this was a vacation and not business trip.

"Damn it, Jamison," he thought, realizing he was dead.

●─────────────────────●

Pastor Zoe concluded his sermon and announced that he was to continue the next part of the tribulation series tomorrow night. Shearson got up from the seat in the balcony and made his way down the steps to the front foyer. Pastor Greg was given the honor of leading the church in a closing prayer.

Pastor Zoe made his way to the back of the church to say goodbye to people as they exited. "Rabbi, it is so good to see you made it to the service," Zoe said.

"I am very happy that I did. You know Paul, I would like to sit down and have a talk with you about these things."

"You mean the things about the end times?"

"Yes, yes. You know, I have been to Petra."

"Interesting place."

"I am fearful that all the peoples of the world will not have much to look forward to in the coming days.

I believe this message of yours needs to be spoken in the synagogues also, not just in the churches. Have you made any time to speak to the Jews?"

"No, I haven't."

"Why not? This Gospel was for the Jews first, then the Gentiles. You should not eliminate anyone from hearing it."

"Rabbi, have you ever heard of a Pharisee named Nicodemus?"

"Yes, I believe I have. He was a member of the Jewish ruling council during the time of the Roman era, two thousand years ago."

"That's the one." Paul put his arm on the shoulder of the Rabbi and led him outside of the church building.

"Rabbi, have you ever heard of the phrase 'born again'?"

"No, I have not heard that terminology before."

"Great, let me tell you about it." Paul continued to walk in the garden of the church with Rabbi Shearson, kindly explaining and talking about the word of God, some from the Torah, some from the New Testament. But all of it was in reverence to the Rabbi.

●────────────────●

The garage door shut as the engine was turned off at the house in Margate, Florida. He locked the car door and began walking into the house. He had just crossed the threshold of the doorway of the kitchen when he was surprised by Joel, who was standing up against the wall. Joel had a gun in his hand pointed right at his head.

"What are you doing?" the General asked. Joel lowered the gun, and sighed a breath of relief.

"Sorry, General. Remember the targets I told you about?"

"Yes."

"They sent reinforcements. It isn't safe for me to be here this close. I am going to have to go. I had to wait till you got back to let the Rabbi know I was leaving."

"I am going to need one of the cars but I didn't want to take one with out your permission, Sir."

"Ok, Joel. You get in contact as soon as you are able."

The General walked out into the garage and lifted the dusty covering off the car that was parked at the end. It was a black sixty-nine Pontiac Firebird. The paint's shine was at least six inches deep with a gloss like a mirror.

"Oh, General, I can't take that. That looks like a collector's piece."

"It is. And you are going to take it, because it's the fastest thing in the south. Now get to the small airport and leave it in hanger fourteen. I will pick it up from there. I will help you make arrangements. Where do you want to go?"

"I must meet a man named Camden in two days, at a place called Lantana Airport."

"Here's the key, Joel. The red piper is mine. She's in hanger fourteen also. Be safe and don't scratch her or I'll come find you and make you pay."

Joel smiled as he jumped in and started the old classic up. The engine turned and spit. Then as Joel turned the key again, she fired up and purred like a kitten. The general opened the garage and Joel put the stick shift in first gear. The whole body of this vehicle shook with power. As Joel let off the clutch, the rear wheels squealed and churned up the street with the sound of a four barrel carburetor thundering down the road. Joel had made it to the corner of the block with no other cars in site as he turned the corner heading south on State Road Seven. A County Sheriff's unit was northbound and saw Joel sitting in the charged up classic.

"Unit three-seven-two-four to dispatch," said the deputy sheriff into the radio microphone.

"Unit, go ahead."

"Do you have a description of the suspect?" the deputy asked.

"Stand by," said the voice on the radio. Moments passed and then the dispatcher came on.

"Subject is dark hair, grew shirt, black pants, golden necklace of a Jewish star. Use caution. Subject is armed and dangerous."

"Dispatch, change my current route to southbound. I believe subject has acquired a vehicle. A black sixty-nine Pontiac Firebird, Give me a second here. I have to find him again."

●─────────────────●

The black chopper came in towards the White House and the clearance was given for landing. Brice looked down out the window as the chopper came to a rest on the White House lawn. "Don't wait here. I don't want you to be viewed by all the political eyes," Brice said to the man with the short crew cut.

"Fine with me, Bloke. I don't particularly care for this sort anyhow."

"This is going to be a long meeting. I will call you. Take the chopper back, get to the private jet and wait for me there."

"Where we headed?"

"We intercepted a satellite coded message from Camden that he was meeting in Lantana, Florida with one of the top key people in the group of E. P's."

"E. P's?"

"Extreme Protectors. Now get going."

"Yes sir, mate." As the chopper lifted off the ground, crew cut guy commented to the chopper pilot. "You know bloke, someday I am going to axe that nasty chap."

•─────────────────•

The door was opened, so he entered. His pace, quick but silent as he walked on the deep blue carpet right up to the rich mahogany desk where the secretary was sitting. She was on the phone with her back to him. He coughed to acknowledge his presence but she held up a finger, not even turning around to look at him. Brice Noland placed his hands behind his back as a trained soldier would. He looked straight ahead at the bright white walls of the inner office, gazing at the pictures of the past era of history. A few moments had passed and then she turned and faced him.

"Good afternoon, Mr. Noland. He is expecting you."

"Thank you," he said, as he entered the office.

The golden presidential seal on the floor was brightened by sunbeams shining in a downward glow through the open window.

"Ah, good morning, Brice," said the President.

"Good morning, Sir."

"Brice, we have a problem and I want it taken care of right away."

"What problem, Sir?"

"I have it from another little birdie, that Kirk Dagon is about to become a rabbit. Find out why. And do it now."

•─────────────────•

The morning had come as most do, never enough time to sleep in. The little rap on the door to see if you're awake, then those words asking the same question every time, letting you know it is time...time to get up and do it all over again.

"Room service," the hotel maid said. But he was still sleepy. His spirit felt drained of all energy. Pastor Zoe did manage to sit up. He saw his Bible lying on the dresser. It was opened to the passage he was reading the night before. He sat on the edge of his bed and rested his elbows on his knees, burying his face into the palms of his hands. The rap on the door sounded as the key was heard twisting in the lock. The door starting to open.

"Room service."

"No, no, please come back in a little while," Zoe said, lifting his face up to look at the door that was slightly ajar.

"Ok, sorry. I'll come back later."

"Thank you and God bless you," he shouted as the door shut. He looked down at the blue carpeting. The cheeks of his face were still buried in his hands, his elbows on his knees. "Dear Lord, please rejuvenate this tired man. The spirit is willing but Lord, my flesh is weak." Looking over at the foot of the bed, he slipped on his slippers with checkered squares. Zoe reached for the red checkered matching robe that lay on the edge of the bed and put it on also. The room was comfortable and the bed was the one thing he really didn't want to leave just yet. He mustered enough energy to walk over to the dresser and look in the mirror. He leaned in close, using the index finger of his right hand. He pulled the skin down under his eye revealing his entire eyeball. He stepped back, opened his mouth and gave a quick gaze at his tongue and hair. He turned to his right, glancing at his middle-aged body in the mirror. "Ok, so I'm not twenty anymore," he said aloud to himself. When Zoe had left the prayer meeting service, he had been obedient to the scriptures. He preached faith, laid hands on the sick and casted out devils, in the name of Jesus. A report of all the healing had finally descended to the lower regions of Hades, where Rokon was overseeing the torturing of unsaved spirits. Rokon turned to see one of the many demonic spirits that had returned via the gateway to the place of Hades.

"What are you doing back here, Addiction?" Rokon was a giant in comparison to everything in dungeon of Hell. His hands alone were able to pick up all the objects of the imagination. The six-foot soul of a man was but the size of a tea cup in his hand. A three-foot imp was but a flea to him. The imp moved back cowering.

"Zoe!" The word alone had power in it. Rokon turned his powerful muscular body to the side as if the word itself had struck him on the face.

"Aaaaaaahhhh! Why did you use that name?" Rokon was fully aware what the name meant.

"Zoe is the one who cast me out," the imp replied.

Rokon was jarred and stretched out his enormous bat wings as the imp said the word 'Zoe' again.

"I have to give an account of why you are back here. The Dark Lord, is not going to be pleased." His voice thundered throughout the blackness of the nether regions.

Inside the cage, he watched in bewilderment as it began to happen again. He was a skeleton with no eyes but yet able to see, the muscles were first, coming back at an incredible speed in no time. Then the skin growing from the shoulders first, moving down to the tips of his fingers; All of it, it was back. He was alive. He reached for the cage as he heard the rumbling. The rumblings from under his feet were the sounds of his sins growing louder and louder, turning the coal black ground to a glowing red cinder. Then it happened again, just as he looked up to see the cage across the way...the glowing red cinder burst into an engulfing flame. The coal black floor on which he stood was now a furious fire. The searing heat of flesh melted upward. The smell of cooked flesh. Yes, he was alive only to feel a daily resurrection of pain for all eternity. He could not faint. There was no room to even fall down in the small confined cage of which he stood. Murphy cried and cursed the day he was born, wishing now he had accepted the gift of salvation from God, Jesus Christ.

Rokon turned and laughed at the torment of souls in the darkness. Their pitiful screams for mercy had no effect on him. He then turned back towards the imp, Addiction. Rokon's yellowish serpent eyes squinted. "I have no room for you, but an assignment I do. Go seek out Doubt. Tell him I command him to destroy the faith of Zoe. Go now before I change my mind and keep you here."

"Yes, mighty Rokon," the imp squealed. As it turned to depart, Rokon picked him up by his tiny tail.

"If you do not do as I ask, I will see to it that your punishment is enforced by me personally."

"I understand, Rokon, I understand."

Rokon let him go as he exited the gates of Hell into the outer darkness. The imp traveled on thought and found Doubt. He had explained everything and even added to the story, a lie to get Doubt going quicker.

"Yes, Rokon said you must go and destroy Zoe's faith. If you don't, Rokon said he will come and get you and torment you for all eternity."

"Is that the right?" Doubt asked the imp adding, "But aren't you a product of the devil?"

"Yes, I am."

"Isn't he the father of lies?"

"Yes."

"You are a liar, too."

"Yes, but do you want to chance it with Rokon? I can go and report to him if you like."

"No, I will do it because I am good at it. Asking questions to make them believe in me...I mean have 'Doubt'. He grinned a wicked smile as he knew what he was saying. Doubt was not a power demon. But he was a 'spiritual wickedness in heavenly realms.' Only a few, even in the spiritual world, knew of his position. He himself liked to keep it hidden. The imp did not care what Doubt's reason was as long as he was doing it. His only thought was no Rokon, no torture.

●────────────────●

Paul Zoe turned his body around to see the other side of his profile in the mirror. "Nope, definitely not twenty anymore," Zoe walked over to the bathroom and turned on the shower letting it run. The steam quickly filled up the bathroom as he entered.

Doubt appeared. His being was like a man but not as contorted as the other angels who were changed during the fall of Lucifer. He had horns of short nubs on the forehead and his beauty was taken from him. Now his appearance was grayish. He remembered having a beard but now all that remained was a goatee on his chin. His once beautiful hands now were enlarged and bony. His fingertips were now pointy, not rounded. His voice that once sung the ancient of praises, now only spoke in raspy whispers. The whispers were the weapons of his new position.

"Are you sure you're doing what God wants you to do?" Paul barely heard the voice but it was there.

"Did you really hear God? Look at yourself, mid thirties, no family, hopping from church to church, living the life of a vagabond. Are you sure you're called to the ministry?"

Paul had heard the questions in his head, just as he was putting shampoo in his hands and beginning to wash his hair.

"Don't you think you're feeling old?"

Paul finished his shower and wrapped towel around his waist after drying off. The mirror was now foggy and he walked over to the dresser, combing his hair straight back.

"See that, you're going bald. Look, look at the corners of your head."

Paul leaned forward and touched the temples of his head. Good, Doubt thought, now I know he is hearing me.

Zoe walked into the bathroom, lifted his arms, put on some deodorant, splashed a shake of baby powder into his hands and patted his chest.

"See that? See that word, (Baby) You could have fallen in love, settled down and had kids. But no! No baby for you. 'Cause you're running around from place to place trying to get the people to hear a two thousand year old fairy tale."

"Stop right there!" Zoe shouted, breaking the tranquility of the room, all but the voice of Doubt talking in the spiritual realm. Doubt had been acting casual and was leaning against a wall. But when Zoe shouted, fear shot throughout his being. Zoe was tired when he had awakened, but now he felt refreshed. His mind was alive. Zoe thought that the questions were just questions he heard in his head, until Doubt made the mistake of calling the Gospel, the 'good news', a two thousand year old fairy tale.

Now Zoe realized that he was under a spiritual attack. He knew his best weapon was the Word of God. He stopped what he was doing and walked over to the dresser and picked up the Bible.

"Spirit of Doubt, I bind you in the Name of Jesus." Doubt was still leaning against the wall when Zoe spoke the words of faith. Suddenly, in the spiritual realm, a beam of light pierced the room from the ceiling over which Zoe stood and two angels of God appeared—Defender of the Faith and Sword of the Spirit. Doubt wanted to leave now. The glory of the two angels was too overpowering, but he could not. One of the angels of the Lord reached into the palm of his hand and pulled upward as if he were pulling an invisible string but it was visible. Visible to the angels and visible to Doubt who was now trembling with great fear. The angels grabbed him and bound him with a cord of truth. Zoe spoke as if he were able to see the whole event.

"Angels of the Lord most High, do His will; Amen."

Zoe sat back down on the edge of the bed, unfolding his hands which were now clasped in prayer. He placed his face back into the palms of his hands as he had earlier, looking down at the deep blue carpet.

He crossed the deep blue carpet walking towards the door. He looked down briefly only for a second as he walked over the golden presidential seal on the floor. Reaching for the door handle with his left hand that had the pentagram ring on it, he turned towards the President.

"Don't worry Sir, I am right on it. Mr. Dagon will see things our way. I promise you that."

"Just take care of it. Good day, Brice."

"Good day, Sir." Brice walked out of the oval office and into the secretarial wing. Reaching into his pocket, he opened a pill bottle and swallowed two pills.

"Mr. Noland, are you all right?"

"Yes, yes. Just a little headache," He leaned down, removed a paper cup and filled it from the purified water cooler. Brice chugged the water and crumpled the cup, throwing it into the small wastebasket.

TWENTY-THREE

The sixty-nine Firebird was now heading east on Atlantic Boulevard from State Road Seven. Joel looked down at the gas pedal made of chrome, shaped in the design of a giant big foot with toes. Turning right at the light, Joel headed south into the boundary lines of the city of North Lauderdale.

Federal Agent Calvin Rust had heard the radio call when the Margate unit had asked for a description of Joel. He also heard the suspect had now acquired a vehicle, an old, almost one of a kind vehicle.

"Dispatch."

"Dispatch, may I help you?"

"Dispatch, this is Special Agent Rust, Federal Bureau. I need an all points bulletin on a black sixty-nine Firebird anywhere within the Broward County area."

"Dispatch to Federal Bureau, that is affirmative."

"Attention all units, be on the lookout for vehicle, make Pontiac. Year sixty-nine. Possible suspect involved in shooting deaths of three law enforcement officers. Suspect is considered armed and dangerous. Use extreme caution. Notify dispatch or supervisor immediately. That is all."

●────────────────────────●

"Hey Chief, Let me ask you something."

"Go ahead."

"Now you paid for the food. Camden paid for the tickets. How come I'm stuck with the bigger bill for the clothes and luggage?"

"Just lucky I guess," Tom said, adding, don't drop that. It has the glass souvenir of the Florida snowman in it."

"Did I pay for that too?"

"Whine, whine, whine. I should have let you sleep on the plane and not have awakened you when we landed. I believe the next stop would have be Panga-Panga."

"Panga-Panga? Where's that?" Steve asked.

"Somewhere far away, where I wouldn't hear you whine."

The bellhop opened the room and rolled the cart in. He opened the closet door, took the luggage off the cart and hung up the garment bag.

"Tip the man," Tom said. Steve smiled as he pulled out a dollar and handed it to the bellhop.

"Maybe I should have gone to Panga Panga. What's the chances we find Zoe before the hit man does?"

The bellhop said, "Thank you," as he shut the door to room 776. He was stepping backwards when he bumped into the gentleman leaving his room next door.

"Oh, I am so sorry," said the bellhop.

"That's ok, no harm. Is my tie on straight?" He brushed it down and straightened it out.

"Yes, Sir. Looks very good and that's a nice tie."

"Well, thank you. Will you let room service know they can come and clean the room now?"

"No problem, sir. I'll let 'em know personally."

"Thank you."

He started to sing a little song as he walked into the elevator.

"Bless the Lord, oh my soul, and all that is within me. Bless His Holy Name." The elevator doors closed as the lights flashed 6...5...4...3...2...1...ding. He approached the front desk and spoke to the clerk.

"Excuse me, do you have any messages for me? Zoe, room 777?

"Yes Sir, just one." The clerk handed him the note.

"Well, I prayed while we were on the plane. I asked the Lord to help us find him."

"Lauderdale is a big place. Lots of hotels."

"Yeah, but we know he is here, close to Margate, right? So we are close to Margate. Get the phone book and find every church in the area. Make a list and let's start calling."

"Ok, Tom."

"Now that didn't sound too encouraging, Steve."

"I have an idea. Let's make these calls from the pool side with some of them little funny drinks with the umbrellas."

"You really hate me, don't you?" Tom asked.

"What are you talking about?"

"You know what Lori would do to me if she even thought I let you get near a Lauderdale pool?"

"Second thought, let's order a pizza and some cokes. Looks like a long night in a hotel room."

The horn beeped twice and then the hanger door opened. Inside was the small airplane. Joel pulled the car in and parked it to the left of the plane.

His name was Cody Dunn. He had served under General Cooper and was one of the best combat fighter pilots in Korea. He wore tan pants and shiny black shoes. He had the appearance of a pilot. You could tell he hadn't shaved in a day or so from the stubble on his face. The sleeveless tee-shirt he wore had grease stains from working on the plane. When Joel pulled into the hanger, he removed a red cloth from his back pocket and wiped his hands.

"Hey, how are you doing?" he asked, as he extended his hand. "Name's Cody...Cody Dunn. The General called. Said you was coming."

"You my ticket out of Broward?"

"Yeppers, me and Maple."

"Who's Maple?"

Cody moved back from the passenger door, so Joel could get a better look at the plane parked in the hanger.

"That's her."

"Ah, just why do you call her Maple?"

"Because she starts off slow, then pours out quick and it's sweet."

"I see."

Cody walked over to his desk and sat behind it. He put his feet up and leaned back in the chair. He took a cigarette out of the drawer and put it in his mouth. Joel walked over to the desk where Cody was.

"What time you want to leave?"

"Now."

Cody reached in the drawer and pulled out a small chrome plated gun and pointed it at Joel. Joel was shocked that he was taken off guard. His mind was flooded with all kinds of thoughts. He knew he still had his bowie knife in the small of his back.

"Aren't you forgetting something?" Cody asked.

"What?"

"The General's keys to his car. He told me to kill you if you put a scratch on it."

"Is that what you're going to do, kill me?"

"What, with this?" Cody pulled the trigger and the top of the gun popped up, revealing a small flame from a lighter.

"Don't think so, but I will take the General's keys."

Joel took in a deep breath and let out a heavy sigh. Reaching into his pants, Joel handed the keys to Cody, who then opened the desk drawer and dropped them in.

"So, where am I taking you?"

"Lantana airport."

"Cool, no sweat, Have you ever skydived before?"

"Yes, Israeli Air Force."

"You know, I thought I detected an accent. You might want to change before we go."

The garage door opened as the car waited in the driveway. When it opened fully, the car moved slowly forward into the empty space. Rabbi Shearson exited the vehicle from the passenger side as his daughter Sandra locked the car door with a remote key.

"What? The crime is so bad, you need to lock the car in a locked garage?" Rabbi Shearson asked.

"Yes Papa, better safe than not. Now, shall we go in?"

"Yes, yes, lead the way. I want to thank you for picking me up from the services last night and for taking me to all the wonderful places today."

"I am glad you enjoyed it, Papa. Which place did you like best?

"I believe the Lion Country Safari was very nice."

Across the street, near the car wash, a black suburban truck with black tinted windows was parked. The black alleyway faced the open street and the house of the Coopers.

"You saw that, right?" Agent Reos asked.

"Yes, I did. One black B.M.W. coming home," Calvin replied looking through the binoculars at the license plate.

"And Johnny, what do we have for our guest today? We have a tag number of three-three-two, David, lima, alpha."

As special agents Calvin Rust and Terry Reos were watching the Shearsons pull into the Cooper residence, the radio silence was broken by a call coming from the Broward Sheriff's communications office.

"Dispatch to Federal Bureau, unit twenty-nine." Terry looked over at Calvin, setting the pad and paper down in her lap. Calvin lowered the binoculars turned toward Terry.

"Answer that."

"Federal Bureau, unit twenty-nine, go ahead."

"At approximately zero-nine hundred hours, a call was received. Black sixty-nine Pontiac Firebird was seen entering the Ft. Lauderdale Executive Airport."

"Ten-four dispatch, we copy," Agent Reos said.

"Think that is our man?" she asked.

"I'd bet you a weeks pay it is," Calvin replied. Calvin set the binoculars down on the seat and took a sip of coffee from the paper cup. He opened the driver's door and dumped the rest out.

"Get your seat belt on," he said.

"It's on, it's on, let's go." Calvin put the truck in drive and mashed the gas pedal. The black truck flew out into the road as he cut the wheels sharply.

Kirk Dagon turned the steering wheel to the left after the light turned green. The red and green decorations along street on all the lights made the city look festive. He was slowed down by an older car driven by an elderly woman. He could tell from the way she leaned forward she was up in her years. The woman reminded Kirk of his own grandmother.

The memories flooded his mind like a dam, breaking and covering a valley. The smells, the sounds...he heard and saw it all in a flash. The middle class home back in Norfolk Virginia. All his family sitting at the dinner table, his brother, his sister, mother and father and his grandmother. He could picture the cooked turkey, honey basted, the sweet potatoes and the homemade cornbread. They all held hands to pray. Prayer he thought, he had almost forgotten what prayer was. He didn't put it down but he just never really accepted it as real either. Yet, the memory flooded his mind anyway. His grandmother prayed. He wondered if the little white haired lady in car in front of him prayed also.

Honk!...the sound made him look up into the mirror. Then he realized that the light had turned green. The elderly lady had completed her turn. Kirk was all alone, in a city full of people. And for the first time in his life he knew it. Kirk drove down the snow covered street, passing the church that Pastor Zoe had held a revival at. Kirk looked, only seeing a lone man crossing the street, getting into a car. He was unaware of the eyes that were watching him. The invisible eyes were of seven angels who stood guard on the footsteps of the Church called upon by Pastor Paul Zoe to lead the lost into the house of God. To beckon the poor at heart, to reach out for damned, to give a notice of clemency.

Kirk wanted to stop and go into the church, but his mind was weighed with the guilt of sin. He was at the "Melting Pot", the night he assisted the late Senator Tinnimen use a poniard dagger to kill officer Murphy. He felt remorse from his nights in a college sorority when he went along with friends to parties that ended up in orgies and then finally to his demise, joining the society. The cult he learned about in college, drinking the blood of innocent and pledging his life to the immortal being, an angel named Lucifer. The shame was a burden he knew; A weight he didn't want to carry.

Brice Noland exited the gates of the White House lawn, walked towards the corner intersection, and hailed a cab. He entered the speed dial number on the phone and waited.

"Hello," said the voice in an Australian accent.

"Dagon is done. Do it now!"

"Hey Mate, I am not near there. You told us to head back to Langley, remember?"

His voice rose.

"Well tell the pilot to turn around. Use the tracker to get close enough and do it. NOW!"

"Yes Sir Mate. I'll get right on it." His accent was heavy but the blond crew cut guy was ticked off at taking orders from this man he considered a pencil neck. "Go back," he yelled at the pilot. The noise from the chopper blades was loud and the pilot wasn't clear on what he said.

"What?"

"We have to go back."

"Ok," he said, shaking his head as he banked the stick to the left, swinging the tail end of the chopper around to head back to city.
Mr. Crew Cut reached into his pocket and pulled out of a pair of silver framed, blue-tinted sunglasses and hid his eyes.

The traffic was flowing moderately at the departure and arrival gates in front of the Ft. Lauderdale airport. A tall man walked out from inside when the automatic sliding doors opened. He looked to the right then to the left, flagging down the local cab.

"Where to, Bub?"

"The name's not Bub; Local car rental please."

"Hey, no offence; that's just the way I talk. It's the Jersey in me. Know what I mean?"

Ashton looked at the heavyset man, observing his clothes. He wore a white tee-shirt with a green fish on it, an advertisement for some hole in the wall nightclub. He had on a brown cap and dark blue uniform pants. Ashton's expectations of Florida grew dimmer by the second. He considered this short trip with his new friend a bit agonizing. Ashton was polished and coordinated, articulate and eloquently presented. He was a man of dignity and had expectations. He was used to being around high society. He was repulsed by the short trip to the rental car parking lot. The cabby turned in the parking lot of Avis and neared to the front door.

"There you are, Bub." That'll a be seven twenty-five."

Ashton handed him a ten, not having any smaller bills on him. He slammed the door.

"Keep it."

"Hey, thanks," he said as drove off.

Ashton felt something hit is nose. He looked at the sky and felt some raindrops fall upon his lips. "Huh, sunny south Florida," he said to himself as he walked into the building. The front desk clerk was a young girl, maybe about nineteen or twenty. She was blond, her hair was pulled back into a ponytail. When Ashton walked in, she smiled greeting him.

"Hello, welcome to Avis car rental, How may I help you?"

"I'd like to rent a car."

"Small, mid or luxury, Sir?"

"Luxury."

"I think we can take care of that. Now if you would just fill out this form for me. How long will you be needing the rental?"

"Day or two."

"Let me just type that in for you, and I'll need to see your driver's license, please."

Ashton reached inside his wallet and handed it to her. She looked up at Ashton, and smiled then quickly looked at his license again. Ashton looked out the huge glass window, and put his hands in his pockets, leaning on the counter.

●─────────────────────────────●

"Is it always this dreary?" Calvin turned into perimeter road of the airport. He drove rapidly around the curve to the north side of the hangers. While he passed an open hanger, he saw a deputy standing near a desk. Inside the open bay, was a sheriff's helicopter.

"Calvin, I don't think our guy is going to be hanging out with the local yokos." Terry said.

"Hey, that's not nice."

"Sorry, I am just a little bit in a hurry here, ok?"

As they drove on down the street, they looked in between all the hangers and in the small parking lots. Calvin looked over at the runway where he saw a plane taxing down the strip.

"Two men were in that plane, right? Not one?"

"Yeah, two."

"Did you see the call letters on that plane?"

"No. But it did say Maple on the side of it."

"What hanger did that come out of?"

"I think that one on the end. Yeah, the inside bay door is opened."

"Let's go see who owns that plane."

"They are still sitting on the runway."

"LOOK! There's the Firebird. That's him. That was Joel."

Calvin cut the wheels and turned the truck around as he headed back the same way he came. The plane he was after was on the other side of the fence and it was clear he was about to leave the ground.

"Federal Bureau, unit twenty-nine to dispatch."

"What are you doing?" Terry said as she looked at Calvin.

"Dispatch, go ahead unit twenty-nine."

"Requesting a poppa unit from your district. Need clearance a.s.a.p."

"That is a ten-four. Chopper unit in district is clear."

Calvin had just pulled up to the hanger when he saw the pilot and co-pilot start to run out of the hanger to the chopper. Another deputy, sitting at the desk, stood up when Calvin approached the hanger in such a swift manner.

"You can't come in here, sir." The deputy held his hand out in a stop position. Calvin raised his badge showing it to the deputy.

"Federal Agents. I made the call for this run."

Calvin continued through the hanger out to the chopper. Terry followed but Calvin turned to her.

"Stay with the truck. I will need you here."

"What are you doing?" Terry yelled over the noise.

"Stopping a take off."

The plane was now at the end of the taxi road and had just turned onto the runway. The clouds were grayish towards the south.

"Looks like a little rain south of here," Cody said. He adjusted his headset and spoke into the microphone.

"C-Q-4-9-2, to tower requesting clearance."

"C-Q-4-9-2, you are cleared for take off," relayed the air traffic controller. Cody pushed the throttle forward, increasing the speed. The plane was heading down the runway when the traffic controller received a new message from the authorities.

"Tower to C-Q-4-9-2."

"Go ahead tower," Cody said.

"Abort take off, repeat abort take off." Cody was already past the point of no return due to the speed he had gathered. Just as Cody had lifted his wheels off the ground, the sheriff's chopper had appeared at great speed, narrowly missing him by inches as he continued lifting higher and higher.

"What the...?" Cody shouted.

Joel looked as the chopper flew by and started to turn around. The chase was on.

Joel now held a gun at Cody.

"It's not a lighter."

He reached into his jacket pocket and pulled out a stick of gum. He felt good whenever he wore his blue blazer. He looked at the note the desk clerk handed him. His last name was on the outer envelope, the name he had used for so many years...'Zoe'. When he opened it and unfolded the paper inside, time seemed to slow down like a pendulum of a wall clock swinging away the seconds. He felt every heart beat within him. His breathing increased as he looked around, searching for someone, anyone who might be looking for him. His eyes began to tear. A flood of emotions came back to his mind. The feel good feeling was gone. In a flash, it was all erased. Now his mind was back at a place he didn't want to remember, to a person he wanted to forget. But someone else knew too. He was no longer standing on the curb of a hotel but was somewhere on an inner city street corner, hearing the voice of the past. Gary's voice, quoting Jesus with his last breath..."No greater love is this than a man lay down his life for friends."

He realized someone in this town was aware. He tossed the note in the trashcan. As Zoe walked away, the polished metal lid of the trash can swung back and forth and with each swing, the note now laid open for all to read..."Happy Birthday, Toby."

●━━━━━━━━━━━━━━━━━━━━━━━━━━●

"Alright, move the chopper in."

"You want me to circle or fly straight?" the pilot asked.

"Mate, just get me near that building. I need to lock a frequency on our dear friend Mr. Dagon."

"Whatever you say."

"That's it, Mate, go to the north by northwest two blocks."

"Yeah, ok. Hold it. That's his car down there."

"What are you going to do? Have him picked up?"

The man with the crew cut hair laughed.

"Picked up? Yeah, gonna have him picked up."

He took off his blue tinted glasses and put them inside his coat pocket. Out of the other pocket, he removed a small black box with a little antenna.

"You want me to hold this position here?" the pilot asked.

"Yes, Mate; Right here."

Kirk's car began to move away from the curb and speed off down the street.

"Stay whiff him, Mate."

"I'll try."

"Don't try it, do it!"

"Yes, Sir."

Several blocks away from the curb, the chopper was following high above. Mr. crew cut lifted a black switch on the box revealing a read switch. He pushed it. Nothing happened.

"Get closer!" He slapped the pilot on the shoulder.

"Ok, ok!" Kirk's car turned left and then right, zigzagging in and out of side streets, making its way to the freeway. The car increased its speed.

"Stay whiff him."

"I am," the pilot said, irritated. The chopper moved in close and crew cut pushed the red button on the black box. The speeding B.M.W. heading down the highway, exploded into a giant fireball, disintegrating the vehicles close to the blast.

Cars were shoved off the road in both directions and began to pile up, slamming one into the other.

"That's it. We're out of here."

The pilot turned and looked over his shoulder and said, "You! You blew that car up! No, no, no! I thought that was an engine kill switch not a detonator."

"You were half right, Mate, it was a kill switch." He said as he sat back. "That's not important now. Mr. Dagon is no more."

The traffic was jamming up on the freeway for miles. Sirens were heard all over the city. Half a dozen or more vehicles were involved in the speeding bomb.

Not far from the accident at the curb where the black chopper first spotted Kirk's car, directly across from the empty parking lot, stood the building. The building where the steps were guarded with seven angels; The steps that led to the house of God; The church where Pastor Zoe had preached, where the seven angels protected and gathered all who passed this way. He could hear the sirens off in the distance, even behind the closed doors. The spaciousness and the stillness of the empty tabernacle were deafening. He stood at the entrance of the inner double doors and stared at the huge wooden cross hanging on the wall behind the pulpit.

"May I help you?"

The sudden question made him jump. He turned to look at the person speaking to him. It was an elderly man with a kind looking face.

"Excuse me?"

"May I help you? Do you need prayer, my son?"

"Yes...I think I do."

"What seems to be the problem?" He asked as the two men strolled into the sanctuary down the long isle.

"I somehow lost track of who and what I really am."

"Times like these are hard to decipher for anyone, especially if you don't have leadership in your life. We all need to know the Shepherd of our life."

"Is it possible to get back to God? To really have a relationship with Him, if you have been so far away?"

"The love of God is everywhere. You just have to look with spiritual eyes to see the truth. Sometimes the things we think are bad are really for our own good. It's just that we really don't see it with understanding yet."

"Yes, I believe you're right."

He turned to shake hands and say thanks to the elderly man. But no one was there. He had just vanished. The man began to tremble. A feeling of eeriness came over him, a lingering terror. The stories flooded his mind again, especially the one his grandmother told him from the Bible. "Forget not to entertain strangers, for by doing so, sometimes you have entertained angels unaware." A chilliness crossed his neck as he turned and hurried out the doors of the church. What he did not see made him want to cry. "Oh, no. My car has been stolen! Kirk Dagon raised his arms up in frustration.

•———————————————————•

    Steve raised his arms in utter frustration, sighing.
"What's the problem?"
"What's the problem? What's the problem? I'm hungry, I have jet lag, I am three thousand miles away from my wife. I'm sitting in a hotel with my nose stuck in a yellow pages book, and every phone number I dial has some pious answering machine! Never a person to talk to, just an answering machine; And you, Chief."
"Don't."
"Don't what?"
"Don't go there."
"Oh, I'm going. You take your shoes off, stink up the whole room, and flop on the bed to nap."
"Oh man, you had to go there, didn't you?"
"Yes I did." Steve grinned knowing he was getting under Tom's skin.
"Well, that's what happens when you're the boss, Steve."
"Really? Well, I quit." Steve walked out of the room. He picked up the ice bucket from the dresser as he left.
"Good, you'll be back," Tom shouted, "Now maybe I can get a nap."
    I stood over Tom as he lay on the bed. Tom placed his hands behind his head. He was too tired to get undressed and he only intended to take a short nap. I was here again to answer the prayer he whispered as he fell asleep. He had prayed, "Dear Lord, help Steve find Zoe." Tom drifted off to restful dreams. I walked right towards the hotel door and then passed right through it. I was now on the indoor terrace balcony that overlooked the tables

and chairs below in the courtyard. I turned to the left and continued to follow the railing. Inside the small area was a soda and ice machine. The one called Detective Steve was filling an ice bucket. The timing had to be perfect. I delayed Steve, placing ideas in his head. From where I stood, I saw the man known as Zoe coming off the elevator walking this way. I whispered to Steve.

"Footsteps, someone is coming. Since you don't have any change, ask this person. Then you can get the soda."

Immediately Steve turned as Zoe had just passed the little room.

"Excuse me sir, do you have..." Zoe turned and recognized the man. "...change for a dollar? Zoe!"

"Detective?"

Zoe had a look on his face. Was this the one? Zoe wondered. Could Steve have been the one to send him the note? No it couldn't be. His demeanor is too surprised to see me, he thought.

"Zoe, is it really you?"

"Praise God, Brother, what are you doing in Florida? Are you on vacation?"

"Nooo. We're looking for you."

"We? Who's we?"

"Tom and I. That's funny, he prayed to find you. Now here you are. Where are you staying?"

"Here in this hotel." Steve started to laugh.

"Now that's funny," he said, as he began to walk along with Pastor Zoe towards his room.

"What room are you guys in?"

"Right here, seven-seven-six," Steve said reaching for the doorknob.

"And you?" Zoe pointed at the room right next door.

"You're joking right? Now that is weird."

"Lord works in mysterious ways, Steve."

"I see that. He must have a sense of humor."

"Why?"

"Why what?"

"Why are you and Tom looking for me?" Zoe asked.

"I'd better let Tom explain that. I'm just the iceboy." He held up the ice bucket.

Zoe scowled with a look of bewilderment.

Kirk sat down on the steps, staring out into the open parking lot, just gazing at the empty space where his car was parked moments earlier. He rested his elbows on his knees, as he leaned forward, letting his hands dangle freely.

"That's what I get for going to church. My car gets stolen and I get stuck." Kirk looked to his left. The city street was almost empty and a light snow began to drizzle towards the ground. He saw car lights off in the distance but they turned several blocks away.

"No cab is coming this way," he commented. Kirk reached inside his breast pocket and pulled out his cell phone. He dialed nine-one-one.

"Washington Police Department. Is this an emergency?"

"My car was stolen." Kirk stood up as he raised his voice.

"Sorry Sir; that is not a life threatening event. That is not an emergency, please hold," she said, as she pushed a button. The communications dispatch desk was in an uproar. The operator who was sitting two stations down was calling for as many units as she could gather to a major accident on the freeway.

A Beamer was involved in an explosion with an eight car piled up, smashing into the guardrail on one side and the center wall on the other.

Kirk sat back down on the steps and wrapped his arm around one knee, keeping warm and holding the phone to his ear.

"Dispatch, how can assist you?"

"My car was stolen. It's a black B.M.W."

T W E N T Y-F O U R

Cody Dunn had just pulled off the ground, elevating to a forty-five degree take-off. He turned the wings to the left to get a view behind him. The sheriff's helicopter was no match against the speed of the small private jet.

"I give up. What's the deal?" Cody asked.

"The deal is this...no matter what they say on that little radio, we are not landing," Joel replied.

"If you didn't notice, a country sheriff's helicopter almost clipped my wing."

"Cody, I have only two words for you...fly faster!"

"Hey, I told you her name was Maple."

"Just get us out to the water and head north."

"You can't outrun the radio, Joel."

"When you have nothing to lose, you don't count the cost. Now listen, Cody. I like you but I will kill you, if that's what it takes to fulfill this mission."

"The mission to stop the second rise of Hitler? Wait a minute. I heard about an elite group when I was in the service called E.P.'s. Never knew any, only heard rumors. When I asked if you jumped, you said commandos, didn't you?"

●─────────────────────────●

Inside the sheriff's helicopter, special agent Calvin Rust was holding the headset over his ears, talking into the microphone to the pilot.

"How long you been flying this bird?" Calvin asked.

"Twelve years, ten of them in military combat."

"Can you get it to go any faster?"

"Sir, that is a Lear jet we were trying to stop and this bird is for observation, not self destruction.

Besides that, they're gone." The pilot switched the radio frequency to another channel.

"Poppa unit to dispatch...returning to base."

"Dispatch to poppa unit, roger that."

Calvin laid his head back against the seat divider. His expectations were not met. He knew Ashton was coming and now he tried to think of the most logical oral report he would give.

"You said Lear jet, didn't you?" Calvin asked. Calvin flipped open his cell phone and called Terry.

"Terry, contact your old friend Mark in the D.E.A. Get a look on the homing device box for a Lear jet named Maple."

"What makes you think that plane's got a homing device box?"

"Because I know that the owner we have under surveillance bought a Lear jet from the D.E.A. auction block for a discounted price a year ago. And the drug dealers who use to own it had a girlfriend here in the States. Every weekend he'd fly up here to Florida from the Islands. But he used to run some of his little businesses inside it. Well, a friend of mine used to date a D.E.A. agent who confiscated the plane under the R.I.C.O. act. He had an informant who was on the plane and planted a homing device. The name of that plane was Maple."

"Ok, so what makes you think the device was left there by the D.E.A.?"

"They don't remove them once planted."

"Why not?"

"Do-do."

The pilot made a face. "What?"

"You know, poop. The informant goes to the head, the toilet he deposits the bug, a little circular piece about the size of a dime, into the bowl and flushes it. The sewage tank of the jet is not emptied for a long time, so maybe the bug is still there."

"How did he get it in there with out getting caught?"

"Taped to the inside of his butt cheek."

"Forget I asked."

●────────────────────────●

Clickity clack, clickity clack, clickity clack. The passenger car swayed gently back and forth as the massive train rolled down the railroad tracks. Rapping on the chrome door, a male voice said, "tickets...tickets, please."

"Just a minute,"

He picked up his coat pocket and removed the ticket. He wore black pinstripe pants, black dress socks, and black dress shoes. He had removed his shirt, preparing to shave the slight stubble from his face. The weather down south was much warmer than the cold of Washington. No need for facial hair. He stood directly behind the door and opened it with his right hand, which also held the ticket.

"Here you go," he said, holding the door ever so slightly ajar. The conductor in the white jacket was unaware that on the other side of the metal door was a forty-five automatic pistol pointed right at him.

"Thank you, Sir. Enjoy the rest of your trip." The conductor punched in the cabin number on his palm pilot organizer and handed his ticket stub back to him.

"Hey, Conductor how many more miles to Palm Beach?"

"About two hours, Sir."

"I need to catch a nap. But I need a wake up call before Lantana. Here's a twenty. There's another quick one with your name on it, if you just rap on the door to wake me when we get close to that stop."

"Yes, Sir!" he said emphatically, smiling and giving a quick bow as he walked away. Camden Pelt turned after closing the metal door. He tossed the forty-five on the lower couch bunk and threw a small hand towel on his shoulder. He walked into the small bathroom, turned on the water, and smeared his face with shaving cream.

He looked at the man in the mirror, seeing the slick back hair and the shaving cream. His sleeveless tee-shirt reminded him of Brando in the Godfather movie. So he imitated him. "I'ma' gonna make youa' offer you canna' refuse." He waved his hands at the mirror as if to say no. He even shook his head.

"Naw, I'd never make it in the movies," he thought.

•————————————•

Rabbi Shearson was in the living room of his daughter and son-in-law's house in Margate, Florida.

"Papa, are you ready to eat?"

"No, not just yet, my dear. After the news goes off, there is something I want to see." Ring...ring.

"Hello? Yes he is. One moment please," she said.

"Papa, there's a man on the phone for you. Says his name is Cody Dunn and he needs to speak with you."

Shearson rose up from the easy chair he was sitting in and walked to the kitchen. His daughter, Sandra, handed him the phone that was attached to the kitchen wall.

"Hello?"

"Rabbi Shearson?"

"Yes, that's me."

"One moment please." On the Lear jet, Cody patched the call into the headset on a private channel so Joel could talk.

"Rabbi?"

"Joel? Is that you? I can barely hear you, a lot of static. Yes, I understand. I am getting ready to watch the six o'clock news now. I was hoping to hear anything from the New Persia. My prayers are...he is not the one, but because of what happened to my David..."

Shearson eyes started to water.

"I pray his actions were not in vain."

"I will tell him. Be careful, Joel."

"I will be back in Jerusalem by Friday."

"Shalom to you too, Joel."

Shearson hung up the phone.

"Hey Chief!" Steve entered the room with Zoe right behind him. Tom sat up quickly then slowed down. He was not used to being awakened so rudely.

"Sorry Tom, but I have some good news for you. I found Zoe." Tom did not look at Steve when he came in. As a matter of fact, his eyes were still shut, as he was slowly awakening.

"Cut the clowning, Steve. You haven't even made one phone call." Steve with his arms stretched out like he was presenting a package on the 'Price is Right' T.V. game show.

"Pastor? You weren't joking. You did find him; How?"

"Can you say that one more time?"

"What? How?"

"Now you know why I call him Chief all the time."

"Alright, smart guy."

"Listen Tom, I am in the room right next door. I'm going to go so you can get yourself together, take a minute to wake."

"You're next door?" Tom asked.

"I said the same thing. Isn't that wild?" Steve interjected.

"Good evening. In tonight's top stories, NATO prepares for uprising, the U.S. President canceled talks in Geneva, and Babylon mourns King Oculus's death. In today's local news, three men were arrested in an attempted bank heist..."

{Click} Shearson turned off the T.V.

"Nothing, nothing, not hardly a word about Oculus.

"Who Papa?"

"Come on Papa, it must be important."

Shearson smiled. "It's not as important as your lemon cake now. How long will you make me wait for it?"

"It won't be long, Papa."

"What's that smell; it's not burning, is it?"

"Oh no, for Heaven's sake no." She ran to the oven quickly checking the cake.

Shearson took the cue to duck out of the conversation and make his way into the bathroom. He turned on the water, pulled a pill bottle out of his pant's pocket, opened it then took two aspirins. He then removed a paper cup from the bathroom wall dispenser, filled it with water, and washed down the pills.

Robert Ashton arrived at the governmental building, where a sub unit of the Federal Bureau of Investigations held offices on one of top floors.

The secretary at the front desk said,

"May I help you, Sir?" Ashton was tired. He really didn't feel like talking.

"I'm the Regional Director. Buzz your boss's office and tell him I'm coming in."

"Yes Sir. Right away, Sir." She scrambled to push the buttons, but somehow in her nervousness, miss dialed the number. Ring...she finally got through.

"Mr. Lutes..."

The call was too late. Ashton was standing at Sean Lutes' office door. The door was opened. Mr. Lutes wore a white shirt with stripes, a red tie and matching suspenders. Sean Lutes was the prodigy of Ashton. Sean's demeanor was the same as Ashton's five years ago. He's a totally committed, arrogant, pompous and ambitious company kiss up.

"Mr. Ashton, won't you come in?" he said.

"Relax Lutes. I am not here to scout out your territory. I'm here for operation M. & M. Affair."

"Well, I uh...I...M. & M. Affair?"

"Don't worry, Lutes, I know you don't know squat about it."

●────────────────────────●

Terry called Calvin back, and had Mark on the line three way.

"Hello?"

"Hey Calvin, how's life with the Feds?"

"Mark, I need a big favor."

"What's all that noise, Calvin?"

"I am in a chopper, about to land."

"Chopper, huh? Nice way to get around. What can I do?"

"Do you still have a bug on the Lear named Maple?

If so; I need to activate it and get a trace."

"No sweat; I can do it from here, I am in the central office, Just give me a second." The phone was silent for several minutes. Calvin could feel the adrenalin flowing. He wanted to make this arrest so bad.

"Terry, you still on the line?"

"Yes, Agent Rust."

"Terry, come back to the sheriff's hanger bay."

"I'm on my way."

She sounds upset. Calvin wondered what was bothering her.

"Cal; you still there?"

"Yes, go ahead Mark. We are on solid ground. Hold on, I am going in the building. Aah, that's better. Now I can hear."

●━━━━━━━━━━━━━━━━━━━━━━━━━━━●

"You don't have to hold a gun on me, Joel. I am here to help."

"I have a plan. I am going to give you a number. You call it tomorrow and five thousand dollars is yours."

"I don't need your money, but I'll take it," Cody said as he smiled.

Then Joel smiled. Cody laughed, and then Joel laughed at him laughing.

"Ok, what's the plan?"

"You fly straight north till you get to the barren heading being due east of the Lantana Airport, but still over water. Slow to a cruising speed of a hundred and twenty miles per hour. I am going to have an early departure."

Cody looked at him. "Are you nuts? This is a Lear jet."

"No, not nuts. Just practical. You're going to fly to this heading after I depart. So, if they are tracking the plane, I will have time to get away. You land, get away from the plane. Call it in stolen."

"Hey, that's not bad...not bad at all."

"How far away from the shore line?"

"Ten miles."

"Ten miles? You're going to swim against the currents, ten miles?"

"Nope. I have a boat ride waiting. That is why I gave you the coordinates to follow."

"Israeli commando," Cody said, as he shook his head.

"Israeli commando!"

"Calm down, Lutes."

"What do you mean calm down? Sir, if you authorized this mission, how come it didn't come to me through proper channels? Did I do something to tick you off? Are you trying to have my head on a platter?" Lutes stood up and put his jacket on.

"I'm sorry, Sir, but I am a little perturbed about this whole ordeal."

Lutes leaned toward Ashton and whispered. "Is this a cover-up or something because it sure smells like the works of something stinky?"

"Lutes; sit down and shut up!"

"Sir, I don't think you can talk to me that way."

"I can and I just did! Now understand this. I am under presidential orders to quell this whole mess."

"Begging your pardon, sir, but the deaths of three federal agents can never be quelled."

"What did you do?" Brice Noland asked.

"Whatdaya mean, Mate?"

"I mean about Dagon."

"I did like you asked. It's been taken car of. We saw him get into his car, we followed and eliminated the moving target."

"It's not taken care of...a call came back from a local dispatcher. The car was reported stolen. It was searched and no traces of the driver were found."

"None? Good."

Mr. crew cut smiled, thinking that he had done an excellent job.

"No, it's not good, you blundering idiot! Who do you think reported it stolen? And the no trace is like no driver at all in the car. None!"

"Hey, we saw him get into it, Mate."

"I don't know who or what you think you saw, but it wasn't Dagon."

"Somebody was in that car and drove it."

"Is that so? Then why didn't they find anything?"

"What you trying to say? It was driven by a ghost?"

"No, but maybe someone had a remote following close by. Maybe the driver exited out, and you didn't see him."

•―――――――――――――――――――――•

The next cab pulled up to the curb. The sky was cold and gray with slight snow flurries. Daylight was starting to disappear at the horizon's edge, giving rise to the shadows of the night. The streets were empty, except for a few cars, which could be seen off in the distance. But most every one turned long before thinking of coming all the way down to this lonely end of town. The cabby wondered if he had the right address as he slowly pulled in front of the church. "Ah yes, there he is." He pulled forward enough to see the man sitting on the steps of the church, trying to keep warm between two short brick walls that were made to serve as handrails on both ends of the steps. He hadn't looked up yet, and the cabby tapped the horn a couple of beeps.

Kirk peeked up from the cradled ball he had wound himself in. He jumped up and trotted down the step, reaching for the back door to cab. He jumped in. The driver turned towards him. Kirk was shivering. The warmth of the cab felt so good to him.

"Where to pal?"

"Diamond Tower apartment complex."

"Nice place. How'd you end up down here, You a priest or something?"

Kirk was getting the feeling back in his toes from the heater blowing directly under the passenger seat. He chuckled a little at the question.

"No, but do you believe in angels?" Unnoticed by Kirk, the cabby rolled his eyes and thought to himself, 'Oh boy, I have a koo-koo on board.'

"Oh yeah, sure pal." Kirk was intelligent and heard the sarcasm in his voice.

"Forget it."

"Hey, where are you going?"

"I said Diamond Tower."

"I know sir, but the freeway is jammed. There was a big wreck not a mile from here. The only way I will be able to get to Diamond Tower is to go around. Unless you want to wait in traffic with the meter running."

"No, that's alright. Go ahead, go around. I just want the fastest way home. How'd you know about the accident?"

"Saw it on the T.V. Wait it's coming on again. Yeah, I already seen it, Here you go."

The cabby pulled the small T.V. off the front seat so Kirk could see. Then he turned up the volume. "...mergancy and fire rescue rushed to the scene. The cause of the black B.M.W. explosion is yet to be explained."

"Oh no, that's my car!" Dagon interjected.

"Miraculously, none of the drivers in the other cars were injured, yet the traffic became congested for miles, due to the location of the accident."

"Really?" asked the cabby.

"Yes, it is. That's why I called you, because my car was heisted."

"In other top stories tonight..."

{click}. Kirk reached up and turned the T.V. off, sat back in the seat, and began to think.

"Thanks for letting me look at that," Kirk said.

"No problem." The cabby took the small T.V. off the dash, and placed it back in the passenger seat.

"Hey, I know you might not want hear this about your car and everything, but maybe it was a gift from God, you know, you not being in it when it exploded. Sometimes the things we think are bad are really good for us."

Kirk was looking off into the distance when the cabby said those words. Almost the same words the man he thought was an angel said earlier inside the church.

"Excuse me, what did you just say?"

•─────────────────•

Tap...tap...tap...

The porter said, "Sir? Sir? You wanted me to knock on the door as soon as we got close to Lantana."

On the other side of the door, Camden sat up at the first knock and had his gun in hand. He slept on his right arm underneath the pillow holding it.

"Yes, just a sec, please," Camden shouted.

The porter stood just outside the door as two attractive ladies walked by.

"Good evening, ladies." He tried to make himself thin in the narrow corridor. Camden heard him say ladies and he mouth the word 'ladies' but let out no sound as he put on his shirt and buttoned it quickly from the top down. He reached into his pocket and pulled out a twenty dollar bill. Camden opened the door and the porter removed his hat.

"Excuse me, Sir. Remember, you asked me to wake you before we got to Lantana."

"Yes, yes, thank you very much." Camden handed him the folded money, then asked how far away are we.

"Not too far, Sir," the porter said.

"Which way to the dining car?"

"To your right; Sir. Two cars down."

"Thank you." Camden handed him another dollar.

"Very welcome Sir, very welcome."

Tom walked out of the hotel room, and there standing next to the balcony was Zoe. He was looking down into the crowd of people eating in the dining area.

"Hey."

"Tom, you awake now?"

"Yes, Sir, I believe I am."

"Tom, why are you guys here looking for me?"

"We have one heck of a story to tell you from that merc Camden Pelt, you sent us to see."

"Camden...that was that brother's name, huh?"

"Quite a character he was."

"You didn't happen to leave a note at the front desk, looking for me did you?"

"No, wasn't me."

"Hummm."

Tom and Pastor Zoe both turned and looked back at the sound of the door closing. Steve was walking out of the room.

"Tom, I got a hold of the office. Nancy says she needs to speak to you right away. Marcy, the lady you mentioned to me earlier, has been trying to get a hold of you. Oh, and I called Lori too. She said you have three days to get me back or she is coming to get you." Steve addressed Zoe by saying,

"Hey, Preach."

"You're right. I won't argue that. But Lutes, there is only one thing I know we must do. That is, get this killer and put a stop to his terrorism. Now I know you understand what a 'Presidential Order' is, so I am sure I will have your utmost cooperation, or will I have to remove you and put one of your subordinates in here?"

Sean Lutes sat back in his chair realizing that he could be terminated from his job in a flash.

"Yes sir, what can I do to help?"

Ashton let out a big sigh.

"That's better."

"Ok Cody, you understand it."

"Yeah, I do. Head west till you're out of the plane then veer due north. Check?"

"Check; It was a pleasure to meet you."

"Stay safe, Joel. Don't forget to fall backwards then roll. Don't get killed by breaking my flaps on the way out."

Joel smiled as he checked his parachute straps, and gave the thumbs up sign to Cody. He removed the door. The heavy sound of rushing wind filled the cabin. Cody had slowed the jet down and set the cruise control. Joel looked at his commando watch and hit the red button on the side.

Cody gasped for a breath and flinched an ouch, when he saw how close Joel came to hitting the rear flap of the plane. Cody stuck his head out to look back at Joel. He was free falling over the blanket of blue water. Joel gave a little wave as Cody reached for the door to pull it shut. The wind noise and air speed jiggled the skin on his face, then a sudden stillness as Cody sealed the door. He made his way up the single isle back to the cockpit.

"Calvin, your Maple is heading directly inbound towards the west. No wait. Now that's strange."

"What's that?"

"Well the Lear was heading north about twenty miles out, and then turned west heading for land. Now about ten miles out, it's turned north again."

"So what's odd about that?"

"Not the direction but the speed. It slowed down its air speed, from about four hundred to one hundred, now back again."

"How can you tell that?"

"Too complicated to explain, but it has to do with the map distance and the location."

Camden entered the dining car, closing the metal door behind him. A different porter was standing near the door, holding a menu in his hand.

"Table for one, Sir?"

"Yes," Camden replied.

Camden took a good look down the long dining car. He saw one bartender standing behind a small black counter top bar, which held the weight of four elbows attached to two men, who looked like sots who had been sipping the samples since Saturday.

The dining car was impeccable, pristine. The linen was crisp as a double starched, white shirt from the cleaners. The tableware had the look of a polished mirror.

"Here, Sir?" the porter asked.

"That will be fine." Camden sat down and placed the brown envelope on the table. He quickly untied the string on the outside of the envelope to open it.

"Can I get you something to drink, Sir?"

"Club soda with lime."

"Coming right up."

Camden opened the package, and began to read the letter. His inside informant was a very reliable source. Not only was the source good at getting the correct information, she was also very much in love with her husband, Mr. Camden Pelt.

Hello My Love:
I miss you terribly. I can't wait to hold you in my arms again. I pray that you're ok and well. Cam, Noland ordered a hit on Dagon. Ashton is already in Florida. New agent, named Calvin, is on case. Your contact, Joel, has escaped with help of General Cooper. Cooper maybe able to help. I need you to hurry and complete assignment. I want to get away from Noland and I can't do so till I know you're done. He has the presence of evil around him. Please hurry. I love you.
P.S.
I sent your friend, Toby, a birthday card. Hope he likes it.

Love, Kelly.

Camden took a deep breath when he read the P.S. portion of letter. He had forgotten to tell his wife Zoe was the name Toby used now. Camden was the only one who got close enough to the information that Zoe had kept secret all these years. Camden looked out the window as the train rolled onward down the tracks, the fields passing by ever so quickly. The light inside the dining car reflected his transparent image in the glass. He shifted his gaze from the fields passing by, to the reflection of himself, sitting at the clean table, one elbow bent holding his bottom lip. Just looking, just reflecting life. Here he was. How did all this come about?

"Your club soda Sir, with a lime twist."
"Thank you."

"Are you ready to order, Sir?"

"Yes, I'll have the beef Wellington, side order of steamed vegetables and a dinner roll."

The waiter smiled, nodded in agreement, took the menu, and exited down the isle. Camden reached for the ashtray and tore the letter he just read into little pieces. He placed them in the ashtray and reached inside his coat pocket to remove an ink pen. He glanced around to make sure no one was watching him, then squirted a liquid from the pen onto the paper. He placed the pen back in his jacket. He picked up the lime and sipped the drink casually as he squeezed the lime over the paper. The acid from the lime and chemical from the pen disintegrated the paper. No smoke, no smell, no evidence.

The sun was starting its descent towards the west. The boat, named 'Dream Catcher,' was rocking in the water. The two men stood on her deck wearing only swimming shorts and tennis shoes, one in red and the other in white. They had on the same kind of watch, black-faced with a band of thick rubber-like material. Both men were in excellent physical shape. Both were dark skinned from the middle-east with dark hair. Both were members of the Israeli commandos.

Beep...beep...beep.

"You got that?" The one in red shorts said as he looked back and down to the lower deck to his friend.

"Yes, three clicks, due north."

"Ok." The man in white shorts picked up the binoculars and began to search the sky northward. After a few passes, he saw what he was looking for.

"There he is." He pointed northeast of where they were located. The driver cut the wheel to the left, and pushed the lever forward. The bubbling blue water churned and turned to a whirlpool of white water, as the powerful boat sped off, moving closer and closer to the parachute falling towards the horizon.

TWENTY-FIVE

Tom looked at Steve then turned back to Zoe. "Paul, I may not understand it all, but for some reason someone is out to kill you. Camden was the one hired to do the job but somehow God must have spared you, by touching Camden's life."

Zoe showed no fear and that alone scared Tom.

"That news doesn't surprise you?"

"Tom, I realized a long time ago that God wrote in the scriptures, 'it is appointed a time for man to be born, and a time for him to perish.' Now why would I be afraid of going home to see my Heavenly Father, the Father of my spirit?"

"Don't you think God wants you to be here, to continue to do His will on earth?"

"I trust in Him, Tom. I have seen what man's violence can do. I have also seen what the grace of the Lord can do, too."

"Alright, I told Camden I would warn you. So I did."

Tom walked away and entered the room, passing Steve.

"Think I'll make those phone calls now," Tom said.

Steve just nodded his head as Tom walked past him.

"What's wrong with him?" Zoe asked.

"Ahhh, just jet lag. Hey, Preach, what do you say we go down there and get a bite to eat?" Steve slapped Zoe on the shoulder and walked with him.

"Did I tell you how glad I am to see you?"

Dagon paid the cab driver, then he reached inside his pants' pocket to retrieve his keys. As he walked up the steps of the luxurious apartment complex, he whispered a prayer.

"Dear Lord..."

●━━━━━━━━━━━━━━━━━━━━━━━━━━━━━━━━━━●

I was hovering over Pastor Zoe and Steve, when I heard the voice of Xenophon call to me saying,

"Septuagint, go and record." I looked and directly in front of me was the White Door. I stepped in, and I was no longer in the lobby of a Florida hotel. Now I was in the lobby of an apartment complex in Washington D.C. Next to a man who was whispering a prayer.

"Lord, I don't know if you want me or even if you can forgive me. But I would like to give my heart to you. I surrender myself and my will to you."

I watched and I recorded all. I saw the ceiling open through all the floors, even the elevator as he stepped inside. Even as it moved upward, it was if the invisible realm and the physical realm had met and become one. The words of the Lord came into my being, alive, and manifesting itself into reality that the Good Shepherd knows His sheep. I saw the oil of anointing fall atop of the man who was whispering the prayer. I looked past his flesh, into his spirit and I watched as the love of God moved on him. He was being washed clean by the words of repentance and the blood of the Lamb. Kirk exited the elevator, and somehow felt all anew. I was standing next to him and I recorded that prayer. It was now sealed with the blood of the Lamb. Kirk Dagon had become a Christian.

He put the key into the door of his apartment, and started to open the door. Kirk had a strange look on his face when something on the inside of the door caught his eye. It was a blue thin wire that was held together by the copper wiring on the inside of the door. As the door was moving to open, the wire split. The explosion was heard for miles. The entire top floor of the Diamond Tower apartments was in a burning blaze. All that was there had vanished in seconds. The image of Kirk Dagon was still standing, holding a key, as if to enter a home. But nothing was there.

He looked around and saw fields of wheat, waist high. Then he saw me. Kirk was no longer in a body of flesh. Kirk was now a spirit, set free.

"Excuse me, did I pass out? I was standing in a hallway wasn't I? How did I get here?" I smiled at his curiosity.

●────────────────────────●

Joel was coming down and the boat was maneuvering to get right into place. He pulled the right handle, making the parachute go to the right, and then he adjusted to the left. He was coming in quick. The boat that seemed to be a white speck was now getting bigger and bigger. Joel lined himself up with the massive cruiser. He stepped on the rear deck, first his right foot, then his left.

"Hey; hey!" The man in the white shorts shouted gladly. A slight wind gust had arisen and the parachute, which was still falling, was now acting as a drag chute, almost yanking Joel off the boat. The man in the white shorts grabbed Joel, and pulled him inward on the deck.

"Quick, help me undo this chute." The two quickly released all the tabs that held the straps on. The chute broke free and the boat moved forward. Joel watched as it slowly sank into the ocean waters.

"Ah, the ocean, she wants you, yes?"
"Yes, my friend, she does."

●────────────────────────●

Tom dialed the number to speak to Nancy, but he called her cell phone, not the work number.

A female voice answered. "Hello?"

"Nancy?"

"Tom, where have you been? I have so much to tell you."

"Nancy, did a man, name Camden call?"

"Yes, he did. I didn't understand it, but this is the message. Society, Circle of Twelve, is meeting in rear of club tonight at nine o'clock. Club is called 'Diablo's Den."

"Anything else?"

"Yes, Marcy has called and called, trying to get a hold of you. She says it is a matter of life and death, but won't say what about, and will only talk to you."

"Tom, the Captain wants me to let him know if I hear from you. I think he is trying to justify the loss of a police cruiser you let get shot up in Chesapeake Bay Lodge parking lot. Who did you tick off? It was riddled with more bullet holes then Bonnie and Clyde's car. The boys in homicide think you and Steve got drunk and used it for target practice."

"Well, officially I haven't contacted you yet. I am calling your personal phone. So you really haven't heard from me. Bye Nancy." Tom hung up the phone, walked over to the chair next to the window, picked up the jacket he was wearing, and reached inside the pocket. He pulled out the ring with the pentagram on it, and put it on his left hand. "Diablo's Den, huh?"

He picked up his gun, and pulled the slide back to check the chamber. He let it snap back then de-cocked the lever, leaving the safety on. He put the gun in the holster, and covered it up with his shirt tail. He looked in the mirror, brushed his hair with his fingertips, and said to himself.

"Time to catch a devil."

Calvin Rust was standing inside the hanger when Agent Terry Reos gingerly walked up to him. He was still on the phone with Mark from the Drug Enforcement Agency.

"Are you sure? Then it turned. Has it stayed at the same speed and course? Thanks Mark." Calvin snapped his cell phone shut.

"Hi." Calvin smiled.

"Hello?"

"He got away?"

"He got away."

Tom picked up the keys to the rental car, as he left the hotel room. He made his way down the elevator to the dining room, where he saw Steve and Zoe. He stood off in the background until he knew Steve had seen him. Tom put his finger to his lips, as to say be quite, and then beckoned his partner to come over near him. Zoe had not noticed that Tom was standing near the door's entrance.

"Would you excuse me, Preach? I need to go to the head for just a second."

Zoe laughed. He liked Steve's candor and forwardness.

"Sure, help yourself." Steve rose up and walked away, looking back to make sure Zoe didn't watch him. As he turned the corner, Tom was standing at the door.

"Hey Chief, what's up?"

"Steve, I'm going to go check something out, at a club called Diablo's Den. I need you to stay with Zoe. Don't lose him for nothing! Understand?"

"Sure Chief, but you sure you don't want me to come with you? I mean, it is a club." Tom reached out and gave a little pinch to Steve's chest.

"Ouch!"

"Don't lose him, no matter what!"

"Ok, ok."

"If you need me, use the cell phone, and I am taking the car. Have the front desk rent you another one now, in case Zoe wants to leave after your dinner."

"ok."

Tom turned and walked out the front door of the hotel lobby. He paused on the steps of the grand hotel, and looked at the beauty of the lights, on the giant water fountain that lined the long circular driveway. He took a piece of gum out of his pocket, and as he removed it from the wrapper to put it into his mouth, he noticed the light of the moon reflected off the pentagram ring on his left ring finger. Tom was alone on the steps and said a prayer of his own.

"Dear Lord, I am not much of Bible thumper, but please help me out here. Protect Steve, and protect me, Amen."

Picking up the pace, and trotting down the steps, then out to the rental car in the parking lot.

"Thanks a lot, pal." Steve said as he turned from the front desk clerk, who had assisted him in having a rental car delivered to the hotel. He looked out the door as he watched his partner going down the steps, out to the parking lot. He rubbed his chest and said, "Ouch," thinking about the pinch Tom gave him.

●────────────────●

"Am I dead?"

"Physically, yes. But spiritually, you were just born."

"What happened?"

I observed Kirk as he paced back and forth, trying to make sense of the whole event. He began to speak to himself aloud.

"I jumped into a cab. My car was stolen. I stepped out of a cab. I came up an elevator to my apartment. No, no wait. I said a prayer in the elevator, and then I came to my apartment. I put the key in the door, then what? Oh yeah, I saw the blue wire. It separated, then, the next moment, I am standing here in a wheat field, in perfect weather, holding my ke...Hey, where did my key go? Who are you?"

"I am Septuagint, Greetings to you." As I was talking to Kirk, the White Door appeared. An angel in all white linen, with a golden belt around his waist, appeared. It was Newfound.

"Newfound, it's good to see you once again."

"Greetings to you Septuagint, I have been sent to help Mr. Dagon home."

"New... Who? Greetings? Help me, what?"

"Peace, my friend all will be explained." Kirk was still a little shaky, but when Newfound opened his wings to full expansion Kirk was filled with awe and wonder. I had completed the assignment. I had recorded the event, the record of Kirk's repentance. I know in the end I shall hand the book of remembrance over to the King.

I watched as Kirk became like a child, holding Newfound's hand and walking away. I saw the tunnel of review slowly appear, as the two slowly walked in and faded from my view. I turned to go back, back to the place where time ticks. Back to the place where sin abounds, back to the blue planet. Back to help the one called Tom.

●———————————————————————●

Joel stayed below deck. He sat at the table made of fine oak. The white tile was complimentary to the brass fixtures on the boat. He picked up the spoon, and placed it inside the bowl of clam chowder. He folded his hands and began to pray in Hebrew. He had just finished and started to eat, when the man in the white shorts came down the steps of the galley and leaned his head in. "Joel, we are docking. Is ok?"

"Yes."

"You call C.I.A. man now? No?"

"Yes, I will call."

"Ok." He turned, walked back up the steps "He is calling now," the man in the white shorts yelled to his friend.

•────────────•

Camden wrote down the instructions that Joel gave him then shut the cell phone. He reached up and tapped on the divider glass of the cab, and told the driver to head towards the marina. The driver who was heading west form the train station, now made a u-turn at the next light.

"Yes Sir. Marina next stop."

•────────────•

Steve came back into the restaurant and sat down with Zoe.

"Hey Preach, you haven't touched your food yet. What, does it smell or something? You didn't see a roach run across the table did ya?"

Steve bobbed his head to the left and right, looking under the table, for a bug that might have spooked Zoe.

"No, no, nothing like that," Zoe laughed at Steve.

"I was waiting for you, my friend. I thought since this might be the only time I get to have supper with you, that I would wait to break bread, and have fellowship prayer with you."

"Oh I see, one of them Godly thing-a-ma-jigs."

Zoe couldn't help himself but to let out a hardy laugh.

"Fellowship prayer. I could use some of that, but if it takes two grown men to break their bread, I ain't eating it." Zoe laughed again, then Steve smiled.

"Just playing, Preach. I would love to break bread with you."

Calvin and Terry walked into the restaurant, walked up to the bar, and sat at the small table for two in the bar area. A waitress in a red and white striped shirt with buttons that had quaint little sayings all over them came up to them.

"What can I get you folks to drink?"

"Two drafts. Buds, please."

"Coming right up." The waitress hurried off. Terry reached inside her purse, as the beeping became louder, when she pulled out her cell phone. She looked at the number and recognized it right away.

"It's Lute's."

"Better let me take that."

"No problem." She handed the phone to Calvin.

"Calvin Rust here."

"Rust...you and Reos are being pulled for a special assignment tonight." Calvin rolled his eyes and made a face. He was tired and after this beer, all he wanted to do was go home and sleep.

"What assignment, Sir?"

"Causal couple...for bodyguard duty. Look for Joel, Israeli commando, tonight at a club called Diablo's Den. Do you know where it's at?"

Calvin sat up straight. This was the first thing that Lutes ever said to him that made him want to work. Calvin hated the fact that Joel had gotten away from him. Now here was a second chance to catch him.

"Yes, Sir, I know where it's at. How did you come by that information, about Joel being there?"

Now Terry became interest in what was being said. She began to make gestures at Calvin saying, "What," but only moving her mouth with no sound. Calvin held up a finger as to say, 'wait a minute'.

"Director Ashton has it on good authority that a meeting is taking place there tonight." Lutes turned his leather chair he was sitting in. Speaking quietly he said, "Ashton is here, in the office. Well he is out in the hallway, getting a drink of water. So don't screw this up." Calvin made a grimace face at the cell phone.

"Yes sir."

"Oh, Calvin?"

"Sir?"

"Be careful and use extreme caution. This guy is a trained killer. I don't want you or Terry hurt."

"I understand."

●────────────────●

Tom was about to turn the corner, but I whispered in his ear, "Brake now," and he did.

The semi-tractor trailer barely missed the front end of the rental car. Tom was engulfed in the thoughts of all that had happened since the phone call that morning Steve told him about the two dead girls in an alley, on the back streets of Washington, D.C. Now, here he was, involved in a case that led all the way to the heights of the political arenas. Tom's mind was buzzing. He had killed the one suspect, a hit man with a smiley face tee-shirt that had almost killed the girl he wanted in his life. He found out that another killer had turned to God, and was supplying him with the information that may lead to the top political leaders. A preacher from no where was somehow tied to all of it. The one suspect he had in custody, a predominate Senator Tinnimen, was released on a Presidential pardon then obliterated in a car explosion, along with his chauffeur and his wife. The ring was on his hand, and it had ties, too. The society, that is what Camden Pelt called it. But the 'Extreme Protector's 'or E.P.s, who were they? How did they manage to make a hit so close to the president? Who was funding them? Tom could not stop thinking about it. He looked over and there up ahead on the right was a small park lit up by the street lights. He pulled in and stopped the car. He wanted to try to think things through. He leaned forward on the steering wheel.

"Lord, I wish I knew you were here with me."

I could not help the desire to console Tom. I let my appearance flash the Glory of White, only for a brief millisecond. Tom jerked his head up, off the steering wheel, thinking that someone had shined a light into the car. But when he rose up, he realized there was no one around.

Tom looked up toward the courtyard. He saw a young boy playing basketball. He exited out of his vehicle, and walked over to the young boy shooting hoops.

"Hey."

"Hello," said the young boy.

"You any good at that?" Tom asked.

"Sometimes? Are you?" Tom was not ready to be quizzed by ten or eleven year old.

"Not bad."

"You want to shoot a couple?" The little boy bounced the ball to Tom. He thought, why not? It might clear his head. Tom took off his jacket, and laid it down on the courtyard, next to the grass. He picked up the ball, and gave it his best shot. The ball circled the rim, and fell into the chain hoop. The young boy picked up the ball, and tossed it back to him.

"You know, its getting kinda late out here. Do you live far?"

"No, not far at all."

"Your folks know where you're at?" Tom asked as he bounced the ball and took another shot. Again it rolled around the ring, and into the chain hoop.

"My father does. Hey, that's not bad. two in a row."

Tom turned to walk away, but the kid said,

"Just one more Mr., please." Tom saw the innocence on the kid's face, and thought how lonely the boy must be, playing ball, by himself this late.

"Ok, Kid just one more."

Tom walked back to the chalked line made by a rock and the boy passed the ball to him. He dribbled the ball a couple of times, stood in position to shoot, and released the ball. It hit the backdrop and bounced up and down on the rim of the goal, then circled and fell in. Tom heard the kid speak behind him.

"Thanks Tom, for being here, I am with you, always."

Tom turned but no one was there. He looked back at the sound of the basketball bouncing on the court. But the ball was gone also, only the echoing of a ball bouncing. Tom got a chill up his spine. He walked over to the edge of the courtyard, picked up his jacket, and put it on, as he walked out to the car.

"If that was a sign, it was a good one." Tom jumped in the car and started it up, put the gear shift in reverse and started to pull out of the park. He looked over at the courtyard that was darken, but silhouetted by a dimmed light. As he turned the steering wheel, he saw the pentagram ring on his hand.

"Diablo's Den." He smacked the steering wheel.

The cab driver smacked the steering wheel.

"Thank you, sir." He held the twenty dollars up to the light, and then stuffed it into his shirt pocket.

Camden shut the cabby's passenger door then started walking down the marina, holding a piece of paper and reading the dock numbers. He stood at the rear of a huge white boat with words "Dream Catcher" written on the back. It was the correct dock number. A man in white shorts was coming around the side isle of the boat, when he saw Camden.

"Hello, hello."

"Hello? Marcy?"

"Tom? I have been trying to get a hold of you all day."

"Marcy, Nancy said you called and it was a matter of life and death."

"Tom, I was in my coffee shop and this couple came in. It was that press guy for the Senator that was killed. I read that you were the arresting officer. Well anywho, I heard her try to offer that guy a certain job, but he doesn't want it. And now he is dead, Tom."

"Dagon? Dagon is dead?"

"Yes, Tom. He was killed in an explosion at his apartment complex. Some say it was a gas leak. But I don't think they have gas stoves in apartments, especially penthouse apartments. Tom, are you ok?"

"What? Yes, I'm fine."

"Can you come over?"

"Marcy, I am in Florida."

"Florida?"

"Did you go on a vacation?"

"No Hun. I am on a case. I will call you when I get back."

"Tom?"

{click} The line was dead.

•―――――――――――――•

"Shalom!" Camden said.

"Shalom to you, please come aboard," Joel answered as he was coming up the galley steps. Camden stepped aboard. He and Joel shook hands. Then Joel led the way down into the galley.

"I have heard you're a wanted man," Camden said.

"Funny, I have heard it from my sources that you are wanted also, my friend."

"We have both made some enemies, huh?"

Joel went over and poured two glasses of Coke then sat one in front of Camden.

"I guess this is true."

"Any word on Circle of Twelve?" Joel asked.

"Yes. They are meeting later tonight at a place called Diablo's Den."

"And just why are they meeting this night?"

"You know about King Oculus?"

"Of course."

"They are going to pray to their god, for his resurrection." Joel turned his head and spat in disgust.

"Their God! The liar of all liars!"

Camden remembered that he once heard the pseudo voices.

"Yep, that be the one."

"The information you brought is very valuable. I will pay the price you asked. Where will you go now?"

"Somewhere sunny, where me and the Mrs. Can drink those funny little drinks with the umbrellas and not have to worry about black choppers or the society again."

"Michael!"

The man in the white shorts came below deck to the galley.

"Bring it."

Michael went down the second staircase to the lower decks. Moments later, he walked up with a chrome case and sat it on the table in front of Joel and Camden. Joel released the levers and turned the case to Camden without opening the suitcase.

"Thank you Michael," Joel said, as Michael left the galley. Camden opened the case to see stacks and stacks of money in large bills.

"It is all there. If you want to count it, you can."

"Joel, I believe you are a man of your word and I am still going to believe it. No need for me to waste the night counting something I know is already there."

"Good, a toast to a new friendship." Joel raised his Coke.

•———————————————————•

The black truck pulled in the driveway, followed by car after car after car. The night club, 'Diablo's Den,' was a very busy establishment. "Twenty bucks," said the young guy working at the parking lot's gated entrance.

"Twenty bucks...For parking? That's highway robbery!" Calvin retorted.

"You can pay twenty to me, or chance parking it out on the main, and getting towed for seventy-five. Maybe, if you're lucky, they'll take the whole car, so you can claim it on the insurance."

"I don't think you know..." Oof! Calvin let out a sudden breath of air, as Terry elbowed him hard in the side.

"Pay the twenty...," she said, through gritted teeth.

"Ok." Calvin handed the young man a twenty.

"Don't blow the cover before we even get in."

"Yeah, alright...Did you have to elbow me so hard?"

"Sorry."

"Are you gonna kiss it and make it better?"

"Only in your dreams."

"Oh really?"

"Really." Terry exited the car and waited at the rear of the vehicle.

●─────────────────────●

The night sky was a perfect backdrop for the royal blue lights that lit up the runway to the private airport. The glow from the tower, where only four men were watching the night skies for incoming flyers, was more than busy with unusual amount of traffic.

"Pete?"

"What?"

"Is there some sort of convention in town this week?"

"Not that I'm aware of. Why?"

"Look at this. This is the ninth Lear I've had come in, and all of them are parking at the end of the runway, near hanger twenty-seven."

"So what? What's so weird about that? They are all black Lear's. None are white."

"Hmmm, maybe it's an AC/DC concert. I heard they painted all their buses black."

"I just think that's odd."

"Q-nine-nine-four-two-one to tower. Request landing."

John covered his microphone and turned to Pete.

"Pete, switch to channel two."

"Tower calling Q-nine-nine-four-two-one. Please identify your make."

"Roger tower. Black Lear, repeat black Lear."

Pete raised an eyebrow at John.

"Copy that Q-nine, request granted. You can land and taxi to hanger four."

"...Negative tower. We were instructed to taxi to hanger two-seven." Pete and John both shrugged their shoulders.

"Q-nine, who gave instructions to you to taxi to hanger two-seven?"

A long pause...

"Repeat, Q-nine, who gave instruction to you..." The door to the tower swung open swiftly. The chief of the F.C.C., who was the boss of the boss of the boss of John and Pete, was standing in the doorway.

"John! My office now!"

"I am landing a plane, Sir."

"That pilot and plane can land on it's own. Step into my office, now!"

John made a face at Pete, like I don't know. He took off his head set, stood up, and follower the chief. Ten limos in all had pulled up to hanger twenty-seven and picked up all the guests. The drivers were all instructed to transport to one location, 'Diablo's Den.'

TWENTYSIX

Tom pulled up across the street, and watched the cars, as they came into the parking lot and parked in the rear. But on the left side, he noticed something different. Limo after limo began to pull on that side, into a private parking area. The scene seemed familiar to Tom. He had seen this set up before at the 'Melting Pot' night club. Tom watched a couple that somehow looked out of place. They were standing at the door, waiting to go inside. The bouncer was being real choosey about who he was letting in. As he watched, he noticed that the couple were both too clean-cut, not rough enough to be in this joint. Tom watched the man and woman go stand in the line. He felt in his gut that the man was a cop, maybe the lady too. Now would be a good time to have some back up, he thought. Tom left the car, crossed the street, and walked over to the line. He stood behind the man, who stood behind the woman.

"Hey, how's it going?"

Calvin turned and gave a quick once over.

"Fine, how you doing?"

"Great, great. Just heard about this place. Thought I'd come check it out. Ever been here before?"

"No, actually, this is our first time, also."

"Funny, you don't have a southern accent, like the other people I've met down here."

"We're from the north," Calvin said.

"Really? You a cop?"

Calvin turned quickly and looked at Tom.

"Yeah, I thought so..."

Calvin smiled.

"Who wants to know?"

"I don't know; Maybe, someone who's looking for a little fraternal, brotherly love."

"you messing with me, Mr.?" Calvin asked.

"No; not at all, that would be a fraternal order type of love, you know what I mean?"

"Yeah, I know what it is. You working or something?"

"Maybe, but it would be nice to have some family I could call on, in a time of need, if need be. Know what I mean?"

"Yes, I think I do. Calvin Rust, Federal Bureau of Investigation," he whispered in Tom's ear, as he shook his hand.

"Sgt. Detective Tom Allen. Washington P.D."

Tom had his left hand atop of Calvin's shoulder, who was facing him, when he whispered in his ear. They were standing under the lighted fixture, when one of the bouncers yelled out.

"YOU, HEY YOU!"

Tom pointed at himself.

"Who me?"

"Yeah, you with the ring; Come here." Tom walked up the steps to the bouncer.

"You can go in Bro." Tom looked back at Calvin and the woman next to him.

"Who is that guy?" Terry whispered to Calvin.

"One of us; A shield."

"Friends of yours?" The bouncer asked.

Tom shook his head, 'yes'. The one bouncer looked at the other, who was sitting on the stool. He looked down at the ring on Tom's hand, and shook his head, yes.

"Then they can come in, too. Hey, you two, come on."

"Believe this? He got us in," she said.

"Ok, so he knows somebody."

"Must know somebody really big," she retorted.

"Maybe the gorilla working the door is his brother."

Camden had his money and was ready for a good night's sleep. He stepped in the hotel with his shining chrome briefcase. He approached the front desk and tapped the little bell on the desk. A clerk who was placing paper in the printer below the counter, stood up.

"Yes, Sir, may I help you?"

"Room please, one with a wall safe."

"Yes, Sir. Please fill out the registry and I will be right with you." Camden filled out the card and turned it back towards the clerk.

"Thank you, Mr...uh...Pelt."

"Room eight-sixty-five."

The clerk rang the bell twice and then cupped it with his hand to stop the ringing. A bellhop, in full uniform stepped out from around the corner with a push cart for luggage.

"Mark, please show Mr. Pelt to room eight-sixty-five.

"No luggage, Sir?"

"No."

"This way, Sir." The bellhop pushed the button for the elevator. Camden looked at his white gloves and high glossed shoes. The elevator stopped on the eighth floor and the bellhop led the way. He put the key in the door to open it. Camden looked down across the open balcony at the two men entering a room. He recognized both men.

"Here, give me the key." Camden handed him a five dollar tip, adding, "Thank you, I can manage from here."

"Thank you, Sir." Camden closed the door and waked towards the elevator. He walked down the one flight of steps, which were next to elevator, and made his way around the corner, to the room he saw the two men go into. It was room seven-seventy-seven.

"Ok, Pal. Who are you and what are you doing here?" Terry asked.

"You know, you ask questions like a cop."

"Hmmm, bright boy we have here, Cal."

"I'm here to find out why the political leaders of our nation are here, taking part in a Secret Society."

Terry turned to face her partner and said, "Ok, he's a nut case."

"Oh, am I? Then why are you here?"

"We are here to...to dance."

"Dance? Yeah, and I'm Santa Claus. The two of you stuck out like a sore thumb. Why do you think I approached you? I knew you were heat. I am here alone and I thought a little backup might help."

"Listen, Joel is ours. I don't care who you know or how you managed to get us in here so fast. He is our collar."

"Joel, Joel who?"

"That's great. Pretend you don't know."

"Listen Calvin, and I didn't get your name."

"Reos, Terry Reos."

"Terry, there are ten limos parked in the back, for V.I.P. parking only. Now if you two came here to dance, go ahead. But I possess the one thing that will get me in the back room. That's this ring. And for your information, this is not about some guy named Joel. This is about the President of the United States being involved in a plot to give power over our freedom to some leader in Persia. A group called the E. P. s, are trying to stop them. Maybe Joel is one of them."

Tom walked off, making his way slowly through the crowd. Calvin looked at Terry.

"You know, he talked pretty straight."

"I know, I know. Let's go find him."

The door opened to the control tower, and Donnie McCreary came in big as life. He walked over to the north control tower seat and plopped right down.

"Hi, Pete."

"Hello, Donnie. What are you doing here?"

"Overtime; recieved a call that you guys were short one."

"Really?"

"Hey, too bad about John, huh?"

"What are you talking about?"

"He was fired. Something about almost running two planes into each other. That's what they told me."

Pete sat back in the chair and thought aloud. "Black Lears."

"Huh? What did you say, Pete?" Donnie removed the headphone set he had just put on.

"Nothing, Donnie, nothing."

Pete had a sick feeling in the pit of his stomach.

"That's a roger. You can taxi to hanger number twenty-seven at the end of the runway."

As he was speaking, Donnie spun around in the chair, looked at Pete and smiled. He held up his coffee thermos to offer some to Pete. Pete just shook his head, 'no'.

Camden knocked on the door and Steve opened it from inside.

"Well, well, well, If it isn't the duct tape man!"

"Come on, now. You're not going to keep holding that against me now, are you?"

"Naw; you lent me your coat."

"Where's Tom?"

"He went to someplace called the den."
Camden turned from the window quickly to look at Steve. "Not the 'Diablo's Den?'"

"Yeppers, that's the one."

"We have to go, right now."

"I can't go anywhere. Tom told m..."

"Right now, Steve, or you may never see Tom again."

Steve picked up his jacket and followed Camden to the elevator. Camden took the steps and Steve followed.

"What's this all about, Camden?"

"Remember those guys I told you about? The E.P.s?"

"Yeah,"

"They know about a meeting of the Society that is going to take place tonight."

"What's that have to do with Tom? Let me guess, Diablo's Den."

I followed Tom in the huge crowd of humans. The place was infested with imps and demonic hoards. My clothes were glowing the brightest of white. I drew my sword, which was flaming, and held it above my shoulder, ready to strike at a moments notice. Everywhere I turned, the yellowish eyes were upon me.

"Hey Pal, what's your problem?" A bald headed man said to Tom, who made it apparent he bumped into Tom's left shoulder, knocking him almost sideways.

The demon, who was sitting on his shoulders, was named Brawler. He hissed at my glory, which shined like a beacon lighthouse on a sea of pitch black darkness. The demon croaked sneers.

"Angel of the Most High, What are you doing here? It is not yet our time. Are you here to do battle? Who has sent you?"

Tom pointed his left hand finger at the large man in the leather vest, who had bumped into him, revealing the ring.

"What's wrong with you, Dude?" A fear came over the man when he saw the ring.

"Sorry, I didn't mean anything, Sir. A thousand pardons a thousand pardons."

The man hurried off in the crowd.

The wicked demon, perched on his shoulder, cried out.

"Join us, Angel. Is that why you are here? You have not made a decision which path to follow?"

I said nothing, but watched the imbedded demon being carried off by his physical host. The whispers of evil were all around. The demons were perplexed at an angel, following a man with the pentagram ring of a druid priest on his hand. Tom looked at the ring and wondered what spooked the guy.

"Hey, wait up," Calvin said, as he and Terry made their way through the crowd.

"What, no dancing? You must be disappointed," Tom said.

"Ok, you win. What else do you know?"

Tom looked around then walked over to the wall near the bar. The crowd was shoulder to shoulder. The music of the band was starting to play when two women had walked passed. One was dressed black leather skin tight pants, high heels, and a white top. Her hair was fixed like a model, and looked ready to walk the runway in a Paris fashion show. The other wore a dress that was red but cut high on one side. The top of the dress only covered one shoulder. She also wore white high heel pumps. Tom was talking to Calvin, when the woman in the red dress touched Tom on the center of his chest and started flirting with him.

"Nice tie, Handsome." Tom nodded his head to say thanks, but she had walked on by without looking back, continuing to talk with her girlfriend.

"Oh, smart and a player," Terry remarked.

Tom looked up at Terry's snide remark. Then he glanced back down the hallway, watching the two women as they turned walking into the washrooms. Now they were gone but Tom continued to look down the long hallway with the black wall to wall, and on the wall carpeting. A man in black was standing at the end of the hall. Another corridor to the right at the end of the hallway would have been undetected, but Tom saw cigarette smoke circling out from the hallway. Tom turned and said to Calvin,

"If I'm not back with in an hour and a half, send in the Calvary full speed ahead."

"Be careful," Calvin replied.

"Don't make me come in there and kick your butt, 'cause you forgot to come back out here in an hour and a half," Terry added.

Tom kinda smirked.

TWENTY SEVEN

The last limo had arrived from hanger twenty seven. It entered the back gate. Two men stepped out of the car, quickly rushed in under the awning, into the back entrance, and walked down the steps to the long corridor hallway. The one man put on his robe first, and then the other followed. It was brown cashmere with a hood, the robe of ancient priests, and only worn during a ceremonial ritual. On the opposite side of the long hallway was a man approaching from the club's side of the entrance. A bouncer stood with his arms folded across his chest. He was about six foot four, and looked like a miniature "Mighty Joe Young". He held up a hand to stop Tom. "No admittance."

Tom held up his hands. "Alright, I'll just have to tell them you're the reason I'm late." The man saw the ring on Tom's hand.

"Sorry, Sir, I didn't know you were with the circle. Usually you guys come in the back way. Your robe is hanging right there in the closet."

"Thank you."

"No problem, Sir. Just down the stairs and straight back, you will see the pentagram on the double doors."

Tom put the robe on and lifted the hood over his head.

•———————————————•

Zoe came out of his hotel bathroom, but the door between his room and Tom and Steve was still ajar. Zoe heard what Steve had said about Tom being at a club called the something den. He also heard Camden say, if they didn't hurry, he might not see Tom again. Realizing the emergency, Zoe called the front desk.

"Hello? Yes, you may. Do you know of any night club called the den something or other?"

"Yes, Sir, there is a club called 'Diablo's Den.'"

"Where is that club, exactly?"

Zoe wrote down the directions as the clerk explained.

"Do you know how to get there?" Steve asked.

"Yes, it is not far from here," Camden replied.

"I want to know everything, Camden, I mean everything."

"Get in." Camden started up the Pathfinder truck he rented after leaving Joel.

"You're kinda fond of these mini-trucks, huh?"

"Yeah, they're alright."

Zoe walked out to the entrance of the hotel as Camden and Steve were pulling out onto the main street.

"Juno seven to Lantana tower."

"Lantana tower. Go ahead."

"Juno seven, requesting take-off."

"Affirmative. Juno seven, you are cleared for take-off on runway three-six."

"Copy that tower. Thank you. Have a good evening." Michael reached up and turned the knob, and then taxied the plane onto the runway. He clicked several switches above him, then some on the dash in front of him, pushing the levers forward until the plane's engine reached the desired idle speed. Then Michael let go of the brake. The plane began to roll at full speed down the runway, and lifted, as he pulled back on the steering wheel. The cargo plane was huge, and in the rear was Joel, preparing for war. Joel was wearing black military cargo pants, a black military sweater and black boots. His face was painted black with green streaks, crossing from the left eye to the right side of his face. He wore thin black leather gloves, a black backpack and a black toboggan cap on his head. Joel took out his gun, pulled the slide back on the model nineteen-eleven military forty-five auto, and let it snap back. Joel holstered the weapon under his left arm. He stood up from the side bench and checked the equipment in the rear of the cargo.

⎯⎯⎯⎯⎯⎯⎯⎯⎯⎯⎯⎯⎯⎯⎯⎯⎯⎯

Tom walked down the stairs and followed the hallway straight back. He raised his head just enough to see the double doors, and the pentagram sign in red, on the door. A picture of a goat was inside the drawing of the upside down star. Tom pushed one side of the door opened and entered. He followed the narrow passage further down. He saw a dark blue haze as he entered the open arena area.

On the floor was another pentagram, a much bigger symbol on the floor. The circle had spots marked for each of the twelve to stand upon. Tom tilted his head just enough to look around. Behind him, in the seating area of the arena, were hundreds of people looking down at the circle. Tom thought, *'they must have entered in here from another entrance.'* All the other members of the circle had their left hand crossed atop of their right, to show the rings. Tom had made a mistake. His hand was crossed but he had right over left. The man standing directly across from him, noticed. Tom kept his head down.

⎯⎯⎯⎯⎯⎯⎯⎯⎯⎯⎯⎯⎯⎯⎯⎯⎯⎯

Camden and Steve pulled up to the outside of the club. Steve saw the line was very long and looked at Camden.

"No way we are never going to get in there."

"Have a little faith, Steve."

"Oh no, don't you start on me, too."

Camden reached in the back seat and opened a chrome case. Then he shut it and slid it under the rear seat.

"I think I know someone who can get us in."

"Yeah, who?"

"A few fellows named Grant."

"Who?"

Steve followed Camden across the street. Camden walked up to the red ropes and turned his back to the long line of people waiting in line. The bouncer standing at the top of the steps saw Camden fan the stack of money, like a card dealer running his thumb over a fresh deck, about to be played. The bouncer walked down the steps and stood near Camden and Steve.

"What can I do for you?"

"My friend and I would like to gain entrance into your establishment and only for a brief time. We are not interested in staying, only finding a friend of ours."

"How long?"

"Hour. Tops."

"Ok, but the green friends stay with me."

"Oh, but of course."

Camden handed him the stack of money as he lifted up the red velvet rope. Camden and Steve walked in the door. The crowd grew upset, mumbling about Camden and Steve waking in. The bouncer walked back up to the top of the steps. He folded his arms in front of his chest. He was a big man and no one seemed to want to argue with him about the decision he made.

●────────────────────●

Joel picked up the headset that was in the rear of the plane.

"Michael, how far are we to target area?"

"About twenty minutes. Are you ready?"

"Yes. Just let me know when we are over the target."

"Joel, do you see a red lamp and a green lamp there?"

"Yes."

"Red is the two minute warning and the green is the go."

"Got it. How old is this crate anyway?"

"World War II. I borrowed it from a friend."

Joel though aloud, "Friends like that, who needs enemies?"

I stood behind Tom. I was in battle mode and my clothes were getting brighter. Everywhere I turned, I was surrounded by the forces of darkness. But then I turned and looked as the last two men walked into the arena. Both men were leaders on different levels.

One a political leader of a nation; The other a leader of the damned. I could not take my eyes off of him. Not the man, but the enormous creature of darkness that was behind him.

It was Gopher. The 'Prince of a Nation.' He was so huge, only half of his being appeared in the arena. I watched as the other demonic hosts shivered in his presence. Gopher was a spiritual wickedness that rules heavenly realms.

I looked to my right, and there appeared Xenophon, then his commanding officer Oracle.

I looked to my left the "White Door" appeared. 'Defender of the Faith' and 'Sword of the Spirit' walked though and entered the arena. All of them surrounded Tom. And their swords were at the ready. I was closest to Oracle and I asked,

"What is going on?"

Oracle replied, "Spiritual warfare; We were summoned here by prayer to do battle, by the one called Zoe."

Camden and Steve were looking around for Tom, when Camden saw someone he knew.

"Hello, Terry."

She turned and was shocked to see him. She tried to straighten her hair a little, but then became a little defensive in her body language and crossed her arms.

"Oh my, my, my...look what we have here," she said.

Calvin turned from the bar and looked to see Camden standing nearby.

"Camden Pelt, Now let's see, when was the last time I laid eyes on you? Virginia, basic training,; Murk, is it? Trained killer?"

"Not tonight." Calvin felt a little uneasy when Terry said trained killer. He looked Camden over and thought to himself. *'Killer, this guy doesn't look like a killer.'*

"Oh, just out to have a little fun?"

"Something like that," replied Camden.

"What are you doing here?"

"A night out with the boys. Who's your tag?" Terry inquired.

"Excuse me?"

"You know tag, Tag-a-long."

"Steve, this is Terry. Terry...Steve."

"He's a detective with Washington Police department."

Terry turned and looked at Calvin.

"Really? You don't happen to know a detective, named Tom Allen, do you?"

Steve was surprised she mentioned Tom's name.

"Yes, I am here to find him. Have you seen him?"

"I think we better talk. We did see him. Your friend asked us to assist him, but to tell the truth, we are on a case of our own. We are looking for a terrorist who somehow got into this country."

"A terrorist?" Steve asked.

"Some guy named Joel," Calvin said.

Camden coughed and raised an eyebrow at that name, Terry took a step closer to Camden and whispered in his ear.

"Now Cam, I know you are very informed. Do you know anything about this guy, Joel?"

A fight broke out near the bar where Calvin, Terry, Camden and Steve were standing. Two men were fighting over a woman. The smaller man had thrown the first punch, a right swing that came from way out in left field. He struck him with a blow hard enough to put a Kirk Douglas dimple in his chin. The man stumbled backward, tripping over a chair and knocking over a table. He managed to stay on his feet, but fell into Steve's arms. Steve tumbled into Camden just as Terry asked about Joel.

"Sorry Pal, I don't feel like dancing," Steve said, as he lifted the man up, and shoved him back towards the guy who had struck him.

Steve turned back towards Terry.

"Forget the terrorist. Where is Tom?" His voice was indignant.

Calvin pointed down towards the end of the hallway where one of the bouncers stood.

"He went down there, He told us that he would be back in an hour and a half. If he didn't show up, he said for us to come in guns blazing."

"How long ago was that?"

"About twenty-five minutes."

"I think we might need to find him before that," Camden said.

"You going to blow his cover?" Terry asked.

"Why?" Steve asked.

"I watched him talk to the gorilla down the end of the hall there. He was pretty smooth about getting by him. He may not appreciate what you're about to do. I know I wouldn't," Calvin said.

"If you knew the whole story, you might be singing a different tune," Camden said.

Terry didn't like the tone in Camden's voice. He was shaky, spooked, and she knew well enough that a C.I.A. mercenary didn't get nervous, unless it was a very serious situation.

TWENTY-EIGHT

In the backroom arena of the building, Tom realized he had the wrong hand in the crossed position, and quickly switched them. The man across from him was one of the two who had come in late. The other man was the one who put on the robe with the markings on the sleeves of a high priest. Detective training over the years had improved Tom's observation skills. He noticed the expensive wing-tip shoes of the man across from him. Tom perceived that the man was someone of character and taste. The gentleman's face was covered with the large hood of the robe.

The lighting was dimmed, except for the bluish glow of the black lights in the arena overhead. The man raised his head up exposing his face. Tom recognized it was the President of the United States.

Tom quickly lowered his head again so as not be seen. Solitude of loneliness entered Tom's mind. The scripture he had read the night before came to his mind. 'Tho has prepared a table before thine enemies'. Tom wondered *If that was the President, then who is this ring leader that stood at the stone table alter? Who was more powerful than the President?*.

A quick shiver ran down Tom's neck. He tried not to flinch but realized that he did. He had felt something. Something had touched him. Yet, he knew logically that nothing was near him. The distance was at least four feet of space between him and the men on either side, and ten feet across for the men standing on the other side of the painted circle on the floor. The crowd in the balcony viewing area all started to chant in unison.

"Dog si eh na tas,/ dog si eh na tas,/ dog si eh na tas."

Tom had it figured out from the start. He had worked cult cases before. He knew that devil worshipers chanted their songs backwards, so he reversed it to understand what they were saying.

"Sa...tan, he is god."

Under his breath, Tom prayed his own prayer.

"Dear Lord, I am in the den of lions. Shut the mouths of the roaring beasts to my ears. I desire, my Lord, only to hear the sweet sound of your angels singing."

Hundreds stood in the arena seats. One stood at the stone alter. Eleven stood on the giant pentagram. Only one of the eleven was surrounded by the 'Holy Angels of God'.

●————————————————————————●

Joel watched as the red lamp came on inside the rear of the cargo plane. It was the two minute warning lamp. Joel put the rigging on over the back pack. The rear of the cargo plane was wide enough for him to test the wing springs. Joel pushed the release switch and felt the quick jerk of the springs. The new device worked perfectly. The glider opened instantaneously. He pushed the compression switch on the left shoulder harness strap and the whole rig collapsed again. The second lamp let up and the red one went out. Joel was over target range. Joel was looking at the lamp when he heard the rear cargo bay open. The wind rushed in with a howl as the bay was being lowered from the cockpit by his friend, Michael.

Joel sucked in a breath, let it out, then did it again on the third breath he started to run towards the open cargo bay that viewed nothing but the darkness of night. Joel felt his boot hit the last edge of metal as he spread out his arms like a kid jumping off the swimming board high dive. In the momentum of the push off, Joel looked down at the lights of the city below. It was December, near Christmas time, and all the bright lights decorating the city proved it. But the only light that concerned Joel was the light the owner had put on the roof of his club. The arrogance of one night club owner may have been his own waterloo. A giant, red, neon pentagram sign, affixed to the roof to show incoming tourists his club, was not the homing device for a night parachute jumper named Joel.

●————————————————————————●

Camden looked at Steve. "Well, go get him."
Steve walked down the long hallway to where the bouncer was, who held up his hand to say, 'stop'.
"Sorry pal. No admittance."
"I have a friend in here and I have to get him out."
"No way, this section is V.I.P. only."
"This is a matter of life or death."
"Sorry friend. Go have a drink at the bar. When he gets done, maybe he'll come and see you."
"Going to be that way, is it?"
The bouncer stood, getting up off the bar stool which made him appear about six foot. Steve watched him as he towered a full six foot, seven inches and weighed about three hundred and forty pounds solid mass, no fat.
"Yeah, it's going to be that way."
"Ok," Steve turned to walk away. He walked up the hallway again to where he saw Camden, Terry, and Calvin.
"Be right back. Don't go anywhere," he said as he walked passed them.
Steve approached the front doors, where he came in, and looked to the right and then to the left. Reaching towards his back, he pulled out Simon. Holding his hand directly above him, he fired

the forty-five auto into the ceiling. The crowd screamed and began to panic, like sheep in a pen with nowhere to run. A mad man was in the house with a gun and he was shooting. At each blast of the gun being discharged, people jolted with fear.

"Simon says, everybody out! And I mean that-away!" Steve pointed down the long hallway to the private area where the bouncer was. Steve had started an old fashion wild west stampede.

Camden looked at Calvin, who had reached inside his jacket to pull out his weapon. "No, no. It's ok." Camden patted the back of Calvin's hand to let him know not to pull it out.

"Your friend is nuts," Terry said.

"I think the kid's has class. Oops, excuse me."

Camden was being pushed by the throngs of people, now packing like sardines in a tin can. They were rushing the bouncer to get out. The entire club area was cleared except for Steve, Camden, Terry and Calvin. Steve walked over to the bar, watching the people at the end of the hallway running over the bouncer.

"I sure hope this place had good medical plan, because that looks like it hurts," Steve said.

"You definitely know how to empty a bar, kid," Camden said.

Steve shrugged his shoulders.

"It was nothing. Now let's see if we can find the Chief."

"Who?" Terry asked.

"Tom."

Zoe had arrived and saw all the people rushing out of the building. He waited as the crowd came out and then he went in. Camden, Steve, Terry and Calvin all walked down the long hallway and went down the steps to the corridor. Calvin had looked at the emergency evacuation plan on the bouncer's desk and saw the place marked 'arena'.

TWENTY-NINE

Joel opened the hang-glider and saw the red neon sign on the top of the roof of the building. He sailed right onto the roof, and with a couple of running footsteps, he landed. He quickly released the glider. He hit the retract button, causing it to fold. Joel saw the back parking lot and the crowd below. The man standing next to alter turned and faced the circle and all who were sitting in the balcony arena. Two men in black robes had come from the opposite side of Tom, carrying a drunken, naked woman. They placed the woman in four point restraints on an alter of stone. The priest facing her had held a silver cup chalice and poured it over her. Tom thought to himself. *'What a bunch of idiots.'*

The priest rotated back and removed his hood. Tom had seen that man somewhere. He then picked up a poniard dagger. He clasped it with both hands and held it above his head, ready to strike. Tom reached inside his shirt and pulled out his gun.

"Alright!" He shouted. "Stop right there!"

Tom removed his hood that covered his face.

"Who is this man?" The high priest asked.

The President started to move to leave.

"Freeze! Nobody and I mean nobody moves!" Tom shouted.

The President yelled at the high priest.

"Do something now, Brice!"

The high priest, Brice Noland, shouted "Gopher!"

The giant spirit moved in the dimness of the light and possessed the man standing next to Tom. It was the assassin with the crew cut. Demonic spirits were all now focused on Tom. None were able to come near him. The glory of the angels who surrounded him began to fight. Xenophon was the first to move at glory's speed. He must have sliced ten imps in half before they even knew they were dissipating into gas vapors. Defender of the Faith and Sword of the Spirit stood their ground around Tom. Oracle, who was huge in stature, fought against Fury and Murder.

Zoe saw Tom, holding a gun, pointed at Brice Noland. Tom didn't see the man with the crew cut pulling a gun on him, but Zoe did.

Zoe ran towards the assassin. He had the gun pointed at Tom's head while he licked his left two fingers, and brushed the front of his hair in an upward stroke. Time seemed to slow down as Zoe made a leaping jump to knock Tom out of the way. He flew mid-air, falling towards Tom, pushing him towards the floor. Tom turned to see a sudden movement out of the corner of his right eye as Zoe knocked into him.

BOOM...A shot rang out.

The bullet fired from the assassin's gun hit Zoe in the back, piercing the front of his chest with a small explosion. Zoe saw the splatter of his own blood gushing out, as he cried out Tom's name.

Camden, Steve, Calvin and Terry heard the shot from the other side of the door. Tom was sliding backwards on the floor from the force of Zoe's shove, but managed to twist towards the shooter and fire.

Zoe finished his sentence. "God help him."
In the physical realm, time stood still. The bullet had just left Tom's gun when the "White Door" appeared. And there he was; The third most beautiful thing to behold, The glory of innocence 'Michael, the Archangel' himself.

He drew his sword and swung it at the man with the crew cut. The demonic spirit, Gopher, tried to get out of the man's body before getting hit, but it was too late. The spiritual wickedness was slain.

And as fast as he appeared, he turned and walked back through the "White Door". The Archangel, Michael, was gone.

The bullet Tom fired continued to travel, and struck the assassin in the shoulder, knocking him to the ground. Steve came in as back-up, as did Camden, Calvin and Terry.

"Stop right there, Mr. President," Calvin said.

Brice yelled, "Gopher! Gopher!" but the power was gone.

Joel came in from the roof and made his way to the balcony. He saw the circle of twelve was broken and he saw Camden down on the arena floor. Camden saw him, too, but didn't say anything to the two Federal agents.

Joel saw no reason to blow up a completely good building if the bad guys were already caught. So he turned and left down the hallway, leaving the black back-pack sitting in a balcony seat. He winked at Camden before he left, to let him know it was there.

Tom jumped up and rushed over to Zoe, who was laying face down on his chest. Tom turned Zoe over from the right shoulder and laid him on his back. Blood was coming out of his mouth.

"Paul! Why man? Why did you do that?"

For that brief moment in time, Paul's memory flashed back to an inner city street where someone else had saved his life. And he held a young boy in his arms, asking the same question. Zoe smiled the best he could as he looked up and answered Tom.

"No greater love is this, than a man lay down his life for friends."

THIRTY

One year later...

Jerusalem:

Joel looked out at the mighty army of commandos he was in charge of training, the elite of fighters for Extreme Protectors. He tapped his pipe against the handrail of the porch from which he gazed. He thought to himself, '*Good looking group of men. They will make fine soldiers.*'

Rio de Janeiro:

Camden Pelt and his wife Mrs. Kelly Pelt, also known as Mrs. Kelly, who quit working for Brice Noland, were toes deep in white sand. Peering over the clear royal blue waters, they were sipping from coconut shells some wild fruity drink with the little umbrellas hanging off the edge.

Northeastern United States:

Steve was sitting on a park bench eating an ice cream cone. The bell rang and a crowd of students walked by. Steve; the big kid he was, just kept on licking, when someone approached him.

"You waiting on me?" Tom asked.

"Yeppers."

"All those books yours, Chief?"

"Yes, I have to get to class. Now what did you want?"

"Lori wants to know if you and Marcy want to come over for dinner Tuesday."

"What time?"

Steve took a lick and dripped some chocolate on his shirt.

"Ooooh, man...around seven o'clock. Can you make it?"

"Let me ask Marcy."

"Ok, get back with me and let me know."

Steve tossed the ice cream cone in the trashcan, brushing his shirt as he walked out to the street, where a young man was leaning on the car.

"Hey sarge, who is that?" the man leaning against the car asked.

"Just a friend, Rookie, now get in. I'll drive."

Tom laughed at the thought of Steve being the boss and breaking in a new partner.

Steve bald and squealed the tires as he pulled away from the college campus,
'The North East Theological Seminary of Ministry.'

Tom walked to his next class and said a Prayer,

"Dear Lord, send your angels to watch over Steve."

In Heaven:

Gabriel turned to the new arrival looked at him with love and said with the sweetest tone of voice...

"We just received a request. Would you please be so kind Toby, to ask your escort to take care of it?"

Paul Zoe also known as Toby turned and winked at me. I smiled, knowing I had to leave to go back to Earth.

So here I am again. My name is Septuagint I am but an angel who has earned his wings.

The End.

About the Author;

Billy Scott was born and raised in Kentucky. At sixteen he resigned of high school and received a G.E.D. diploma. At seventeen became a licensed hairstylist and also began a business in the underworld of nightclubs. Being supernaturally called into ministry he became a minister by the age of twenty three. He graduated from Rhema, Broken Arrow, Oklahoma majoring in evangelism. At the age of twenty five and relocating to Florida, Billy Scott joined the Broward County Sheriffs Office and conducted what he called "*Undercover ministry*" for next sixteen years as preacher hiding in a cop's uniform. He says, "*They never saw me coming and then Pow! I hit them with the word of God, besides, cops only listen to other cops.*" He has written several works of literature, songs, and novels. He is currently working on his novel **"Masquerader"** a follow up in the **"Angelic Rage"** series. He now resides in the southeastern part of the county.